THE GOOD HUSBAND

A NOVEL

JOHN KAINE

For Charmaine

Also by John Kaine

American Homemaker

The Seven

1

Zoey Finch was cheating on her husband because he didn't deserve her loyalty.

She crossed the lobby of The Herbert Hotel, reassuring herself that her blouse was buttoned properly, her skirt wasn't unzipped, and that she'd fixed her makeup. Out on the sidewalk, she went past the Sag Harbor Fire Department and the brick structure of the Municipal Building. She focused on her loud stride, glanced down at her Miu Mius— patent-leather crystal-embellished pumps, drawing the eyes of random gawkers away from her face. People were just magpies. *Look!* Shiny. She threw her shoulders back, chin out, Bulgari Flora sunglasses shading her eyes from any betrayal of guilt. At thirty-eight, the walk of shame was a thing of the past—the tramp trot, the slut strut, whatever it was called these days. No, with each step, her confidence grew. She didn't look around as if she was trying to spot someone who'd recognize her. That was the hallmark of a true amateur. Peripheral vision was acceptable, anything else was *too much*. Instead, her head was locked forward and her walk was blameless, strong, her heels striking the sidewalk as if she were renting it to everyone else. All it took was momentum. Once your head was tilted slightly upward and your hips were rolling, the initial hesitation faded—she had come to know it as the guilty stutter. She was just another Hamptons resident taking a morning stroll. Or, as she'd told her husband: "I'm going to get some coffee, some breakfast at The Blue Lemon. You want anything?" He had said "No, thanks," just as he always did.

A sudden chill developed along her spine despite the clear blue sky, the rising temperature. *Is that Peyton Ellis?* She told herself to remain calm. It *was* Peyton, and she was just across the street. But she was looking down at her iPhone. Zoey walked faster, and now her underwear was riding higher, getting stuck between—

Goddamn you, don't panic. Why am I worried? Because she knows me, and she'll know I did … something.

Now she wasn't convinced her blouse was buttoned as it should be. Now she felt her skirt wasn't zipped. She could swear it was a bit loose. She had combed her hair in the hotel, but had she? Was it standing up in all the wrong places? Marcus was a hair puller. She wasn't complaining … was the hectic redness on her neck and chest gone?

The Blue Lemon Café was closer, its red awning a promise of safety. Zoey glanced across the street, watching in horror as Peyton looked up from her cell. Her heels were too loud now. And the guilty stutter was taking effect. She tried to take the weight out of each step, but she was trying to increase her pace at the same time and realized she must look like somebody who had a pebble in her shoe. Peyton Ellis, a member in good standing of her book club, socialite, could smell infidelity on a penguin. She had a nose for it. It was the way her eyes probed you when you were in conversation with her. How many times had she guessed correctly who was being unfaithful in the Hamptons? Zoey suspected it wasn't guesswork, it was insider knowledge. She was well connected.

Adrenaline drove her forward, her heart heavy and quick like a rabbit caught in a snare, watching as the wolf approached. She flicked her eyes sideways and glimpsed Peyton looking down Main Street. *Thank God, she didn't see me*, she thought, her hand curling around the door handle. She entered the café, staring at Peyton through the glass, continuing to swipe at her iPhone. If Peyton casually mentioned to Jon that she had seen Zoey entering The Blue Lemon at this time, she'd have some explaining to do. The Village Book Club was meeting tonight, and she would get Jon out of the house, just to be on the safe side. She was sure Peyton hadn't seen her. But you never knew. Zoey didn't want to get caught. Yet. She couldn't be selfish. She had an eleven-year-old son and a seven-month baby girl to think about.

2

The nanny was late. And Zoey wasn't home yet. Jon Finch showered, leaving the en suite bathroom door open and the volume on the baby monitor turned up, even though he would be able to hear her if she cried. His daughter was in her Minnie Mouse rocker in the master bedroom, quiet the whole time as he shaved, wrapped in a towel. Where was everyone this morning? he wondered. He knew Zoey had gone out to get breakfast, but she'd probably seen one of her friends and they'd ended up chatting in the middle of the sidewalk. It was even possible she'd met more than one of her friends—Zoey was popular. But the food would be soggy if she didn't hurry back, a breeding ground for bacteria as it got warmer … He went into the bedroom. Jane was asleep. Maybe the sound of the water from the shower had helped her drift off. He had survived the trauma of changing her loaded diaper when he got out of bed, retching only once. He put on a dry-cleaned suit. He was late for work.

Jon went to take his shoes from the closet and stood on something. He lifted his foot, picked up a black button and dropped it into his pocket. He sat on an armchair to put his shoes on, which he'd polished to a high shine the night before, then carried Jane to the adjoining room that served as his office. He turned on the three monitors mounted on brackets above his workstation and his laptop, started typing and brought up his charts onto the screens.

He couldn't leave the business entirely. Even though they didn't need the money, Jon wanted to work. He had semi-retired from Aquarius Asset Management at thirty-one. That had lasted a month, after which he returned to the hedge fund he had cofounded with Zoey. Now, at thirty-nine, he was taking three months off. So far, he had gotten through the first month just fine. He'd decided not to base Aquarius on Wall Street. Instead, he rented office space on East Broadway, on the other side of the Brooklyn Bridge. The last thing he and Zoey wanted was to tell people in polite conversation that they were Wall Street bankers.

Day trading was risky, even if you knew what you were doing. But Jon Finch had spent most of his life managing risk, appointing himself senior risk manager and general partner at Aquarius. Zoey took on the role of prime broker, in charge of custody and execution services, acting as an intermediary between Aquarius and pension funds who'd loan them shares for the purpose of short selling and convincing commercial banks to cover margin loans. She was good at it, too. He suspected Zoey was the reason venture capitalist and fund manager Charles Shaker had decided to provide them with the seed money to get Aquarius up and running. Even though Shaker's investment was equivalent to holding bundles of cash over an open flame, near enough to become warm but just the right distance away to avoid combusting, he'd seemed remarkably casual about handing over the required capital. Zoey had been persuasive and charming. She hadn't glossed over the potential pitfalls of investing in their new (and untested) business, either. Shaker had responded to her honesty.

The market was a precarious place. You couldn't eliminate risk completely, but you could take steps to minimize it. Jon was done with being careful. His caution in business had bled into his personal life. He wouldn't let his son run in the house or let him ride his bicycle without wearing a helmet. Deep down, he knew these were common-sense precautions. But he was sick of being sensible. Now he thought he was suffocating his family by managing *their* risk. He had asked his wife not to drink as much wine, afraid she was drinking herself towards cirrhosis of the liver. Quietly, he was ashamed. Zoey had the right to do whatever she wanted. And here he was, ruining everyone's fun. She didn't even drink alcohol most days, except when her book club met every Friday night. Those women drank wine like it was about to be rationed. He vowed to try and pull back. The last thing he wanted was to make Zoey and Cody unhappy. *What if?* kept tormenting him, though. What if Cody fell off his bike and cracked his skull? Then what? What if Zoey got so drunk one night, tripped, hit her head and ended up in a coma? Or worse: brain damaged. He had visions of feeding her through a straw. He'd do it, too, but the horror of it all … He had to stop asking himself that small, evil question. What if? It was rooted in fear. He just didn't want anything bad to happen to his family. He felt he had been exceptionally lucky, fortunate, and he had the sense, no matter how irrational, that his good fortune was like some financial products: their return diminished in the long run.

He was tapping the keys on the keyboard, not as focused on the task of buying and selling equities as he should have been, and he glanced down at his daughter. A wave of love passed through him. Being protective of your child was normal, and he had felt the same way about Cody when he was a baby. But shouldn't it lose some of its intensity as they got older? That was one of his problems—he hadn't become less protective. He worried about Cody far too much whenever his son's foot crossed the threshold to leave the house, hang out with his friends and ride his bike in the street.

His cell phone vibrated and he snatched it off the desk, checking to see if Jane had stirred. She was asleep, thank God.

He whispered, "Hello."

"Jon, hi." It was the nanny, Candice Fersh, who was late.

"Having trouble getting here? You okay?"

"Actually, Jon, I'm not feeling so good. I think I have the flu."

"Oh, I'm sorry to hear that." *The flu? In late June? It's possible …*

"I could come in tomorrow?"

"Better not, until you feel better. I'll give you the week off. Just go see a doctor, and bring me a note confirming you have the flu. You might have to see a doctor before you come back here because I can't expose Jane to something as dangerous as influenza. If the doc says you're clear, we'd be delighted to welcome you back."

Silence on the line.

Then: "I *have* to see a doctor?"

"Yes, I'm sorry but I have to insist. I can't have flu in my house."

"Okay … aren't I entitled to sick pay?"

Jon was willing to let it go at that. He almost did. But *entitled* was like barbed wire being dragged across his senses. He blinked hard. *Entitled.* Jon Finch had never been entitled to anything in his entire life. No one owed him anything. He had planned to give Candice full pay for the seven to ten days it would take for her to recover, perhaps even a little extra. It wasn't her fault she had the flu. But now … "Candice, I have to call you back. Please give me five minutes."

A hesitant note had crept into her voice. "Uh … okay … is everything okay?"

"Yes," he said, "everything is fine." He hung up and dialed Eve's, a bar on the opposite end of Main Street, and asked to speak to the head bartender. Jon didn't drink alcohol, not much, anyway, but he frequented the bars around Sag Harbor, ordering only a club soda, and left generous tips. "Jim, were you working the bar this week?"

"Yeah. Something wrong, Jon?"

"No, not yet. Was Candice there last night?" Jon and Zoey, on occasion, asked Candice to join them for drinks when a babysitter became available. She was part of the family, friends with Zoey.

"No, it'd be hard to miss her if she was." Candice's latest dye job was electric blue. Jon didn't care what she looked like as long as she did her job and took care of his children.

"All right, Jim, thanks."

"Anytime."

He called Murphy's Bar on Division Street and spoke to Julia, the owner, and asked her the same question.

"She was in, stayed late, her and a couple of friends."

"Thanks, Julia. I'll drop by the bar soon."

"I didn't get anyone in trouble?"

"No, *you* didn't get anyone in trouble." Which was true. Candice had gotten in trouble all by herself.

He brought Candice's name up in his contacts, and she answered on the first ring.

"Candice?"

"Yes." It was a slow *yes*.

"I have to let you go. I'll pay you for the rest of the week, even though you're not *entitled* to more money. I'll give you a reference so you can get another job. Thank you for your services." He put the phone on his desk, leaned back in the chair, hands in his pockets. His hand touched the button, squeezed it between thumb and forefinger.

3

Lizzy Jenkins was on her way to work. She bowed her head, especially when a car drove past, watching the sidewalk on Garden Street unreel before her. Praying to the sidewalk, her husband called it. Not in a mean way. She walked by the eighteenth-century Custom House and as she approached the Sag Harbor Whaling Museum, a Greek revival building with fluted Corinthian columns, she moved to the edge of the sidewalk. The white fence surrounding the museum had pointed stakes. She was afraid of losing her footing, falling and becoming impaled. It was a well-worn routine. Every morning she did the same thing as she neared the intersection with Main Street. It was automatic now; she didn't have to think about it, her body knew what it had to do.

She stood on the corner, checking for traffic. Lizzy squeezed the tennis ball in the pocket of her cardigan. She had stripped it of its green felt. Her fingers were jittery and her legs trembled. It would probably take another twenty minutes for the Limbitrol to take effect. It was a new antidepressant her doctor recommended she try.

Lizzy loved her job, and yet her nervousness didn't make any sense. In the past two years she had experienced the same fear every day as she crossed Main Street to the John Jermain Memorial Library where she was director of adult services. She wasn't any closer to understanding why she was scared.

She entered the library and hurried across the terrazzo floor, heading for the women's bathroom. Lizzy locked the door in the stall, removed the tennis ball and a razor blade she had packaged in a piece of greaseproof paper. She sliced the ball in half and peeled the edges of the rubber. Her eyes became wet as calm slackened her muscles and her face drooped. She clenched her jaw too often, and sometimes it hurt. Now it became unhinged. Her mouth fell open. The blade carved another sliver of rubber, dropping to the flattened grease paper on top of the cistern. The smooth sensation, the lack of resistance as she pared the dull rubber was … was *tranquilizing*.

Lizzy blinked; a tear rolled down her cheek. She swiped at it absently and collected herself. It was Friday. She would be finished work at five. The book club was meeting later to discuss Thomas Harris's novel *The Silence of the Lambs*. Lizzy was looking forward to it. Her doctor had told her many times if she had something to look forward to, she'd have a renewed sense of purpose. Lizzy already had purpose in her life. She had a daughter and a loving husband to look forward to every single day. A husband who kissed her on her upper arm (at her request, not on the lips; in fact, why didn't he just leave her entire face out of the gesture) as he left for work in the mornings. A daughter who respected her, even though Lizzy didn't completely approve of her choice of boyfriend.

All she had to do was get through the day. And hope no one played a prank on her. That no one tried to trick her.

But no one has tried to prank me or trick me since I've worked here.

There was always a chance someone would, though. Because some people liked to play pranks on the vulnerable.

I am not vulnerable. I. Am. Not.

She put the remains of the tennis ball into her cardigan pocket with the tightly wrapped shavings.

Lizzy reminded herself of the things she should look forward to, listing them in her mind in no particular order.

I'm looking forward to the book club meeting tonight.

I'm looking forward to hugging my daughter.

I'm looking forward to helping people find books.

I'm looking forward to seeing Zoey.

I'm looking forward to greeting Marcus when he comes home and cooking him a meal and hugging him, too.

Marcus understood. He gave her hope. He said she was young. At thirty-eight there was a real possibility she could get well again. She just had to take her medicine.

4

Coconut Grove, Miami, Florida

"Why are we dealing with this lawyer?" Ken Brooks turned the van onto Loquat Avenue, a quiet, residential area of detached homes. His friend, and employer, didn't answer immediately. Ken glanced at Benny Cooper, who was in the passenger seat next to him, adjusting his shoulder holster, then his sport coat.

"I get it," Benny said. "You don't like the guy. But if liking everyone was a prerequisite for doing business, we'd be poor."

Ken looked in the rearview mirror. George Howard was sitting on a bench in back, his eyes closed. "What do you think?" Ken asked. "George, are you praying?"

"I'm meditating, asshole. Andre is slippery. He's being investigated by The Florida Bar's Lawyer Regulation Department. That's the word, anyway. My contact used phrases such as misappropriation of client funds, not complying with trust accounting rules, and some ethical issues unrelated to same. That may not be a complete list."

"See, Ken?" Benny said, "The man's a thief. It's not as if he's a rapist, at least if he was, we could shoot him on general principles and call it a night."

"He's probably been siphoning off cash from his firm, too," George said.

"Is he being investigated by the cops?" Benny said, sitting up and looking at George in the rearview.

"Yeah. The cops and the Florida Bar—that may not be a complete list, either"

Benny's cell phone buzzed. He answered. "It might be nothing," he said, after a pause. Then: "Keep me updated. I can plan—you already have a plan? Call me later. I'm working." He hung up and turned to Ken.

Ken slowed the van to a crawl. "Take note of the walls," Benny said, "George, walk the perimeter when we get inside. The gates are electronic, high, vertical bars; the front of the house can be seen from the road."

"Got it," George said.

Ken called the lawyer. A moment later the gates opened. He stopped halfway up the driveway and George jumped out. Ken checked his mirrors. George was clear of the van, and Ken headed towards the front door. He shut the engine off. Lights came on in the hallway, and Andre appeared in the doorway, a silhouette moving from one foot to the other.

"I want to talk to you later; if not tonight, in a few days," Benny said.

Ken looked at him. "Everything okay?" Ken didn't think he'd done anything wrong. And yet he sifted through his memory in search of a mistake, a misstep, or some inadvertent offense he may have caused: he would *never* offend Benny on purpose. There was nothing.

"We might have a new client at some point, lot of money at stake. There's no contract yet. But I want to figure out the details, be prepared." On one hand, Ken was relieved he hadn't displeased his boss; on the other, he was concerned by Benny's troubled frown. Ever since he'd hung up the phone, he'd assumed a contemplative air, more so than usual. When Benny lost his grip on his normally serene disposition, his temper frayed easily. He hoped this lawyer wasn't a moron. On first meeting him, Ken had agreed with George that Andre had been a bit jumpy, nervous, which was understandable, given the circumstances. But there had also been an erratic quality to Andre's vibe. Something *off* about the guy. Or as George had put it, Andre was suffering from a disturbance in his aura, whatever in the Christ *that* meant.

Ken saw George walking across the lawn, as if he was out for a casual stroll and not making a mental map of the layout. Benny took a brown envelope from the glove compartment and exited the van. Ken followed.

As he got closer to the door, and the lawyer doing his impatient little dance from one foot to the other, Ken knew it was going to be a long night—Andre was either drunk, or he'd vacuumed an eye-watering quantity of blow up his nose, quite possibly both. He stuck out his hand for Benny to shake. Benny ignored it. Ken followed Andre's gaze; he'd seen George coming around the side of the house.

"Hey, what were you doing back there?"

"I had to take a leak, couldn't hold it."

"You pissed in my grass?"

"Are we going to stand out here all night?" Benny said, and Ken heard jagged edges in his voice. Andre turned and all three followed him, Ken unable to take his eyes off the lawyer's feet. Ken nodded at George, who headed for the stairs. They entered a room at the end of the living room. It appeared to be used for entertaining guests. There was an octagonal poker table in the middle of the floor and a huge sectional taking up an entire corner. The wall mounted flatscreen was blaring a sitcom. Ken looked up at the pecky cypress ceiling, lowering his eyes to the walls. His mouth dropped open.

Benny sat at the poker table, and Andre eased into the chair opposite him. Ken took a seat between the two men. Benny, elbow planted on the blue felt of the poker table, bent his wrist, a forefinger pointed at the TV. He said, "Shut that shit off." Andre picked up the remote and the screen went dark. Benny was furious, and Ken knew why. He looked at Andre's feet under the table.

"So," Andre said, "did you have any trouble finding me?"

Andre was uncomfortable with silence, Ken noticed immediately, or perhaps it was just the current silence. Outside the open door of this room, George was opening and closing doors all over the house, checking if there were any unannounced guests, maybe a visitor or two that Andre had forgotten to mention.

George came back into the room, nodded at Ken, closed the door and stood in front of it. Ken watched George's eyes widen as he scanned the walls, and smiled briefly.

"Would you gentlemen like a drink?" Andre asked. Benny still didn't say anything, and Ken held up a hand.

Andre turned, and said, "How about you?"

"No thanks," George said, "I'm on a dopamine fast." Ken rolled his eyes, and quickly returned his full attention to the two men at the table. Andre was not as drunk as he'd first appeared. There was a bottle of bourbon on the table, but it was almost full.

Benny pointed at the bag on the table. "You have something for me?"

"Half. I need a few days to get the rest."

"Then we'll come back in a few days when you have the other half."

Benny started to get up, and suddenly Andre achieved an alertness that revealed just how desperate he was. "Please," he said, "please, just have a seat. Some of the half right here is gold bullion, I'm a collector. I need to liquidate some assets, but I need a new identity, otherwise I'm in serious trouble…I'll include twenty-thousand, on top of what we already agreed, you know, for the inconvenience." Benny sat again. Ken hoped Andre knew what he was doing, for his own wellbeing; otherwise, things could get messy.

Benny said, "Ken, check the bag." Ken picked it up, counted the bullion (still in their plastic packaging), and the cash.

"It's half," Ken said, "plus a little extra with the gold."

Benny placed an envelope containing a new identity—passport, social security number, driver's license—on the poker table, which Andre eyed, until Benny reached inside his sport coat and brought out a Glock 43 and put it beside the envelope. Ken watched Andre's eyes widen. Blood drained from his face.

For as long as he'd known him, Ken had wondered what Benny's deal was: he didn't drink alcohol, smoke, or do drugs, so what was he into? Was he single? There was no way of knowing because Benny didn't invite questions about his personal life. But now, as his gaze alternated between Benny and Andre, Ken had the answer—crime. He hadn't seen it before and it was right in front of him: Benny was a criminal down to the spiral strands of his DNA. Crime was his deal, *all* of his deal. As Ken looked at him, he saw Benny was curious, and interested, in how this meeting had developed. Andre had made a bold move; Ken knew it and evidently, so did Benny. The only question on Ken's mind was whether or not Andre was going to be alive in the next few seconds. That was another facet of working for Benny: you never knew what he was going to say or do.

Benny pushed his chair back from the table, lowered his head slightly.

"What kind of man answers the door in his bare feet?" Andre appeared to be puzzled by the question, but judging by the set expression on Benny's face, Ken guessed he was expecting a reply.

"I don't…I mean, um—."

"Let's discuss your character," Benny said, "from my perspective. You answer the door, you're not wearing shoes or socks, your suit is rumpled and creased, your tie is loose. What message are you sending me? That the social norm of wearing shoes to a business meeting doesn't apply to you, or doesn't apply to this specific instance? Do you meet clients in your office barefoot? No? Are you a hippy, masquerading as a lawyer, or vice versa? You've got powdery dandruff under your nose. The picture I'm painting of you, Andre, is one of slippage. Am I an early witness to your professional and personal decline, counselor?"

It's like being an umpire at a tennis match, Ken thought, as his eyes flitted from Andre to Benny, and back to Andre, who was sweating heavily; he kept glancing at the bottle of booze beside his elbow. Ken reached for it, poured the brown liquid into the tumbler, filling it. Ken knew Andre was scared, but when the lawyer picked up the tumbler, sloshing and spilling liquor as it made its torturous journey to his lips, Ken revised his initial impression—Andre was terrified. His eyes had taken on a jerky quickness. A low grade shudder seemed to have developed across his entire body, even his feet were affected. His bare feet.

"I'll tell you what kind of man answers the door barefoot and disheveled—an animal. I should shoot you, take the half as payment for wasting my time, and I might just do it...but let's play. Show me how you're going to pay me."

"I have shares. Stock certificates, in my safe."

"Give the code to George." Andre did, and George left the room. He returned a few minutes later carrying bundles of stock certificates.

"Are they good?" Benny asked.

"They're good."

"Cash them in, and you can pay me the other half, but bear this in mind—if you're late, you'll see me again. I'm not yet certain how your day is going to end, Andre. That all depends on how you answer the next question: why do you have pictures of O.J. Simpson all over your walls?" Ken was curious about that, too. Andre was pictured in two photographs that took pride of place high behind the bar, blown up to an unmissable size, his arm around the Juice, both of them smiling. There were posters of Simpson in his Buffalo Bills days in various action snapshots, either running with a ball or catching one, and dozens of glossy photo reproductions from the trial of the century.

"I met him twice," Andre said.

"Okay, but *why*?"

"I'm a fan. He's a nice guy."

"You think he's innocent?"

"Oh no. But he really is one of the nicest people I've ever met."

"I'm not judging you, Andre. I've broken some of the Ten Commandments myself…you don't think this is too much? A little creepy, maybe?"

"It's a conversation piece."

"Are you a contrarian, Andre? Are you trying to challenge the notion of what is acceptable bad taste? Your guests don't find this objectionable?"

"I don't know what to say."

Benny got up, expelling a weary sigh. He was done toying with the lawyer. He sat on the edge of the table in front of Andre, grasped the end of his tie, rotated his wrist until it was wrapped around his hand: he had reeled the lawyer in like he was a fish. Benny leaned forward, his forehead no more than an inch from Andre's, and said, "Don't be late with my money, counselor, or I *will* judge you."

Ken stayed where he was for a moment after Benny and George left.

He said, "Whatever you do, Andre, pay that man. If you don't, dying will be the least of your problems."

5

Zinco Sciences, Cambridge, Massachusetts

He's looking at me like I sold him a used car.

Dr. Arthur Dunhill breathed through his nose and rolled four marbles together in his big left hand as he stared at his accuser—*persecutor*—across his vast desk. For a moment, he thought he'd captured, however briefly, a satisfying moment of discomfort in Dr. Roger Berris's steely exterior: just a slight movement of the shoulders, a kind of sideways shifting the average person might not notice. But when you were at the very top of the food chain, looking down on lesser animals, any sign of weakness fortified—*encouraged*—an apex predator such as Dr. Arthur Dunhill. Roger was in *his* office, waiting for *him* to speak; Arthur was going to draw the silence out for as long as he possibly could, until he had induced peak mortification in his former friend and now Number One Adversary. Roger was no longer *on board*, which meant he had to find a way to push the other man *overboard*. He grinned at the idea, but sobered instantly when he remembered that he didn't have the power to jettison the piece of deadwood regarding him coolly, defiantly—

"I know what you're doing…Arthur."

The marbles stopped turning. "Really? What am I doing…Roger?"

Roger sighed. "I'm asking you, again, to drop the application. You've forced me into a corner. The worst part of it is I can't believe, or even process the fact that you think you're going to get away it."

"Nothing was ever achieved by taking the cautious approach."

The marbles began to turn in Arthur's fist. "I once knew a man," Arthur continued, "He had an audacious streak a mile wide and it grew wider by the day. That was you, Roger. Now you come in here like a crybaby, talking about ethics, almost as though you get to decide what is and what isn't ethical."

"No damage has been done yet. But you should step down. Resign, Arthur, do the right thing."

"How dare you." Arthur clenched the marbles in his fist. "Get out," he said, quietly, between bared teeth.

***

Dr. Berris returned to his office, adjacent to Arthur's, and promptly searched online for Zoey Finch and her husband, Jon. In the past week, he had learned as much as possible about his potential new partners. They had the social and professional cachet to guarantee that Arthur's scheme was his last.

6

"You fired her?"

Zoey stood in the doorway of Jon's office, that day's mail in one hand and a brown bag in the other. She had bought herself a whole-wheat wrap with turkey, baby spinach and scrambled free-range egg whites, and a whole-grain roll with scrambled free-range eggs and turkey bacon for him, even though he hadn't asked for anything.

"I did," he said, "she's unreliable. She lied to us."

"You shouldn't have done it. So she had a few drinks, but she knows our kids and they know her. We trust her with them." Despite her hands being full, they formed fists and came to rest on her hips. "You have no right to let her go."

"Well, it's done now."

"No, Jonathan, it isn't. You should've consulted me first." Jane started crying, giving voice to an impressive bawl. She watched him reach for her, cradle her in his arms, rocking her back and forth. The screaming died down a little, and Zoey examined his face. Something wasn't right. Did he make a bad trade? If that was the case, how much did he lose?

"Is everything all right?" she asked, her voice losing its edge. "You look like you've seen a ghost."

He manufactured a quick smile. Zoey didn't see any warmth in it.

"I'm fine, just feeling a bit tired." Jane had quieted, and Zoey couldn't suppress a rising swell of jealousy. He had a way with her, there was no doubt about it. When she cried in the night, he got up and soothed her. She had tried it a few times, lifting her out of her bassinet and caressing her head, making cooing sounds and giving up in the end and calling Jon to take over. Zoey glared at him as Jane placed a small hand on his newly shaved chin and left it there. She felt a wave of hatred for him, then. It was fleeting, but there was no mistaking it.

"Where's Cody?"

"He went out early to meet the Jenkins girl. Now he's out back, in his treehouse."

"You have to have the Talk with him, Jonathan."

"Me? Why do I have to do it?"

"Because you're a man."

"What does that have to do with anything?"

"You're his father, Jonathan. The Talk is a man-to-man type of deal."

"He's only eleven."

"Yeah, well she's twelve. At least talk to him."

He sighed and Zoey was satisfied. He had given in to her.

She softened and said, "I brought you some breakfast. Take a break, come on downstairs and eat."

"What took you so long?"

She watched him watching her. There was a steadiness in his eyes. She didn't like it. At all.

"I got talking to some people … Come on, let's eat. I'll take a shower, I'll be fast. It's so hot outside."

7

Jon had changed out of his suit, put on sweatpants and a T-shirt, ate breakfast and watched Zoey open the mail, her face a mask of boredom.

"Anything good?" he asked.

"No ... Jonathan, do you think Cody spends too much time alone?"

"No. Why would he want to hang out with us? Some of his friends are on holiday. He's finding his way. I wish I'd known what I wanted to do with my life when I was eleven."

"Airline pilots don't make a lot of money, Jonathan."

"Who cares, if it makes him happy, I don't see a problem." When had she stopped calling him Jon? Now it was *Jonathan* this and *Jonathan* that. How long had she been doing it? Was she even aware of it? And why hadn't he noticed before?

Zoey ripped apart another envelope, harder than was necessary. "You should talk to him. See how he is."

Why don't you talk to him? See what kind of person he's becoming, because, you know, he's your son, too.

They had been sitting at the breakfast table for a while and she hadn't looked at him once.

He stood and went to Jane, bending to gently squeeze

her tiny hand. She was awake, making baby sounds, her legs pumping at the air as if she was riding an invisible bicycle.

In the backyard, he walked by the swimming pool, deep blue, dazzling in the glorious sunshine. It was a simple rectangle, nothing fancy, at his request. It had been installed by Marcus Jenkins, pool builder to the stars. Jenkins and his brother had cornered the Hamptons market for recreational additions, including tennis courts. Jon didn't swim anymore, but Zoey used it, sometimes at night.

The treehouse faced Upper Sag Harbor Cove and was elevated twelve feet above the ground. The turret, which served as the dining area, was shingled in red cedar; wide windows wrapped around its curve giving a 180-degree panoramic view of the Cove. The construction company had made it appear as though it was growing out of the eastern red cedars grouped together like a three-pronged plug. He climbed the staircase that led to the roomy deck. One of the eastern reds rose out of the timber floor. He knocked and entered.

Cody was sitting at a small natural oak table in the turret, parts of his model airplane spread across it. Some of the smaller pieces had been cut from the plastic sprue with an X-Acto knife and laid out, ready to be stuck together. Cody had opened all the windows. Jon hadn't tired of reminding him to work in a well-ventilated area.

"Hey, Dad," he said, putting down a tube of model cement next to jars of acrylic paint. "How was work?"

Jon had made just over a thousand dollars during the short time he'd traded that morning. He could have made more, but certain distractions had broken his concentration.

"It was fine, son. What're you building? Looks complicated."

"Nothing's complicated when you have a plan, Dad."

Cody picked up a sheet of paper from the bench and held it up. It had lines and numbers on it.

Jon nodded. *Look at my little philosopher*, he thought. *Kid's eleven and has life figured out already. How dumb was I when I was his age? Exceptionally.*

"So what is it? A 747?"

"It's an Air Japan Boeing 787 Dreamliner. Neat, huh?"

"Yes, it's great."

You can do this, Jon.

He took a deep breath and sat on the bench, moving a bottle of cyanoacrylate glue, or CA glue as Cody called it, and a Kwik CA de-bonder, in case he glued his fingers. Jon had insisted on the de-bonder. He didn't want to come looking for Cody one day and find him stuck to the table, or himself.

"Everything okay, Dad?"

"Yeah, I'm … I just wanted to talk, if it's all right with you."

Jon's palms were sweating. *Jesus Christ, this is awkward.*

Cody nodded at him, waiting. "It's all right, Dad. You can talk to me."

For a moment, he was overwhelmed with love for his son. He shifted his eyes downward, staring at the wood grain on the tabletop. Jon thought Cody could see he was struggling, and he was trying to make it easier for his dad. Sometimes he thought Cody was older than his eleven years.

"Um … so you went to see Mia Jenkins earlier, huh?"

"Yeah, I brought her some of the cupcakes Mom bought."

The kid's a legend, bringing his female friend baked goods. Why didn't I ever think of that?

"Good. Great. Yeah … Yes, it's … um … Cody, I really hope you don't mind if I talk to you about the birds and the bees."

"You mean the sex talk?"

Stunned, Jon just stared at his son.

"It's all right, Dad. They gave us the talk at school already."

Jon's shoulders slumped forward. He attempted to hide his relief. He slapped his knee. "Great. Yep, glad you know about … all that." *Thank you, God, for sparing me this conversation.* "Okay. So you're sure you know where—?"

"Babies come from? Yeah, Dad."

"All right, then. Subject closed. You need any help here?"

"Not if you're busy."

"I'm not, son. Put me to work." Cody handed him a section of the fuselage, a paintbrush and a jar of paint. "I don't know, Cody. I might mess it up."

"It's okay if you do. It's not a real plane. I'll show you how."

Jon smiled at him in admiration and respect. "Let's begin," he said, twisting the cap off the jar.

8

Ken had cabin fever. He needed to get out of the hotel, have a drink. They were lodging at the Mayfair until Benny decided the fate of a certain officer of the court. Andre still had time to prove he was of fair character, according to Benny, who had admitted to a not insignificant curiosity as to how Andre would proceed: would he choose Door Number One and pay up? Or Door Number Two—flee Coconut Grove with his new identity and a large, unpaid bill?

"George, keep a lookout for a parking space." George nodded, and Ken gritted his teeth as he cruised down Main Highway, listening as the man in the passenger seat munched on a rice cake and sipped almond milk. Ken desperately needed a whisky. Or several.

"Why do they even call it milk?"

George looked at him. "What?"

"Almond milk. You ever seen an almond with udders? You get milk from a goddamn cow, not a nut."

Unruffled—which irritated Ken even further—George produced a blasé shrug, and said, "Guess it sounds better than juice—almond juice, or almond drink. Doesn't sound right, does it?"

Ken clenched his jaw, harder. He glanced at the younger man, and said, "But it's factually incorrect."

"Factually, who gives a fuck?"

"And you're eating rice cakes."

"So?"

"So they make you hungry, it's like eating fresh air—."

"There, *there*!" George was pointing at an empty space across the road from Gemini Beer and Whisk(e)y House. Ken swung the wheel hard to the right, and the Ford Edge made it into the slot. Someone behind him leaned on their horn.

"Jesus, Ken, what's the matter with you?"

Ken shut off the engine. "Sorry," he said, "I'm in a strange mood."

"Yeah? All right then. Apology accepted…something on your mind?"

"I've been thinking about Andre."

"How long have you been having these impure thoughts?"

"Can you be serious for a second?" Ken said. "If you don't want to hear it, just say so."

"All right, all right." George held up his hands. "I'm listening."

He relaxed his shoulders, putting conscious effort into the task, aware that George was watching him. Ken said, "Andre's not going to pay."

"How do you know? You *can't* know that."

"I was sitting right there, at the table with Benny," Ken continued, "Andre was scared. No doubt about it, he was terrified of Benny. Call it instinct, whatever you want, but I got the impression Andre was scared just for that moment.

As soon as Benny was out of sight, I'd bet Andre's fear wore off like whatever he snorted before we arrived."

"Does this little anecdote have a point?"

"The second Andre told Benny he only had half the money, Benny knew he wasn't going to pay the rest."

"You're speculating, Ken."

"I watched Andre closely. I know how guy's like that think: he's sitting in a house that cost maybe a million five, maybe two?"

"Yeah, somewhere around there. It's not Munroe Drive, on the waterfront, but it ain't too shabby, either."

"Exactly," Ken said, "he's got the high walls and thinks he's safe. I saw it in his eyes, and Benny caught it, too. Andre is a lawyer, living behind walls, and he doesn't believe Benny has the guts to whack him."

George held up a hand. "Hold on. He's not just a lawyer, he's a criminal. I told you already he might have embezzled eye-catching amounts of cash from his own firm—."

"Why didn't Benny shoot him on the spot? He knew Andre wasn't going to pay—."

"He didn't want to create a crime scene, Ken. You know how it is."

"Okay, fine. Let me tell you what I think: Benny's going to let Andre think he got away with stiffing him, then when he least expects it he's gonna show up…" Ken paused as realization dawned on George's face.

"I get it," George said. "You're saying this is sport for Benny. That he takes pleasure in it. If that's true, so what? It doesn't change anything. What difference does it make? By the way—I disagree: you can't know Andre isn't going to pay. A hundred dollars says you're wrong."

"I'll take that bet," Ken said.

"Why does it bother you, anyway?"

"I just wonder about someone like Andre," Ken said, "the mindset of a guy who *had* it all. He's a lawyer, living in a wealthy neighborhood, he's a bachelor, living the dream…and somehow, he fucks it up."

George sighed. "You're thinking about things too deeply, Ken."

"It fascinates me. I was annoyed, watching him, struggling to process how someone who has the world in the palm of his hand sabotages it all—for what? A quick buck? Then he made things weird with pictures of the Juice. Are they a metaphor for something I don't understand?"

"Why are you asking me?"

"Because you eat rice cakes, George. You drink almond milk, which technically doesn't exist, and you're about the same age as Andre, so maybe you know."

They sat in silence for a moment. Then: "You shouldn't try to figure him out, Ken. I backed out of that dead-end street years ago."

"Who are you talking about?"

"Benny," George said, "give it up. You're not going to gain any insight into the character of someone like him…are you sure there's nothing else bothering you, Ken?"

Ken considered telling George he was worried about his upcoming physical exam, or that his doctor had warned him he might have to increase the dosage of his blood pressure medication on his next visit. Instead, he asked, "What the fuck is a dopamine fast?"

George held up the box of rice cakes.

9

Lizzy's mood had improved. No one had tried to trick her today. Nobody had played a cruel prank on her. She was glad to be home, relieving the babysitter and paying her without making eye contact. Lizzy knew Audrey Moore thought she was weird, but she could live with it. Audrey, it seemed, had gotten used to her. And Mia liked Ms. Moore, even though Mia recoiled whenever Lizzy referred to her as the babysitter. She wasn't a baby, Mia would complain, she was *twelve*, practically a grown-up.

Marcus had called her at work to tell her she didn't have to cook; they were having dinner at his brother's house in North Haven. Lizzy had asked Mia to get changed; her dad would be home soon and they had to be ready to leave.

As usual, Lizzy went to her bedroom and crawled into the back of the closet to hide the day's shavings. She unzipped a sports bag half full of green felt and sliced rubber. When the bag was full, she dumped everything into the garbage, hiding it in the household waste. She had filled and emptied the sports bag dozens of times.

Lizzy had a quick shower and put on a simple chambray tunic dress, slate gray. She went downstairs and came to a dead stop as she approached the kitchen island. There was a single cupcake sitting on its granite surface. She heard Mia coming downstairs, and turned, pointing. "Where did you get this?"

"Mom, Cody brought it this morning."

"I see. Please be careful, Mia. You know boys are only after One Thing."

It, she thought, they want *it* all the time. Except Marcus, who had somehow managed to go without *it* for two years.

"We're fine, Mom. Everything's fine. What do you think?" Mia twirled, her hair and yellow summer dress catching air.

"Looks good."

"Won't you be late for your book club?"

"No, it starts at nine. Plenty of time." They headed for the front door at the sound of Marcus's SUV in the driveway.

10

Zoey was standing behind Jon when he answered the door.

"What're you doing here?" he said.

"Zoey asked me to come over." Candice Fersh leaned sideways and waved at Zoey. Jon glanced at his wife. Zoey was certain she saw hurt in his eyes. Betrayal? Possibly a hint of humiliation? It was there. She sensed it coming off him in waves. She could almost taste it. Well, who did he think he was? Firing her nanny? Without asking her first?

"Why are you here?" Jon said.

"Go inside, Candice," Zoey said, "check on Jane." Candice slipped past him, head bowed, watching him from the corner of her eye. Zoey turned, and when Candice went upstairs, she looked directly at her husband and said, "Don't make an issue out of this. She made a mistake."

"She's unreliable."

Pouty, petulant, whiny—Zoey was familiar with *that* tone.

"You don't make mistakes, Jonathan? Are you saying you're infallible?"

"What's happening to you? Where is the anger coming from? Only an angry person would do this."

He was right. But there was no way she'd tell him why she was angry.

Some people didn't deserve answers, even when the answer was date- and time-stamped in her memory.

"I thought you were going out?"

He looked at her then. Really stared, searching, trying to read her. Zoey was familiar with that look, too. But she wouldn't give anything away. She had given too much already.

Zoey saw someone coming up the path. It was Lizzy Jenkins, eyes downcast, shoulders slumped, hesitant.

"Come on in, Lizzy," she said, and Jon blinked.

"Hi, Lizzy," he said, and the woman barely looked at him. Instead, she muttered a greeting. Zoey left him standing in the doorway and ushered her friend into the living room, an arm around Lizzy's shoulders.

***

Jon was on his way to Murphy's Bar for a club soda. Zoey wanted him out of the house tonight, but she wasn't direct about it. She'd say things like, "You should go out, catch a football game on TV at a bar."

Hands in his pockets, head lowered, he stared at the sidewalk and only looked around when someone whistled. His friend and neighbor, Peggy Dawson, was on her porch, magnifying glass raised. "I thought I recognized you, handsome stranger. Come on, pull up a chair." If anyone else had made the offer, he would have walked on. But he couldn't say no to Peggy.

He climbed the steps to the porch and sat next to her on the bench, which was covered in some type of memory foam cushion. Peggy sat out here a lot, watching the street, especially in summer. Jon hardly saw her in the winter, except when he stopped by with some soup at least once every week and to check if she had enough provisions. Peggy was always dressed impeccably. She wore a regal blue suit, smart shoes, and pearl earrings. Her hair was meticulously permed. She looked ready for business rather than someone just relaxing as the sun sank lower and the evening drew in. Jon wondered if she missed her old job. Peggy had been a partner in the biggest marketing firm in New York City for thirty years. Retirement must have been a hard adjustment. He didn't know how old she was. Seventy? Whatever her age, it was a closely guarded secret.

"You want a drink?" she said.

"You have any beer?"

"Yep. Why don't you walk your way inside? You know where the fridge is."

Jon returned a moment later with a bottle of Budweiser. "I didn't know you still drink this stuff," he said.

"I don't. I keep it for nostalgic reasons. Can't sup them like I used to. Gives me gas ... I thought you didn't drink alcohol?"

"I don't. I'm thinking about taking it up. You don't seem the nostalgic type, Peg."

"Yeah, well, even a tough old broad like me has a weakness."

"I don't believe you."

"Uh-huh. You looked like a man with confession on his mind."

"Just brooding on a problem."

"Yep. You should brood harder. Whatever's on the gray matter looks like it's about ready to trip you up and steal your wallet."

37

"Does it look that bad?"

"I've known you a long time, Jon. Yes, it does."

Jon paused, took a sip of beer, and said, "Can I ask you a question?"

"Sure, but I can't guarantee I'll give you an honest answer."

"You and Gabe were married a long time."

"Forty-five years."

"Were you ever cruel to him?"

She squinted, placed her hand on the cane propped against her leg. "No," she said, "we had disagreements, don't get me wrong. Even arguments. But cruel? No. Gabe was a sweetheart. We had a good marriage, sometimes great, and he loved me and knew me like no one else." Gabriel Dawson had had a stroke that had sent him to Stony Brook hospital in Southampton two years ago, and another shortly after arriving in the emergency department that sent him to Green River Cemetery in East Hampton. Jon and Zoey had eaten dinner prepared by Gabe many times and Jon remembered how envious he'd been of his culinary skills, wishing he had progressed further in his cooking than being able to fry an egg. Some people just had a natural touch for it, and Jon had learned to accept he wasn't one of them.

"Okay, Jon, what's wrong?" Peggy turned her sage, knowing gaze on him.

"Probably nothing," he said.

She nodded, as though he had given a full answer.

"Marriages go through phases," she said, "even the best of them. Keep it in mind. Things get stupid when people don't talk. Don't let things get stupid."

"Why haven't you joined Zoey's book club? It's not as if she hasn't asked you."

"My bulbs aren't as bright as they used to be." She held the magnifying glass to one eye. "Don't let things get stupid, Jon. Follow that, and you'll be fine."

11

The van took a hard turn and Ken clamped a hand to the wall behind him and pressed his foot into the floor. The muscles in his jaws twitched; he was nervous. They were minutes away from perpetrating a serious crime, and he was responsible for making sure they weren't discovered. Benny was driving, talking to someone on the phone, but saying very little. Benny didn't leave even scraps of conversation that someone might be able to piece together to form a picture.

George's face was lit by his cell phone. He was dressed in black, from head to toe.

"Are you on Instagram?" Ken said.

"Just logging out, baby."

"Where's my money?"

"Oh." George dug in his pockets and brought out some bills, counting them. "Here." He leaned across and handed them to Ken.

"Don't bet with me, George," Ken said, smiling.

"I'll keep that in mind, bitch."

"Two minutes," Benny said, "masks down, scanner on." Ken and George lowered their ski masks. Ken switched on the scanner, keeping the volume low.

"George, good luck."

George looked at him and nodded.

Up in front, Benny killed the headlights. It became even darker inside the van.

Ken spoke into a two-way radio. "Test one." He heard his voice transmitting from the radio on the dash.

The van came to a stop. Benny climbed in back, putting his arms through the straps of a book bag, and crouched by the side door. George slung the tactical ladder over his shoulder and Ken took up position in the driver's seat. He looked at his watch. It was 3:41 am.

He checked his mirrors, watching Loquat Avenue in front, and behind.

"Go," he said, and tilted his head to look in the rearview. Benny slid the door open carefully, and closed it when George got out. Ken looked in the side mirror; two shadows streaked across the road at impressive speed. George laid the ladder against the wall, adjusting it until he had the required height. He climbed a few rungs up, then pushed the retractable half of it over on its hinge and another ladder extended, dropping to the ground on the other side of the wall. It was designed and built by Benny; its non-reflective black paint made it almost blend into the darkness. Once Benny and George were inside, Ken allowed sixty seconds to elapse and retrieved the ladder. Back in the van, in the dark, he allowed himself a dry smile as he settled in to wait for Benny and George to drag Andre out of his house, something Benny could have done the first time around. But the pictures of O.J. Simpson had saved the lawyer's life, giving him an extra few days to luxuriate in the mistaken belief that he was going to run out on his debt to Benny and live happily ever after. It hadn't escaped Ken that even though Benny found the photographs of Simpson to be in bad taste, he knew his boss respected—at least, temporarily—Andre for not backing away from his assertion that the former football star was a nice guy, worthy of a place on Andre's wall. But it was more than that: Andre hadn't apologized for his odd veneration of Simpson, and Benny, he guessed, could not help but respect him for it.

How ironic, he thought, that of all the people in the world, O.J. Simpson had bought Andre an extra few days of life.

Benny had called him as he was eating breakfast yesterday and he'd told Ken that Andre was preparing to flee. As he'd driven by Andre's house with George, lo and behold, there was a moving truck parked in the driveway of the mansion, the largest house on Loquat. How Benny came by this information was a mystery, but George had merely shrugged and hadn't offered any comment, even when Ken had wondered aloud how Benny knew that Andre had purchased a one-way ticket to Brazil.

He had warned Andre, but the lawyer hadn't listened. Ken had no sympathy for him; in fact, he was looking forward to dealing with Andre personally.

***

George led the way to the rear of the property. Benny followed, both men moving low and fast. They bypassed the covered lanai, heading for the door that opened directly into the kitchen. "Is this it?" Benny whispered.

George nodded. During his walk-through of the house, he'd seen a key that Andre had left in the back door, and Benny hoped it was still there. Benny had shaken his head at this careless lapse in security, but it didn't surprise him at all. Andre was one of those people who believed he'd never become the victim of a crime. Even if the key wasn't there, Plan B would work just as well: he would break the glass in the lanai door with the hammer and punch in his book bag. It would make a lot of noise, and they'd have less time to make a quiet getaway; one way or another, Benny was getting inside the house.

He took the duct tape from the book bag, rolled a strip across the glass. George hovered by his side with a blade, cutting each piece. Benny pushed the tape hard into the small section of glass nearest to the door handle, using his fingertips, making sure it gripped. He added one more layer, held the punch like a pencil, drew back with the hammer and tapped the rubber cap on the end of the punch. The small window collapsed, and with his gloved hand, he forced it inward, reached down, and turned the key. George had told him that the sensor on this door was broken. They were in.

In the kitchen, Benny discovered that Andre was not entirely reckless in matters of home security—he had set the intruder alarm. At the upper left hand corner of the door leading into the hall, George placed a small magnet in the center of a clear square piece of tape over the receiver, a reed switch, disrupting the signal between the sensor and the magnetic contact that was screwed into the door. The alarm system was old and could be easily defeated. George's survey of the house had been very useful.

There was no guarantee that the alarm wouldn't trip when George opened the door, Benny knew, and he held his breath as George pulled it wide.

Silence.

They glanced at each other in the dim light. Benny entered the hall, taking the weight out of each footfall, and climbed the stairs, three at a time.

Benny moved toward where George was pointing, the last door on the left of the hall.

They stopped outside the door—Andre was snoring.

Benny didn't waste precious seconds. He went into the room, leaned over the sleeping lump. He grabbed a handful of Andre's neck and squeezed. Andre's eyes shot open. He tried to scream. Benny brought his head closer to Andre's face, and said, "You look surprised to see me, Andre. Scream and I'll cut you." He waved a razor blade in front of the lawyer's eyes. Andre choked, gurgled and struggled. Benny dragged him from the bed and slammed him into the floor. He moved aside slightly, sensing George at his side. George duct taped Andre's mouth, punched him in the throat and turned him over, taping his hands behind his back.

Benny hauled Andre to his feet. "Ups-a-daisy, counselor. Let's take a walk. You're going to open the gates."

12

It was a hateful way to live, with your anger on a constant low boil. But Jon deserved it. He deserved to be undermined, humiliated. Betrayed. After all, it was his treachery that had caused her to treat him this way—Zoey had hired Candice again to punish him. Perhaps she shouldn't prolong his torment. She had considered divorce many times, yet she couldn't bring herself to do it. She had to think of others, her children, for one. There was another reason, too. A rogue, pathetic part of her still loved Jon. The utter absurdity of it … She had a right to her anger. It was a grubby indulgence, but it was earned.

So what if he caught her? What would he do? Probably nothing at all. Whatever he did, it would have a negative return. After all, Jon was a risk manager, and some losses were unacceptable. And he'd lose, of course, especially when she held a mirror up to him and demanded he take a closer look. Zoey had lost already. Her own investment—emotional, physical and monetary—had all been all for nothing. The only thing that hadn't soured was her love of books. As she watched the other three members of her little club take their seats the old certainty hit her hard—she had chosen the wrong career. Her dream had started when she was twelve and it hadn't dulled with the passage of time: she had wanted to be a book reviewer. Telling her parents at dinner what she wanted to be when she grew up had been a mistake. She remembered the way her father had knitted his fingers under his chin, looked at her with supreme patience and something she later recognized as indulgence, and said, "Oh, sweetie, there's no money in it. Finance, that's where you need to focus your talent." She'd felt stupid, in her pretty dress and her perfect shoes, because everything grown-ups said sounded true. Her face had become hot and she had dropped the subject, vowing not to speak of it again. The main reason she had gone to Harvard Business School to get her MBA was her father, Edward (never Eddie) Harman. He had approved of it, her mother, too. And it was all she had wanted: their approval. Which was probably why she carried within her enough self-loathing to last three lifetimes. She didn't blame her parents for controlling the reins of her destiny. She had one life, and it was hers. And it was her fault for not making her decisions her own. It wasn't even as if she wasn't strong enough … trying to please everyone was paving the road ahead on the way to regret. Because it was impossible to satisfy everyone. Her father had been right, though—there *was* more money in finance. She wasn't quite a billionaire yet, but the gap was closing.

She was angry with Jon for another reason: because he had found success the hard way. He had worked on building sites in his teenage years, he had gotten his hands dirty, whereas she had interned at Goldman Sachs straight out of college. Jon's route to investment banking was circuitous, to say the least, and not without hardship. He had paid for his own education, holding down three jobs. Her parents, of course, had made sure their only daughter had an easy entrance to the hallowed halls of academia. But it wasn't solely envy that burned with the intensity of sun-fire inside her; it was raw, immovable regret. Zoey wished she'd had those three jobs; instead, her parent's money and influence had bought her frictionless passage through life ...

No. *No.* She knew exactly why she was angry with Jon, and it had nothing to do with his working-class roots. It wasn't her fault she was born into a wealthy family.

Peyton Ellis caught her eye as she lowered herself daintily into Zoey's Ralph Lauren writer's chair, its brown leather creaking. Then Peyton propped her legs on the matching ottoman.

Jesus Christ, make yourself at home, why don't you?

Zoey tried to read her face, searching for a knowing look, anything that might indicate Peyton had seen her slut shuffle outside The Blue Lemon. But Peyton's usually expressive face was inscrutable—was that a sign? It was one of the worst things about cheating on your husband: persistent paranoia.

She had invited Peyton into her home many times, and yet Zoey watched her behave in the same curious way she always had: she looked around the living room as though seeing it for the first time. Was it a tic? Or was it not-so-subtle criticism of the décor? Peyton's eyes went from the sisal rug on the floor to the dark oak beams in the ceiling. Zoey had convinced herself Peyton's open examination of her colorful throw pillows and the lack of distressed timber furniture in limed oak and the omission of wicker chairs and linen sofas (she had opted for brown leather) and blue-and-white china and soft neutral tones was a sign of disapproval because Zoey had gone off course and decided the

47

Hamptons-style interior was not for her. Yes, she kept some elements, such as the sisal rug, yet her bookshelves weren't Dulux white but a deep chocolate walnut.

There was something unselfconscious in the way Peyton looked around that irritated Zoey. Being self-conscious was probably a vague, alien idea she'd heard about but never actually experienced.

Lizzy, on the other hand, was visibly uncomfortable. Thomas Harris's masterpiece, *The Silence of the Lambs*, was sandwiched between her knees and her arms were wrapped tightly across her chest. She was sitting forward, and for some reason Zoey expected her to start rocking back and forth. A deep wave of sadness rose in her gut and swelled in her throat as she watched Lizzy. She picked up her glass of merlot from the black coffee table (another example of her spitting in the eye of the Hamptons style and those who championed the overuse of white furniture) and took a long drink. Myrtle Shaw, the oldest member of the Village Book Club, was staring at her, as if to say, *Let's get started already.*

"Okay," Zoey said, "we'll begin."

13

Lizzy felt safe—no one would play a trick on her here. She kept her gaze on Zoey, zeroed in on her kind eyes. Zoey wouldn't let any harm come to her. The Village Book Club was having an Eighties Thriller Week, and Lizzy was just glad she was invited. She'd thanked (at last count, nine times) Zoey for urging her to take part until Zoey had made her promise to stop thanking her. Promises to Zoey were easy to make and keep. After all, she was Lizzy's closest friend.

"Did anyone have a favorite character?" Zoey asked.

Peyton answered immediately. "Jack Crawford," she said, "it was the way he took care of his wife. I thought it was sweet … but I couldn't help feeling there was some chemistry between Clarice Starling and Crawford. Did anyone else get that?"

Lizzy looked at the paperback in her lap. Heat was rising in her face. She didn't want to discuss the Sex Thing, or chemistry, especially the sexual kind.

"What book were you reading?" Myrtle asked, and sniffed, hard.

"This one right here," Peyton said, holding up the hardback and waggling it. Everyone except Lizzy had read the hardback. She preferred paperbacks—she only had two wrists and wanted to keep them in good working order.

"Okay," Zoey said, "I get what you're saying, Peyton, but nothing happened between them."

"So why do I get the sense they wanted something to happen?"

"I'm not saying you're wrong. In fact, you may be on to something."

Peyton removed her legs from the ottoman and sat forward, both feet planted on the floor, as though her next point was built on solid ground. "I know I'm on to something. Crawford was interested in Starling and she was interested in him. Young woman has romantic notions about an older man in a position of power. Shock! Horror! It's the whole Daddy complex—"

"Okay, okay," Zoey said, and Lizzy caught the concern in her glance, "let's keep it clean."

"There's nothing clean about this novel," Peyton said, elbows resting on her knees, head lowered, almost as if she was aiming her body at Zoey. "Thomas Harris laid bare the human psyche in all its true ugliness. *The Silence of the Lambs* is just another example of how there's no limit to what humans will do to humans." Peyton slid backward into the chair and put her feet up on the ottoman, the hardback on her thighs, hands intertwined on her midriff, and Lizzy was sure she had just seen a small victor's smirk pass briefly over her lips.

Lizzy reached for the lemonade on the table and drank. She didn't consume alcohol like the other women. It wasn't recommended for someone taking antipsychotic drugs. But there was another reason: when she was drunk, she wasn't in control of herself, which was frightening. She wouldn't deliberately enhance the sense of not being in control already present.

She wasn't at all surprised things had gotten a little heated. It had been a lot worse last month when they'd reviewed Liane Moriarty's *Big Little Lies*. Myrtle and Peyton had come down on the side of a character suffering from domestic violence, and Lizzy and Zoey had taken the controversial position that the character with the abusive husband was wrong to accept such treatment. Lizzy thought anyone passing on the sidewalk outside would have heard the arguments. But she never felt unsafe. She was used to what Zoey referred to as "lively debate," although Lizzy recognized plain old altercations when she heard them.

"Did anyone not see the movie?" Zoey said, and nobody raised their hand. "All right, so everyone's seen it. Did seeing the movie detract from your enjoyment of the novel?"

"No," Myrtle said, "I've seen the movie five times. It's impossible to say everyone on the planet has watched it, but it *is* that famous. The book had more depth."

"Do you agree with Peyton about Jack Crawford?" Zoey said.

Myrtle considered the question for a moment. "No. It was nice the way he took care of his wife, as any husband is meant to, just as any wife is meant to. He used Clarice." All eyes were on Myrtle. "Clarice was my favorite character," she continued, "and Crawford allowed the monster to probe and prod her mind like she was in the cage and not Lecter … Clarice was barely cooked, and she was thrown to the lions and here she is having spunk thrown at her by a lunatic and all because the Big Boss Man used her to poke the beast and she's the one who got poked. You can't wash that out."

Lizzy gaped at her, mouth open in awe. She'd just heard a sixty-two-year-old woman say a dirty word, before a small audience, and not even blink. Her cheeks burned but she wasn't going to remove her thick cardigan. In fact, she pulled it tighter around her shoulders. A thrill of excitement contracted her gut. Which was fine, this was controlled excitement. These women weren't going to have a fistfight in a pleasant Hamptons home. At least, she hoped not.

The silence stretched out until eventually Zoey cleared her throat and said, "It's an interesting way of looking at it."

"Are you saying I'm wrong?" Myrtle said.

"No, no. This is a book club, there are no wrong opinions."

Lizzy glanced at Myrtle, who seemed a bit more relaxed. Then she looked at Peyton, but had difficulty reading her facial expression, which could have been anger or amusement, she didn't know.

"Did anyone find Hannibal Lecter charming?" Zoey said, and Lizzy had a strong sense that she wanted to change gears, move on.

"I did," Peyton said, "he's the kind of person you'd invite to dinner, not to talk to, but to just listen to."

"What if you ended up on the menu?" Myrtle asked.

"As long as he didn't sprinkle tarragon on me, I wouldn't complain. I hate tarragon." Zoey and Myrtle laughed, and Lizzy was glad the atmosphere had become more relaxed. It didn't last long.

"I liked him," Zoey said, and now the sound of Myrtle breathing through her nose made Lizzy uneasy. The air whistled through her nostrils. Lizzy didn't look up from her lap to see if anyone else heard it. "I know he's a cannibal,"

Zoey continued, "but I was charmed by him." The nose whistle grew louder. "Lizzy, what did you think of Dr. Lecter?"

The temperature in her face increased by several degrees. Everyone was looking at her, paying attention to her. Two things were guaranteed to make her skin crawl: the Sex Thing and being the center of attention. But it was Zoey's gentle tone that gave her encouragement.

"Hypnotic," Lizzy said, "I thought he was hypnotic."

Peyton nodded, as did Zoey, as though Lizzy had perfectly encapsulated the Hannibal Lecter effect with a single word—hypnotic. Lizzy was pleased; she was taking part, engaging in the discussion. But most of all, she was just glad that Zoey had smiled at her.

"Who did you sympathize with more—Lecter or Buffalo Bill?" Peyton said.

"Buffalo Bill. I felt sorry for Jame Gumb—he just wanted to be pretty." Lizzy noticed the air had stopped whistling in Myrtle's nose. Why was everyone staring at her? Had she said something awful? She was being honest. Her face was on fire, and the excitement no longer felt controlled. Her stomach fluttered and the pulse in her neck quickened and her body prickled with a horrible itchiness. She reached into her pocket and touched the smooth rubber of a skinned tennis ball. Oh, how she wanted to cut it ... She squeezed it instead.

Lizzy was relieved that Zoey didn't let the stunned silence linger. There was something merciful in the way her friend said, "Thank you, Lizzy. We all have unique ways of interpreting a character. Anyway, we move to matters greasy: Dr. Chilton."

Peyton groaned at the mention of Chilton. Lizzy's focus drifted back to Jame Gumb. Even though Gumb had done terrible things in the novel, Lizzy couldn't help but admire the craftsmanship of his grotesque creation. Gumb's attention to detail was just as mesmerizing as Thomas Harris's most famous character, Dr. Lecter.

The voices of the other women became faint. She was *in her thoughts*, as her mother would have said. *Don't mind Lizzy, Mrs. Fitch, she's in her thoughts.* As if she was somewhere else. Lizzy supposed she probably was, but she couldn't remember going there. Wherever *there* was.

***

Myrtle Shaw was furious. That anyone could think Hannibal Lecter was anything less than a monster was shocking to her. Charming, they'd said. Dr. Lecter was *charming*. If she had her way, Lecter would have been executed, twice, just to make sure. As Peyton prattled on about the sleazy lecher Dr. Chilton, growing more animated by the second, Myrtle considered a deeper question: why were so many women fascinated by murderers? She herself was a true crime addict, and most of her friends were, too. She read books about serial killers, fictional and very real. She watched TV shows about husbands murdering their wives and vice versa. Why were so many women fascinated by the perpetrators of violent crimes? She believed she had stumbled on the answer: because we hope we'll be able to recognize our own Hannibal Lecter if we ever see him.

Myrtle wasn't preoccupied with being the victim of a crime except perhaps at a dim, low level of awareness—the possibility was there, but it was less likely here in Sag Harbor.

The crime rate was low, and she got daily updates from her husband, Vincent, the Chief of Police, who was kept busy in the summer busting brawling drunks. But other than that … She had to admit *The Silence of the Lambs* had gotten under her skin. There *were* people like Buffalo Bill and Hannibal Lecter in the world, ordinary monsters who went to church on Sunday and who had regular jobs and helped their neighbors with a smile on a human face hiding inhuman desires. Her favorite character in Thomas Harris's novel was Barney, the orderly, because he was compassionate. Barney was better than her. He treated Dr. Lecter with dignity, more than she would have afforded him. Barney was recognizably human. There was something reassuring about that.

She could forgive Lizzy's comments about Buffalo Bill just wanting to be pretty, but not Zoey and Peyton. She didn't fully understand what was wrong with Lizzy, but whatever it was, she at least had an excuse. Or maybe Myrtle just didn't like bankers. Hated them, in fact. And Zoey was a banker. If some people had short memories, she was grateful hers was intact. Zoey was probably one of those people who believed that because her office was not on Wall Street she was somehow less culpable for the past and present swindle concocted by men and women in suits. Of course, Zoey was different. But she wasn't. Myrtle loved books, enjoyed being part of a book club, but she wouldn't let Zoey borrow a cup of sugar. She *would* drink the free wine, though.

She looked at Lizzy from the corner of her eye and felt a surge of sympathy for her; she hoped she would find peace. The reason—the real reason, anyway—she still took part in the Village Book Club was to check on how Lizzy was doing. Myrtle liked the young woman, felt protective toward her. Coming here was a way for Myrtle to tell Lizzy in person that if she ever needed anything, she knew where to find her. She couldn't not come here. She felt she had an obligation, a responsibility. She didn't want Lizzy to take her life the way her sister Sandra had, who had left only a two-word, unsigned suicide note: I can't. Lizzy had sought help, though, and she was on medication, so she had a chance. Lizzy bore a striking resemblance to Sandy, not in her features, but in her eyes. Lizzy had the same look she'd seen in her sister: pain, buried deep but bobbing to the surface briefly, long enough for her to catch a glimpse of it. She had lived for more than six decades and she was no closer to understanding people. But she was trying. The real mystery wasn't the nature of the universe or the meaning of life, it was people.

Since she had arrived she had wondered why Zoey was watching Peyton. Watching her in a quiet, searching way that intrigued her. Then Myrtle caught her gaze and held it. Zoey had a nervous, hunted look. As if she had done something wrong.

14

Peyton had met Zoey at the Met Gala when she had been invited as a contributing writer for *Vogue*, where the theme for that year was Manus x Machina: Fashion in an Age of Technology. Madonna had stolen the show with her Givenchy outfit, which exposed her buttocks and breasts, although she had applied tape over her nipples in an admirable display of modesty.

She had known Zoey was a regular fixture on New York's social scene, attending exclusive parties, being photographed with the rich and famous. The couple fitted perfectly into the glossy magazines. They were young, rich, attractive and smart. Peyton found out just how clever Zoey was when they somehow started discussing the mathematics of probability. Peyton lost the thread of the conversation almost immediately. In her teenage years she'd thought math had been created specifically to make her life miserable. Peyton had done her part, nodding politely as if she knew what Zoey was talking about. She couldn't even remember how they'd gotten onto the subject. But she was relieved to discover that Zoey's real passion was for books. The way her eyes lit up as they had discussed their favorite authors and the novels they enjoyed the most. Peyton soon discovered they were neighbors, and that was when Zoey had asked her if she would like to start a book club. Peyton had agreed right there in the Metropolitan Museum of Art, standing in the Temple of Dendur room, to get together just as soon as she got back to the Hamptons. Those years of the Village Book Club had been some of the best in Peyton's life. Their mutual love of story had bonded them together in a tight friendship. Yes, tempers frayed from time to time, but they were passionate in their opinions and they always made up in the end.

She had grown weary and somewhat cynical lately about the fashion world. There was no doubt in her mind: some of the outfits she'd seen in the course of her work were nothing short of works of high art, stunning examples of the imagination at its most inventive. Then there was Chanel's fetish for clear plastic knee-high boots, gloves, coats, and see-through wide-brimmed hats. Peyton didn't care which label was attached to these items; they still looked cheap because they *were* cheap. The transparent look just didn't do it for her. And soon the trend would fade away as people came to their senses and realized how ridiculous they looked.

Her dream job had soured. Or maybe it wasn't even the job itself, but the dimming spark of her enthusiasm. There was something awful about that feeling, the way you could unexpectedly lose your passion for your chosen profession. On the other hand, her husband, Peter, was the vice mayor of Sag Harbor, and someday—with her support—he was going to be mayor. They were equals, and therefore they would have their policies enacted equally. Political power, even at a local level, was far more appealing than writing for a magazine, even if it was *Vogue*.

Jon Finch had supported her husband's political

ambitions, donating large sums of money to Peter's campaigns. At first, Peter had viewed Jon as just another donor, until they became real friends. Peyton didn't understand Jon: he hadn't asked for anything in return for his money. What kind of contributor to a political campaign didn't ask for a favor? She had seen Jon at various events and parties over the years. He didn't shun the limelight, but he didn't seek it out, either. Peyton decided that he just didn't care about it the way Zoey did. After all, during the whole Anglo Pharma episode, it was Zoey who had toured the TV studios explaining her short position to CNBC and Bloomberg News. Jon had worked quietly in the background—probably using every hour in the day to borrow yet more shares—while Zoey took care of the unpalatable business of dealing with the TV people, as she had heard Jon refer to them more than a few times.

So what was Peter going to do when she told him Zoey was cheating on his friend? Could she bring herself to tell him? Because that was the only explanation for what she'd seen earlier. Peyton recognized the walk of shame when she saw it, since she had participated in said walk on many early morning occasions herself.

Her job—no, vocation—wasn't the only thing that had soured. Her friendship with Zoey was under strain.

She glanced at Zoey as Zoey asked her, "Does Dr. Chilton have any redeeming qualities?"

Peyton shook her head. "No," she said, "Thomas Harris created a real shit-weasel, and if that was his aim, he succeeded."

What happened to you, Zoey? Who are you cheating with?
She would find out. Jon was her friend, too.

15

Lizzy kept glancing at Myrtle, as if to make sure the older woman was still beside her. It was a pleasant evening to walk home, the air was mild and the first starlight appeared in the darkening sky. Traffic was thin on Main Street and the moderate wind rustled the leaves in the trees.

Already she couldn't wait until next Friday when the Village Book Club would meet again. She needed these women in her life.

Afterward, as everyone was preparing to leave Zoey's house, Peyton and Zoey had hugged her. She felt a warm flush of love for them in her face despite a sudden cool breeze. Even though there were sometimes heated exchanges—especially between Zoey and Peyton—they left as friends at the end of the night. The hearty consumption of Zoey's wine had probably contributed to differences in opinion being forgiven and forgotten. Lizzy had enough self-awareness to know that she could be awkward, and that she often said things that silenced those listening. But she'd gotten much better at not apologizing, thanks to Zoey.

The pale fluted columns of the Whaling Museum appeared through the trees like a ghostly gateway into the underworld. The embers of twilight had burned out and the remnants of clouds resembled old, strewn ashes. Lizzy didn't want to be out here in the deepening dark much longer.

They stood on the corner of Main and Garden Street. On the opposite side of the road was the John Jermain Memorial Library and Union Street, where Myrtle lived.

"Did you enjoy yourself?" Myrtle asked.

"Oh, I did, I really did. I wish we could do it every day."

"Jeez, Lizzy, you've got to give us time to read!"

"I know, I'm sor— I had a great time."

Myrtle looked toward Union, then back at Lizzy. "I'm only two minutes away, Lizzy. Anytime you need to talk, why don't you just wander on over? You don't need a reason to come see me."

Lizzy smiled and her eyes became hot. "Thank you, Myrtle." They embraced, and when Myrtle released her, she said, "Keep taking your medicine, Lizzy. You seem like you're in a good place." Lizzy looked at her shoes. Even though Myrtle had seen her at her worst, her most distressed, when the mutiny taking place in her mind seemed unstoppable, she was embarrassed. She was *mentally ill*. It even sounded awful. She had sat with Myrtle on Myrtle's kitchen floor being comforted as she had cried on so many occasions she'd lost count, all while Myrtle had reassured her that the mutineers were flagging, ready to surrender. But Lizzy didn't want to be a burden to her friends. She understood there was a limit to everything, and she couldn't stand the ordinary kindness shown to her, because it was limitless, freely given, and *extraordinary to her*. She hated being treated as if she was special. She wasn't, she was just Lizzy. A little different, perhaps, but just Lizzy.

"Have you given any thought to getting a puppy?"

Myrtle said. Myrtle had been asking her to get a service dog at least once a week for two years.

"You really believe it'll do me some good?"

Myrtle nodded. "It's up to you, but why not? You have the space."

"Okay, I promise I'll consider it seriously."

"That's good enough for me."

"See you soon," Lizzy said, raising a hand in a timid wave. She headed down Garden Street, head bowed, hugging the paperback copy of *The Silence of the Lambs* to her chest. She only looked up at the sound of a vehicle's engine. Further down the street, a van was turning away from her house. She knew who it belonged to and again raised her hand in a half-wave, but the driver didn't see her. A puzzled frown creased her forehead. She glanced behind her and saw Myrtle standing on the corner, watching her, making sure she got into her house safely. Lizzy was ambivalent about the gesture. On the one hand, she was grateful. On the other, she was slightly annoyed. She was a grown woman capable of walking the short distance home without panicking, *mentally ill* or not. But then she thought she had the best friends in the world.

16

It was good to be home. Safe from the night. If Lizzy had lived alone, she would have slept with the light on. But she had Marcus, who reminded her that there was safety in the dark, too, especially when he curled his arm around her in bed. Marcus kept the nightmares at bay.

She found him in the kitchen. The construction plans for a long rectangular swimming pool were spread open on the table, the top corners held down by salt and pepper shakers. When he saw her, he got up and went to her, kissed her on the cheek (she tried not to recoil too much) and hugged her. Over his shoulder, Lizzy saw the bottom two corners of the plans curl inward.

"Sorry," Lizzy said, "I didn't mean to interrupt your work."

"Nonsense," he said, "it's fine, just going through a few details in case I forget anything for the job on Monday."

"Was that Lewis I saw leave?"

"Yeah, he brought the plans, forgot to give them to me. I swear that man would forget to put on his pants if he didn't have to put his shoes on afterward. How was the book club?"

"It was great. I can't wait for next week." Lizzy beamed at her husband, so overwhelmed with love for him that she fought the rising lump in her throat. "I'm going to check on Mia. Did she eat anything while I was gone?"

"Lizzy, stop worrying. Our daughter knows where the fridge is."

Lizzy nodded.

"How're you feeling?"

"Right now, amazing. Marcus, I think I'm getting better. I'm having a lot more days where I feel positive. Sure, some days are not great, but I'm hopeful. I believe I can get well."

Marcus gathered her into his arms, squeezed the air out of her. Heat blossomed in her neck … and in other places, too. Something … sexual. She backed away from him, from his swelling … area, burying that ugly desire. She was being selfish, her body betraying her when she should be checking on her daughter's well-being.

"I love you, Marcus. I'll be back in a minute."

"I love you, too."

***

And he did. Lewis might doubt it, but Marcus Jenkins loved his wife so much that sometimes telling her he loved her seemed insufficient. Never mind his brother—and employer—no one would believe it.

He sat at the table again, the stiffness in his pants subsiding.

How dare Lewis come to his house with his holier than thou attitude? Somehow, Lewis knew Marcus was having an affair, and he had unleashed a self-righteous tirade on the immorality of adultery. What did he know? But then Lewis had a comfortable black-and-white view of the world, and shades of gray were nothing more than convenient excuses to him. Just because Lewis had helped him when he was hopelessly addicted to the one drug that had consumed him, stolen his heart, his body and soul: cocaine. Of course, Lewis hadn't said anything about *that*. Then why did he get the distinct impression that it was hanging in the air, directly over his head? Not a day went by that he didn't crave it, despite being clean for seven years. Some addicts in NA had promised him it would get easier, but they had lied. Until his dying day, the need to shove all the coke in the world up his nose wouldn't cease. Sometimes he woke in the night, a pulling sensation in his gut, as though it were filled with iron filings and a magnet was being held over his core, *pulling …* The only reason he stopped himself from using again was the certainty that this time it would kill him. He knew it as surely as he knew the sun would come up tomorrow. The reason was simple enough: he would make up for all the coke he hadn't consumed in seven years in the span of a week or two. He'd make up for lost time. He would jam the stuff into his nose with such furious abandon he wouldn't realize when death touched him on the shoulder. *Hey, buddy, party's over.* He reached across the table and folded the old construction plans. He had been afraid Lizzy would return home and see Lewis, and he needed to be ready with an explanation.

Where was the carefree woman he had married?

The suddenness of Lizzy's illness had shocked him. One day she was her usual happy, funny self and the next she had discarded her stylish outfits in favor of cardigans and longer dresses and sensible shoes that looked like they belonged on a sixty-year-old woman with bad arches. Even though she had made a convincing effort to remove her sex appeal,

Marcus still found her attractive, because Lizzy was
beautiful. He recalled the terror of being woken at four in
the morning, Lizzy's body contorted in a screaming fit, eyes
huge, scared, unseeing … and he had held her until the
tremors had passed. Lizzy insisted there was nothing in her
past that had caused the change in her—that she knew of,
anyway. Whatever it was, it had frightened her to such an
extent that she wouldn't speak about it. He suspected she
knew what had caused the sudden shift in her behavior. He
couldn't be sure, of course. He had no choice but to accept
her assertion that she was as clueless as he was. He had even
suggested hypnosis to get to the root of the matter. Lizzy had
flatly said no.

Lizzy's illness had changed Marcus's view of himself as a
confident, sure-footed man. Not just changed it, but
challenged it. Drug addiction aside, for the most part,
Marcus had believed he had some control in his life. But
trying to help Lizzy had tested his resilience, had made him
finally see that he was not in control, that he was, in fact,
helpless. And frustration had a sneaky way of breaching the
previously solid walls of his devotion, his love for his wife.

His anger toward Lewis fizzled. It wasn't his fault. He
was probably right, in the bargain. He should stop while he
still could.

***

Mia went to her mother when she entered the bedroom,
taking her cold hands in hers. "How'd it go, Mom? Are you
okay?"

"It was fine. You don't have to ask me if I'm okay every
five seconds."

"It's just a habit, I guess." Mia was close to coming undone. She'd been lying on her bed, thinking about Cody Finch, considering the possibility that she might be in love. She was nervous and giddy at the prospect of Cody finding out she loved him. What if he didn't love her back? Then Uncle Lewis had dropped by.

Mia was terrible at hiding her true feelings. She couldn't look at her mom. Mia's face began to lose its calm façade, breaking out in a spasm as tears fell in fat drops down her cheeks.

"Oh my God, what's wrong?" Mom brought her toward the bed and they sat on its edge.

"It's nothing, Mom … it's … it's stupid."

Mia cried harder, but quietly when her mom put her arm around her shoulders.

"A problem shared is a problem halved. What is it, Mia?"

She'd lost control and now she had to lie. Had to.

"Cody—"

"I knew it! What did he do?"

"Nuh … nothing. We had an argument."

"Boys are bad news, Mia. They're only after—"

"One Thing, I know."

They sat in silence for a moment. Gradually, Mia's tears stopped and her breathing slowed. *I'm sorry, Cody, but I had to.*

"It breaks my heart to see you upset, Mimi." Her mother was the only one who called her Mimi. She said it with such gentle concern and love that Mia almost lost it again.

She hated lying to her mother and she especially hated herself for making Cody look like the bad guy. She had wanted to say hi to Uncle Lewis and instead she had detected the grave tone of their discussion in the entrance hall and overheard the conversation. She had heard everything: her father was having an affair, and Uncle Lewis had tried to convince her Dad to end it.

17

Zinco Sciences, Cambridge, Massachusetts

It was Dr. Roger Berris's third lap of the fifth floor and there were still a few stragglers, people finishing up for the day. He checked his Rolex, a Cosmograph Daytona, with a mixture of guilt and disgust. It had been a gift to himself after he had made his first million, and now that he was older, if given the chance to go back and slap some sense into his younger self, he'd do it at a low run. He pulled the cuff of his shirt over the watch's green face. It was too blingy for a man backing up against sixty. Baldness had come to him late. His hair had gone gray at fifty-five, then white, thin at the sides until he had shaved it all off. Despite being on nodding terms with his sixth decade—he would be on speaking terms with it in two days—Roger fancied he could pass for fifty. Regina, his wife, seemed to think so, and that was good enough for him.

He cursed the right-angled-triangle shape of the building: three long corridors, three corners, not enough to hide behind quickly.

Two scientists passed him, white lab coats flapping. Roger tilted his chin at them in his usual greeting. He hoped they were headed home. These were the last days of Zinco Sciences, a company he had formed with Dr. Arthur Dunhill, and Roger didn't want anyone to see him skulking along the corridors, casing the place before he brought it down. People would remember the moments leading up to his betrayal, although Roger didn't think he was betraying the company, or Arthur. After all, it was Arthur who had put him in this position.

Roger had spent much of his academic career in an arms race with a deadly enemy—antibiotic-resistant bacteria. As far back as the early 1990s, he'd recognized the public-health implications of common antibiotics becoming useless in the fight against infections. Some shared his concern, but most of his colleagues (including many of his closest friends at Harvard Medical School) had shrugged and moved on to more profitable areas of drug discovery. So far, the bacteria had outsmarted everyone, evolving defense mechanisms faster than they could come up with new ways to destroy them. The most famous example was probably MRSA. And when he had synthesized Zinbactin from soil samples collected by his scientists in North Carolina in the labs on the lower floors, excitement had rippled through the entire building. Roger, on quiet reflection, admitted to himself that he had gotten swept up in it. Arthur's enthusiasm and media savvy had caused massive public interest. Soon, the funding came in from every direction, millions of dollars that left Roger reeling, and was perhaps the main reason he'd become anxious. He had to be certain Zinbactin would not precipitate resistance in bacteria samples. One of Roger's few heroes was a man who had specialized in an entirely different branch of science, the physicist Max Planck. As soon as

Planck discovered his constant, he had set about trying to prove that he was wrong. Planck, of course, was right. So Roger set the course of his research in that direction. If he couldn't prove he was wrong, then he had to be right. He recalled performing the confirmatory tests to establish whether he had a usable drug or not. As it turned out, Zinbactin was highly bioavailable and killed both gram-negative and gram-positive bacteria. Of course, the lightbulb went off in Roger's mind. If Zinbactin stopped the growth of gram-positive bacteria, it might also stop MRSA in its destructive path, too. So he set up a simple experiment with very few moving parts and therefore less chance of it going sideways: he repeatedly exposed samples of Staphylococcus aureus to Zinbactin over a span of months. At the same time, he exposed rats to S. aureus and treated them with the new compound. Initial results had been promising—Zinbactin killed Staph aureus. And then it didn't. The number of colonies surviving the drug just grew and grew. The horror of watching a life-threatening bacterium develop resistance to a powerful drug was fresh, even months after observing it in the lab. He had informed Arthur of his findings immediately ... well, after he'd calmed down somewhat. Roger had been badly shaken by the experience, the failure. They were all facing a formidable enemy and no one had any answers. Or, at least, the answers Roger had for Arthur were unsatisfactory. Roger had dismissed his reaction as understandable disappointment. Arthur had told the world (prematurely) they'd discovered the silver bullet, the longed-for solution to incurable bacterial infections. He had pumped millions of dollars into research. Now he had to walk it all back. But he wasn't going to do it easily. Arthur had had their senior scientists replicate Roger's experiments, and they had found his analysis was solid. And Roger had sensed their disappointment: they had hoped he'd made a mistake. Nobody wanted to tell Arthur that Roger's results were unimpeachable.

Arthur's behavior surprised Roger. Developing a new drug was nothing short of high-stakes gambling. Sometimes you won, sometimes you lost. And if you came out on the losing end, the share price tumbled for a while, but you dusted yourself off and got back in the game. Arthur, however, pursued FDA approval for Zinbactin. His actions were erratic and a genuine source of concern for Roger because Arthur continued to sell the drug as one that didn't make bacteria resistant to it. Roger had seen the paperwork on Arthur's desk when he had gone into his office to speak with him and found he wasn't there. He had read the application—and taken photographs of the documents with his cell phone—to the FDA and knew that he couldn't say or do anything to change Arthur's mind. Arthur wouldn't step aside; he wouldn't change course. It was time for him to act. When his business partner left his office, Roger was going to try to take the original documents. Arthur was single-handedly driving Zinco Sciences into the ground. And Roger wanted to avoid any repercussions from its eventual—inevitable—wind up. He didn't have the stomach for being hauled before Congress to explain himself. He saw how it was going to play out and he didn't want any part in it. Arthur, on the other hand, actually believed he could get away with his deception.

Roger shook his head sadly as he entered his office, which was right next to Arthur's. They had other drugs in the pipeline, and progress on the development side had slowed, all because Arthur couldn't let Zinbactin go. Was it so difficult to admit defeat? Yes, Roger thought, for some people it was impossible.

As he waited for his desktop to boot, he called his broker's private cell in New York City and arranged the disposal of all his 2.2 million shares in Zinco Sciences, instructing his broker not to pull the trigger until Roger gave the order.

Arthur's eyes had acquired a worrying glaze over the past five months. For the first time, Roger was concerned about his safety. He'd have to be far away when Arthur blew up, and he would, that was a certainty.

He typed the name from memory into Google and a photograph of Zoey Finch appeared on his screen. The door to the office beside his slammed shut. That was new in the past few months, too. Arthur left for home every day by slamming his door so hard the force of it reverberated in the walls. Roger figured he had twenty minutes in which to stuff as many reports and test results into his briefcase as would fit before security locked all the doors. A wave of sadness passed through him. Arthur wouldn't believe that Roger had not enjoyed this. But Roger knew the truth: he was distraught.

18

Cody had been through Mashashimuet Park many times alone and with friends, and there had never been anything special about it. There were tennis courts, baseball fields, their grass short and sparse from use, now yellowed by the sun's glare. But walking with Mia seemed to give the park significance, as if the ground itself had been hallowed by her presence.

He shifted the soccer ball from under his arm and rolled it from one hand to the other. It was a relief to have something to do with his hands. Cody was nervous, and all he wanted in the world was for the girl next to him to like him. He would settle for her not hating him, but he'd consider himself lucky if she liked him. When she smiled at him, Cody experienced shyness he didn't think he had. No other girls had that effect on him.

They were breathing heavily after their one-on-one soccer match. Cody had used rocks as makeshift goalposts. He couldn't help but be impressed. Mia was an amazing player, better than him, and she'd won 4–3 after making up their own rules and playing the best of seven goals. She could kick the ball in a straight line, unlike his best friend Bobby Holcomb, who was on vacation in Florida. Bobby looked the part of a soccer player—strong, athletic, great hair, sporting actual muscles, but he couldn't kick a ball straight to save his life. It always ended up in the tall grass or in someone's back garden, and once it had landed in a neighbor's swimming pool. He had gotten into trouble for that. Cody's dad had given him the speech about respecting other people's property, and Cody guessed he was right. He had been sorry. He didn't want anyone being mad at him. He'd just wanted Bobby to feel some sense of achievement by kicking the ball straight, but every attempt ended up being a banana shot that curled wildly off course. In a way, it was fascinating watching Bobby's determined efforts to get it right. The more he tried, the worse it got. Cody couldn't understand why it was so difficult for Bobby to kick the ball in a straight line until he had played golf with his dad. Cody played golf the way Bobby played soccer, and he finally understood. Different people were just good at different things.

The further they walked, the more agitated he became. Cody touched the cell phone in the pocket of his shorts. He wedged the ball under his arm and his free hand opened and closed. But no matter how hard he clenched his hand he couldn't get rid of the restless sensation in his fingers. Some days were better than others. He was frustrated because the urge had returned with a vengeance. His addiction to social media was degrading and trivial. Cody knew there were people out there in the world who had to deal with real problems, real addictions, and he felt guilty whenever the stupid compulsion seemed to take up all the space in his mind and the desire to tweet overwhelmed all thought.

He wouldn't have brought the phone with him if his dad hadn't insisted he carry it at all times. Cody didn't blame him; dad was a worrier and he wanted him to be able to call for help if he needed to. He hadn't sent a tweet in two days and he was having trouble sleeping. The weird thing was, he didn't even enjoy it as much as he once did. Yes, calm was restored when he pressed Send, but it didn't last long. The satisfaction he got from engaging in social media made no sense to him. Most of his posts were about model airplanes, sometimes sports. He was worried he might be wired wrong.

It wasn't as if it was Twitter's fault. If it didn't exist, he would've found another form of social media. Or just created a blog. Or built his own website. Cody was obsessed with model airplanes and the mechanics of flight, so how could one obsession feel good and another feel bad? It was confusing. He wished he could put all his energy into one activity, but it seemed too many things were vying for his attention. He loved TV, watched shows on Hulu and Netflix, often for hours at a time. He read his mom's books, he played soccer, he studied aerodynamics … why did his attention seem to be in many different places and why was it a cause for concern? He didn't know much about his dad's work, except that he was successful at it. He had asked his dad two months before why he was successful. Dad had frowned at him (he always frowned at Cody's questions, or so it seemed to Cody) and considered his answer. After a while, he'd said, "Focus. That's all it is. I have the ability to focus on what I'm doing for long periods of time." Cody was fascinated by the simplicity of it; it was like a recipe but with only one ingredient.

"That's it?" Cody had said, wondering why he had been sure the answer was far more complex. But what if it wasn't? What if it really was that simple?

"All right, Cody, what's on your mind?" Cody had told him he lacked the kind of focus his dad had, and that he might have attention deficit disorder like some kids in his class.

"You don't have attention deficit. You're young, and believe it or not, I was eleven once, too." Cody had smiled at that. It was indeed hard to imagine his dad as a kid. "It's natural for your attention to be in different places," his dad had said. "When I was your age I was interested in many things. Then you get older, and if you're anything like your old man, you develop focus with laser-beam precision. There's nothing wrong with you, son. You're normal, and if you're not normal, that's fine, too. But you don't have an illness. Focus comes with age, Cody. You're already crushing it with your model airplanes. Do you think I have the dexterity needed to build those planes? Or the patience? I wish!" The message Cody had taken from that conversation was to stop worrying. He'd started to think of his dad as a kind of wizard problem solver. It was reassuring, just knowing he could talk to Dad about anything—it was like having an invisible hand on your shoulder everywhere you went, guiding you in the right direction. But Cody hadn't told him he was possibly addicted to social media. Because it was shameful, and he couldn't explain why. He didn't think Dad would judge him unfairly, and yet he didn't want to take the risk, even though he didn't have any evidence to support the notion that Dad might be angry and disappointed in him.

Something touched his fingers. Unable to disguise his surprise, he looked at Mia. She had reached for his hand, and held it. *She was holding his hand.*

77

"Uh …" he began. *God, I'm such a moron.*

"It's okay, Cody." He believed her. Everything was going to be okay. And tonight, he'd switch off his phone. Tomorrow he would get through the day by going for a walk. Given enough time, it seemed possible to at least quit obsessing about how many likes he got on Facebook. He hoped the itch to tweet would pass, too.

For a brief moment, Cody forgot about the strange atmosphere that had taken root at home. But it wasn't so far from his thoughts that he forgot about it completely. He rarely saw his parents laughing together like they used to, and sometimes he caught his dad watching his mother with a cold steadiness that made him uneasy. Something had happened, but Cody was in the dark. On a few occasions, he'd seen his dad staring at Candice, and there was blackness in that look, an absence of sympathy. Cody was glad he was out of the house. The air felt thick but brittle, and if something broke, the sound would be loud. Cody knew what divorce was—some of his friends' parents were divorced—and whenever it surfaced in his consciousness, a shadowy thing climbing out of a deep well, he forced it down, out of sight. Divorce meant The End. He had heard his parents argue many times in the past, but this felt different. It was the lack of arguments that scared him. In a weird way, he wished they'd shout and scream at each other. It would at least demonstrate that they still cared.

They came to the tree line and Mia said, "You wanna go to Long Pond? I'm gonna take some photos."

Cody would have agreed to almost anything just then. "Sure," he said. They found the trail that branched off the main one, the Paumanok Path. The dense woods closed around them and Mia said, "Ah, it's so much cooler."

Cody smiled, becoming aware of her hand in his, her skin touching his … *God, if you're recording this to watch later, thank you!*

The intensity of his shyness had eased a little. Bobby Holcomb had said that girls liked confidence, and they hated shy guys. True or not, he didn't want to take any chances. He rolled his shoulders back and stuck out his chest.

"You okay?" Mia said. "Is your back sore?"

"Oh, no, just stretching it a bit. I was just thinking about one of my douchebag friends."

"Bobby, huh?"

"So you know he's a douchebag, too, that's great." Mia laughed and squeezed his hand. "He's in Florida, he goes there every year, and every time he comes home he's sunburned, like a strawberry with legs."

Mia was giggling. "Doesn't he use sunblock?"

"Yeah, his mom has to put it on him as if he's a baby, but he wipes it off."

"Why?"

"He says it's greasy. Two summers ago, he came home from vacation with skin peeling off his neck and shoulders."

"Eww."

"I know. His folks keep threatening not to bring him, but I guess they didn't make good on it. So now they make him wear a hat, a sombrero, I think. But he can't keep that on, either. He says it itches."

"And sunburn doesn't?"

"Told you he was a douchebag." Mia laughed again and it occurred to Cody that if he could make the way he felt now last forever he'd never be unhappy.

The vegetation became thicker, fuller, the further they went. It was easy to imagine they were in the middle of nowhere, far from home. But the faint sound of car engines and the hiss of tires on asphalt served to remind Cody that Main Street was a ten-minute walk west, and that he wasn't guiding the girl to a place of safety in a dystopian landscape away from the clutches of alien invaders.

I'm such a geek.

Yes. Yes, I am.

They paused at the intersection of three narrow dirt tracks. One snaked straight ahead, the other wound its way east, and the final one would bring them out onto Main. Cody headed east, and soon the rotted swamp stench drifted to him through the trees. They were close.

"Thanks for coming out here with me, Cody."

Cody nodded, a big *aw-shucks* smile stretching his face wide. "You take a lot of pictures?"

"Yeah. Anything that looks interesting. I post the pictures on Instagram and Facebook. I know for sure I won't lose them if they're already online if I lose my phone."

"How many phones have you lost?"

"Four." He stared at her for a moment as they meandered along the uneven path. Then they laughed, hard, Mia supporting herself by gripping his shoulder. *Four cell phones!*

"Your mom must've had a fit."

"Oh, she doesn't know. My dad buys me a new one, and I keep promising I won't lose it. I'm seriously trying to be more careful. He knows I don't mean to do it."

Cody had met Mia's mom. He didn't know what was wrong with her, but something was definitely … off. Missing.

Cody stepped into the clearing first. Behind him, he heard Mia's gasp. Long Pond was impressive. Its surface was covered in bright green algae as far as the eye could see. Mia ran toward an enormous rock overhanging the swamp, climbed it, and said, "Take a photo, Cody." Cody obliged, taking one, and as Mia struck a new pose, he took another.

He watched her take photographs of the pond from atop the boulder. Then she came back to him, smiling. Cody felt good when she smiled.

"It looks like a comic-book swamp," he said.

"It's awesome, and so are you." Before he had time to react, she kissed him. On the lips. His stomach flipped with excitement and his skin prickled with electricity.

Okay, calm down, it's no big deal.

But it was a big deal. The kiss had made all his worries and fears evaporate in that moment, made them seem smaller, even a little stupid. Dumb kid problems. He was stunned, and when the power of speech returned, he almost thanked her and stopped himself in time.

I'm such a geek.

"That was amazing," he said, which he guessed sounded a lot less lame than *thank you.*

They sat on an old mossy log, Cody brushing loose bark from the spot where Mia would sit. She reached for his hand, and Cody gave it to her. This was the best day of his entire life. If he had the power to determine how his day was going to pan out, he wouldn't have changed it. It was already perfect.

"So how's your mom?" Cody asked, before he could reel the words back. He was nervous and trying to hide it. This was a special day, but it felt suddenly fragile too, like the atmosphere at home. He didn't want to say anything to ruin the mood. He looked into her eyes and saw them lose some of their light; he regretted his question.

"She's fine. It's hard when you catch a glimpse of how she used to be. Some days her illness is front and center and sometimes she's just normal. Do you think it's possible for someone to be convinced they're unwell? Like they hold on to it because it's what they've come to know?" Cody was struck by the intelligence underlying what she was saying to him, and intimidated. Out of his depth. He understood airplanes; people were a different kettle of exotic fish he couldn't understand.

"Um … you mean it's all in her head?" It was the best he could do. He was trying to negotiate a way out of the conversation, steer it on to lighter topics. But he had fallen into his own trap, even though he'd set it by accident of nerves.

"No, she's sick. I've seen it. What if she believed she could get well?"

Was it possible for a person to cure a malfunction of the mind through believing they could? Cody was doubtful. He thought Mia was grasping for solutions. Even though her tone had been even, Cody heard desperation underneath her words.

"I'm not sure belief, by itself, is enough," he said, "but it might work with the help of drugs."

"I hate pills. I've got this suspicion that they make her worse." He felt the intensity of her frustration then, and marveled at how well she'd hidden it.

"I don't understand brain mechanics," Cody said. "I'm not convinced the people who study it know, either. They know more than me, they just don't know everything. What do I know? You could be right. Maybe belief is enough." Cody had the impression that Mia wanted to talk more, but she didn't. She was holding something back, and whatever was troubling her was big.

She wasn't staring at the ground anymore but at him.

"Wanna take a few more photos and watch *South Park* in your house?"

"Sure, sounds great." She snapped to her feet and ran toward the rock jutting over the pond. Her sudden exuberance surprised him and made him smile at the same time.

Got to be careful; can't go round depressing the girl of your dreams.

He pulled out his phone and took up position close to the rock, focused the camera, and said, "Say *South Park*!"

"*South Pa—*"

She disappeared from his screen.

19

Lizzy wasn't so sure a makeover was a good idea. But she had agreed to it. If anyone other than Zoey had asked she would have refused. Lizzy knew Zoey was only trying to make her feel better, despite Lizzy insisting she was balanced, emotionally. The urge to scream at her friends that they didn't have to worry about her mental state was exhausting. Yes, they didn't talk to her in the way some people spoke to those in a wheelchair as a result of a disability, bending over with their hands on their knees, asking if they were okay in a voice that sounded as though it had been summoned for a child or a dog. If that ever happened, she'd lose it. Finally tell them all to quit treating her as if she couldn't spell her own name.

It's L-I-Z-Z-Y: Lizzy. I am Lizzy.

They were sitting in front of the vanity mirror decorated in gold leaf, on French armchairs. Not only was her face painted but she was wearing a short black dress that climbed high above her knees. Her eyes kept dropping to her exposed cleavage. Lizzy glanced in the mirror again. At the red lipstick plastered on her lips. *Whore lips, that's what they are.* Just like the lips of that pop star in the poster hanging on her daughter's wall.

It was a disgusting vista, scandalous. Loathsome. And yet there was something familiar about the woman looking back at her, almost recognizable. She tugged at the hem of the skirt, pulling it down from its repeated attempts at an upward journey, as though the dress itself was determined to expose her … her womanhood. Just the idea of … of *that*, sent a shiver through her and her bare arms became suddenly cold.

She looked at her friend's face. Stretched into a full smile. Tears stood in her eyes, and most disturbing of all: adoration. Lizzy Jenkins didn't want to be admired by anyone. It was as though God had personally delivered her to Zoey and ordered her to worship Lizzy. Except God was ignoring her, He wasn't wrong; she was an aberration.

She said, "Come on, Lizzy, stand up and see how great you look."

Lizzy hesitated. She didn't want to see how slutty she looked from head to toe. But Zoey was her friend. She only wanted what was best for her. Zoey wouldn't play a trick on her. Dressing up in such a disgraceful manner didn't feel like a trick, just a misguided attempt to make her see how pretty she really was.

Lizzy rose from the armchair and moved it aside. They moved a few steps backward so that the mirror could see all of her.

"My God, you look amazing," Zoey said, and Lizzy saw her catching a tear with her finger as it rolled from the corner of her eye. "You'd be right at home in any party in the Hamptons." Then why did she feel so gawky? Awkward? Self-conscious? In this outfit, she felt her thoughts had developed a stutter. As if her mind had had an accident.

Now *she* was the Sex Thing. And oh God she felt unclean inside, dirty. But Zoey was standing next to her as if she was witnessing the single greatest event of her life. It was difficult to reconcile how she felt with what she was seeing—Zoey kept telling her how pretty she was, yet she had never felt uglier. *Dirtier.*

Lizzy conjured the image of a tennis ball, and the feeling of ripping its green skin off and carving its hard rubber core. She needed to get home. She longed for the sensation of cutting.

A sudden question entered her mind, edging its way to the surface of her consciousness with all the smoothness of a snake—what was Mia doing with Cody? She'd believed for a long time now that she was in danger of becoming her daughter's friend instead of her mother. A true parent would tear down that poster of the lascivious pop star on Mia's wall, would forbid her from seeing that boy because boys were only after One Thing. Were they doing the Sex Thing? *No, goddamnit, no!*

"Lizzy, are you okay?"

"Um, I'm fine. I don't think this is me, Zoey."

"Two years ago, this *was* you. Don't you remember?"

She didn't know what Zoey was talking about. It was strange … Zoey wasn't lying to her, that much she knew. Which meant she must be telling her the truth. But the woman in the mirror was a stranger. Lizzy hadn't seen her before.

The day had taken on a dream-like quality.

Her left hand trembled.

Zoey's cell phone rang. "Give me one minute," she said, and she closed the bedroom door.

Lizzy stood there in the middle of the floor, staring at the impostor in the mirror. The lipstick was wrong … she dragged the back of her shaking hand across her mouth, smearing a red streak onto her cheek. She immediately relaxed, sensing the return of the Lizzy she knew. With her other hand, she wiped it over her mouth again and caught her eye in the mirror. The clownish smile was grotesque, the backs of her hands those of one afflicted by stigmata. But she felt the presence of the real Lizzy Jenkins, and that was all that mattered.

The door opened behind her. "Oh my God," Zoey said, "I'm so sorry, sweetie. This was a bad idea." She plucked some wipes from a box on the table and began to clean Lizzy's face. "I'm really sorry," she said, "I was just trying—I didn't mean to try and change who you are now, I wanted you to remember who you were, that's all." Lizzy's cheeks burned with embarrassment. She was a child again, a girl who has discovered her mother's makeup and made a mess. But with each cool touch of the wipes on her skin, she felt more like Lizzy and less like the person in the mirror, whoever she was. Less *dirty*.

20

Cody dropped his cell phone. When he heard the splash, every instinct that wanted to protect Mia kicked in and his heart hammered high and fast in his chest and a tremor worked its way into his arms and legs. He tore his T-shirt over his head so hard it ripped, and tossed it aside. He stepped out of his Nikes and ran in his socks toward the pond, arms pumping, air whistling into lungs that seemed bigger than usual, and launched his body into the water, not afraid for himself, not really caring what happened to him, but terrified of what might happen to Mia. How could that feeling be worse than being scared for himself? He didn't know, he was only sure that it was.

He swam underneath the overhanging shelf of rock and dived.

He saw bubbles rising toward him and paddled downward through the murk.

In the dimness, he spotted her hair, given a ghostly, wavy quality by the water.

He reached for it, grabbed a handful to stop her sinking even further.

Her eyes were closed.

She's gone.

Cody wrapped an arm around her waist and headed

upward. Driven by sheer panic, he thought he was closer to the surface than he actually was. Mia's limp body was heavier than he expected it would be. He fought the urge to take a breath. His lungs were no longer as big as they had seemed earlier. The water was much colder than it had been. It was still dark. And it felt like the end. His vision blurred. Cody wished he had been faster and stronger.

Daylight dazzled him and air slammed into his lungs. Strings of algae clung to his face in a slimy veil. His free hand probed for Mia's head and he held it above the water. He swam toward the shore. The moment his feet touched mulchy earth, he dragged Mia free of the pond, laid her down gently, and began CPR, counting the hand compressions aloud.

"One, two, three …" Every sinew was tight and every muscle seemed to contract in his exhausted body. He had to concentrate and not press down too hard and risk cracking her ribs.

His school had bought CPR in Schools Training Kit from the American Heart Association. He had watched and listened dutifully, not believing for a second he would ever have any need for it. Now he was glad—grateful—he'd participated. He wasn't sure if it was going to save Mia's life, but it was better than standing around and watching her die.

"Please, Mia, please wake up." The hands-only method wasn't bringing her back. He bent over her, opened her mouth and checked her airway. He wasn't trained to give rescue breaths, but he'd seen people do it on TV. And what else could he do?

He cinched her nostrils closed between thumb and forefinger, tilted her head slightly upward and sealed his mouth over hers. He breathed into her, twice.

Nothing.

Please, Mia, please come back …

He began chest compressions again, the low grass-fire of panic growing higher, warmer.

Some water dribbled from her mouth.

He put his mouth over hers, and this time he rotated his head before he blew to see if her chest would rise. It did.

He pressed down on her chest. "One, two, three …" As he was about to begin the fourth compression a guttural watery choking sound erupted beneath him.

Cody swayed as Mia looked at him. He turned her on her side and said, "I'm so glad you're back … Mia."

Spent, Cody slumped flat to the ground, looking up at blue sky. In the distance he heard coughing, before consciousness swam away and he fainted.

21

Lizzy was glad she was wearing flat shoes and not the heels she'd tried on at Zoey's house. They would have prevented her from running to Mia, embracing her daughter as she lay on the emergency department bed, tubes snaking out of her arm and nose. She couldn't remember the car journey to Stony Brook University Hospital: a low drone seemed to have taken root in her mind, driving out thoughts and images. Whatever it had been, the monotonous sound had had the weight of something actual, and comforting.

She held Mia's face in her hands, gently pressing her cheeks, making sure she was there, then kissed her forehead. The light in the room was strange. It gave her the urge to check if anything was real. Lizzy touched her own face. *Yes, I'm here.*

And so was the one responsible for almost killing her daughter. He was in the next room. The doctors had told Zoey he was being treated for shock but otherwise he was fine. They had reassured her that Mia was going to be okay, too. She was *out of danger.* Lizzy couldn't rid herself of the memory of the doctor's voice on the phone: two tourists had witnessed Cody pulling her daughter out of the water. He had given her CPR. Lizzy had stiffened at the mention of a boy putting his mouth on Mia's. Had Cody tricked Mia? A slow chill uncoiled along her spine at the thought. But Lizzy was growing more convinced that the Finch boy had tried to murder her only child. Lizzy had been a bad parent and she promised herself she would improve. She should have insisted Mia stay away from Cody, from *boys*, because little boys played tricks on little girls.

Lizzy sat on a chair next to the bed, knees together. Little boys not only tricked little girls, but they lied, too. And Lizzy knew they lied.

Now she was facing a serious problem: how to persuade Mia to stop seeing *the boy* and remain friends with Zoey, who had driven her to Stony Brook, that much she did remember. She didn't think she could cope with being a bad friend, which was a lot worse than having no friends. She was wedged fast in that fabled barren wasteland known as a rock and a hard place. She had to improve her parenting, but didn't want to do it at the expense of her friendship. Lizzy *loved* Zoey. It wasn't even Zoey's fault she had spawned a demon child who had almost drowned her daughter. She wasn't convinced it was an accident. Lizzy knew what little boys were capable of. After all, hadn't they—

"Mom?" Lizzy looked at Mia and stopped wringing her hands together.

"Um … yes, Mimi?"

"You look really pretty." And suddenly her eyes fixed on the short, tight dress, the way it revealed every curve and too much leg. The foundation on her face, which she hadn't had time to wash off. The skin underneath the cake itched, and she swallowed the urge to scrape it off with her fingernails. Her hair seemed to have more volume; she felt it. So much volume that it seemed to lift off her head like some kind of sinister halo.

Lizzy was confused. "What?"

"You look really good, mom. Can't you see it?" Lizzy didn't want to see it.

"I don't know what you mean."

"You look great, that's all I'm saying."

"Stop it!"

Mia flinched and Lizzy instantly regretted raising her voice. She didn't mean to snap; she just didn't want Mia to think this was appropriate dress for a woman. Or even a store-window mannequin.

"I'm sorry, sweetie," she said, "I'm a little on edge. I've had a huge scare today."

Lizzy turned toward a sudden commotion outside. Someone was shouting, then running, the soles of their shoes squeaking. Marcus filled the doorway, breathless, shoulders quaking, eyes widening as he saw Mia. The blood dropped from his face, and he trembled there for a moment, an expression of pasty disbelief dawning. His mouth opened, closed, and Lizzy almost giggled as she was reminded of the goldfish—named Goldie, coincidentally, may he rest in peace—she'd had when she was eight.

He went to Mia, squeezed her hand. "Careful, Marcus, she's fine, I don't want you breaking her bones."

Marcus turned to her and she watched him freeze.

"Lizzy? What …? I mean, you look fantastic."

Why does everyone keep saying that? Why don't I believe them?

"Don't worry, I'll be changing into something else soon."

"You don't have to," he said, and there was something genuine, heartfelt in the way he said it that made Lizzy want to cry.

22

The doctors had kept Mia overnight for observation, running various tests that showed she hadn't sustained any lasting damage from the "accident." Lizzy had kept her suspicions to herself—the boy had tried to kill her daughter. It was all an elaborate trick: Cody Finch had gone into "shock" to deflect attention away from his crime. Why was Mia colluding with the little tyrant? Lizzy settled on the idea that her daughter was scared—*terrified*—of Cody.

The mocking, sarcastic voice in her head had grown louder.

Do they think I'm stupid? So they'd recommended the boy stay overnight, too, to get over his "shock." The kid's a good actor, I'll give him that ... but Mia is a terrible liar.

The experience of being in the hospital had been nightmarish. Everyone had stared at her, probably wondering how a mother could walk around in public, dressed *like that*. The moment she had set foot across the threshold of her home she had excused herself, gone upstairs and shimmied out of the dress, discarding it in a pile on her bedroom floor and regarding it as though it were an alien skin she'd managed to shed. She felt she had been through a battle, and there was no clear winner. But she had survived.

Breathing hard, she retrieved a tennis ball from the closet and the razor blade, put on a bathrobe, went into the bathroom and locked the door.

She sat on the lip of the bathtub, her hands already shaking. Lizzy slit a jagged smile into the green felt, poked her forefinger underneath it and yanked upward. It tore; the hairs on her neck stood erect, and goose pimples broke out on her arms. When the ball was in two pieces, she began slicing strands of rubber, collecting them in the lap of her robe. Her vision blurred and her pulse slackened. Saliva dribbled from her mouth but she didn't care. There were no problems. The world was awash with promise. Except …

The blade paused. She was back in the hospital. Jon and Zoey had come to check on her, on Mia. She had been so busy trying to conceal her embarrassment, her shame at having her thighs on public display, constantly pulling the dress down as it tried to ride higher, that she almost didn't notice the look that had passed between Marcus and Zoey.

Jon had spoken to her as if she was well, in a non-pitying way that she'd been grateful for. Talked to her as though she was just a normal person who wasn't sick. Everyone seemed to be commenting on how pretty she was, except Jon, who, according to Marcus on the car ride home, didn't think any woman was pretty unless she was entirely composed of hundred-dollar bills. She had told Marcus he was being unfair, that Jon had treated her like a real person. And Marcus had insisted they all treated her that way, that they all loved her and they all thought she was pretty. Lizzy thought they were all lying, especially about her being pretty. If she was so pretty, how come she didn't *feel* pretty?

But the look between Zoey and Marcus … *that* look. Lizzy sliced through the remaining pieces of rubber. Her vision had cleared.

23

Roger cruised past the sign that said SAG HARBOR, and underneath the letters there were more: SETTLED IN 1707. *They should've added White Picket Fence Country underneath that.* Every house on Main Street seemed to have one. He glanced briefly at the men on the all-weather green of the tennis court and continued along Main. Roger's own picket fence was in Newton, Massachusetts, and whiter than most, he fancied. He applied a coat of paint to it once a year, even though it didn't need it. But he wasn't willing to take the chance that it would become weathered, grubby, and flaky. Thus, Roger spent a few days every year painting his fence, much to Regina's consternation. Why didn't he hire some kid to do it? Well, because Roger didn't see himself above manual labor. After all, that was how he'd become wealthy. And Roger wanted to stay rich. Why pay someone to do a job he was perfectly capable of doing all by himself? Regina might have developed amnesia due to their lifestyle, forgot where they'd come from and how hard they had struggled to get where they were now. But Roger hadn't forgotten. He had seen Regina sometimes watching him from one of their many windows as he painted their fence carefully—arms folded, shaking her head. When he was finished, there was always the satisfaction of knowing he had done it well. He had tried to explain it to his wife, but Roger was old enough to understand that some arguments weren't worth the effort. However, what he was about to do *was* worth the backlash that was sure to come from a single source—Arthur Dunhill. Arthur might be able to fool the FDA, but the moment a fellow scientist examined Arthur's forged analysis and replicated the experiments Roger had performed, there would be questions, and Roger didn't want to be standing in front of the news cameras explaining himself, his bald head shining under the lights. Arthur believed he would get away with his fraud, and that was what disturbed Roger most. If Roger could see the flaw in Arthur's swindle, then how could Arthur not see it? It was inevitable that the lie would be found out … His thoughts turned to the Glock he kept in a safe in his closet for home protection. He regretted not practicing at the range more. Then Arthur had forced his hand, and as a result there hadn't been time for detailed preparation.

Roger wasn't a gambler, but if he were betting on a horse, he would at least study the form sheet first. And Zoey Finch had form, as did her husband, Jon. The whole Anglo Pharma debacle had been a story of drug-price gouging, embezzlement, insider trading and an intricate web of bad practice followed by a five-course helping of lies and double-dealing. Zoey had—rightly—shorted the company and it had fallen spectacularly. Any pharmaceutical corporation that relied on inflating the price of its drugs to prop up its share price instead of investing in research was paving its own road to ruin.

Easy come, easy go.

Now Arthur was on the scent of the quick buck, and because of his odd behavior, the course he had set was sideways, a trajectory that would lead him to financial disaster and quite possibly the penitentiary. It was amazing to witness. Roger had stood in Arthur's office (he'd refused to sit) and outlined all the horrible possibilities that lay in his business partner's future. Unable to reason with his former friend, Roger wasn't left with many choices: get in the same lane and deal with a guilty conscience for the rest of his life or topple the whole rotten edifice. Roger believed in ethics, even though Arthur had labeled the notion "old fashioned" and, perhaps even more sinister, "naïve." He tried to recall when he had noticed the change in Arthur. It was before Michelle had divorced him. Nothing had stood out, except a general hardening of his attitude. In his youth, Roger would have tried to solve the mystery of why Arthur had become this sudden weird stranger, unrecognizable as the man he had known for forty years. Now that he was older and knew a little more about life and people, he'd concluded it would be a useless exercise, delving into the murk of someone else's mind in an attempt to detect the ghost of reason, perhaps even untangle his twisted motives. It was futile. People like Arthur only ever let you get close enough to glimpse who they were, but never to see.

It was early but the parking spaces in front of The Blue Lemon were occupied. Instead, he slid the car into a diagonal spot outside Capital One and walked back up the street. The feel of the briefcase's handle in his dry hand was comforting. How things had changed, he mused. Back when he was a cheap-suit-wearing nobody looking for investment his hands had always sweated as he stood before panels of people trying to decide if he was a risk worth taking, some of whom seemed to be wrestling with a dual dilemma: whether or not to give him the money he was asking for and also if he really was what he appeared to be—human garbage wrapped in a cheap suit. At least, that was how it had felt to Roger at the time. One venture capitalist (whose palm had been bone dry when he'd shaken Roger's wet hand) had approached him after he had been denied funds yet again to inform Roger that he admired his balls, *coming in here looking for money with no track record*. Which hadn't made any sense to him. How could he have a track record when no one was willing to give him a chance? It hadn't taken long for Roger to realize his mistake: never rely on other people for your success. If he were ever to give a lecture on being successful in business, those would be the first words out of his mouth.

Roger entered the café. A man and a woman were seated against the far wall, already watching him.

24

Jon was worried about Cody. After the accident, he'd stayed in his room and only came out when he was hungry. Zoey didn't seem concerned, insisting their son would "snap out of it" and continue as normal. Anyway, she had warned him not to go near the ponds in the woods. Even the one across the road from their home was out of bounds, Otter Pond. If she hadn't told him once she'd told him a million times to keep away. Jon thought it was strange, the way she had reacted to their son saving the life of his friend, congratulating him in a distracted, almost dismissive manner. Jon had decided to refer to Mia as Cody's *friend* because he knew Cody didn't want Zoey to know Mia was his girlfriend (although Jon knew his wife was aware that Cody and Mia were more than friends) accurately gauging that his mother wouldn't approve of him being in a relationship with a girl who was older than him. *He's too young*, she would say. Jon wasn't going to rat him out. He had loosened the reins, giving Cody more freedom, and it had been difficult to ignore every protective instinct that screamed for him to keep a closer watch on him. He didn't want to smother him, restrict his every movement to within his sightline. The accident had rattled him, though. Cody could have drowned out there in the woods. It would have taken days to find his body …

He could've, but he didn't.

He had made Cody promise him that if he wanted to hang out around ponds again, to let his old man know and he would take him. He had tried to make himself sound casual, dropping the edge of anxiety that kept creeping into his tone. Jon sensed his son had had a lucky escape, and for some reason, Zoey didn't appear in the least concerned. She had changed the subject, talking about how much she was looking forward to Friday, and hosting another round of "vigorous" discussion of the latest novel the women in her book club were reading. It was a peculiar quirk in her personality: when something awful happened, rather than address it, she brushed it under the carpet and moved on to a more palatable topic.

Jon recognized Dr. Berris from his internet search. He was tall, thin, dressed in a tailored three-piece suit, its dark gray tones broken by a red bow tie. As he came toward him (Jon had no doubt the good doctor had done a little internet browsing on him, too) he maintained eye contact. Jon respected him already. He was fascinated by his impression that the pharma CEO didn't seem to cut the air; rather, it parted before him. There was an oily smoothness in his approach. He rose from his seat, hand outstretched, and glanced at Zoey. She didn't acknowledge him. Her features had molded into an expression with which he was familiar— *let's cut the bullshit and get down to business.* Jon knew the reason for it: Zoey didn't want anything from Dr. Berris, so why waste precious energy being phony in his presence?

Jon shook Dr. Berris's dry hand and exchanged brief

pleasantries. He looked at his wife. She merely nodded at Dr. Berris, an impatient frown lifting her eyebrows skyward.

"Dr. Berris, would you like something to eat or drink?" Jon said.

"Coffee, please."

Jon caught the attention of the server and when the large cup was placed on the table in front of Dr. Berris, he popped open his briefcase, removed a large brown envelope, and handed it to Jon.

***

Roger had passed the envelope to Jon because his wife looked as though she'd bite his hand off if he aimed it in her direction. She had the same aura of those panelists back in the day, regarding him with a mixture of mild curiosity and impatience, wondering why he was taking up space in their vicinity and why he had the audacity to stand before them, asking for their cash.

He hated these people. Not because Jon's wife was ice cold and had the poise of a predator—they were both short sellers, and Roger despised anyone who bet large sums of money on failure. At its most basic, that was short selling: a bet on a company's failure. And in Roger's world, they were parasites. Some believed short sellers kept the market honest, in balance, but Roger didn't buy it. They were opportunists—tier-one gamblers who made Vegas look like an oversized bingo hall with lights. They didn't produce anything of tangible worth the way a farmer produces crops and meat. The way a pharmaceutical company produced drugs. However, he needed them now. He might feel unclean for a while after dealing with them; in fact, he was sure the sensation of being contaminated would last a long time before it eventually washed away, as most things did in the end. But Roger's pragmatism overrode his distaste for these bankers. He needed to get a job done, and Jon and his wife were just the type of people to do it, even if they were eyeing him with open suspicion.

Roger had made up his mind—he would explain what he wanted, but he wouldn't pretend to like Jon and especially his wife while he did so. He wouldn't smile at them, cajole or persuade. Plan B was simple: if they wouldn't do it, then he'd find someone who would. And there was no shortage of opportunists in the world. They were a dime a dozen.

"What am I looking at here?" Jon said.

"Test results for Zinbactin. The text and diagrams highlighted in red were falsified by Arthur Dunhill." Roger kept his amusement in check as Zoey Finch sat up straight in her chair, a Wall Street meerkat scenting dollars on the wind. He had her attention now. "Zinbactin was a promising drug at first. Effective against MRSA until resistance developed. I informed Arthur but he wouldn't listen. He insisted I was wrong. In fact, he said I was wrong so many times I began to doubt myself and I went back and did the experiments again."

"Let me guess: it still didn't work," Jon said.

"It *is* an antibiotic—it just doesn't work the way Arthur wants it to. He's going to market Zinbactin as a cure for MRSA." Roger watched Jon's eyes flit from sentence to sentence, occasionally glancing at Roger. Jon handed the file to Zoey.

"Why did you ask us here?" Jon said.

"As I told your wife on the phone, I have a guaranteed investment opportunity I wanted to put to you."

"Which is?"

"I want you to short Zinco Sciences."

They both stared at him. Then Jon said, "I hope you don't think I'm being nosy ... but why would you want us to short your company?"

Roger realized that this couple was probably cynical of such outdated concepts as conscience, doing no harm, and guilt. Rather than paint himself as a moral crusader—which he wasn't—he tried a different approach. He said, "Arthur will be caught, eventually. The second another scientist goes through the results, does the experiments, the cat's out of the bag. My point is, he'll be found out, that's a certainty."

"And you don't want to be in the crosshairs, I get it," Jon said, "but he won't slip it past the FDA." Roger almost laughed. For just an instant, he thought Jon was naïve, and dismissed the idea because Jon was in charge of one of the most successful funds on Wall Street, even though his offices weren't located on the street itself, but he was a member of that cabal of bankers. Even if, Roger surmised, Jon was fooling himself into believing he wasn't part of the germ line.

"You don't know Arthur Dunhill," Roger said. "If he wants it to happen, it will. I've known him longer than my wife. Let's just cut to the chase here because I can see you're not buying all of what I'm saying, but I'm sure you'll buy this—I'm going to dump over two million of my own shares in Zinco. Not today, but soon."

Now I've got two meerkats.

Roger was trying to keep his spirits up, to mask the whole filthy, soul-destroying business. What he'd done would hit home soon. But not today. It made no difference that he was doing the right thing. It didn't make the imminent demise of Zinco any less awful. Roger would cope with the sleepless nights that were sure to feature heavily in his future, but the notion he had been forced to sabotage his own company that he'd worked so hard to build … that would take far longer to get over.

Zoey leaned forward, elbows planted on the table. "Why us?" she said. "Why lead us to the pot of gold at the end of the rainbow?"

"I saw what you did to Anglo Pharma, or rather, what they did to themselves. I saw those video clips of you selling your message on Bloomberg News. The market listened to you and they'll pay attention again."

"I know this is an obvious question," Zoey said, "but I have to ask: why don't you just go to the FDA and inform them of your findings?"

Maybe I've been too quick to judge these two.

Roger sighed, and said, "You're right, I could do that. Option A—shorting the company, and Option B—present the doctored results to the FDA … both scenarios will have similar outcomes. Once the FDA released its statement to the media, investor confidence will drop, as will Zinco's stock. I don't want Arthur Dunhill in charge of another pharmaceutical company in my lifetime, that's why shorting Zinco will guarantee it. Arthur can defend himself against the FDA, he can cling on at the top for a while, might even be for longer than a while. But not even Arthur can stop an avalanche in the stock market. He can't bullshit his way out of that one. He can't sway market sentiment once it has a foothold." Roger decided to omit the fact that Arthur was quite possibly a sociopath and it had taken him forty years to see it. It was a poor reflection of his ability to judge the character of a person, especially someone he had been so close to. Roger had to put Arthur out of business permanently. He was unstable, unpredictable ... and Roger had a feeling that Arthur's sleight of hand wouldn't stop at Zinbactin. What would he forge next? What kind of fraud was he dreaming up in his office as he stared into his fish tank, which he'd purchased to help relieve stress? Roger didn't think it had worked: Arthur still sat in his office, grinding his teeth together, squeezing a handful of marbles together in his fist. Roger had seen him like that many times. And Arthur didn't seem to care that Roger saw. It was eerie, Roger recalled, standing in Arthur's office doorway as teeth and marbles were ground together, both producing a very similar noise. Pent up murder—that was always how it sounded to Roger.

"Let's say what you've said has some validity," Zoey said. "What's in it for you?"

"Nothing," Roger said. "I'm retiring, it's long overdue. I tried to produce a drug that would help kill MRSA and it didn't work. But I tried."

"So you don't want anything?" Roger held Zoey's skeptical gaze. He had been right, up to a point. This banker had no grasp of conscience, no understanding of doing something simply because it was right.

"I don't know what to tell you."

Zoey got up to leave, leaving what looked to Roger like half the money to pay the check. Plus a tip. "It's been fascinating, Dr. Berris. We'll let you know when we decide if we're taking your offer." Zoey crossed the café's floor;

there was a gasp of air as she pulled the door open and left. But Jon remained in his seat, staring at him.

"What's on your mind?" Roger asked.

"You said you've known Arthur longer than your wife."

"So?"

"So I'm guessing he's a friend as well as a colleague. How can you sell out a friend like that?"

"He was a dear friend. You're mistaken if you believe this is easy for me."

Jon nodded. Then he said, "I'll do my usual due diligence, Dr. Berris, and let's say I believe you. You're betraying your friend—excuse me, *former* friend—is that okay with you?"

Roger didn't rise to the bait, even though his temper flared. Softly, he said, "I'll have to live with that. Arthur is embedded in his position, and nothing I can say to him will change his mind."

"We're probably not going to see each other again, Dr. Berris, so I have to ask: I'm curious how you can be friends with someone for such a long time and betray him when the wind blows in a direction you don't like."

Roger smiled stiffly. "Loyalty means a lot to you, doesn't it?"

They stared at each other across the table for a moment.

Jon rose, placed more bills on the table and he left, too.

25

Zoey was sitting in the driver's seat when he went outside. Jon knocked on the window and it hummed down halfway. "Want to take a stroll down the Wharf?" he asked.

"Why?"

"Why not? It's a nice day." And it was. It was going to be a scorcher.

"I don't know …"

"You have somewhere else to be?"

She glanced at him quickly. "What does that mean?"

"Look, I'll buy you an ice cream. With sprinkles." He winked at her, catching her off guard.

Zoey smiled. "Okay, okay."

He gave her the file tucked under his arm and she put it in the glove compartment.

They were walking past the Municipal Building when Zoey said, "Do you think he was lying?"

"Yes. His whole spiel was odd. There is some truth in there somewhere, but we'll find out later. I need to look deeper into this."

"The way he looked at us, Jonathan, like we're the Illuminati fucking with his life."

Dr. Berris's vibe hadn't gone unnoticed. It wasn't as

109

dramatic as Zoey had just described it. It was far simpler than that; it was raw, undisguised disdain, naked distaste. Jon had made up his mind already that he wasn't going to hold it against Dr. Berris. It was an honest reaction to meeting the enemy. He understood it, but it made no impact on his life. He had become a hedge-fund manager not to make friends or change the world for the better, but to make money. It didn't matter that he had donated millions of dollars to various charities for years, quietly and without fanfare. He had done it not because he believed he was a bad person in need of absolution, but out of empathy. He had been at the bottom once, too. When he'd needed help, he had accepted it. But Dr. Berris would never know that. Jon didn't need a pat on the head from anyone—*there's a good boy!*

"Since when did we care what other people think about us?"

"All right," she said, "fair point."

"Let's assume some of what he told us is true," Jon said, noticing how pleasant it was, just two elder millennials taking a leisurely, unhurried walk by the awning-shaded storefronts, the sun warming his skin. "This Arthur Dunhill sounds like a nasty piece of work. We have to do it."

"We need a scientist to examine the content of the file," she said. "I don't understand it."

"All I saw was a bunch of red marks similar to the ones I used to get on my science reports."

She looked at him. "You were bad at science?"

"At first. I didn't appreciate it until later. How about you? I bet you were awesome at it, though."

"I was." They looked at each other, almost in a strange kind of surprise, and laughed.

"To hell with being humble!" Jon said, and Zoey punched him lightly on the shoulder. Jon was glad he'd talked her into this aimless ramble.

They'd had a stressful year, Jon knew, but he wondered whether he had underestimated how severe it had been. Jane had cried a lot during the first four months, as babies do, but it had tapered off somewhat. They were sleeping better, and although they were still woken in the early hours by Jane's bawling, it was a lot less frequent.

"Did you ever experience post-partum depression?" Jon asked.

Zoey considered the question for a moment. Then she said, "No. I was crabby a lot, tired, but nothing as bad as being depressed."

"I wanted to ask in case I might have overlooked it somehow." There was another reason, but he wasn't going to tell her what it was.

"Candice certainly helped." Realization dawned on her face and she lowered her gaze to the sidewalk. Jon chose to ignore it. He didn't want to traipse back over old battlefields.

At the corner of Main and Bay Street they crossed the road; Jon bought himself a vanilla cone and something called a Mississippi Mud for Zoey in Big Olaf's on Wharf Street. They followed the sidewalk to Long Wharf and sat on a bench, looking out at the yachts and ships in Sag Harbor Bay in silence. Then Jon caught Zoey watching him from the corner of her eye as she licked the melting ice cream, because he had been watching *her*.

26

Mia didn't have any reason to be afraid of her mother, but when Mom entered the kitchen and sat across from her at the breakfast table, she sensed a shift in the atmosphere. It was something in her posture—shoulders raised, head stooped forward, her gaze locked on to her, eyes narrowed. Mia dropped her half-eaten slice of toast on her plate, next to the apple she'd diced into chunks. She didn't eat a big meal in the mornings, just like her dad, who had told her in confidential tones once that he couldn't understand how anyone could eat after waking, that normal humans such as them needed at least three hours for their guts to realize they were awake. Mia had giggled, sometimes wondering why she remembered those small stupid conversations with her dad and why they seemed so important not to forget.

She wasn't scared, exactly, but she swallowed the remaining bread in her mouth with a gulp that sounded too loud. It wasn't Mom's stare that made her nervous, it was the concentration in it, as though she was desperately trying to solve a puzzle.

"Mom, are you okay?"

She blinked and said, "I don't want you seeing that boy anymore. I've been scared before, but I haven't felt the kind of fear I went through when you were in the hospital."

For some reason, Mia knew this last statement was a lie. She didn't know how or why she was sure of it, but it was there and the feeling in her stomach persisted. Dad called it instinct, and he'd said many times, "Always trust your first instinct," as if he were imparting some kind of sacred, special knowledge to his only daughter. He had explained to her that sometimes first instincts could be wrong, but not often. And he was right more often than not.

"I don't want you seeing that boy anymore," Mom said, repeating herself as though Mia hadn't gotten the message. Now there was a horrible, determined finality in her words.

Mia felt her eyes fill. "Mom, he saved my life," was all she could say. Keep calm, she told herself, she's just having an episode.

"That's what he wants you to think," Mom said, and she cocked her head, tilting her ear toward the ceiling, listening. "Little boys are all … pigs … yes, *pigs*."

In a voice that was very small and distant, Mia said, "Mom, what happened to you?"

"I'll tell you what happened," she said, and there was challenge in her tone. "I shirked my responsibility as a parent for too long. You're my daughter and it's about time I behaved like your mother. Do not see *that* boy again."

"Why? *Because he's a pig?*" The tears fell freely, streaming down Mia's face. "He's not a pig, he's my friend."

"Don't you see? That's what he wants you to believe!"

Mom stood, her face flushed a deep, dark red, quivering with rage, her hands balled into fists. Mia was in shock. Simple nervousness had become real fear.

"Stay away from him," Mom said, her voice lowering to

a sinister whisper, "or you'll be punished. If it means punishing you to protect you, I'll do it."

Mia watched her mother stalk out of the kitchen, bent forward, hands clenched. She felt her mouth moving, unable to form a plea, to beg her mom to reconsider.

27

Cody hadn't been sleeping well since the accident. When he closed his eyes, all he could see was Mia's beautiful liquid hair floating above her head as he swam to her in the darkening water. The whole experience had destroyed his belief that he was invincible. Death was real, and it sometimes tapped eleven-year-old kids on the shoulder. Diving into the pond had finally convinced him that he was mortal. Worse than the memory of almost dying, of reaching to grab a handful of Mia's hair, was the abject foolishness of believing he wasn't going to die, ever. He was annoyed that the idea had even occurred to him at all. He had actually walked around with the notion that he was immune from the cold touch of death. Hot, burning embarrassment flushed into his face whenever he thought about it, which was often. For the first time in his life, Cody seriously wondered if he was stupid. Unfit to pilot a plane. They didn't allow morons to fly the public to their destinations.

He had been sitting at his desk for hours. A large black-and-white poster of Chuck Yeager standing next to the Bell X-1 he had piloted past the sound barrier hung on the wall he was staring at, but Cody wasn't seeing it. Instead, he was wondering if he'd ever rid himself of the awful memory of his deep dive into Long Pond. His MacBook was open, the prize for washing his dad's car for ninety consecutive days last summer, as well as mowing the lawn and the backyard so many times he had lost count. Dad had said something about understanding the value of a dollar, and Cody had caught his father's expression of total disbelief when Cody had asked for a computer, followed by The Speech: "You just want me to buy you a computer? Without doing any work for it, you want me to walk into a store and hand over good money for no work? You can't expect to get something for nothing, not in this world." At the time his dad's reaction had seemed harsh to him, but he'd come to accept the lesson he was being taught. Dad was rarely mean, seldom lost his temper unless there was a good reason for it.

Mia was calling him on FaceTime. And just like that, his low mood had lifted. He answered, and his smile froze. She was in her bedroom, and she had been crying.

"What's wrong?" he said.

"Cody … my mom won't let me see you anymore." He watched her wipe her eyes with the backs of her hands. He felt cold dismay, distressed to see her upset.

"Why?"

"Cody, it's not you, it's her. She's not well. She—she's sick, that's all. She doesn't know what she's saying."

He paused, tightness circling his throat like a noose. Then he said, "What did she say?"

She was clearly struggling to get the words out. She started to speak, stopped, and began again. "She thinks you're a bad influence. She's convinced you tried to kill me."

Cody felt his mouth loosen, drop wide. He couldn't believe what he was hearing. Surely Mia was mistaken. She was fumbling for something to say, unwilling to let her last devastating statement hang in the air. That was another reason Cody liked her a lot, she was such a sweetheart and didn't want to hurt him. "She's been acting strange," she said, "I don't know what it is. She's stopped taking her medicine. But I'm not going to do it, Cody. I'm going to see you. We just have to make sure she doesn't find out."

"Doesn't she know ...?" He paused, considering his words. He almost said *doesn't she know I saved you* and immediately thought that was a douchebag move. The last thing he wanted was for Mia to think she owed him anything. She didn't, and at some point he would let her know he had simply done what he'd had to. He couldn't watch her die out there in that stagnant pond. He had rescued her more for the sake of his own conscience ... who was he kidding? He was falling in love with her.

He cleared his throat and said, "Doesn't she know what happened? The police told her it was an accident."

"I told her, too. I remember falling in, but nothing after that. It's my fault, Cody. I shouldn't have ... I was so stupid. What was I thinking? I knew the boulder was slippery with moss. I'm sorry I put you through so much."

"Don't be sorry, it's no one's fault."

"I want to see you."

"But your mom—"

"I'm going to talk to my dad. He needs to know Mom's behavior is weird. He usually talks her round. I don't know what's gotten into her ... but it's worrying me. I haven't seen her like this for a long time. Let's go biking, I've been stuck in the house too long."

"Let's maybe avoid ponds and stuff for now," he said,

and the sound of her laughter was awesome. "Okay," he said, "we won't tell your mom 'til she gets better."

"She just needs her medicine and she'll be fine."

28

Peyton Ellis parked her husband's new car outside Schiavanni's Market. The slanted slot was ideal for observing The Herbert Hotel. Yesterday, she had waited for Zoey to leave her house to collect breakfast, as she usually did every morning. But instead of buying food, Zoey had walked past several cafes, entered the hotel and hadn't left for over an hour. Then she had emerged, attempting a sedate getaway, but her legs had betrayed her and she broke into a hurried stride toward home. Peyton had almost headed for home, too, but she hesitated, her head twisted sideways, fixed on the entrance. It had been worth delaying for ten minutes, because Marcus Jenkins had exited the hotel. Coincidence? No, Peyton didn't believe it. And now here she was, developing a bad case of neck strain in order to confirm her suspicions.

Two parking spaces further up, she spotted movement in a burgundy Ford Expedition. She couldn't see who was in it—the windows were tinted—but she saw the outline of a man wearing a baseball cap.

There she was. She'd recognize Zoey's confident walk anywhere. And she was whoring it up—knee-high boots, short dress, the buttons on her blouse undone, giving the locals and tourists a tantalizing vista of her cleavage. How did Jon not notice his wife was picking up breakfast dressed like a streetwalker? Peyton shook her head slightly. She wouldn't be seen in public in such scandalous attire. Except for some parties in East Hampton, and for most of her twenties, and the occasional dinner party at her home, Peyton Ellis didn't cheapen herself by walking into esteemed hotels in a hooker's uniform. *Some people have no class*, she thought. Was Jon stupid or did he not care? It didn't make sense. How could a guy that successful not notice? Was he too busy? She knew he worked most days, and the rest of his time was spent looking after his daughter, Jane. But, really … She had brought her husband's car because Zoey might recognize hers; in the end, she didn't have to worry. Zoey's head was tilted high, locked front and center. Peyton watched her go into the hotel as though she owned it; she certainly had the money to buy it …

Five minutes later her mouth fell open as Marcus Jenkins approached the hotel from the opposite end of Main Street. It wasn't a coincidence, after all. Peyton felt there was something reckless about Zoey's behavior. It was as though she wanted to be caught. Jon may not have seen the glaring clues to his wife's infidelity yet, but how long would it be before he blinked and finally saw?

Marcus followed Zoey into the hotel and Peyton looked straight ahead, massaging her aching neck, squeezing the muscles. What exactly was she going to do with this information? She let the question hang in her mind as the Expedition two spaces over pulled out hard and sped away. Again, she tried to see who was inside. The light shining off the tinted windows made it impossible.

Poor Lizzy. How could Zoey be so treacherous? She's Lizzy's friend.

She started the engine.

Perhaps there was a way to solve this.

Peyton reversed, hoping Myrtle Shaw was home.

29

"Jesus *Christ*, Marcus, you're ripping my fucking blouse!"

As soon as he set foot inside the door, Marcus was on her, tearing at her clothes. He yanked her underwear down with so much force his thumb had gone through the delicate material and the elastic had broken. A bruise would no doubt blossom on her upper thigh ... but Zoey didn't care. She had to stop him from tearing the buttons from her blouse, though.

"Let me do it," she said, undoing the buttons. In an instant, he had scooped her off the floor, carried her to the bed. He was kneeling behind her and pushed her head into the pillows. She gasped as he entered her, and Zoey was certain that anyone passing in the hallway outside their room could hear the sound of flesh slapping flesh, maybe even people on the street below. One cup of her brassiere, hanging half off, rocked back and forth as Marcus thrust hard. Zoey bit the pillow, muffling moans that were getting louder. She could feel it ... she pressed her face deeper into the pillow, stifling an ecstatic scream. Behind her, she felt Marcus's body become tense. He groaned and slid out of her. It took a moment for Zoey to realize how disheveled she looked. Her skirt was around her waist like a belt, her brassiere was hanging askew, and she had one boot on. She couldn't even remember how she'd gotten the other one off.

She glanced at Marcus. He was sweaty and breathless. He was rough, crude, vulgar, and exactly what she needed.

"I have to go to work," he said, "or Lewis'll be bitching again."

"You two had a fight?"

"No, not really. He just wants me to turn up at the job on time." Zoey sensed he was leaving something unsaid. She wasn't sure if it was deliberate, if Marcus was cultivating an air of mystery to keep her curious. Whatever he was doing, it was effective.

"How's Lizzy?" she said.

"Acting weirder by the day. Mia's worried about her, more than usual. She thinks her mom's off her pills."

"Is she?"

"She said she wasn't."

"But you don't know?"

"Only Lizzy knows."

She propped herself up on an elbow, and said, "Marc, find out if she's not taking her medicine. It could get serious."

He nodded. Zoey would keep close watch on Lizzy later; it was the book club's final meeting before she went to New York City.

30

Lizzy parked the Chevrolet Spark a short distance from the intersection with Garden Street and Main, close to a resident's white picket fence, in the shadow of overhanging trees, despite the NO PARKING ANYTIME sign jutting out of a thin strip of grass next to the sidewalk. She had cursed Marcus's poor taste when he'd given her the car as a gift last year for her birthday. The car was covered in some mess trying to pass as paint called Mediterranean Blue Metallic but could be more accurately described as turquoise, or phlegm green. The color yelled *look at me*. And the last thing in the world she wanted was for anyone to notice her, especially now.

Marcus bought me a nice gift and I'm cursing him.
I'm sorry, I didn't mean it. I'm grateful, I promise.

She was sure Marcus hadn't envisioned her using the vehicle as a means to spy on their daughter, and therefore minded to purchase her something in a more subtle stakeout-friendly shade.

She was concerned about Mia. Marcus was not a disciplinarian and neither was Lizzy. But she had to take a firmer hand with her; she loved her only child, and she didn't want her seeing *that boy*. She recalled the strange way the three police detectives had exchanged looks amongst one another. Looks she couldn't fully read, but she knew sympathy, concern, and incredulity when she saw it. She had been frustrated, asking herself why she was the only one who was convinced that boy was a bad influence on Mia. As each day passed without her pills, she felt her perspective was becoming clearer. The pills had dulled her senses, made her miss important things. And Marcus and Mia were giving her a hard time; they wanted to watch her take her medicine. She had refused; she wasn't seven years old anymore when she could be cajoled—*tricked*—into a situation where she had no control.

Her vacation had come at the right time. They weren't going anywhere this year. It was her decision, proof she had some control over her life. Marcus hadn't argued with her, which was odd, since he loved Saranac Lake. Mia had seemed indifferent and hadn't complained, either.

Suspicion had taken root in her mind, stubborn and deep-seated. One of her doctors had taught her to recognize negative emotions and let them pass. Suspicion must be one of those emotions that were extremely difficult to get rid of, because it wouldn't leave.

Then she saw Mia at the intersection, next to the Whaling Museum, one foot on the ground and the other resting on the pedal of her bicycle, looking both ways for traffic. For a moment, Lizzy was scared. But she recognized it as a negative feeling, stared it down, and it passed.

She started the engine, checked the rearview and pulled onto Main, following Mia at a discreet distance. When she got too close, she slowed, let Mia continue ahead of her, and resumed tailing her.

Lizzy parked on the side of the road. The boy was waiting on the sidewalk, and she watched in disgust as her daughter embraced him. They mounted their bikes and rode away together, side by side, past Otter Pond.

Is suspicion a negative emotion if you're right?

What am I doing?

I'm trying to make her see that boys can't be trusted. They're only after One Thing and I have to make her see.

See what?

Boys are pigs. They're all pigs.

She was seven again and terrified.

Little pig, little pig …

But underneath the terror she felt another negative emotion that somehow made her feel better: anger.

Lizzy was breathing hard. She caught of glimpse of her face in the rearview. Shadows had fallen over it, like quick clouds passing across the moon.

31

That whore!

Myrtle was rubbing her neck and she couldn't stop. It got red and blotchy when she was nervous. Or in shock. The chamomile tea on the dining table was cold. She rose with a groan and expertly plucked a bottle from the cabinet over the sink, poured out some of the tea and replaced it with a large measure of cognac.

"You want some?" she asked.

Peyton held up a hand. "What are we going to do?" she said.

"Are you absolutely sure?"

"I'm positive." Myrtle believed her. She cast her mind back to the meeting of the book club, and the hunted look she had seen in Zoey's eyes as if she had done something wrong. And here it was—the *wrong.* It shouldn't have been far-fetched that Zoey would cheat on her husband. Perhaps it was her own bias at work. She couldn't let go of the fact that Zoey was a banker, and therefore predisposed to all manner of wrongdoing. But to cheat with her best friend's husband. That was low, even for a Wall Street whore like Zoey Finch, who took pains to remind them from time to time that her office wasn't *on* Wall Street. It was just like her to split hairs. Myrtle felt sick. She took a long drink from the chamomile-cognac concoction and it was horrible. But it did help take her mind off Zoey, if only for a moment.

Her thoughts turned to Jon. Myrtle didn't know him well. On the few occasions she had met him, he had struck her as quiet, eager not to be in the way. He carried around a quiet, unassuming air that bordered on reticence. He didn't like to talk about himself, the complete opposite of Zoey. And the way he cared for Jane, the baby, was charming. Not like *her* husband. Vincent Shaw would have grown up their infant son Aaron if he'd had magical powers. Zapped him into an adult on the spot, like in the movie with Tom Hanks, *Big*. He couldn't tolerate a crying child. Now Aaron was somewhere in New York City and he rarely visited, except for the occasional Christmas if he wasn't busy. Jon, on the other hand, seemed to take to parenting with ease. She had observed all of this over the past few months; she'd seen him for brief periods before Zoey shooed him out the door before the book club got underway. What had he done for his wife to cheat on him? She regretted it the instant the thought occurred to her. *Great, blame the guy that got cheated on.*

"Myrtle, what're we going to do?"

"Do? We're not going to do anything. What are *you* going to do?"

Why did she tell me this? Myrtle wondered. Was it because Peyton didn't want to get her hands dirty and tell Lizzy herself? Why had this socialite chosen to share the burden with her? But it didn't have anything to do with sharing. Peyton was passing the baton to her hoping she would finish first in the race to tell Lizzy her husband was cheating on her with her closest friend. That wasn't going to happen.

"We have to tell Lizzy."

"Do we now? Okay, go ahead and tell her."

"I mean, you should do it, you know her better than me."

I knew it. Why are there no surprises left in the world?

"I'm not doing it, Peyton. It'll send her over the edge. You know it will."

"So we don't say anything?"

"It's the only way we can protect her." Peyton seemed relieved. She didn't have to get her hands filthy. Or maybe Myrtle was being too hard on the younger woman. She felt the older she got, the meaner she became. Myrtle didn't think there was anything wrong in that, but she sometimes had to remind herself to hold on to her compassion. Show a little empathy. It wasn't Peyton's fault she was a socialite, a career low she'd been unfortunate enough to fall into and from which she hadn't been able to extract herself. Attending even celebrity parties had to get tiresome at some point.

"What about the book club tonight?" Peyton said.

"What do you mean?"

"We're going?"

"Peyton, it'll look weird if we didn't show up."

"It'll be the last time, though."

Perhaps she had judged Peyton unfairly. Beneath the glossy exterior, behind the celebrity friends, there was a human being, after all.

32

Lizzy couldn't understand the downbeat mood. Was the novel that grim?

She sat forward, a weighty paperback copy of Tom Wolfe's *A Man In Full* balanced on her knees, looking around Zoey's living room at the other three women who were watching her, waiting for her to answer Zoey's question, "What was the most memorable part of the story?"

"The horse," she said, "And Fareek 'The Canon' Fanon. He was very … vivid." For most of her life, Lizzy had been trying to say the right thing, but all she got in return was the furtive exchange that passed between Myrtle and Peyton, a look that said *See how crazy she is?* It was difficult not to take it personally. She was amongst friends. In any other situation, she would have choked. She was improving, mentally, since she had stopped taking her medicine. The woman in the old photographs that Marcus said was her was still a stranger, though, with her loose full hair and glamorous clothes.

Little pig, little pig—

She blinked, drifted briefly.

"Sweetie?" Zoey said. "You okay?"

"Yes," she said. "The other memorable part was Conrad Hensley. His story was startling, to think how a person could

130

be one short step away from disaster."

Peyton leaned forward on the writer's chair and said, "I liked him. He was my favorite character."

"But he failed, and he blamed his failure on Charlie Croker," Lizzy said, silencing the room again with the finality of a truth delivered, flat and undeniable.

***

Zoey was only silent because she was pleased to see someone finally render Peyton speechless, a feat worthy of respect. She was keeping one eye on Lizzy. She was worried about her. Zoey couldn't decide if the manic light in her friend's eyes was excitement or something worse. But she couldn't tear her attention away from Peyton for long. Zoey was feeling the first flutter of nervousness. Peyton was staring at her, hard, burning holes in her. What had she done? She hadn't said anything to offend her. And she had noticed that Myrtle hadn't met her gaze once since she'd arrived.

The ambiance had soured, and she couldn't understand why. Did Myrtle and Peyton think she was lording it over them? Zoey was a High-Net-Worth Individual, but she hadn't assumed a superior attitude or reminded them of how much money she had earned. She wasn't ostentatious; she had not hired a butler or a maid, just Candice to babysit her children. Were they jealous? If that was the case, it was unbecoming for adult women, book lovers, to behave in such a tawdry manner. *Unbecoming.* How dare they come into her home, drink her wine, and pollute the atmosphere with their sullen disconnection. She was being excluded, and was disturbed by the strong feeling that they were withdrawing from her. They were supposed to be reviewing a great story, yet both women had managed to foment an air of discord for no apparent reason. They'd had disagreements, differences of opinion, but those events had been the result of their passion for story, the need for stories and how they affected people. This was different. She had the distinct impression that whatever was going on in their minds, their perception of her had shifted, changed irretrievably.

She wasn't about to give up on a rescue attempt, though. She said, "One of the most horrible characters in the book was Charlie Croker. Did anyone else want to push him down a flight of stairs?" Good, she thought, keep it nice and light.

Lizzy surprised her and, it seemed, everyone else by giggling. "He was awful," she said, "and I couldn't bring myself to hate him because he failed, too, but he didn't let it defeat him. Conrad failed *better*, though, if such a thing is possible." She shook her head, then continued. "I liked the novel, its Stoic philosophy."

Peyton nodded. Zoey watched her drag her eyes—with great effort—away from her and focus on Lizzy.

"So, for you, the novel is about failure?" Peyton asked.

Zoey turned to Lizzy, who said, "Partly, yes, but it's not all of it. It just stood out to me. I could see characters rising above ruin, whether it was self-made or by accident of circumstances." Zoey was confused as she caught the emotion rippling across Peyton's face. *What in the hell is going on?*

"Myrtle," Zoey said, "what do you think?"

Without looking at her, Myrtle answered, "It's too real. It had too much cold honesty. But it was funny. It made me feel sad too, made me miss the nineties."

"Oh, come on, Myrtle, isn't that a little OTT?" Zoey said.

"I don't know what OTT is, but by Christ, I wouldn't read it again."

"But time moves on," Zoey said. "Why is your reaction to it so strong?"

"Because I hated the bankers in it," Myrtle said, crossing her arms across her chest. "Charlie Croker made bad decisions, but he was at least vaguely human. Those bankers, though—*they* were the 'shitheads.' So you tell me, Zoey, why on earth do *you* like it?"

Zoey had finally gotten Myrtle to look at her, but she wasn't sure anymore if it had been worth the effort. Now everyone was staring at her. Lizzy's usual contemplation of her feet or the floor was replaced by an intensely curious watchfulness.

"All right," Zoey said, "I liked it because it was entertaining. There, that's it, that's all I needed it to be." She had a lot more to say about the book. However, she kept her opinion of it short, because she was furious—was Myrtle calling her a shithead through the side door?

***

Myrtle didn't believe anything Zoey had said. She had never been more certain that she was in the presence of a woman capable of incredible deceit. She believed Peyton. Zoey was the type of person you had to take a second and third look at, like a painting you kept coming back to, seeing it anew, discovering a previously unseen detail. There was no doubt in her mind: Zoey was cheating on her husband with the husband of a woman she claimed was her friend. It was overwhelming, difficult to process the sheer audacity of this banker: she didn't even have the decency to distance herself from the woman she had betrayed. The only explanation that seemed reasonable to Myrtle was that Zoey Finch was a sociopath. She had to be. How else could she face Lizzy with that fake concern, those soft eyes that now looked decidedly remorseless, cruel and uncaring? She was *seeing* Zoey. It occurred to Myrtle that she should view people like paintings. Take a second, closer look. How often had she met someone in her life and not *seen* who they were? It was an uncomfortable thought.

Myrtle wanted to leave and take Peyton with her. She wasn't confident that the younger woman could contain herself; she was bursting at the seams, probably furious at the unfolding charade. And she didn't blame her. But it wouldn't serve any useful purpose if she lost her temper and confronted Zoey. Myrtle wanted to avoid that, not for Zoey's sake but for Lizzy's ... And yet, a tiny voice—inconvenient because she'd made up her mind—the part of her that balked at the idea of unfairness, allowed room for doubt. She did believe Peyton, but what if she had misinterpreted the situation? What if she was wrong? She drowned out that voice, raised belief above fairness and facts, and leaned back in the armchair, watching Zoey from the corner of her eye in silent condemnation.

***

"What did you think of Charlie Croker?" Zoey asked.

Peyton's heart was racing, pushing blood into her neck, making it feel swollen. She had an iron grip on a handful of leather, noticed, and released her hand from the armrest.

Myrtle was staring at her with such unwavering concentration—with such weight—that it took a moment for her to realize it was the only thing keeping her from leaping out of the chair and strangling Zoey.

Peyton didn't know who Zoey was. It was almost as though *she* had been cheated. She could forgive Myrtle if the older woman decided not to believe her: Zoey's performance was so convincing. She was the picture of innocence. Who would have the gall to sit there and discuss a book, knowing she had cheated with her friend's husband? Zoey Finch. This wasn't the woman she'd met, the person she had liked. What in God's name had happened to her?

Myrtle wasn't the only reason she remained seated—Jon was upstairs; she had heard him singing to Jane earlier, perhaps in an attempt to get her to sleep. Underneath the anger, there was fear. She was afraid of dropping a grenade into the middle of Jon's life, as well as Lizzy's. She didn't want to do it. After tonight, the least she could do would be to avoid Zoey. Behind her riches and her big house lay a wanton tramp who didn't have the guts, the decency, to divorce her husband if she didn't love him. Or was it simple greed? Zoey just wanted it all—the money, the family, and yes, even the husband, a man indistinguishable from the shadows in his own home, and just as easy to ignore. Peyton had noticed that whenever she saw Jon and Zoey together, it was as though she didn't see him. He was the invisible man. He'd discover his wife's infidelity at some point. There was nothing worse than looking like a fool.

The backs of her eyes were hot as she turned her gaze on Zoey, and said, "Croker brought his misfortune on himself. He was irresponsible, overextended and arrogant. He was no different from those bankers."

"Not all bankers are irresponsible and arrogant," Zoey said, giving voice to a small, nervous laugh.

"No, maybe you're right, could just be the ones I've seen on the TV news and met in real life."

They glared at each other. Peyton caught a glimpse of Lizzy shifting uneasily on the armchair.

"Please, let's be calm," Lizzy said, and the fight in Peyton wilted.

She got out of the chair, flung the door open hard. It struck the wall and bounced. The reverberation could be heard throughout the house. She slammed the front door as she left.

33

When she wasn't sitting out on her porch, Peggy Dawson sat by the living room window, watching people pass on the sidewalk as she calmly contemplated suicide. Most were summer people, but there were plenty of locals, too. She could tell the residents apart from the vacationers: those who lived in Sag Harbor year-round had a sure-footed purpose that the visitors lacked. It was subtle, but it was there. She enjoyed watching people walk by her home, although sometimes it made her sad—her days strolling carefree into the village were over. Peggy had osteoarthritis and her eyesight was failing. She was in constant pain, but she refused to let the world see it. And she was getting tired of propping up her image as a Tough Old Broad. It was just plain inconsiderate to encumber others with your suffering. Peggy had had enough.

The real reason she hadn't joined Zoey's book club was simple—she couldn't see the print on the page. And the technology they had these days frustrated her. She had tried audiobooks and had decided they weren't for her. She assumed she was just built differently, that her internal wiring was of a bygone era and not meant for the Digital Age, or the spoken word, which somehow wasn't the same as the printed word. It wasn't the only reason she hadn't participated in Zoey's little club. Peggy was an early riser and always brought her coffee to her armchair by the living room window. Zoey Finch had to pass Peggy's house to get to her own home, and Peggy knew the walk of shame when she saw it. She had known for a long time that Zoey was probably being unfaithful to Jon. But Peggy didn't believe in interfering in anyone's marriage, least of all that of a close friend. Because Jon *was* a friend, someone she trusted. She recalled Jon asking her if Gabe had ever been cruel to her and she'd said no because it was true. She had wanted to tell Jon that he should begin planning his exit strategy, that a partner displaying signs of cruelty was a sign they were looking for a way out. But she had changed her mind. She was going to let Jon know that his marriage was over, or at the very least, close to the precipice. It was up to him to confirm it for himself, but she had to inform him of her suspicions. She didn't know for sure if Zoey really was cheating on him, but she would be surprised if she wasn't.

She leaned forward and composed a letter to Jon, refraining from pressing the pen into the paper too hard. Peggy shifted the notepad into a more comfortable position on her lap. Her hand hurt, possibly an introductory twinge from yet more arthritis or some other horrible condition. In her good hand she held a magnifying glass, moving it back and forth to achieve just the right amount of focus.

Her body was in constant pain. Even worse, she was lonely, cringing inwardly at the bitter taste of failure contained in the word. She was certain that if she'd told Jon this, he'd come around more often. But it would be mortifying and undignified to reveal such a thing. She would rather confess to murder than admit she was lonely. She had been beset by loneliness ever since Gabe had died. She missed him every day. It was awful at night. Thinking about him, the contrast of his serious, even severe expression in the boardroom and then chasing her around the house, threatening to tickle her, and both of them laughing like a couple of teenagers. No one knew how warm Gabe had been except her. No one knew how kind he was, how thoughtful, and how much they had needed each other. There were rare moments when she thought she was recovering, that grief had softened its grip, ceased its endless pursuit of her. But it didn't last. She kept remembering being unhappy in her teenage years and how Gabe had made her feel young and happy again. She cried so often at the memory of him that she barely noticed the first sting of tears anymore. Peggy would have ended her life already if she hadn't known that Gabe wouldn't approve. But she was desperate now. Desperately seeking an end. There was an old .38 in her lockbox in her bedroom, purchased at Gabe's insistence. He had worried about her being home alone (which was rare, since she had been just as much a workaholic as her husband) when he was away, meeting a client, or closing a deal, and he'd wanted her to be able to protect herself. However, she didn't want to leave a mess. The one thing that annoyed her more than daytime TV was inconsiderate people. What about the unfortunate person who would find her body? And it would most likely be Jon. He didn't allow five days to pass without checking on her. As rich as he was, his judgment was somewhat lacking. Money couldn't buy everything, apparently. Peggy didn't know what had happened between them. She only knew that she was very fond of Jon. He didn't talk down to her and he didn't pity her. Instead, they joked about her various ailments and his concern when he expressed it was honest. She owed it to him to let him decide for himself whether he wanted to forgive his wife or start a new life without her. If Jon was really that bad a husband then Zoey should have divorced him.

She had pills, bottles of opiates in her medicine cabinet, except it seemed like such a chickenshit way to go out. She wouldn't make a mess, though. But the gun was quicker, the better option. She hoped Jon understood that she wasn't trying to make a statement. She'd make it so the debris of her death was easy to clean.

In a hand that trembled, she wrote Jon's name on the envelope. Groaning, she rose from the armchair, leaning heavily on the cane. She placed the letter on the table in the entrance hall and began her slow ascent of the stairs. Everest. It might as well have been. How funny it was, she thought, the way the ordinary has a mind to become the extraordinary, remembering she had often bounded up those stairs with the grace and litheness of touch of a ballet dancer. Her bones crackled now. The pain lancing through her legs and hips blurred her vision and stole her breath. Halfway there. And it was strange: she felt Gabe's disapproval. He would not want her to do this. As tough as Gabe could be in matters business-related, he had been surprisingly philosophical. He'd believed that pain was temporary. Bad times came and went. Peaks and troughs. All things passed. A view she had shared until the pall of his death had lingered, stubborn and immovable. At least she hadn't taken to the bottle. That was something Gabe would have been proud of. He hadn't touched a drop of alcohol in his life, yet somehow he had been carried off by a goddamn stroke.

She paused near the top of the stairs. Just five more to go.

She hadn't opened the door on her life and allowed the whole world to look in on her pain. That was something *she* was proud of.

Peggy had put her affairs in order. She had purchased a plot right next to Gabe's in the Green River Cemetery in East Hampton.

Two more steps.

Her chest heaved with the effort.

The agony twisting through her body unearthed a steely defiance in her.

Come on, you bastard, do your worst.

She set her foot down on the upstairs landing and a giddy sense of triumph coursed through her. She wouldn't have to do this every night. Peggy could have moved into a bungalow, but she didn't want to. She could have done a lot of things to make life easier, but she chose not to. She was living and dying the way she wanted ... Gabe would understand. He wouldn't be satisfied being able to work and live at half his capacity, and she was no different.

She held on to the newel post, leaning forward on the cane, catching her breath.

For a fleeting moment, she considered letting herself fall backward down the stairs. An accident. Old Peggy lost her balance in a tragic accident ... No, *no*. Besides, even with her condition, she might survive the tumble. The thought made gooseflesh ripple up her arms and she got moving.

She made it to the bedroom, out of breath and exhausted. Their bedroom. She sat on the side of the bed, rested her forehead on the hand that gripped the cane. All she had to do now was put on a nice dress, something Gabe had bought her, always in the right size.

She didn't know how long she remained like that, but when her breathing returned to normal, she went to the closet. It was hard to miss Gabe's white leisure suit, similar to the one worn by John Travolta in *Saturday Night Fever*, with the shirt's huge collar. It was long out of fashion, but Gabe—and she—didn't have the heart to throw it out, or donate it, although she couldn't imagine anyone would wear it now. But in the seventies there was nothing unusual about it, at least not to Gabe. She saw her own 1920s black-and-gold flapper dress, in which she had last graced the dance floor in 1978. She put it on, but it was a painful process that drew grunts and curses from her. She had plenty of medicine, and she had taken the pills, but they laid her mood low, deepening the darkness every day.

She looked at herself in the mirror. Not bad, she thought, but not great, either. It was a dress designed for a younger woman. With dreadful slowness, she applied makeup at her vanity table, then removed the cold steel box from a slim drawer. The gun was old but the bullets were new. All cylinders were full. As she made her way down the hall toward the bathroom, she felt as though she'd engaged in an epic battle, one she had lost. Old age and the illnesses it brought was the ultimate competitor, a formidable opponent. And she had lost. But there was resignation in defeat, not bitterness, only steadfast acceptance.

The bathroom was tiled, and therefore easy to clean.

She struggled to climb into the bathtub, but determination and the remains of her former grit rose within her and she persevered. It was oddly comfortable, lying in the tub, gun resting on her gut, rising and falling rapidly but becoming gentler as her breathing slowed. In the end, it came down to simple concerns: she didn't want to deteriorate to the point where she would have no choice but to be bathed by a home helper. She didn't want some stranger wiping her ass or feeding her like a child or talking to her as if she were an infant. She imagined it all, all the horrible possibilities as her body broke down and her independence diminished and became a fading memory ...

Peggy cocked the gun fast, turned it, and jabbed it hard into her breastplate.

34

As he entered Harvard University, slowing as he made the turn onto Oxford Street, Jon was keenly aware of time passing. Despite a bumpy flight from La Guardia, the moment he disembarked from the plane at Boston International he had sprinted to the car rental desk and didn't waste precious seconds keeping within the speed limit. Adrenaline soared through his blood, high and kicking a steady beat into the backs of his eyeballs. He felt some of his former self emerge, just below the surface: the risk taker, willing to take a blind leap of faith and hope for a soft landing, but not afraid if he found the ground was hard and unyielding. Roger Berris had called and demanded he execute the plan or he was dumping his shares and taking his chances. Jon had somehow managed to placate him, calm him down, and convince him that the payoff would be larger if he just had a little more patience. But Jon was against a ticking clock and he knew it. He sensed that holding Roger off was no longer an option. Zoey was in New York City, probably already talking to the people from Goldman Sachs, but she was due to appear on Bloomberg News and CNBC later in the day. She needed a phone call from Jon or none of that would happen. He had called Henry Larson at

Aquarius, told his chief financial officer what was about to go down, to lock all the doors and "Don't talk to anybody." His instructions were met with concern and confusion and even a note of alarm. In the end, Henry had promised, however reluctantly, to carry out the tasks given him. He was mildly irritated at Henry—his colleague knew him, and had doubted him. Ten years together wasn't enough to inspire trust. His irritation was brief, though. He felt sure Dr. Berris wasn't lying, but he had to confirm it. He glanced at the file sitting thick and heavy in the passenger seat.

Jon didn't have fond memories of Harvard. He had kept to himself, for the most part, resisting all efforts to get him to join a fraternity. Not because he was unsociable (although that was part of it; he couldn't relate to people who'd had everything paid for them in life by a rich daddy, though he'd thought even then that was a harsh generalization) but because he had odd jobs during term-time and worked construction in New York and Boston in the summer to pay his tuition fees and send money home to his mother in Canarsie, where she still lived on Seaview Avenue, right across the street from Canarsie Park.

Two years ago, he had tried to persuade her to upgrade, to move to a bigger house, and when that didn't work, he'd tried to convince her to accept home help, have someone look in on her at least once a day. But Meredith Finch was stubbornly independent and was horrified at the notion of having some stranger in her home. And besides, Jon had given her enough money to last at least two lifetimes. She didn't want anything else from him, just to see her grandchildren every six months or so. Jon had always sensed that if he hadn't married Zoey, his mother's visits would be more frequent. Whatever misgivings his mother had about his wife, she'd kept them to herself.

Apart from the construction job, Jon had had a small sideline selling weed. Nothing big-time, and certainly nothing stronger than marijuana. It was to help pay for gas and other incidentals. Looking back at it, he could hardly believe he'd taken such a risk. It was the recklessness of youth, the inability to see any consequence greater than possible expulsion, but it had been necessary. He had been smart enough to keep his weed-selling business off campus, though. Both of these jobs were enough to motivate him to get his MBA. Roofing in July and carrying bags of cement up scaffolding only served to remind him that if he didn't apply himself to the task of earning his degree, he would be an old man by the time he reached fifty. He'd seen firsthand the toll wrought on the bodies of his fellow construction workers: aching limbs, back problems, alcohol addiction, men who looked ten years older than they were, weathered by the sweltering heat of summer and the merciless vagaries of winter.

He parked the rental near the Laboratory for Integrated Science and Engineering. He checked his cell, making sure he had Zoey on speed dial, and brought up a photograph of Cody holding his little sister, Jane. He didn't like to be away from them for long, and already he was thinking of home. His children were never far from his thoughts, and he missed them. It was the strength of this feeling that made him blink, come back to himself and the urgency of the situation.

Focus, goddamnit.

He took a deep breath, tucked the file under his arm, crossed Oxford Street and followed the sidewalk past the

Hoffman Laboratory toward the redbrick structure he recognized as the Department of Chemistry and Chemical Biology. He had been here before, to see one of the few people he'd actually become friends with, Lisa Edwards.

He ran up the steps, and in the entrance hall he told a woman behind a desk who he was. She pointed him toward a hallway, and said, "Room 8, about halfway down."

He thanked her and left. When she was out of sight, his stride quickened. He paused outside Room 8, patted the cell phone in his pocket, making sure it was there, and smiled at the name and title on the door: Professor Lisa Edwards. He was glad she hadn't decided to become a lawyer, an idea she had toyed with when they were freshmen. Although Jon suspected even then that she was toying with him. She'd had a twinkle in her eye as she had watched his horrified reaction that she might go over to the dark side.

He knocked and went in. Lisa glanced up from the papers on her desk and her eyes widened briefly. She came out from behind the desk and hugged him. They had gone on two dates. It was on the second date when they both realized how ridiculous it was for them to be anything more than friends.

She stood back from him, openly looking him up and down. Jon couldn't help but smile.

"My God," she said, "who let you out of the house? Well dressed, better looking now than when I knew you—"

"Oh Jesus, Lisa. I'd be hunted with pitchforks if I said the same to you."

"You're such a charmer," she said, laughing her confidential laugh, as though they were sharing a secret joke only the two of them understood.

Lisa resumed her position behind the desk, and said, "You come bearing gifts?"

Jon was momentarily confused, until he remembered the file. "Oh," he said, handing it across the desk to her. "I wouldn't call it that."

She arched an eyebrow, her eyes alight with curiosity.

Jon waited and watched as she turned to the first page. Her dark hair was tied back with a strip of material that looked as though it had been torn off an old blouse. She hadn't changed much. Yes, she had gotten older, but she still seemed like a student to him. She dressed in much the same way now as she had all those years ago. Jeans, blouse, and hair tied with a hank of something she'd found around the house, the knot loose enough to qualify as an afterthought.

He occupied himself by looking at the photographs on the wall as Lisa examined the documents. A smiling man holding an equally beaming child of about five or six years old hung from a frame in the middle of the wall. Jon guessed this was her child, and the child's father. He glanced over at Lisa, trying to spot a wedding band. Then he saw it as she turned another page. He was glad she had a family. They seemed happy, which somehow made him feel more relaxed, despite his eagerness to get out of there. All he needed was confirmation. He imagined Zoey sitting somewhere in the Goldman Sachs building in New York City, waiting for him to hurry up and call. He wasn't going to rush Lisa. She was doing him a favor.

"Huh? That's odd," she said softly, more to herself than to him. Jon wondered if she had even noticed she had spoken aloud. He wanted to ask her what she had found, but he pulled back, waited, watched her turn the pages, her frown deepening, her bottom lip curled as she bit into it.

He slipped his phone out of his pocket, glanced at the time and was shocked to discover thirty-five minutes had elapsed since he'd stepped into Lisa's office.

Then her head snapped up and she looked directly at him, closed the file and tossed it on her desk. "It's wrong," she said, "the medicinal chemistry is fabricated. I'll need more time to decipher exactly what was altered and why, but whoever did this did a poor job of disguising whatever fraud is going on here. The person who did this," she tapped the file with her forefinger, "can't possibly believe they'll get it past the FDA. It's laughable, but not one bit funny. Jon, where did you get this?"

"I can't answer that yet, but I promise when my work is done, I'll call you. Or you could just watch Bloomberg News later tonight."

"I see … I must say, I haven't seen chemistry so sloppy— carbon rings where they don't belong, designed to make this drug seem more effective than it is." That was it. Confirmation. "The thing is," she continued, "there *is* a drug underneath the false statements and hokey chemistry, just not the one presented here."

"You're sure, Lisa? I have to make absolutely certain because the stakes are pretty high."

"I'm sure, Jon. If I cut through the pasted-on chemistry, there's at least two mechanisms by which this antibiotic could—and would—develop resistance. Even a cursory glance would alert a sleepy sophomore that something is wrong. That's what I don't get. If the person responsible for this has even an undergraduate degree in chemistry I don't know how they think they could pass this off and get away with it." Perhaps Roger Berris was right; Arthur Dunhill really wasn't playing with a full deck.

He spoke with Professor Edwards for another ten minutes, and when he had thanked her and got into the hall, he walked fast. And when he got outside, he broke into a headlong run toward his rental car.

35

Arthur Dunhill understood natural selection. As he ground three marbles together in his left hand, he used his right to tilt the tumbler of whiskey toward his lips. It had been a long day and he was glad to be home, even though there was no one to come home to. His wife, Michelle, had divorced him two years ago because he had refused to see a therapist. To Michelle's credit, she had toughed it out with him for three years. His ex-wife couldn't sleep with the light on, and Arthur couldn't sleep with it off. If he slept in the dark, Mr. Pinch would visit him, the man Arthur Senior had promised would pinch the soft, tender flesh on the insides of his arms if Arthur Junior ever forgot what *survival of the fittest* meant. Mr. Pinch had no face, but Senior had promised that if the value of being an Important Man ever slipped Junior's mind, Mr. Pinch would reveal his face to him, a prospect so terrifying that Arthur never forgot. To make certain his son remembered just how scary and hurtful Mr. Pinch could be, Senior demonstrated the pain his son would feel by pinching the soft meat on the inside of his arm and his son had screamed. When his father had stopped pinching, he'd told his son to quit being a little girl, which was somehow worse, even more painful than being pinched. Sometimes, when his father had judged him to be weak, a sin worse than murder, Arthur did see Mr. Pinch, crawling from the closet on hands and knees, its face a black malignant mass beneath a dark hood, the fabric of its tan trench coat rustling as the younger Dunhill hid under the blankets, his breath stopped in his swollen throat.

From the time he was six until he was seventeen, Arthur Senior had come home from his job at JP Morgan in Boston and sat his son down to explain, again, how life was beautifully simple and consisted of two kinds of people: the Weak and the Successful. To be Successful, you had to be Strong. No son of Arthur Dunhill's was going to be Weak, and therefore a Failure. *It's dog eat dog, son,* the elder Dunhill had said, reading from the same script he'd memorized with years of constant repetition: *In the real world, no one cares about you. It's survival of the fittest out there. No one's going to pat you on the back for being a good person. Results are the only thing that counts. Never forget that.* And of course, Arthur Junior hadn't forgotten.

He was in such a deep state of distraction that he hadn't realized he was sitting in one of the two armchairs facing his executive desk, in his executive office. Arthur blinked, looking around, thinking he was on the wrong side of the desk, the Supplicants' Side. He rarely received visitors these days, and if he did, they were usually investors. He had made what in his father's view would be a cardinal mistake—Arthur had forgotten his rightful position in the world. And yet, he found he didn't care. He had larger problems to deal with.

He turned the marbles in his hand around and around, taking in his mahogany wood-paneled home office, a place he used to relax, if such a thing wasn't a sign of Weakness, although his instincts told him it was. Relaxing was for slackers and people who thought a job half done was better than the job not being done at all. But Arthur had discovered a loophole he was comfortable with and one he was sure his father would have approved of: thinking was not slacking or relaxing. Thinking was important. This was Arthur's Thinking Room, even though he was certain that that prissy little architect from Manhattan with the hairless hands hadn't considered *thinking* as a possible function of this room when he had designed it. Arthur recalled the architect—Edgar Fields; even his name sounded pretentious—trying to convince him that walnut would be a better choice, and the little architect had stood before him, excessively polite, all the while wringing his hairless little hands together and Arthur had been almost mesmerized as he'd stared at the bald backs of Edgar Fields's hands ...

He realized, with something reminiscent of disgust, that he was refusing to deal with the problem, and that problem had a name: Roger Berris. It was clear to him that Roger was no longer *on board*. At first, he wasn't angry, just dumbfounded at his friend and business partner's quiet betrayal. It was true that he had envied Roger, a man who had climbed to the top of the tree solely on the strength of his intellect and not his daddy's money, whereas Arthur had had his education paid for by his father, who had introduced his son into every social circle that mattered, a necessary evil accomplished by Roger based on his easy, natural charm. But Arthur's envy of his friend hadn't been toxic. If anything, it was mild and fleeting. Deep down, with his eyes closed against the light as he tried to sleep every night,

Arthur just wished he was self-made the same way Roger was. Roger had come from nothing, whereas Arthur had inherited his father's wealth when he'd finally, mercifully died. And where was the sport in having everything in life handed to you? Although Arthur felt as though he was paying for his inheritance and whatever he had achieved in life, but in a vague, indiscernible way.

Yet it wasn't Roger's all-American rags-to-riches fairy tale that troubled him; it was that he suspected Roger saw himself as *morally* superior to him. It was Roger's self-righteous attitude that grated on Arthur. Roger seemed to have forgotten that while it was true that he had started at the bottom, it was also a fact that Roger was now a paid-up member of the One Percent. He needed to remove his friend—*former* friend—from Zinco Sciences, and he was at a loss as to how he should go about it.

Roger hadn't said or done anything to cause him concern, yet. But Arthur was tuned in to whatever frequency his colleague was putting out: Roger disagreed with the path Arthur had taken and Arthur's usual four hours of sleep each night had been reduced to two. All he could think about now was how and when Roger was going to sabotage his plans. What made the situation even more lamentable was that Roger knew they were neck high in a public-health emergency. Antibiotic resistance was a clear and present danger that needed to be confronted. The economic damage and the health-care costs caused by resistant strains of bacteria ran into the billions. But it wasn't a sexy news story, so it didn't get a lot of press.

Arthur's plan was simple: when Zinbactin was approved, the publicity would drive investors to Zinco Sciences so that they could reinvest the money into synthesizing analogues of Zinbactin, which may be even more effective than the original drug. Arthur was looking at the bigger picture, an ability ostensibly absent in Roger. The situation called for drastic measures. They were running out of drugs effective in treating many bacterial infections, and at some point their last line of defense, the world's top-shelf drug, vancomycin, was going to be useless, too.

His cell phone vibrated in his pocket and when he saw the name displayed on the screen, he frowned. It was his vice president of research and development, Deanna Marshall.

"Deanna, what's wrong?" he said, sitting up straight.

"Is your TV on?" She sounded...scared?

"What?"

"Turn the TV on. Bloomberg news. Arthur, we're in trouble. It's over."

"What—" But Deanna had hung up. He stared at the phone, confused and curious, watching his hand. It was trembling.

He went to his desk, picked up a remote control and pointed it at the wall behind him. A mahogany panel opened with a soft hum and the flat screen appeared. He sat, trying to see everything at once and not seeing anything.

Goddammit, calm down.

A man was interviewing a woman. Her name was Zoey Finch, and she was telling the anchor she had just shorted Zinco Sciences. His eyes dropped to the ticker at the bottom of the screen, and the name Dr. Roger Berris caught his eye. He missed some of it, but he got the general idea: Roger had dumped his entire shareholding in Zinco Sciences, and he had accused the standing CEO of fraud.

He dropped the marbles. They made a hollow sound as they rolled on the floor, and he began punching numbers into his cell phone.

36

Miami Beach, Florida

Andre Rowe had eight fingers left. And by the time Benny
Cooper was done with him, all ten digits would be removed—
if the sweaty, bloody, mewling lawyer couldn't convince Benny
that he was going to pay. On the other hand, even if he could
convince him, Benny wasn't in a forgiving mood.

Rowe's remaining fingers were nailed to the small table
with galvanized staples, the U-shaped kind used for fencing.
Ken Brooks and George Howard were standing by each of
his shoulders. Ken was holding a blood-streaked carving
knife at chest level, blade tilted skyward, primed to strike
again, feet apart on the floor of the panic room. The blank
gray steel walls created just the right ambiance, perfectly
conducive to changing the hearts and minds of debtors.

Benny held up his pinky finger. Ken approached the
wretched, slumped lawyer and placed the blade over his little
finger. Benny casually stuffed the soft silicone earplugs
hanging from the cord around his neck into his ears. There
was no reason to neglect health and safety precautions. He
had flawless hearing, and he wanted to keep it that way. This
job was hazardous at times.

But he could still hear Andre's muffled screams—"NO! Please, please, no, *NOOO!*"—and the irrevocable crunch as Ken leaned on the blade with the heel of his other hand. Now Andre had seven fingers to work with.

Benny's main business was smuggling cocaine from Colombia via the Dominican Republic. But it wasn't his only source of income. As an ex-convict, he understood the importance of a fresh start, a clean slate. So he provided ex-cons with new identities, clean social security numbers ... and lawyers who were looking at serious jail time for embezzling vast sums of money from their own firms. His anger stemmed more from the difficult task of getting rid of Andre's body than Andre running out on his debt. The lawyer had inconvenienced him, placed an insupportable burden on his shoulders. He was forcing Benny to kill him. It was an unusual situation. Benny had supplied dozens of felons with a second chance in life, and only one had decided not to pay; he had ended up weighted deep down in the Everglades. He was having a hard time understanding why this lawyer thought he could stiff him and get away with it. Benny had tried to help Andre. *Had* helped him. His mother had been right: no good deed ...

He waited until Andre's screams died down before removing the plugs. There was no danger of anyone hearing the ruckus, anyway. The panic room had ten-inch concrete walls and a six-inch steel door, with added soundproofing. A person walking their dog on Meridian Avenue outside, or a golfer across the road at the Miami Beach Golf Club would remain undisturbed by the grisly death throes of one Andre Rowe, esquire.

Bent over the table, Andre whimpered, spittle hanging in

strings from his gaping mouth. "I have to know," Benny said, "why did you do it?"

But he mustn't have heard the question. His head was bowed, his shoulders shuddering, gasping mewls of pain erupting from his throat.

"Andre? You get to keep the rest of your fingers if you tell me why you ran out on us."

The promise piqued Andre's interest. He raised his head, swayed from side to side, and looked at Benny. "Do you mean it?"

"Yes," Benny said, a sudden tone of compassion finding its way into his voice, "I mean it. Really, I do."

Andre swayed some more, then he said, "I didn't think I'd get caught."

"Just like you didn't think you'd get caught dipping into the company till? You're a bad criminal, Andre. You had a career path. You should've stayed in your lane."

"I had—I mean, I owed people."

Benny shook his head, dismayed, sympathetic. "You had a gambling problem?"

Andre nodded. "I can get you the money," he said, "please, let me go, I'll get you the money."

Benny sighed. "You see, we operate a trust system. You tried to game the system, Andre, and as a consequence, you hurt my feelings." He looked at Ken and George. "Are your feelings hurt?" Both men nodded quickly. "So now you get it, Andre," Benny continued. "You destroyed our system of trust and hurt our feelings. I feel like you don't respect me. You *offended* me." Benny scanned the table, calculated the price he'd extracted: a forefinger, a middle finger and a pinky. He looked directly at Ken, and said, "The thumb."

He inserted the earplugs, watched Andre thrash and buck and scream, sweat flying in every direction. The trouble Andre had forced him to endure was unforgivable. Benny had had to abduct the lawyer from his Coconut Grove home, transport him across I-195, careful not to violate any traffic laws, with two large men, Ken and George, keeping watch on the slippery embezzler in back of the van, hoping they wouldn't be stopped by a cop. It was funny, he thought, how he hated lawyers more than the police. It was the reason he had spent time in Florida State Prison—an incompetent lawyer. If not for his brother helping him, Benny would still be incarcerated in Raiford.

Andre had six fingers left.

He was about to give Ken the signal to remove another digit when his cell vibrated.

"George," he said, "tape him up."

George stepped behind Andre, ripped a strip of duct tape with his teeth, the same gray color as the walls, and plastered it across his mouth. He looked at Benny and said, "You want the full package, boss?"

"Yes, George, I would like that very much."

George tore another strip of tape off the roll, and this time he covered Andre's nose. The *full package* usually took three to five minutes to arrive at its final destination. It wasn't as messy as stabbing, Benny mused.

He answered the phone and listened, watching Andre suffocate, trying to break free. But the table and chair were bolted to the floor. Andre sagged, his head lolling, as though his neck was made from cooked pasta. Benny was losing interest and frowned, focusing on the caller.

"Problem?" he said, "What kind of problem?"

37

Jon spent most of the journey home glancing at his cell phone propped on the dash as Zoey appeared first on Bloomberg News and then on CNBC, telling investors worldwide that Zinco Sciences was nothing more than a fraud built on false promises and faulty research, taking aim at its chief executive officer, one Arthur Dunhill, calling him a liar, but making sure to add she had evidence that he had lied. Jon wished she had left Dunhill out of it. He was on the ground, bleeding, possibly mortally wounded. It wasn't necessary to continue kicking him.

He kept returning to his meeting with Lisa Edwards, and her blunt incredulity that such a misrepresentation was even attempted. Perhaps Dunhill's arrogance outweighed his common sense. He thought he could get away with it, even though Lisa had told him the FDA would see how Zinco and Dunhill had fabricated their results immediately.

He had spoken to Zoey briefly after her interview on Bloomberg. The excitement in her voice had been a welcome change. He had missed that buoyant tone, flushed with the prospect of a surefire win. As well as keeping a close eye and ear on Zoey's TV appearances, he'd maintained a keen vigil on the Zinco Sciences share price. At the start of the day's trading, it had been holding steady at over one hundred dollars. When the New York Stock Exchange closed, ZNS, Zinco Sciences ticker, had dropped to less than thirty-five bucks. It was only a matter of time before Dunhill's pharmaceutical company went all the way to zero. Jon had shorted bad actors before, companies whose foundations were built on sand, hype and over-valuations. But he hadn't encountered such blatant self-sabotage as that engineered by Arthur Dunhill.

Roger Berris had dumped his entire shareholding in the company he'd built with Dunhill, spooking investors and beginning the rout of ZNS stock. Berris had roused Jon's curiosity. He was trying to process the scale of Roger's betrayal of his friend and colleague. Even though he understood it, he didn't like it. Self-preservation was part of the survival kit in business, Jon knew. Recognizing a sinking ship when the water was up to your ankles was also essential. Jon had spent years swimming alongside sharks; banking was a winner-take-all-eat-the-stupid open-air knife fight. But Berris wasn't one of *them*, circling the chum in the water as frenzy built around him. Had Roger ruined Arthur because he was following his ethical duty or was Roger just doing the right thing for Roger? He suspected it was a little bit of the former and a lot of the latter. Jon smiled at the uselessness of the question—and his ironclad cynicism— since the end result was the same. He hadn't betrayed anyone in all his years running Aquarius. His conscience wasn't entirely without blemish … but he wasn't a rat. That was what it came down to in the end—Roger Berris was a snitch, and therefore garbage. Jon couldn't respect him. Throughout this whole scheme, it had bothered him how quickly and easily one friend could turn on another. Yes, Jon had taken full advantage and didn't regret his part in demolishing a rotten company. But Roger had come to him. Now Berris was lying low somewhere and, according to the news, he couldn't be contacted for comment. People had been murdered for a lot less than revealing questionable research, and if Roger was correct and Dunhill was as unstable as he had claimed, then it was probably a good idea for Roger to stay low. After all, what did Arthur have to lose since he'd lost everything anyway?

He pulled into a parking space outside Gerry's Bistro on Main Street. Zoey would be home tomorrow; she'd had a long day and Jon had told her to get some rest, congratulating her on a great job. She had asked him to buy champagne and they would celebrate when she got back from New York. Things were turning around for them. Jon hoped so, and made a solemn vow that he would be a good husband, or at least try harder. Whatever was wrong with Zoey (and something *was* definitely wrong) Jon wouldn't win Husband of the Year. He wasn't in the running, but he would step up his efforts.

He was looking forward to seeing his children. Candice was babysitting Cody and Jane. As he got out of the car, his mouth twisted into a sour grimace as he recalled the humiliation of having fired her and then her being rehired by his wife. He shoved the feeling down, deep, and ordered hot soup for Peggy. He would check on her, make sure she was all right. She might be in a lot of pain. And she wasn't fooling him, no matter how much she had tried to disguise it. He was backing out of the lot when he realized he'd forgotten the champagne.

***

Peggy's tears had dried into a delicate crust on her cheeks. Before she pulled the trigger, she felt she had to acknowledge the main reason she was in her bathtub, a loaded gun resting on her chest, which was rising and falling rapidly and the heart beneath was beating too fast. Apart from the constant pain, something even worse had turned the occasional sleepless night into chronic insomnia: she had dishonored her late husband by gambling everything they had worked for their entire lives. The money was gone. She had plundered their investments, too. Blew it all on online poker, bingo, roulette and anything else she could bet on. She hadn't gambled when Gabe was alive and didn't know why she had started when he'd passed. Even now, as she prepared to end her life, she viewed her actions with a kind of horrified wonder. More than physical pain, disgrace had brought her to this point.

Sorry, Gabe. I really am.

All she needed was a little courage and it would be over: the misery, the sleepless nights, the unbearably long days.

She reached to turn off her hearing aid. If only she could switch her thoughts off, too, and her fear. But shame was persistent; it had burrowed so deep there was no excising it. Peggy picked up the gun.

***

Jon knocked on Peggy's door. No answer. He shifted the container with the soup in it to his other arm, knocked harder. After the sixth rap on the door, he became worried. She could have fallen down the stairs. Could have tripped, fallen and broken a bone. He had never used the spare key she'd given him in case of emergencies. But now his hand was itching to pluck it out of his wallet.

She's probably on the ground, injured and can't call for help.

He took the key from his wallet and went inside. There was an envelope on the table in the reception hall. He frowned as he read his name on the front of it.

***

She had promised herself she would stop crying. It was useless, the helpless, wrenching sobs growing louder as her decision firmed in her mind. She was glad she could barely hear her own dismay. Her heart thumped in her chest. It seemed to be getting louder.

The bathroom door opened.

***

Jon stopped dead, his horror sudden but his understanding of the scene before him dawning by degrees, as if realization was registering in small installments: Peggy was fully clothed, in her bathtub, distressed, the short barrel of a gun aimed inside her open mouth. The container dropped from his grasp, spilling hot cream of chicken soup on the tiled floor. He held his hands outward, as though to ward off imminent catastrophe.

"Peg," he said, gently, "please don't do it." Her eyes were on his lips. Good, but that meant her hearing aid was switched off.

She moved the gun away from her mouth, and said, "Don't come any closer!"

"All right, all right, just listen to me, Peg." He pointed a finger at the side of his head and watched her reach for her ear.

"It's on," she said.

"Peg," he said, reminding himself to keep using her name, a common tactic of salesmen everywhere that seemed to say, Hey, we're good buddies, old pals, I'm a nice guy and I know your name and I keep using your name because this is called the personal touch and this old Honda gets great mileage I can't believe I'm selling it for such a low *low* price … Except Jon wasn't trying to sell her anything. The tremor in his legs was real fear. His only thought was to get the gun away from her. When she looked somewhere else, glanced at the ceiling or blinked the tears out of her eyes, Jon moved half an inch closer. If that was what it took, he'd do it all day.

"Peggy, don't call time yet," he said, "whatever's going on, it can be fixed."

"No, it can't. Leave, Jon. Please."

"Peggy, we love you and I can't leave. *I* love you. You're not alone. What's wrong?"

"I can't tell you," she said, and as she looked away, Jon moved half a step toward the bathtub. "I don't want you to think less of me, Jon. That's why I can't tell you how badly I messed up."

Jon knew he was going to make a sprinting dive for the gun at the first opportunity, so he quickly scanned the floor, making certain there wasn't any spilled soup he could slip on and break his neck.

If he'd opened the door a moment later than he had, he would be looking at a dead woman. As he stood in the doorway, examined her face, he saw a kind of blank acceptance that was both downright creepy and unutterably sad; it had the unmistakable quality of finality. Peggy had been a second from pulling the trigger.

She was watching him, waiting for him to speak. "It's never as bad as it seems, Peg. I've been facedown in the dirt a few times, but you just keep getting back up. That's the secret to life. All the self-help books in the world and gurus out there won't tell you that because it's simple. The answer usually is. You keep getting back up and each time you get stronger, you become a little more battle-hardened. The good days do come along, but you have to be around to see them. Don't throw in the towel. I want to show you that it's worth it. I promise, if you give me the gun, you won't regret it. You have to trust me. Please."

She was watching him carefully now. That horrible acceptance he'd seen earlier was receding, but it wasn't gone completely. "You're a good man, Jon, and I know you mean well. But I've got nothing left … it was a nice little speech, too."

"That's why I love you. Giving me shit in a situation like this. I believe in that little speech, Peg. Tell me I don't."

Their eyes were locked together, and Peggy's were probing his. In the silence of her searching, the urgency in his gut only increased, and he knew he had to get the gun. The tendons in his neck felt as tight as piano wires, and his muscles were rigid with adrenaline. It had been a while since he'd felt fear of such intensity. The births of his son and daughter were close, but this was different, heightened, every nerve ending seemed to be alight with a kind of white heat.

"I guess you do believe it," she said.

"Peg, please give me the gun. I'll make us a drink and we can talk about things."

"What things?"

"We're going to find a solution to your problem."

"What if there is no solution?"

"There is," he said, firmly, "there always is … Please, Peggy, give me the gun."

Her resolve was softening to resignation. Jon might not have to leap at her and wrestle the gun from her hand, after all.

"It's going to be all right?"

There was something sweetly childlike in the way she asked the question that he was thrown off balance briefly, but he regained his composure, and said, "Peggy, I promise you. It's going to be all right." Her arm swung slowly over the side of the bathtub and Jon caught her wrist, removing the gun from her loose grip. The moment he had the revolver, the dead weight of relief turned his muscles to jelly. He opened the cylinder and shook the bullets into his sweaty palm and pocketed them, stuffed the Smith & Wesson into his belt and sat on the edge of the bathtub.

"The next order of business is to get you out of there," he said. "Just give me a second."

"I'm sorry I caused you any trouble, Jon."

"I'm just glad … you didn't do it."

She reached for his hand and squeezed it. "Thanks for not laughing at me."

Jon couldn't hide his surprise. "Why on earth would I do that?" The moment the words emerged from his mouth, he realized she was terribly embarrassed. He patted her hand. "Okay," he said, "let's do this." He leaned toward her and she folded her arms around his neck. When he felt some clearance beneath her, he scooped both arms underneath her and pulled. "Bend your legs if you can," he said, and she could. He turned, easing her onto her feet.

"If you need to hold on to me, grab something." She gripped his upper arm. Progress was slow, but eventually they arrived at the top of the stairs. "One step at a time, if that's what it takes." Jon did his best not to wince whenever Peggy gasped in pain, which was on almost every step down. He asked her after each of her stifled moans if she wanted to take a break and she refused. But they did pause when they finally reached the hallway.

"That was a rough one, huh?"

"Not for me, Peg. Let me know when you're ready for the final leg."

"Okay, I think I can make it."

He lowered her gently into her armchair and asked her where she kept her pills.

"Far-left drawer, the top one, on the display cabinet." Jon went into the kitchen and headed to the display cabinet, which was filled with photographs, some in black and white, of Gabe and Peggy. He found the pills, poured water into a glass and stopped, looking at the floor, countertops, and dining table. Everything was clean, spotless. How had she managed? He glanced at the laptop on the dining table and frowned. He hadn't seen it before.

"Here, Peg," he said, handing her the pills and water.

Jon sat in the armchair opposite her, near the window. "Better?" he asked.

She placed the glass on the small occasional table between them. "In an hour or two I should be," she said. "Thanks, Jon."

He waited for her to settle, for her breathing to return to normal. Then he said, "Okay, Peg, it's time to tell me what's going on."

She sighed, wrung her hands together. "You won't like it."

"Try me." Peggy remained silent for a time, and Jon knew this wasn't going to be easy. He said, "Peg, please don't make me drag it out of you."

"All right … I gambled everything I had away. It's all gone. I've got nothing left … You don't seem surprised."

"If you saw some of the things I've seen recently, you'd understand why. First things first—I'm going to send someone to see you a few times a week, to start, a physical therapist."

"Jon, I can't pay for it."

"I'm not asking you to."

"No, Jon, I can't—"

"I'm going to send her round anyway. It's up to you if you want to let her in. But Peg, don't fight me on this. I know you don't want to accept my help—I understand it. Just do this for me, for yourself. As for how you get back on your feet, money-wise, I'm going to help you there, too … I saw your letter in the hall. It was a note for me?"

"Yes, it was. You didn't read it, did you?"

"Of course not. But I'm guessing you don't want me to read it now."

She nodded.

"The laptop in the kitchen—you used it to gamble?"

She nodded again.

"How about I just take it with me?"

She looked at him and Jon saw the fear in her eyes. He said, "Just think of it as me borrowing it until you feel better. Deal?"

"Okay." He reached into his pocket and pulled out a piece of paper.

"I need your bank account details. I'm going to deposit money into your account, make sure you're okay for a while."

"Jon, please don't—"

"We all make mistakes, Peg. Every last one of us. Somehow, I think you've been punished enough. It's time to let yourself up off the mat."

"Jon, you really shouldn't …"

"Just one friend helping another out."

"You're a good man, Jon," she said.

"I'm not. I'm no better or worse than anyone else … But I need something from you. A promise."

"I won't gamble again."

He raised an eyebrow.

"Okay," she said, "I promise."

38

If Peyton thought Lizzy was going to forget she had stormed out of Zoey's house she was very much mistaken. Alarm bells were ringing inside Lizzy's head. The sound had started low but was gathering volume as she observed Peyton sitting at her kitchen table. Mia was in her room and not allowed out for the rest of the night. The sad thing was that Mia didn't understand how much it hurt Lizzy to punish her.

She couldn't distract herself. She'd deal with the squalid, sordid business of *that* boy sniffing around her only daughter soon. She would demand cooperation from Zoey, insist she keep control of her family ... and yet the idea of having an argument with Zoey scared her. Zoey was her best, most trusted friend.

Why was Peyton having difficulty looking her in the eye?

"What happened for you to leave Zoey's house the way you did?" Lizzy said.

Peyton looked into her herbal tea as though she had seen something floating in it.

Lizzy glanced at the clock on the wall. Marcus still wasn't home.

"We just disagree on the direction of the book club, that's all," Peyton said, eyes downcast.

"What direction are you talking about?"

"Uh … well, Zoey wants us to read more horror and I prefer thrillers. It's stupid, I know, but people have had arguments over less." Something about Peyton's explanation rang false. It sounded lame, simply unbelievable. Lizzy knew she had mental issues, but that didn't mean she was stupid. And if there was one thing that irritated her it was anyone thinking she was dumb.

She had called Peyton earlier, asked her to come by. The way she had hesitated on the phone caused Lizzy some concern. No, a lot of concern. Peyton looked like someone who had discovered a secret so awful that just the weight of knowing was crushing her. Now that Lizzy had stopped taking the evil medicine prescribed to her by those mind quacks who had the nerve to call themselves doctors, she was seeing the world as if a clear but blurring veil had been lifted. Something was wrong. Her reawakened, reenergized gut was picking up warning signals, it seemed, on a minute-by-minute basis. It was as though the entire atmosphere of her world was changing. She had emerged from the fog, blinking into the sunlight. But things were going to be different. She had dropped the ball as a mother and a wife. She was going to pick it back up and bounce it from one hand to the other as she figured out why she felt it was going to rain when there wasn't any precipitation forecast.

"You're coming to the book club on Friday?" Lizzy asked.

Peyton gave her a brief flash of her eyes and then lowered them to her tea. "No," she said, "I'm going to leave the book club."

"Why? Because you had a silly falling out with Zoey? Can't you two work it out?"

The sound in Lizzy's head had multiplied, going from the ringing of one alarm to the sound of several bells jumbled together in a frightening siren scream.

"Lizzy, do you love Marcus?"

Lizzy blinked at Peyton, mouthing the words silently as though trying to taste their meaning. *Do I love Marcus?*

Peyton seemed beyond simple nervousness; she was visibly scared.

"I shouldn't have said anything," she said quickly, but Lizzy recognized a backward scramble when she saw it. "I don't know what I'm saying."

"What do you mean? Of course I love Marcus."

Peyton stood without warning and headed toward the kitchen door. Lizzy looked after her. "What do you mean, *do I love Marcus? What do you mean?*" She heard Peyton's hurried footfalls in the hallway and the front door opening. "WHAT DO YOU MEAN, DO I LOVE MARCUS?"

39

Zoey took a limousine from the Bloomberg building on Lexington Avenue to the Four Seasons a short drive away on East 57th Street. But her business at the hotel would have to be brief. She had to get back to Sag Harbor. Zoey had just made the deal of a lifetime today. Depending on when Jon chose to sell the shares, they stood to gain hundreds of millions of dollars. She should have been happy, and she had given that impression to Jon on each of the calls he'd made to her. Her mind wasn't on the deal or its impending rewards. It had turned toward her marriage, and how everything seemed fair on the surface. She and Jon kept separate bank accounts so that one would not have financial leverage over the other. They split the bills evenly. Jon was a great father, she had to admit. And since she was being honest with herself, she regretted betraying her only true friend, Lizzy. Her treachery wasn't something that was easy to live with it. She wanted to end the affair but couldn't. Marcus had made Jon's butter-wouldn't-melt good-guy façade at least bearable. She was the only one who knew what he'd done. Someday he would pay for it, even though every time they'd spoken on the phone she'd felt the old excitement—she and Jon looking for an angle, a way to make money for their clients and the rush of seeing something no one else had. The old gut flutter was undoubtedly there, despite her efforts to shove it down, out of sight. Now she found herself balanced precariously on the fence; on one hand she had decided her marriage was over, but on the other, she wasn't entirely convinced. She wondered if they could somehow make it work. It was disconcerting when previously hard certainties became limber, lost their firm outline and their hard edges. Before this deal, she'd had one foot out the door. On one of her phone calls today with Jon she had a moment of panic when she discovered she missed him, even blinking at the force of the feeling.

Zoey was worried. She had called Peyton several times since her sudden departure on book club night. But there was no answer. What did she know? The possibility Peyton had discovered her affair had occurred to her so often it had lost its chilling effect. How did she know? Had little miss high-and-mighty-failed-socialite tramp followed her?

Myrtle had canceled the next book club meeting, giving some lame excuse about a plumbing disaster that she was "monitoring carefully" and could take a while to resolve. But Zoey had immediately detected the cagey tone and noticed Myrtle's lack of gossiping about her neighbors, something she always engaged in whenever she called, a sure sign something wasn't right. Did she know, too? Had Peyton told her? Or had they both suspected and then followed her? The book club was over; Zoey just wondered how she was going to come up with a credible explanation for Lizzy as to why the Village Book Club was no more.

She sent Marcus a text message.

When Zoey arrived at the hotel, she told the driver to pick her up in an hour.

She opened her room door and closed it fast behind her. She didn't want anyone who happened to pass by to see Marcus, naked, sitting on a sofa facing the door, an enormous erection pulsating in his lap. Zoey stepped up on the coffee table, kicking magazines and the TV remote onto the floor. She bent over on all fours on the table, pulled up her dress, and said, "You know what to do, Marcus. Pull my hair, too. Pull it *hard*."

40

Peyton got as far as the Whaling Museum and had to pull over. Tears of guilt and frustration had blurred her vision and she was afraid of getting into an accident. She shouldn't have left Lizzy the way she had. The look of utter confusion and fear on her friend's face was like an afterimage; it came into focus, faded, came into focus again ... She was right—she shouldn't have left Lizzy in distress, and she was sorry for walking out, but she shouldn't have gone over there in the first place.

She tried to view the situation dispassionately: could she blame Marcus? Something was wrong with Lizzy, so if his marriage was dead, why didn't he leave? Peyton suspected Marcus hadn't abandoned ship out of some misplaced sense of obligation. Or he actually cared about Lizzy and was afraid of what her reaction would be if he divorced her. She could see how Marcus might believe his leaving would send Lizzy over the edge. And Marcus just couldn't face the cruelty of the tipping point. He'd have a front-row seat to Lizzy's disintegration.

Peyton wished she had kept out of it. Now, she regretted knowing.

But she had to tell Lizzy her husband was cheating on

her. The pressure of knowing was too much. Ever since she'd discovered the affair she felt different, didn't sleep well, and her temper frayed easily. She would tell Lizzy for the right reasons, too. Not because she sensed Zoey's view of her was that she was just another bimbo wannabe, a has-been, an also-ran, an intellectual inferior. Peyton had made mistakes—no one got through life mistake-free—but *she* wasn't having an affair with a married man. She had once met a minor celebrity who had a tattoo on his forearm that said *No Regrets* and had marveled at the lie rendered in indelible ink, a permanent untruth. She wondered how long before the poor guy had his tattoo removed by laser.

She wiped her eyes with the backs of her hands and attempted to summon the courage needed to return to Garden Street and just tell Lizzy … but she was going to take the cowardly route and call instead. She hated herself for it; the idea of watching a fragile friend destroyed was too much to bear. She was selfish, and she was vividly aware of her selfishness. The torture of this moment was all she deserved because she had stuck her nose in business that wasn't her own. A dry smile stretched her lips, the kind that came with cold realization: she had been wrong to spy on Zoey, goddamn super-whore that she was; it was Zoey's fault she was now scrolling through her contacts for Lizzy's number.

She paused, thinking about Jon. Whenever she saw him, he was smiling, as though everything in his world was tranquil and right. Peyton felt sorry for Jon, too, because he was utterly clueless. She believed he might be good at his job and that he was smart, but his domestic intelligence was seriously lacking.

I'm one to talk. She cringed inwardly as she recalled asking

Lizzy if she loved Marcus. She couldn't make any sense of it, and didn't know why she'd said it. The question was out of her mouth before she could put it back in. *What was I thinking?*

She began to consider the consequences of revealing the awful truth to Lizzy. No one liked the bearer of bad news. Would Lizzy ever speak to her again?

She scrolled back through her contacts and called Myrtle, and said, without preamble, "Myrt, I have to tell her."

"Don't do it, Peyton."

"If your husband was cheating on you, would you want to know?"

"You'll regret it, Peyton. Where are you?"

"Let me put it another way. If I knew your husband was being unfaithful to you, would you want me to tell you?"

There was a pause on the other end of the line. Then Myrtle said, "Don't do it, Peyton. *Please* don't do it."

"I think I have my answer."

"No—"

Peyton hung up. Rather than sit there and talk herself out of it, she instantly dialed Lizzy. A small voice said, "Hello."

"Lizzy, I'm sorry for the way I walked out earlier. I'm really, *really* sorry."

"What's going on? You scared me."

There was no other way to do it. "Lizzy, Marcus is having an affair with Zoey."

In the silence that followed, there was a strange hum on the line.

After what seemed like minutes, Lizzy came back. She said, "Is this a trick?"

"What?"

She flinched as a loud crashing and scraping noise filled her ear. "Lizzy?"

Then it dawned on her—Lizzy had dropped the phone on the floor.

41

Arms straight down by her sides, her hands balled into fists, Lizzy stomped upstairs, head bent, eyes forward, shoulders raised against her neck, which was throbbing, making the cold watery film that had formed on her eyes pulsate, keeping time to a troubling beat. She threw open her bedroom door; it bounced hard off the wall—the marital bed was made, the room was tidy. Nothing about it raised suspicion.

She was being tricked, pranked, and she was determined to get to the source of whatever trickery had been concocted by Peyton.

She pulled the covers slowly off the bed and watched them fall to the floor in a pile. And then it hit her: the way Zoey and Marcus had exchanged a peculiar look at the hospital when Mia had fallen into the pond (no, she was pushed by *that boy*), the memory of their eyes meeting hadn't quite let go, even though she'd tried to dismiss it, passed it off as insignificant and she was reading too much into it. But now … now it kind of made sense. What if Peyton wasn't playing a cruel trick on her at all? Was Peyton a co-conspirator in whatever devious scheme had been devised by Marcus and Zoey to … to disappoint her? But

Zoey was her friend, a real, true friend. She loved Zoey and Marcus. They were careful *not* to trick her.

She became animated suddenly; adrenaline flooded her muscles, and she pushed the mattress off the bed.

Nothing.

She went to the bureau and yanked open drawers. She lifted the first drawer out completely and turned it upside down, showering the floor in her underwear.

Nothing.

She threw the drawer across the room; an edge of it struck the wall and left a dent in the plaster like an inverted pyramid. Lizzy emptied Marcus's sock drawer, watching the pairs that he'd rolled into a ball rain down on the floor. She froze, her body filled with sudden stiffness. One pair of socks had landed differently than the others; it seemed heavier. She knelt and picked it up. There was an object concealed in the socks, and it was solid. She peeled one sock away from the other, revealing a disposable cell phone. She sat on the floor, slumped, and turned it on. Heat radiated from her neck to her face. Her skin itched with an unpleasant prickling sensation, as though she'd stepped into a field of static electricity.

As she scrolled through the pictures, water dripped on her forearm from somewhere. All the muscles in her face went slack. Her mouth dropped open, and a disturbing thought occurred to her as she stared in horror at the pictures: *I should close my mouth. What if something got in?*

In one picture, Zoey was naked from the waist down, waving at whoever was taking the photograph. And she was smiling. In another, either Marcus or Zoey had taken a selfie of them kissing.

A horrible, ratcheting scream came from her. Which was

strange, because it seemed to be coming from someone else, adding to her confusion. Lizzy didn't scream, she was quiet and didn't trouble anyone, ever. But the awful shuddering sound persisted. And someone was beating the world's biggest drum—it sounded as if that sickening rhythm was inside her head. Her thumb seemed to have a mind of its own as it clicked on text messages that were nothing but pure smut, unadulterated filth.

She *was* being tricked, after all.

42

Mia was frantic and scared. She wasn't afraid of her mom, but now she couldn't deny it—she wanted to escape from this house, even if only for tonight. She had heard her mother's blood-chilling scream. It hadn't been a scream of pain, but was one of frustration and anger. *Rage.* There was no mistaking it. She feared for her safety if she remained in this house any longer, which was why she climbed out the window onto the extension at the back, clung to the gutter by her fingers and swung gently back and forth, and let go, landing on the kitchen windowsill. She immediately jumped backward to control her fall because there was nothing else to hold on to.

She rode her bicycle to Main Street, realizing too late that the night was cool and she should have put on a hoodie, and stopped outside the redbrick John Jermain Library and called her dad. It just kept ringing. She hung up and tried again. Still no answer.

Mia was sobbing when she called Cody and he answered on the third ring. "I need to come over," she said.

"Mia, are you okay?" Something about the concern in his voice somehow made her feel better, as though she were important to him.

"Fine, I just need to come over."

"I'll be in the treehouse." She pedaled away from the curb and her entire body seemed to shrink whenever she heard a car behind her, convinced it was Mom, who had discovered she wasn't in her bedroom and was determined to bring her home, whether she liked it or not.

Her legs pumped harder and the chill air cooled the little beads of sweat that had sprung on her face. In other circumstances, she would have enjoyed a bike ride at night, not many people around, blasting past one house after another … Tears continued to stream down her face. There was something seriously wrong, she felt it. The atmosphere at home had shifted; it felt as though some permanent change was coming, and she was afraid of it.

She didn't slow as she neared Cody's house. Even when she was turning into his driveway, and there was a brief moment of panic as she felt the bike wobble. But she held on, passed the swimming pool and headed for the treehouse. Cody was waiting for her, a hesitant arm raised in greeting, a nervous smile at half-staff.

***

Lizzy blinked, emerging from a state of suspended animation. Her body was functioning fine, but she was experiencing a complete deficiency of thought. She remained in her sitting position on the floor, waiting for her mind to fade in again, to obtain some kind of function. She was *seeing* now, looking at the scattered underwear and socks, the debris of discovery, of a secret held up to the light: irrefutable evidence that she hadn't been mistaken—her husband and best friend were having an affair.

A thought, a blessed coherent thought came into focus in her mind as if it had been there all along, just waiting for her to see it: she had a daughter to think about. She was so grateful for the clarity of simply thinking that tears welled in her eyes. A thought without fuzzy edges and with hard lines was something she appreciated; it felt like a gift.

Mia.

Then the memory of seeing Marcus and Zoey in those photographs caused her to blink again. It sat before her, exuding a palpable air of evil. The phone held an aura of menace unlike anything she'd ever experienced. It seemed to throb, giving off waves of malevolence. The things—*pig things*—Marcus and Zoey were doing to each other in those pictures were so extreme it was Satanic. Yes, despite the fact she hadn't seen any symbols of devil worship, those images had the disgusting flavor of the occult.

She attempted to move her legs. They were numb, and she was unsure how long she had been sitting here, in this position. She flinched when she saw she wasn't wearing any shoes or socks; she couldn't remember taking them off. The bigger question was *why* were her shoes placed next to Marcus's archived perversions.

She glanced around and the bedroom looked as if a tornado had blown through.

Lizzy grunted, stood, and waited as returning blood flow tingled in her legs.

I have a daughter to think about.

"Mia," she whispered aloud, and the sound of her voice in the silence following the aftermath of chaos was eerie. She had to check on her, make sure she was all right. Lizzy hoped she hadn't scared Mia. She was desperate to tell her she was fine now. It wasn't the truth, but it would be better than telling her daughter her life was in pieces. And that Marcus, her dad, wasn't coming home.

She had never hurt anyone in her life, even when those … *pigs* …

Was she being punished for being a bad mother? The idea was ridiculous. She was trying her best.

Feeling had returned to her legs and she headed towards Mia's bedroom. She knocked gently on the door, pushed it, stared at the open window and the empty bed. Sudden rage swelled in her chest and spread outward to her limbs until her arms and legs shook with the instant deluge, as if her body was dispersing the force of her anger.

Lizzy walked out of the house, the sidewalk cold and uneven on the soles of her feet.

Her fingernails dug into her palms and she ignored the wetness in her clenched hands.

She knew Lewis had lied to her all those times she'd called, asking where her husband was. Marcus wasn't working late—*he was with that slut*. Were the people she had considered friends all in on the conspiracy? Yes, they had all tricked her.

As she marched up Main Street, she thought about ways to defend herself from further trickery. Several ideas surfaced, taking some of the heat out of her. There was always a way if you were willing to *see*.

The outline of a plan was forming in her mind, and by the time she arrived at the Finch house she had calmed down, a little, anyway. She knew exactly where Mia was, and who she was with. She didn't even need to go near the house itself. Lizzy power walked up the driveway toward the rear of the property, and when she was standing outside the treehouse she shouted at the top of her lungs, "Mia Jenkins, you get down here this minute!"

She sensed she was being watched, turned, and saw a man standing beneath the porch light, half his face in shadow. Jon. His hands were in the pockets of his slacks, and he looked like a weird still image. He didn't move, scratch his nose, or move his head. For a moment, she thought he might not be real. She blinked. But he didn't disappear like a mirage. She couldn't quite put her finger on it, but in that brief backward look there was something formidable about Jon, a man she was very fond of, one who didn't treat her as if she was somehow abnormal. The way the rest of them treated her, like she was mad, a non-person that had to be handled, a precious vase that if dropped would break into a million pieces.

She craned her head upward at the treehouse and said, more uncertain this time, "Mia, I'm not mad at you, just come down so we can go home."

Why didn't Jon say something? Why wasn't he asking her if he could help?

***

Mia took Cody's hand and led him to the couch. Cody was worried because something had happened to Mia and he knew he had to put his feelings aside and comfort her. He didn't believe there was anything worse than seeing someone you loved unhappy or hurt. And he *did* love her, he was just waiting for the right time to say the words.

"My mom," she began, and that was as far as she got. She was crying, and he felt inadequate and awkward. He was out of his depth and didn't know how to respond, so he leaned forward and took a packet of cookies from the coffee table and handed them to her. "They're nice," he said, and he felt a sheepish smile on his lips before he could stop it.

She looked at the cookies and then at him. "I'll eat them later." His face was burning and he was annoyed at himself for his inability to console her. She took his hand in both of hers, and said, "I don't know what to do, Cody. Mom's gone off the rails, but this time I think it's way more serious. I heard her trashing her bedroom and then she screamed. I was so scared I almost pe—almost had an accident. I can't contact my dad, but it has something to do with him. I can't tell you how I know, but my mom and dad are not in a good place. I don't want them to get a divorce. My dad has been very nice to me lately, he always is, but he's being *extra* nice for some reason. I was going to ask him if everything was okay, but I was afraid he'd lie to me and tell me yes, everything's fine. My mom needs real help. Part of the problem is she won't accept it. All those doctors and pills haven't done anything for her."

"Do you want to sleep at my house tonight?"

"Could I? Your dad won't mind?"

"Of course not. My mom might, but she's on a business trip in New York so she doesn't have to know … I think."

"I wanted to call Uncle Lewis and tell him to send my dad home because he's working late but I had to see you first. My mom … she hasn't come around to the idea of us seeing each other at all. I had this feeling if I didn't see you now it could be a while before I see you again. Mom's gonna notice I'm gone and I'll be grounded—"

"*Mia Jenkins, you get down here this minute!*" They froze,

stared at each other. The feeling of being helpless and the frustration that followed it began to build in Cody. Mia must have caught a glimpse of some of it, because she said, "Don't get mad, Cody. I'll handle her. Once she calms down she'll be fine. I'll call you later, okay?"

"Okay," he said, and she squeezed his hand and kissed him on the cheek. She turned quickly and was out the door. Gone. But he understood: if she delayed, it would be difficult for her to leave. She'd see his sadness. The best thing for them both was a quick exit, just like his dad had done when Cody had first started school. The crying would stop, eventually. And it had. Although, once, when he'd thought his dad had left, he had seen him peeking outside the door, as if he was making sure Cody was really okay. For reasons he didn't understand, it was the last time he had any difficulty getting through the school day tear-free. But the tears were burning in his eyes now and he reminded himself that he wasn't a baby anymore. Airline pilots didn't cry because the weather was bad. They went around the storm, or above or below it, and sometimes they steered into it. He drew in a deep breath and held it, waiting for the stinging to abate, for the tight ache in his chest to loosen.

There was a light knock on the door. "Yeah," he said, "come in."

His dad appeared, and he placed a cup of steaming hot chocolate on the table. "It might make you feel better." Cody looked at him and knew instantly his dad didn't believe it.

"Why do grown-ups say things they don't mean?" Cody said.

"Because we mean well, for the most part."

"Oh." Cody didn't understand it, but he let it go.

"Rough night, huh?"

"Yeah. You saw Mia's mom?"

"I did."

"Was she really mad?"

"I think the walk up here took the mad out of her. It's not your fault, son."

"Then why does it feel like it is?"

"People are complex, Cody. Lizzy has a lot of problems, but it has nothing to do with you. I'm asking you to trust me. Whatever issue Lizzy has, you don't play any part in it."

Cody looked at him and knew he was telling him the truth. "What's wrong with her, Dad?"

"I wish I knew. You remember what she was like before?"

"Yeah. She was normal, just like a regular mom. Then she changed."

"None of us are normal, Cody. We just appear that way. Like I said, people are complex. But I came up here to tell you this: it'll take you years of experience to realize that it does get better. This situation you're experiencing right now, it won't last. I'm not sure if it'll make you feel better, but I've been there and I found a way through, and so will you."

Cody nodded, and he did feel just a little bit better.

43

It was a long walk home. Mia kept glancing at Mom's bare feet, and prayed her dad would be home soon. She already missed Cody, and wondered how her mom was going to punish her. It was unsettling, walking down Main Street with her mom *sans* shoes, glad no one had passed them on the sidewalk. But it was Mom's silence that made her uneasy.

"I'm sorry, Mom," she said, just to say something. Mom reached for her hand, surprising Mia. They held hands the rest of the way home, and once inside, Mom said, "Come on in the kitchen, we have to talk." Mia followed her, avoiding the bloody footprints left in her wake.

"Mom, your feet are bleeding. Let me get the first-aid box."

She retrieved the first-aid kit from underneath the sink. Mom watched while she put on blue latex gloves and held up the alcohol pads, pulled a chair toward Mia, propping her feet on it. Mia got down on one knee and said, "It'll sting a little." But Mom only winced slightly when Mia cleaned the soles of her feet, then applied antibiotic cream and Band-Aids of varying sizes, and brought a pair of flip flops from the hall. "Put these on," she said, "you've only got small cuts and they should heal but try to keep off your feet to give them a chance."

"Mia, thank you." Mia was startled as tears glistened in Mom's eyes.

"Mom, it's okay. We're going to be okay."

"I'm the one who should apologize. My behavior was unfortunate. I'm sorry, Mia. For everything. You're my only child and I want the best for you. I'm sorry if I scared you. I'll make more of an effort to be a better mother. I had to go get you, bring you home, for a few reasons. What happened to me … I don't want you to go through what I went through. I'm having trouble explaining myself. But I'm figuring it out, Mia. Our lives have changed today. I don't want to say why but I have to. You're going to realize what's going on even if I don't tell you."

"Mom," Mia said, her tone gentle, soft, "I know you think you're explaining yourself but you're not. You're confusing me. Did something happen?"

"Yes, Mimi, something happened. I'm so sorry to have to say it—"

"Mom, you're scaring me."

"I don't mean to … your dad and I, we can't live together anymore."

Mia felt her eyes fill. "Why?" Mia knew why, of course. Her mom had found out her dad was having an affair. What else could it be? But she couldn't allow Mom to know she'd known all along.

Mom shook her head from side to side.

"Did he do something wrong?"

"Yes, he did. But he's your dad and I can't tell you what he did."

"Mom … did he … is he seeing someone else?"

Mom had been making an admirable effort to hold on to

her composure. Now it was broken and she wept openly. Mia went to her, hugged her. Some people would say—her dad being one of them—that it was just another one of her delusions, a word she had heard spoken between her parents far too many times over the past two years, often enough for her to look it up in the dictionary. But it wasn't a delusion. Mia had kept the secret of her eavesdropping because she had wanted desperately to avoid this situation. She had hoped her dad would see sense eventually and stop cheating on her mom, but the secret was out. How it had happened didn't matter to her. She knew, just *knew*, Mom wouldn't forgive her dad. She didn't have it in her. And Mia didn't blame her. They would get divorced. That *did* matter to her. So she spent the next hour trying to convince her mom that she was mistaken. Whoever had told her that Dad was being unfaithful was a liar. She knew it was wrong, but she was desperate and scared.

44

"I know what you did." Lizzy sat on the end of her bed, phone pressed to her ear, glad Mia was in the kitchen, eating breakfast. She had called Marcus fifteen or twenty times last night and he hadn't answered. He was probably concocting an excuse, a reason for why he hadn't come home. It was clear, too, that Lewis had lied for him, and he was therefore a co-conspirator in the Grand Trick. She didn't know where Marcus was, she was only sure he wasn't at work. What kind of swimming pool was built through the night? Was a tennis court so special it had to be resurfaced into the small hours? No, of course not. Marcus had been with *her*. And Lizzy knew she had to convince Mia her father had been unfaithful. The reason was clear—Mia thought she was mistaken, and if she kept accusing her dad with no evidence to back up her claim, Mia would stop humoring her and her daughter's quiet patience would quickly turn into resentment, then anger. No one believed a lunatic. Oh, she knew how they saw her. Crazy old Lizzy, let's all tiptoe round fragile, broken Lizzy. Let's lie to her and tell her how much progress she's making. Let's all pat her on the back and tell her how brave she is. And when she's not looking, let's all play a cruel trick on her.

She wasn't crazy, and even if she was, it didn't mean she was stupid. The curtain had been lifted on their evil scheme. What were they planning on doing to her? Was it really an attempt to drive her over the edge once and for all? *Yes!* The voice in her mind shouted the affirmative with such conviction, such enthusiasm, that it couldn't be wrong. After all, the voice sounded remarkably similar to hers. *Yes!*

Lizzy was aware of her shock, and its numbing effect. Wasn't that further proof of her sanity? Self-awareness? The full weight of the betrayal wasn't crushing her yet, but it was coming, she felt it.

The look that had passed between Marcus and Zoey at the hospital returned to haunt her thoughts as she let the silence on the other end of the line play out. She was in no hurry to break it. She was curious to see if Marcus was going to deny all of it, some or none of it. But hadn't *she* denied their affair? It was the look between them when *that boy* had almost drowned Mia. Hadn't she known then? Denial was an irresistible force, and she was as susceptible to its magnetic pull as anyone.

Then there was Zoey ... the pretend friend. Who else knew Zoey was making a fool out of her? Did Myrtle know? Peyton knew, so it was a safe bet she had told Myrtle. The deceit was bad, the treachery of her husband and former best friend was worse, but the cherry on the sundae was that she was the clown, standing in the center of a three-ring circus while the audience pointed and laughed at her. Except Jon wasn't in the crowd. He was yet to discover his life had been burned down by that common whore he called his wife. But Lizzy wasn't going to tell him. She could barely bring herself to show Mia proof of her father's infidelity. But the bridge was getting nearer, and sooner or later she was going to have to cross it. But first, Marcus. "What's wrong, Marc, cat got your tongue?"

Lizzy heard the sneer in her voice. It was repulsive and … and satisfying.

"What's going on, Lizzy?"

"Do you have anything to confess, Marcus? Anything at all?" Lizzy was surprised by her calm tone. Despite the rage that made her vision shimmer, her voice sounded casual, almost friendly.

"Lizzy, sweetheart, you need to take your medicine. You don't sound okay."

Sweetheart!

"Sure I do, Marcus. I sound okay to *me*."

"Lizzy, what the Christ is going on over there?" Good. For the first time in years, there was real fear in Marcus's voice. And annoyance, the same kind of put-upon, petulant tone he adopted when she complained about him dropping cigar ash on the back porch where he went to smoke every morning at 3 a.m. It was a disgusting habit, but she'd let it go because Marcus had insisted cigar smoking was helping him with his insomnia. Now, she thought it had probably been helping him with a guilty conscience.

"I found your phone, *sweetheart*."

"What …? What—"

"Don't stutter, Marcus. It's unbecoming for a big strong man like you. Don't come home. Find somewhere else to squat. Maybe you can shack up with your whore. She might be smart, Marcus, and successful, but she's no less a whore. You can have her."

"Lizzy, please—"

"I know I'm not easy to live with, Marcus. I'm crazy, or so those quack doctors say with their eyes. But I'm finding my way back, Marcus. Mia knows, too. I'm sure you'd deny it if I didn't have proof ... poor crazy Lizzy, babbling about an affair, it's all in her head. But I've seen the photos, Marcus. Or would you prefer *Marc*? It sounds younger. Because that's what you want, isn't it? To be eighteen again."

"Lizzy, goddamnit—"

"The locksmith will be here any minute, *Marc*. Don't come around or I'll call the police. You won't want me telling anyone who'll listen how you're fucking the smartest whore on Main Street." The derisive tone in her voice was new, and Lizzy liked it, the confidence in it.

You can have confidence without mocking somebody. You caught him with his hand in the cookie jar, take your foot off his neck ... Why should I?

"Lizzy, are you there?"

"Not completely, *Marc*, judging by the thoughts running through my mind, but I will be there, don't worry. Not all the way there, but some of the way is better than nothing."

"What ...? Lizzy, listen. Let me explain."

"There's no need. You, of all people ... you're the ringmaster, the Chief Trickster."

"What are you talking about?"

"You can shout, you can scream, but those pictures on your phone say everything about you ... and *her*. Don't come around, Marcus, I mean it, or I'll distribute those cute photos of you and her to the four winds. Goodbye, Marcus."

"Lizzy, don't hang up—"

Lizzy hung up, picked up Marcus's smut phone, and scrolled to the least objectionable photo of Zoey and Marcus with their filthy lips locked but fully clothed. Marcus's first order of business would likely be to turn Mia against her, tell her daughter that it was *all in her mind*. He'd said the same thing many times before, so she was going to show the photograph to Mia, even though she didn't want to, just as soon as the locksmith was done changing the locks.

***

Lizzy was sitting at her kitchen table, drinking tea, when movement caught her eye. She looked around, and was startled to see Jon Finch at her back door. He waved.

She opened the door. "Can I come in?" he asked.

"Uh, sure. Okay."

He sat at the table. "Mind if I ask for some coffee, Lizzy?"

Somewhat flustered, she said, "Oh, I'm sorry, yes, I'll make some."

"It's just that we have a lot to talk about," he said, "we may be here a while."

45

Jon was waiting by the window with Cody, cradling baby Jane in his arms when the cab pulled up outside and Zoey emerged smiling, waving at them. They returned the greeting and went outside.

The cab driver helped Zoey remove bags from the trunk and set them down carefully on the sidewalk. She paid him and handed the driver a hefty tip. Zoey wasn't a big tipper, which Jon found odd. He tipped often and generously. She didn't believe in it, apparently. But it seemed she was awash in the afterglow of having struck the mother lode because she was smiling, beaming, enveloped in an aura of happiness, of accomplishment. Jon understood it—there was nothing quite like the thrill of the hunt. The excitement, the anticipation of throwing all your chips on the table knowing you were making a calculated gamble, but the possibility always existed that you could be wrong. It was doubt that amplified the joy of the win.

He looked at the bags and knew why Zoey was late coming home—she had gone on a shopping spree. And by the looks of the bags, she'd traipsed all over New York City buying him and Cody clothes, computers, phones and God knew what else.

Passersby had to detour around them as they stood there, expensive gifts at their feet, and Jon was becoming steadily more embarrassed, dropping his eyes as he acknowledged people with a nod and a hesitant half-smile. In his soul, he was and would always be a poor kid from Canarsie. Any day now, someone would knock on his door and tell him the dream was over, that his illusion of riches was just that: an illusion.

All his internal rambling paused when Zoey kissed him. On the lips. And lingered. He was momentarily stunned. It had been so long … He heard Cody groan and mutter, "Oh, Jeez." It was strange, funny. There was no exasperation in it; there was even an undertone of relief.

When they parted, Jon looked at his son, who had both hands covering his eyes. "Are you done?" Cody said. Jon laughed and Zoey joined him.

"Okay, kiddo," Jon said, "we're done. Help carry these bags inside."

"I'll call Candice," Zoey said, "so we can talk and have a nice evening."

"Sure," Jon said, "we've a lot to talk about."

Zoey kissed baby Jane on her forehead and said, "How's my little angel?"

"Missing her mommy," Jon said.

"Well, we get to spend a lot more time together now."

46

Arthur Dunhill had driven by the Finch residence eight times, but it was on the ninth pass when he spotted the cab, and the happy family gathered on the sidewalk. He took note of the boy, and the newborn held so lovingly by Jon Finch, the man partially responsible for his ruin. His research into the Finches hadn't said anything about them having children; this was a bonus.

He kept the Cadillac Escalade at a reasonable non-suspicious thirty, baseball cap pulled low, eyes quick and raw behind his sunglasses. The SUV had tinted windows, an added layer of protection. As long as he wasn't seen, he would proceed with his plan. Then he'd deal with Roger, because there was no way the Finches could have known the internal business of Zinco without privileged input from his old colleague. There was no way it was mere coincidence that Roger had dumped his entire shareholding in the company they'd founded together on the same day Zoey Finch had appeared on the money channels: Bloomberg News and CNBC. And there was no way a winner like Arthur Dunhill was going to let it slide.

He had checked into The Herbert Hotel and rarely left his room. He kept the baseball cap low, shielding his eyes, which had become dry to the point they stung, and he constantly had to blink hard in an effort to force some moisture into them.

Arthur knew it was over. As a man who understood natural selection, he knew he had been beaten by stronger, smarter animals. He wasn't at the top of the food chain anymore; he had become prey. And that was disagreeable. He was glad his father was dead, to spare him the spectacle of his son being dragged from his perch at the top of the tree by a hedge-fund manager and his prime-broker wife, disemboweled before the world's media by two new superstars of high finance, smacking their lips as they fed on his guts …

Don't be a crybaby, Arthur. I'm not raising a blubbering crybaby.

The voice sounded real in his mind. It was the same voice his father had used as he'd chased him into a corner in the Dunhill living room, wielding a piece of garden hose folded in two to teach young Arthur a lesson. The outcome of the lesson was straightforward, so simple even a crybaby like Arthur could understand it: don't let anyone bully you or you'll get a beating ten times worse when you get home. The memory was cruelly fresh, to the point he could see Arthur Senior's facial expression when Arthur Junior had told him the reason why his lip was split, and why some of his schoolbooks were missing. The look of utter disbelief, of something akin to wonder on his father's face, was no less frightening now, even though time had put a safe distance between himself and that awful day. "You were bullied by a kid named Timmy? What the fuck is wrong with you?" It was the slack wonder in his father's tone that had scared him most. Apart from the painful strokes of the folded garden hose, the thing that hurt him almost as much as the beating was that he had viewed himself from his father's perspective, and the shame hurt, as brutal and vicious as the long, wide bruises and lumps that had appeared all over his body later that day and the next. It was the indignity of being bullied that made him believe he had deserved to be punished. Arthur Senior had taken him out of school for a week, claiming his son could go back to his education when he learned it wasn't his station in life to be stepped on. And young Arthur *had* learned. After the beating, Arthur had returned to school, a different look in his eye, a daring glint, a challenge, a hope that someone would take a shot at him. But no one ever did. The air of danger, of someone who would go further, lingered. The other kids sensed it, and that was all right with him.

His eyes were leaking now as he searched for a parking space near The Herbert Hotel. But he wasn't crying. He wasn't a crybaby. He shouldn't have been worried about getting caught, either. It was over, anyway. He *was* afraid of being arrested before he could get to Roger Berris. And he would get to him, sooner or later. His father would no doubt be proud of him. He was Asserting His Dominance. His plan wasn't set in stone, it was subject to change. The ropes and duct tape and glue in back, nestled amongst other equipment, were optional extras, although he would love— *dearly love*—to glue Zoey Finch's mouth shut, just to keep all her vile lies in, to mute her slanderous remarks.

Beneath the chaos in his mind, a certainty emerged— clear, with sharp edges and a distinct shape: if he stood up for himself, if he confronted the bullies, then Mr. Pinch wouldn't visit him anymore. He could sleep peacefully, for once, with the light off.

47

The air of excitement in the house was a welcome change from the indefinable frostiness of the past few months. The living room floor was littered with gifts, and when Zoey extracted a huge model airplane from one of the bags Cody yelped, did a little dance, his face a picture of happiness and awe. Jon thought Zoey's gift was acceptance; she had come to terms with her son's chosen career path. And Cody seemed to think the same. Jon caught him knuckling a tear out of his eye before it could fall and possibly open the floodgates. "Thanks, Mom," he said, and they hugged. Jon believed then that happiness was transferable; he *felt* how happy Cody was, and it lifted him. They had to celebrate.

"Okay, I'm going to the store to get the champagne I forgot," he said.

"Sounds great," Zoey said, "but hurry back."

"Dad," Cody said, "can I have some champagne?"

Jon almost laughed. "No," he said, "when you get a commercial airline pilot's license, then you can have some." He left, and Jon held on to the image of his smiling son as he got into his car and backed it out of the driveway.

It had been so long since he had felt this good. He thought the last time he'd experienced happiness like this was when his daughter was born and he had picked her up and made a silent promise to her that he would make sure she had a good life, promised he'd protect her. Today might be the turning point. He was optimistic that he and Zoey could get past whatever black cloud had fallen over their marriage. Jon suspected (though he wasn't fully convinced) Zoey had suffered some kind of post-natal depression— despite her insisting otherwise—after Jane's arrival into the world. But if she had, it seemed to have resolved itself. He had tried to pinpoint the moment their relationship had stalled. He couldn't be certain, but if he had to pick a time, it was during a Christmas party at Aquarius's offices in New York City. Everything had changed after the party and he didn't know why. He and Zoey had taken a cab to their hotel, and he had been subjected to a stony silence which he'd never been able to explain, and he hadn't asked Zoey for an explanation. When she was dragging him over hot coals with her silence, he knew better than to ask what was wrong or was she all right. He hadn't wanted to be on the receiving end of her if-looks-could-kill Death Glare.

As he parked outside Francesco's Fine Wines, across the street from The Herbert Hotel, he stopped dead, as though his life was a movie and someone had pressed pause. He watched the man exit the SUV and remove his sunglasses. Jon would have recognized him anywhere, even with the baseball cap. He had searched for him online, seen many photographs of him, and here he was, Arthur Dunhill, frozen just like him, his eyes wide and his mouth open. They stared at each other as traffic passed on the road. The encounter couldn't have lasted more than a few seconds, but it was enough time for Jon to see recognition dawn in Arthur's oddly bulging eyes.

His face was twitching, too. Jon straightened, and as soon as he had a chance he had to call Zoey. He got back into the car, pretending he had forgotten something just as Arthur was pretending he hadn't seen him. Jon watched him walk toward The Herbert Hotel, although it couldn't really be described as a walk, it was more of a skulk.

Zoey answered on the fifth ring. "Jon?"

"Zoey, lock all the doors. Don't let anyone in or out. I'll be there soon."

"What's wrong? Are you okay?"

"I'm fine. But don't answer the door. Tell Candice, too. I'll be there as fast as I can."

"Jon, what's going on?"

"I just saw Arthur Dunhill. I'll explain when I get there." Jon glanced in the rearview mirror, then turned around, trying to see if Dunhill was still watching him. But he was gone. He committed the tag number on the SUV to memory. Hadn't Roger said his business partner was unstable? In a way, Jon wasn't surprised to see Dunhill. His company was tanking, and he was obviously seeking revenge. There was no chance him seeing Arthur was a coincidence. He wasn't on vacation. Maybe Arthur was in hiding from the media or the law—probably both. But of all the places he'd chosen to hide out ... No, Jon was taking the handgun from the wall safe in the master bedroom and keeping it next to his side of the bed. If Dunhill wanted revenge, Jon would be waiting for him.

***

Arthur knew the game was up instantly when their eyes met, at least temporarily. He wasn't about to fold his tent and run home. What would Senior say if he quit? How he'd chuckle, because his father wasn't given to laughter, although he was partial to a chuckle, which was often laced with mockery. Arthur wasn't a beaten dog. Even though Finch had seen him, it wasn't a good reason to abandon his plans, just tweak them a little. He would have to wait to pay them a visit. What else did he have to lose? His life? *He* almost chuckled.

It was time to check out of the hotel. For now.

48

Myrtle wasn't sleeping. It had been five days since she'd spoken to Peyton, and the more she thought about the failed socialite, the angrier she became. It wasn't Peyton's place to right a wrong, to interfere in a marriage. But that was the world she was living in. Everyone, it seemed, was minding someone else's business. And yet she felt guilty. The worst part of it was how irrational it was—she hadn't been disloyal to Lizzy. Yes, she had known Zoey Finch—*rampant scumbag and wanton tramp*—had betrayed Lizzy, but she was just protecting her friend.

If she was blameless, then why didn't she answer when Lizzy called? And by her last count, she had twenty-three missed calls from Lizzy. Each ring was an ice pick between the shoulder blades. Now Myrtle peeled back the scabbed-over layers of denial and admitted that as well as protecting Lizzy, she was doing it to spare herself the heartache of listening to the devastation she was sure was waiting on the other end of the line when she answered. She knew Lizzy didn't want to be pitied. But that was exactly what she would feel if she spoke to her: pity. After years of being pitied, Lizzy had a keen ear for it.

Peyton was extraordinarily naïve; Myrtle put it down to

youthful inexperience. But in a decade or two Peyton might reflect on her mistake when she realized marriage was like nature—there were no straight lines in it, the terrain was often rough, sometimes smooth and frequently isolating. Her marriage to Vinnie had had all of those moments, but each hairpin turn along the way had brought experience and insight and they had never been stronger than when they were together.

She had all day, every day to think about Lizzy. Vinnie was out chasing down speeders, and all the true crime shows and documentaries on TV were no distraction. Before Peyton had trodden all over her peace of mind, her days had been pleasantly mapped out. She checked windows and doors were locked after Vinnie had left for work, afraid of an intruder breaking into her home and bludgeoning her to death with her silver candelabra on the mantelpiece in the living room or stabbing her repeatedly as she tried to scrabble to safety and somehow her shoes had come off during the attack. Usually, her fear ebbed away as she did some housework, read at least fifty pages of a true crime book, and then watched her true crime shows. She wasn't sure if it was the fear of being murdered or how her body would be found that disturbed her most. Above all, she did not want to die with no shoes on. The rational part of her knew how ridiculous this fear was, but the irrational part of her was a dark-haired stranger with eyes that made you just *melt*, and was far more persuasive. Myrtle's fear of dying with no shoes on was something with which her husband was well acquainted. And she knew she was no picnic to live with. Some people were afraid of spiders and heights and dogs and marzipan and pink Jell-O and wrongly orientated ornaments, but the idea of being dead and shoeless was terrifying beyond measure. Vinnie had the patience of a saint, and he'd been very kind. He hadn't dismissed her fears as the ramblings of a crazy old woman, and she was thankful. He was always just a phone call away. As he kissed her on his way out the door he always reminded her to call if she was feeling afraid. Vinnie was the only person in the world who really knew her. On the surface, she had a hard exterior, could be seen as prim and proper and a no-nonsense type of woman. She wished she was some of those things. Vinnie had even suggested she stop watching her true crime shows, but that was a bridge too far.

She had a boxset of *48 Hours* on standby and she was about to press Play. Then another layer of denial peeled away. The only other person she had told of her fear of being dead with her feet exposed was Lizzy, and she hadn't laughed at her or mocked her. Lizzy had taken her concern seriously, patting her on the shoulder, even though she knew Lizzy hated to touch people. She felt guilty because Lizzy was her friend and she hadn't been there for her when she was needed most. She should have talked to Lizzy. Whenever she was confronted with a difficult issue her mind rambled, avoided the subject. And as she sat on the sofa in her living room, scanning the ornaments on the mantel and in their display case, checking they were facing in the correct direction and that she hadn't accidentally moved them by nudging some with her hand as she was dusting each one, she picked up the phone.

Lizzy answered on the third ring. "Hello." Myrtle was suddenly nervous. Her friend's voice was thick, cracked, *strained*.

"It's me, Lizzy. Myrtle. I was calling—"

"You knew." It wasn't a question.
"Lizzy, do you need me to come over?"
The line went dead.

49

Jon spent the next few days after his unscheduled meeting with Arthur Dunhill checking windows and doors were secured at night and that the intruder alarm was set. He slept with a loaded gun on his nightstand. Zoey seemed to think he was overreacting, although she didn't complain as he walked through the house, making sure they were locked in and the Arthur Dunhills of the world were locked out. When he had come home that day and told Zoey about Dunhill's poor attempt at a disguise—baseball cap and glasses, which he'd made the mistake of removing—there was a noticeable glint very similar to excitement in her eyes, and something perhaps even worse: recklessness. It was there and gone in an instant, but he had seen it. He didn't know what it meant, only that it troubled him.

He stood at the living room window and glanced at his watch. It was almost noon. He dialed Henry Larson. Zinco Sciences had lost eighty-six percent of its value since he'd shorted its stock, and it was time to sell. It had more than enough room to fall further, but Jon wasn't greedy, even though he knew if he said so to anyone who didn't know him they wouldn't believe it. Zoey would be upset, no doubt, but Jon's finely tuned instincts told him it was time to fold and walk away from the table. He had to put all his focus into figuring out what Dunhill was planning, because it was now a hard certainty—Dunhill was out for revenge.

Larson answered on the sixth ring. "It's time to sell, Henry."

"Are you sure?" Jon would have lost his temper then if his attention hadn't been drawn to the woman dressed in a uniform walking up the path to Peggy's house. It was the physical therapist, and she was right on time. Good.

Larson was ten years older than Jon, and despite the fact Jon had made Aquarius Asset Management tens of millions of dollars and made Larson a wealthy man, he still had the gall to question him as though he were a young inexperienced upstart who needed a little guidance to avoid making foolish calls. Larson had ambitions to open his own fund. It was the worst kept secret in his offices in New York City. Everyone knew. But Jon didn't care. Larson's inability to accept he was a numbers guy and lacked the foresight and intuition needed to run a successful hedge fund wasn't his problem. It probably hurt Larson's soul that he was working for a younger man. Henry was effective, Jon gave credit when it was due, but if he thought he was indispensable, he was sorely mistaken.

"What makes you think I'm *un*sure, Henry?"

A pause, then, "All of it?"

"Yes, all of ZNC."

"But it hasn't reached the bottom yet."

"Yes … yes, it has. For me, it has. I won't take up any more of your day."

"Wait, listen—"

"No! You listen, Henry. I'm not asking you, I'm *telling* you. Do it." He hung up, and even though he found Larson distasteful for many reasons, as long as he did his job Jon didn't care about his flaws or shortcomings or habits or his personal life or his ambitions. Henry Larson wasn't happy or even content because he wanted more, more, *more*. Enough would never be enough for someone whose problems were at murky depths Jon had no intention of exploring. There were no real friends in banking. At least, not anymore, not since Charles Shaker went missing. If Larson had been a man with even a shred of decency at his core, Jon would have given him a helping hand up the first two rungs of the ladder on his way to becoming a fund manager, just as Shaker had reached down and pulled him up. But Jon knew Larson would betray him given the first opportunity. Which was too bad, because Jon had a surprise in store for his soon-to-be erstwhile CFO.

He called Roger Berris, not expecting him to answer since he hadn't returned any of his calls all week.

"Hello?"

"Dr. Berris, how good of you to accept my call. I feel honored."

"Ha fucking ha."

"Why didn't you tell me Arthur Dunhill is a lunatic?"

"I did. Not in so many words, but I did."

"I saw him here, in the village, last week."

"What happened?" He could imagine Berris leaning forward in his leather armchair, phone pressed tightly to his ear.

"I was getting out of my car and there he was, across the street, shades in hand and wearing a baseball cap. He recognized me, Roger. Should I be worried?"

"Did he say anything to you?"

"No. And I'm going to take that as a *yes*."

"Look, Jon, I knew Arthur was unstable. It's not a coincidence you saw him, either. I had no clue just how far gone he was."

"He's planning a move, Roger. I don't know what he has in mind, so maybe you know."

"Jon, I swear I didn't know he was this close to the edge. I mean, I knew he wasn't right, something was amiss in his personality. But I didn't really believe he would … Jon, do you have a gun?"

"I do."

"I don't know what to say other than to be vigilant. It might only be an attempt to unsettle you."

"Roger, you don't even believe what you're saying."

"What am I supposed to do? An indictment is on its way for Arthur, maybe not today or tomorrow, but it's coming. Until then, batten down the hatches."

"You think you're not in his sights, too?"

"I've thought about that already. I know I'm high on his shit list."

"So you're just going to wait him out, is that it?"

"He hasn't committed an act of violence or threatened anyone. Yet."

"Do me a favor, Roger. Why don't you sit out in your front yard and act as bait to draw him away from us? After all, you're the stupid sonofabitch who decided to fuck with a maniac."

"Fuck you, too, Jon."

"No, fuck you, and good luck sleeping at night with the knowledge Dunhill is prowling around outside, waiting for you to stick your bald head out far enough for him to get a clear shot."

Really, Jon? Calling the guy bald?

Jon admitted to himself that it was a low blow, but he didn't regret anything else he had said. As he hung up, he doubted he'd hear from Berris again. His thoughts turned to Zoey, and how happy she had seemed ever since she'd returned from the city. *Glowing*, was probably the right word to describe her now, despite it making him cringe inwardly. He was glad the house was quiet. Candice had put Jane in her stroller and taken her for a walk in the park. Zoey was shopping, and Cody was in his treehouse, assembling the airplane Zoey had bought him.

Although he had reason to be concerned about Dunhill, he found himself enjoying the silence with such active intensity that he felt a smile curling his lips. Just sitting there on the sofa staring at the wall was sheer luxury. He would trade a stay at the world's fanciest hotel, the greatest spa, for moments like this. He was almost embarrassed by how much he appreciated the quiet. And he knew why he was grateful for it—it rarely lasted.

50

It had taken Cody nearly a half hour to get from his bedroom to the bottom of the stairs without making a sound. He could hear his parents talking and laughing as they watched TV. It was an odd sound. Laughter leached the tension from the air, the sense of things unsaid. It was a pleasant change. The atmosphere in the house had been laden with an odd heaviness for months. Ever since his mom had returned, bearing gifts, the coldness in the house had turned to warmth. He wasn't complaining, just confused.

He sidled up to the doorway of the living room and peeked. He saw the backs of his parents' heads, but he could also see they were in an embrace. When was the last time he'd seen *that*? He couldn't remember, but he figured it must have been an age.

His mom's head turned and Cody ducked, then slowly resumed the peek.

They were kissing.

Okay, too much.

He headed to the kitchen on tippy-toes, breathing in short soundless breaths through his nose and mouth. Cody was glad his nose didn't whistle when he exhaled like his dad's sometimes did. He had asked his dad why his nose made a sound like their kettle boiling on the stove, and Dad had replied, "You'll get bigger, son, and then you'll understand the struggle that is the hairy nose. A man's nose is a battleground, and if he neglects his duty to trim the overgrowth, you get a sound like this." Cody had been delighted as Dad forced a hard breath through his nose and it whistled. He'd said, "Dad, I'm *not* trimming my nose hair if it makes that sound." And Dad had laughed. Now, Cody was trying not to laugh at the memory. And he tried to ignore the guilt he felt with each careful step as he sneaked toward the back door. This was the last time he would do it. Mom and Dad trusted him, and he wasn't treating their trust in him with respect. He'd still be in his bedroom if he hadn't sensed something was seriously wrong with Mia. He had spoken to her briefly, then for some reason she couldn't talk anymore and they'd sent text messages back and forth. The worrying part of their conversation was that Mia was pretending nothing was wrong. But he would get it out of her, whatever it was.

He hurried toward his bike. It was lying on the ground next to his treehouse, which was framed against the big night, the sky dark but tinged a bruised purple in places.

He headed out, pedaling fast around the side of the house, and onto Main Street. He'd ridden his bike at night a few times now. He enjoyed it more at nighttime, probably because there were so few cars on the road and the mugginess of the day had passed, replaced by cool dewy air. Or it could be the haunted-house feel of the Whaling Museum, its pale columns in the gloom like the bones of some enormous mysterious creature. Maybe it was the creepy Custom House, with its unlit windows, hoarding shadows. And perhaps something walked within, a woman in a flowing gown, its hem disturbed by a wind not of this world.

Come on. Quit it.

He was scaring himself and diverted his gaze to the road as he turned onto Garden Street.

Mia was waiting for him at the far end of the backyard. He spotted her pale hand beckoning him towards her and he thought about the ghost of a woman he'd just imagined. He shivered.

Cody didn't want to spend long here. Mia's mom already didn't like him, and he didn't want her to dislike him even more. He wouldn't hold a grudge against Mrs. Jenkins. He didn't blame her for wanting to protect Mia. She just couldn't see that he wanted the same thing.

He lowered his bike to the ground, and whispered, "Hi, Mia."

"You're not going to let this go, are you?"

"What do you mean?"

"Cody, what if I said I didn't want to tell you what's going on?"

"I'd say fine. But I think you *want* to tell me."

He watched her look at the ground. Then she raised her head, and said, "I can't tell you all of it. Most of it, though. My parents broke up."

Cody felt a lump in his throat and gulped it down.

51

Lizzy was sitting at her kitchen table, the lights turned off. At first, she thought the sound of conversation was coming from inside her own head, which was strange because she hadn't formed a complete thought in hours. Images flitted through her mind with formless rapidity, uneven monstrosities that bore no semblance to the familiar.

She stood, clenched fists by her sides, and went to the window, squinted. Mia was in the yard, talking to *that* boy. Lizzy was done arguing with her daughter.

She marched upstairs and picked up Marcus's secret phone on the nightstand. There was one cell number in his contacts. She dialed it. It rang seven, eight, nine times, and she imagined Zoey leaving Jon's side as she hurried out of earshot, probably to the swimming pool or the treehouse.

She didn't turn on the lights, but remained standing by the window, pushing aside the drapes to watch for the boy. He had to come out sometime, push his bike down her driveway and cycle home …

… *ring … ring … ring …*

"Marcus, I've been waiting—"

"Shut up, cocksucker. What's wrong? Expecting somebody else?"

"Lizzy?" Slowly. Ever so slowly. Lizzy's name poured from her mouth like the world's thickest syrup. A humorless, vicious smile crumpled Lizzy's face. It was funny in a non-amusing way, she thought, since it felt like her face hadn't experienced any expression in years. It felt *good*. Little by little, Lizzy's shock was wearing off. The numbness had become a mild whole-body tingling. It would fade, and when it did, this Double Cunt on the phone with her heavy breathing, the square root of cuntery, Cunt Cubed, was in for a surprise. If Zoey thought she was taking The Trick lying down she was mistaken. Lizzy imagined the anger, red laser beams of hate shooting into her pores, and it fed her, raising her head, dropping her shoulders back just the way Zoey did, as if she was afraid every Tom, Dick and horny Harry would miss her perfects tits.

"Yes, it's Lizzy. I found Marcus's porn phone, the one he uses for slut dialing."

"Lizzy, you don't sound like yourself—"

"That's what they all say. *You don't sound like yourself.* Take some more pills."

"Please, Lizzy, you don't understand—"

"Why? Because I'm stupid? Because I'm *not well*? You can trick your husband, but not me. Sooner or later, you're going to pay for this, for your *sluttery*, with interest, *pretend friend*. I've never felt more like myself. In fact, I don't believe I've seen things with such clarity. You think you're so clever. Well, we'll see … I'll see you around." Before Zoey could spew more lies from her filthy lips, Lizzy hung up. The boy was leaving, pushing his bike down her driveway. Just as she had expected.

52

Cody felt guilty for leaving Mia, but he had to get home. It was only a matter of time before his parents realized he wasn't in bed, asleep. If he was caught, he'd be confined to his bedroom for a week. His dad wouldn't like to do it, and yet Cody had no doubt he would. Even worse, he'd be banned from using the internet and his cell phone would be confiscated. He would have no way of contacting Mia.

His usual enthusiasm for riding his bike on deserted streets was gone. His speed had reduced considerably until he was barely above walking pace. The one thing he feared most had happened not to him, but to Mia, and that was just as bad. In the past few months, he had often believed that any day now his parents would announce they were breaking up. Somehow, whatever was going on with his parents had taken a turn in a positive direction. He didn't understand why things had changed, only that he was grateful they had.

He hadn't wanted to push Mia for more information because he'd seen how difficult it was for her already. The ache in his heart had sapped his strength; he missed Mia terribly, so much he considered turning back. She had embraced him as he was about to leave. He couldn't shake the idea that she had tried to comfort him even though she was the one who would have to deal with her mom and dad and the dreaded D-word, divorce. It even *sounded* heartless, callous, and evil. The worst part was helplessness. He couldn't find the words to make everything okay, despite knowing nothing he said would reduce the horror of an end to something so important. Cody was annoyed and distressed as the realization solidified into cold certainty that there were some situations in life no words could mend. It was his first real experience of a bleak fact: not all problems had solutions. There was something utterly horrific about facing this stout, immovable truth—it resisted all his attempts at dismantling it, at finding a weak point. Cody suspected life had a way of throwing up these walls on occasion, and that even expert climbers had difficulty reaching the other side. Sometimes, the wall was too high.

Great. When did I become a pessimistic asshole?

Cody felt his old self coming back, the Cody Finch who refused to accept hopelessness because it had no value. That was straight from his dad's mouth to his ears: *hopelessness has no value; emotional, intellectual or otherwise. It's the psychic equivalent of a black hole. It sucks you in and you only think you can't fight it, but you can.*

He wasn't quite sure what it all meant, but he had picked up on the steadfast conviction in Dad's voice when he'd said those words.

There was a car behind him and Cody moved further to the side of the road and sped up slightly. The last thing he wanted to do was block somebody who was trying to get home.

But the car didn't go around.

The road was clear and awash in the whiteness of the headlights' full beams.

Cody pedaled onward, wondering why his throat was tightening and his heart was pumping faster than his suddenly stony legs.

The car stopped and Cody glanced over his shoulder, breathing hard.

What's happening?

He pedaled faster and faster.

The car's engine idled.

For a moment, he felt silly. What was he running from?

But his body disagreed with his emotions. His body felt it was in danger.

Then the sound of rubber gripping the road in a burst of acceleration reached him and sudden terror seemed to bloat his limbs, his head.

The car roared toward him, too fast to avoid. It struck Cody, throwing him high into the air. He didn't make any sound, but things below him were breaking, crunching, and as his body slammed into the asphalt, other things broke too. But he couldn't feel anything. He was sure he was dreaming. It was just a dream.

And yet he could see and smell the exhaust fumes. The brake lights.

As he lay on the ground, paralyzed, Cody watched, unable to alert the driver, as the car backed toward him.

53

Peggy had been getting up from her chair by the window to warm a pot of milk on the stove before bed when she heard high revs from a car. Then there was an impact. And the sound of the car's engine revving again. Maybe somebody was having car trouble ... but a deeper instinct, the one you learned to trust as time's passage became experience, told her to be cautious.

She picked up her cane and her cell and dialed 911 into the phone, finger poised on the Send button. Peggy was still in pain, and she hadn't stopped taking her pills, but she was using fewer of them. She made it down the porch steps with relative ease, a feat that would have been impossible a week ago. But now, Peggy felt the progress she had made. And it was all thanks to Jon, who'd sent her an angel: Alice Grundy, who had retired early as a registered nurse and retrained as a physical therapist. It would take a few more weeks until her range of mobility improved, according to Alice, and there would be pain along the way, but Alice was determined to have Peggy walking without a cane, although she had cautioned that she didn't want either of them "counting our chickens before they hatch." Peggy had to repay Jon somehow, despite his predictable response if she suggested such a thing: a stubborn refusal to hear of it. But Peggy Dawson wasn't in the business of accepting freebies, even if it was from a friend.

She had torn up her letter to Jon and she had tried and failed not to spend every waking moment despising his wife.

As she made her way slowly toward the sidewalk, a car screeched away, accelerating at speed.

What in God's name is going on?

Her finger remained pressed to the Send button. At last, she was on the sidewalk, looking at the road. About twenty yards down, she spotted a bundle. Someone had dumped garbage on the road. She could hardly believe it. And if it was garbage, Peggy was going to go through it in hopes of finding a bill with the dumper's name on it and report them.

She headed toward the pile, her eyes constantly adjusting to the streetlights and pockets of darkness untouched by the light.

She was less than ten yards from the object when she stopped hard. It wasn't garbage. She recognized a human leg when she saw one, even though it was grotesquely twisted at impossible angles. Her gaze jumped to the bicycle some distance from the body, because it couldn't be anything else. She didn't want to go any further but found herself powerless to stop or look away. She pressed Send.

"There's a body on the road," she said. Her voice sounded odd in the stillness, as though she'd shouted in a library or spoken out of turn in church.

"Please, it's on Main Street, a—" She had been getting closer as she talked to the woman trying to talk over her with questions of her own. She saw the upturned, bloodied face, and the bike with the bent front wheel and made a horrifying connection in her mind.

Cody.

Peggy screamed and dropped the phone.

54

There had been a part of Zoey that wasn't afraid of being caught. The prospect of divorcing Jon didn't worry her; in fact, the idea was enticing. At least, it had been. She had wanted to show Jon he wasn't the only one capable of keeping a secret, to prove she, too, was not above deceit. Now she wasn't so sure. Jon just had a way of growing on her, or *re*growing. She wasn't excusing what he'd done, and she wouldn't forget. Zoey thought the past few days were the best she'd had in a long time, but she was trying to persuade herself it was a fluke, and that it would take a few more days for hatred and disgust for her husband to return, in vivid color. She *wanted* to hate him. She had wasted enough time being sad and disappointed. There was something comfortable about hating him. It was almost as though she had gotten so used to hating him that she missed it. And the anger—she missed the anger most of all. It was easy to meet Marcus in a hotel room with anger and hate balled up in her gut. Easy to enjoy the fact that Jon probably thought his secret was safe and that his little dutiful wife was probably depressed but faithful.

She was giving her children more attention, too. She spent most of her days cradling Jane, carrying her around the house and making baby sounds at her. She understood why Jon would have believed she was suffering from post-partum depression, not realizing he was the direct cause of her aloofness these past few months. But Zoey regretted neglecting Cody and Jane to focus on her anger toward Jon. It was the ultimate in selfishness: putting her own feelings before those of her children.

She had tried to discourage Cody's obsession with becoming a pilot. She'd thought her son was meant for better things, but what if being a pilot *was* the better thing? He hadn't grown out of his preoccupation with flying and it didn't look as though he would.

Zoey was watching Jon from the corner of her eye, and had been for the entire night. *The Real Housewives of New Jersey* was on TV, and Jon hadn't sighed heavily and loudly once. He seemed content to suffer through it. He hadn't folded his arms tightly across his chest in some kind of unconscious attempt to block out the misadventures of the housewives. She wondered how long he could maintain his impassive, calm air—she would find out when *The Bachelor* came on, another one of her favorite shows.

She felt a smile curl her lips. She wasn't being malicious, just mischievous.

Her cell rang.

"Oh, good," she said, "it's Lizzy. Be back in a sec."

***

Jon knew she was testing him. He glanced at her as she left for the kitchen, phone in hand. Zoey had probably made a quiet wager with herself, betting that he would lose his patience with the housewives (which was an oxymoron, as far as he was concerned—these women were the furthest thing from being real housewives) on TV, but it wasn't going to happen. He'd seen all the episodes of *The Real Housewives*, whether they were filmed in the Jersey Shore, Atlanta or Orange County. He wondered why she had to watch them *twice*. No doubt she thought he hated her viewing choices, but she was wrong. They were shows like any other, they just weren't meant for him. He wasn't the target audience. And Jon had more important matters on his mind: Zoey had kissed him for the first time in months. It felt like a breakthrough, as though they had recaptured the warmth that had been absent from their marriage for so long.

Twenty minutes had passed and Zoey hadn't come back inside. He'd heard her, vaguely, speaking to Lizzy, then the conversation had paused. He was about to get up and check on her when she returned, ashen-faced.

"What happened? Is everything okay?"

"Uh, yeah, yes. Everything's fine. I'm just worried. Lizzy is off her pills."

"She stopped taking them?"

"Yeah. She's rambling, incoherent, not making much sense at all."

"Marcus is there to take care of her, right?"

"Right." Her smile was weak and she looked haggard, her face drawn in worry and concern. She bit her lower lip.

"Hey," he said, rising from the sofa, "are you all right?" He went to her and folded her into his arms.

"She's so sick, Jon. She might be a danger to herself. You should've heard the nonsense things she was saying. It's just upsetting, that's all."

He embraced her in a tight hug, gave her a reassuring squeeze.

A blood-chilling scream came from outside.

They broke apart and stared at each other. "What the hell?" he said.

"We have to check it out."

He headed toward the front door, Zoey following close behind.

On the sidewalk, Jon looked both ways. There were no cars on the road. He saw lights were on in Peggy's house, which was odd; Peggy was usually in bed by now. He walked further down the road.

What in God's name …?

Peggy's front door was wide open. He nudged Zoey gently and nodded in the direction he wanted her to look. She saw.

"Zoey, dial 911 into your phone and get ready to call." Zoey typed the number in immediately. Pale yellowish light spilled onto Peggy's porch. Whatever was going on, he hoped his friend was all right.

He came to a sudden stop as he made out the shape of a person standing in the middle of the road.

"Jon, who's that?" The fear in her voice made Jon's skin stretch tight across his chest. He shrugged. He didn't want to speak, because he might scare Zoey even more if she heard the fear in his voice.

He edged forward and Zoey grabbed his arm. "No," she whispered, sharply enough to get his attention.

He touched her hand, gave it a caring caress and found that he couldn't stop. He was drawn forward, as though propelled by unseen hands. He recognized the outline of the person in the road. It was Peggy, and she was standing over something, looking down, weeping loudly.

"Peggy?" he said, and his legs carried him forward faster without any conscious input from his brain.

She turned, and the horror he saw in her eyes quickened his heart into a heavy gallop. He looked past her, and the screaming that started at his side was drowned out by the strange sounds coming from inside his head. Hands grappled for him but he was on his knees, next to Cody's broken, misshapen body.

"Cody," he said, "get up. You should be asleep by now. Don't you know what time it is …? Wake up, son. I promised I'd help you build your model plane tomorrow. I promised. Come on, wake up, son. *Please wake up*." He cradled Cody's head in his arms and it was odd the things you noticed when your life developed gaping chasms right down the center … Cody's head was heavy. Very heavy. He kissed his son's forehead. "Please, Cody, get up, let's go home." He was vaguely aware of red and blue strobing lights, but there were no sounds, just that peculiar ringing that seemed to radiate outward from a fathomless part of his mind, a black starburst of sound.

55

It had all started with Milo Grainger's pig.

Lizzy lay on her bed in the dark, covers pushed onto the floor. The skinned tennis ball in her hands shed slice after slice of hard rubber as the razor cut fine shavings into a gathering pile on her stomach. Saliva dribbled from the corners of her mouth. Mia was asleep in her room, the house was quiet, the silence thick enough to transport her to 1989, when she was seven years old. Lizzy attempted to resist this loathsome mode of time travel—memory. It was useless, though. She was down the rabbit hole and couldn't back her way out.

The morning was bright, the mid-July temperature already in the high eighties. Lizzy was sitting at the breakfast table, eating her cereal with relish, and kicking her legs back and forth beneath the chair. Her feet didn't reach the floor yet; she was impatient to start growing. She was the smallest of her friends. Her ankle was almost healed; she had rolled it when she'd run down the driveway to help Mom carry the groceries inside. It had swollen to an alarming size, and once the drugs had taken effect and before the doctor had strapped bandages around it, Lizzy had delighted in showing her friends how wonderfully gross it was, displaying her injury with bottomless pride and taking pleasure in Zoey's exclamation of disgust—*Ewwwuh!*—and her backward step of revulsion. It still hurt to stand on, but in two weeks she wouldn't need the crutches anymore. Lizzy had put all her weight on it yesterday, and while she did wince in pain, it had faded on her second attempt. She had made progress, but decided not to stretch her luck too far and continued using the crutches.

There was a knock on the door. Mom went to answer it. Lizzy followed her. Zoey, Marcus, Sage, and Lewis were on the porch, all wearing T-shirts, shorts, and sneakers. Lizzy felt Mom stiffen beside her. She rolled her eyes upward in an effort to decipher which of her friends had caused this sudden wariness, this instant distaste. Mom's gaze was trained directly on Zoey. Despite the Incident, Mom hadn't forbidden her from seeing Zoey. But it hadn't been Zoey who was responsible for the Incident, it had been Zoey's parents.

After school, two months ago, Lizzy had arrived home after visiting Zoey's house. Lizzy had been upset, dumping her book bag on the floor. She was crying, but she was angry, too. It had taken Mom an hour to get it out of her, but eventually she did: the Harmans were not keen on feeding someone else's child. Lizzy hadn't asked for food; it was Zoey's idea that she come in and eat, even though Lizzy had protested that she must be getting home, Mom would be worried. But Zoey had coaxed and cajoled until Lizzy gave in, and when the Harmans returned from whatever country club they'd been at, Zoey had received the scolding of her life for feeding Lizzy.

As Lizzy had recounted the story, including snippets of

Mr. Harman's tirade, Lizzy had watched Mom's eyes grow to the size of saucers when she'd quoted Harman as saying, "We're rich, Zoey. Feeding random waifs isn't the way to maintain our wealth." Lizzy had even included the emphasis on *maintain*.

Lizzy was becoming more afraid as she had watched her mother. Mom's face had flushed a deep, dangerous red. Her eyes were large, and she seemed far away. Then, in a breathless whisper, one word emerged from Mom's mouth, which had tightened as though someone had pulled a drawstring on it. "Bastard." Lizzy winced, not knowing what it meant, only that it was bad. Mom had noticed Lizzy's fear, put a hand on her shoulder, and said, "I'm talking about Mr. Harman, sweetie. You didn't do anything wrong. But don't go near that house again. Ever. Understand?" And Lizzy had nodded. There was no way she was going to disobey the order, either. Mom's body seemed to hum, *vibrate* with the power of her fury. It had taken several minutes for Mom to compose herself, and when she did, she said, "That sonofabitch. They're not better than us, Lizzy. Don't believe it for a second. They swan around in their big foreign car as if their shit don't smell. They're people, just like us. They belong to a country club, but there's nothing exclusive about them or their stupid little club." Underneath the rage there was something Lizzy recognized as astonished disbelief. Mom blinked, looked at Lizzy. "Don't ever repeat any of those swear words, Lizzy. Those are bad words, and I had a Bad Spell. You know I get them every once in a while. Promise me."

"I promise, Mom." Lizzy kept her promise for several years, until she moved into her own one-bed apartment on

Division Street, within walking distance of Sag Harbor Bay, and received her first flurry of utility bills and the obscene sums demanded by said utility companies. All the bad words had been free-flowing that day. She was just relieved that her mother wasn't going to march over to the Harmans' house, as she'd seemed poised to do, to give Mr. Harman *a piece of her mind.*

"Time to get you some ice cream." They hadn't spoken about the Incident again. But whenever Mom saw Zoey, Lizzy sensed a renewal of Mom's rage, and the enormous effort she expended in containing it. Mom was a Christian, but her values didn't extend to turning the other cheek, and Lizzy was instructed not to allow Zoey inside the house to eat *their* food.

Mom had quickly turned away from the door and gone to the kitchen as if she was trying to fight off one of her Bad Spells, leaving Lizzy to greet her friends.

As she was about to leave, Mom called from the kitchen, "Don't be out too late, Lizzy."

"I won't, Mom."

***

Lizzy had gotten used to the crutches quickly, swinging herself back and forth like a human metronome, but not their sound. It was similar to old bones crackling, almost identical to the snap and pop her grandpa's had made whenever he rose from his armchair. Grandpa had passed and, according to Mom, he was in Heaven, arguing with the angels. Lizzy missed him, though. He'd never argued with her.

All five children walked down the driveway, out onto

Joels Lane, the trees lining both sides of the road several different shades of rich green. Sage and Lewis were walking close together, and Lizzy thought it was funny because she knew they wanted to hold hands but didn't—Marcus and Zoey would tease them.

"Where are we going?" Lizzy asked.

"I want to look at Milo's pig," Marcus said. Lizzy had spotted Milo Grainger around the Village, usually from a distance, but not often. On the few occasions she'd actually seen him, he had been carrying a suitcase. The luggage suggested Milo was going somewhere, maybe on vacation, but he always ended up returning home. Lizzy was saddened that he was considered the Village weirdo. He contributed to this view with his hunched back, long neck bent forward in a permanent bow, and his grizzled, unshaven appearance. His clothes were dirty, too; his blue jeans were caked in dried mud, engine grease and God knew what else. His plaid shirt had holes in it, and its original red-and-black color had faded. There was a navy blue blotch over the chest pocket, as though a pen had burst eons ago and Milo had bigger things to think about rather than removing the stain. Lizzy was glad Mom saw Milo the way she did: a hardworking man who ran a small farm and took good care of his animals. Mom had often commented on how healthy his pigs were when she passed by the Grainger farm, sometimes catching a glimpse of Milo feeding his charges.

Lizzy had wanted to know why people looked at him the way they did and if there was something wrong with Mr. Grainger and Mom had responded, "People can be ignorant. It doesn't mean they're bad, just flawed. As for something being wrong with him, let's just say Mr. Grainger has seen far more of life than he ever bargained for." And Lizzy had had no idea what any of it meant.

"Ew," Sage said, "who wants to look at a pig?"

"I do," Marcus said, and Lizzy was suddenly nervous. She didn't want to trespass on anybody's property, least of all Mr. Grainger's, whose troubles appeared to literally weigh him down, to bend his body. Lizzy had seen Milo muttering to himself and was mortified when she remembered pointing at him and asking her mom, "Who is he talking to?" Mom had scolded her for such a display of bad manners, and as she swung her body back and forth, the crutches filling the stillness with their sound of infirmity, she felt she deserved it. Lizzy hadn't pointed at anyone ever again.

She had heard the rumors about Brutus. Legend had it that Milo's pig was enormous, and so bad-tempered it had to have a pen of its own because it had attacked and killed one of Milo's prized sows. Lizzy didn't know if this was true or not, and Marcus seemed determined to find out if Brutus really was the beast of lore. "Seriously, guys," he said, "I want to see Brutus for myself."

Lewis gave his brother a doubtful glance, and then Zoey said, "I want to see it, too. Come on, it'll be fun."

"I don't know," Lizzy said, "we shouldn't."

"Scaredy cat," Zoey said, "just a quick look. It won't take more than a few minutes."

It seemed she was outnumbered. Marcus and Zoey were in; Lewis and Sage were loath to argue. They were all looking at her. Under the weight of their collective, expectant gaze, Lizzy caved.

"Okay," she said, "a few minutes is fine. But we can't stay long—my foot is beginning to hurt." It wasn't, but she was prepared to use it as an excuse if she could shorten the duration of her imminent trespass.

They arrived at Milo's farm. There was an old Ford F-100 in the front yard. It had black patches on its front quarter panels and the hood, as though rust had eaten holes in the metal and Milo had tried to fill them in. There was a dent in the roof, and Lizzy wondered what had caused it. Had a tree fallen on it? She couldn't put her finger on it— the Ford pickup made her feel sad and she couldn't figure out why.

"The place looks deserted," Marcus said. It certainly had an air of abandonment, but Lizzy wasn't sure she trusted it. In the far distance, she heard grunts: Milo's pigs were awake.

"Come on, you guys," Marcus said. "I think the old dude is asleep."

With a heavy heart, Lizzy followed her friends to the rear of the house.

In the backyard, Lizzy paused to take in the pigpen. The animals snuffled contentedly and grunted. Nothing out of the ordinary. Beyond the pen, there were neat rectangular rows of newly sown crops. Lizzy didn't know what Mr. Grainger was growing, but it looked as though it had taken a lot of work. She was quietly impressed. Mr. Grainger had done all this by himself?

Her gaze was drawn to a circular pen and its padlocked door. It had been built from what looked like railroad sleepers standing vertically, except these were taller. The thick wooden planks were dark brown and black, and Lizzy smelled oil in the early morning heat. Stairs led up to a platform, the steps made from the same timber as the pen.

Lizzy spotted the chicken coop near the back porch, then

she heard Marcus's harsh whisper, "Come on, Lizzy. What're you doing?" Lizzy's friends were climbing the stairs. Marcus was waiting for her, and she thought it was sweet how he was going to help her to the platform above. He was waving her toward him, and the clicking of her crutches in the dirt twisted a knot in her stomach. It was the sound of frailty, of vulnerability. But there was a large part of Lizzy that was convinced she was immortal. She didn't believe in death. Despite her sprained ankle, the possibility that she could ever be seriously hurt was remote, absurd.

Marcus helped her up the stairs. Lizzy was surprised at how strong he was; he lifted her to the platform and ran back down the steps to fetch her crutches.

Lewis and Sage were the first to swing their legs over the lip of the pen, followed by Zoey. It looked like a bad idea to Lizzy. What if they fell in?

"Look at that thing," Zoey said, and Lizzy looked. Brutus—if that was his real name—was enormous, his furry brown coat glistening. There was a patch of mud in the middle of Brutus's circular prison. An orange soccer ball sat next to it with some soft toys. Maybe Mr. Grainger had hosed it down. Lizzy's grandpa had explained to her once that mud was like sunscreen for pigs, and that it kept insects from biting.

"I'll boost you up," Marcus said, and before Lizzy could protest, she was sitting on the lip of the pen, too, right next to Zoey.

"How big do you think he is?" Lewis asked no one in particular.

"Has to be prob'ly seven hundred pounds," Marcus said.

"No way, douchebag," Lewis said, "maybe six hundred."

Lizzy was watching Brutus. The pig had seen them, and didn't seem pleased. He began making noises deep in his throat, menacing, guttural sounds that made her nervous. The swine backed up, and suddenly it charged, slamming its body into the side of the pen. Everyone laughed. But Lizzy didn't find any of this funny. She wanted to go home. Wanted to get back on the platform instead of sitting here with her legs hanging over the side. Her injured foot had developed an itch, and she leaned forward to scratch it.

Lizzy didn't know who pushed her. She had been sitting with Zoey on one side and Marcus on the other, then she was falling through the morning heat, arms scrabbling frantically at the empty air, a scream caught in her throat, her stomach where her heart should have been.

She hit the floor of the pen.

The impact knocked the air out of her.

It's a dream just a dream it feels like a dream a nightmare—

But it wasn't a dream, just a sense of unreality, of disbelief. Shock.

They were laughing. Someone yelled, "Little pig, little pig." Above her, the sound of her friends laughing stunned her. She looked up, just before the pain in her shattered ankle registered, and saw them pointing and laughing.

Pointing and laughing.

Lizzy screamed, the force of it silencing all other sounds. The pain in her ankle was far worse than it had ever been.

The world swam in and out of focus.

She tried to stand and stumbled.

And the sound of menace, of harm, was getting closer.

Brutus was staring at her from the other side of the pen. When they made eye contact, Brutus took a step toward her.

Then another.

He charged, shoulders rippling, his squeal filling her head.

Black dots floated across her field of vision, like soot.

She was frozen in place, panic-stricken.

And suddenly she was flying through the air again, tossed around as though she had no substance, no weight at all. Lizzy believed in death. Now she knew it was more than possible. She wasn't immortal.

The noises erupting from her throat were alien to her. She didn't know she was capable of producing such frenzied, miserable pleas for mercy, for someone to help her.

Teeth sank into her thigh.

Brutus was dragging her.

Her shorts and underwear tore, and she caught Marcus peeking over the top of the pen, staring at her nakedness. She saw the Sex Thing in his eyes; her mother had warned her about it. Then Marcus was gone.

Mouth wide in an agonized scream, tears blurring her vision, Lizzy believed she was dying.

Brutus bit down harder. She was screaming but no sound was coming out of her mouth. The power of this beast was elemental, the power of nature itself. Fighting against it would be useless.

But she had to try because she was going to die if she didn't.

She attempted to launch a kick at Brutus's head and missed.

Lizzy tried again. She was going to pass out. The world around her was dim; it had lost its color.

She threw her leg out again, and Brutus let go of the one

he was biting into and clamped his jaws on her uninjured leg. Lizzy screamed again, and again there was no sound, just a voiceless gasp of air. Through the haze of tears, she saw the pig's red feral eyes and knew she was going to be eaten alive.

A shadow fell over her, as though there had been a solar eclipse.

But it was Milo Grainger, his arm around the beast's neck, wrestling it toward a chain hanging from a wall.

She listened to the struggle between man and beast. It didn't last long. Lizzy was fading in and out of consciousness. She had fainted once, possibly twice, she didn't know. When she came to she was in sunlight wrapped in a blanket, being carried, the animal squealing, but it was far away.

She looked up at Mr. Grainger. There was no expression on his grizzled face.

Lizzy faded out briefly, fighting the urge to sleep forever. Then she heard Mr. Grainger talking to someone. She couldn't see where he was. There was something in her eyes. The smell of blood was so strong it made her stomach roll.

Lizzy tried to speak, but issued a wheezing wail of pain instead.

"Don't talk," Mr. Grainger said, "the ambulance is on its way. Give me a minute, I'm going to get a wet cloth to wash the blood out of your eyes."

56

Milo Grainger had saved Lizzy's life. As the first light of a new day dawned, Lizzy sat up in bed and pulled out her cardigan to catch the shavings from the tennis ball. Old habits were hard to break, but she was going to try. She emptied the shavings into a paper bag, went to the closet and removed the tennis balls. She carried them to the backyard where she dumped them in the trash.

Mr. Grainger had stood by, silent, watching, as she had been carried out of his home on a stretcher. He had cleaned the blood from her eyes and she was grateful, trying to thank him as she was conveyed to the ambulance, but the words had emerged in monosyllabic rasps that hadn't made any sense. Even though she had trespassed on his property, Mr. Grainger hadn't reprimanded her, hadn't said she deserved her wounds for interfering in his business. He had even visited her in Stony Brook, but she had been too sick to take visitors. At one point during her dazed confinement to a hospital bed, she had seen her mom and Mr. Grainger in conversation. She had caught a glimpse of her mom touching his arm—a friendly gesture. Then she'd fallen asleep.

When she was discharged from Stony Brook three weeks later, Lizzy had wanted desperately to thank Mr. Grainger for rescuing her. She made dozens of attempts to walk toward his small farm. Once, she had even made it as far as the end of his driveway. She wasn't sure if it was fear that had kept her away or guilt: a rumor had circulated in the Village after the attack that Milo had shot Brutus. It had also occurred to Lizzy that although Brutus was dangerous, she remembered the orange soccer ball in its pen, the soft toys that squeaked when they were bitten, the kind a dog owner might buy for their pooch. And the itching post, a piece of steel pipe added to the pen so that Brutus could scratch whatever itch maddened him. What if he knew Brutus was bad and Milo was only trying to rehabilitate him? The thought horrified her. She had wanted to thank Mr. Grainger, but she also wanted to apologize. She was sorry. She had listened to her stupid friends and regretted the fact that she could be so easily swayed, talked into dumb escapades, persuaded to take part in a foolish caper. Lizzy couldn't face Mr. Grainger, no matter how many times she had tried. She hadn't found out for sure if Milo had euthanized Brutus or not. It was probably best not to know.

But the strangest thing had happened in the years following her less than auspicious encounter with Brutus— Lizzy forgot about the incident. Completely. As though she'd been stricken with a peculiar type of amnesia. It had happened around the time when Mom had started talking to the floor, the dining table, and baking bread at 3 a.m. some mornings, talking up a storm, even though there was no one there. Eleanor was losing her mind, and Lizzy witnessed her distressing decline. Then, for no reason she could think of, the memory had resurfaced, full force and unabridged, two years ago.

It was time to clean house. If her home was clean, tidy, ordered, then perhaps her mind would take its cue from her efforts.

Lizzy saw the problem—she had asked for too much from life. She had asked for a good man, a good husband, and instead she was given Marcus. There was a way to mend the broken cogs in her mind. She saw the way forward, as she lined up cleaning products on the kitchen table.

Lizzy knew exactly the steps she needed to take in order to rectify the wrong done to her. The betrayal. The old, timid, *poor Lizzy she's not well,* was gone. She had discovered her real self, had caught a tantalizing glimpse of her own strength. And she was reaching for it. Because she remembered who had pushed her into Brutus's pen.

57

Vincent Shaw, Chief of Police in Sag Harbor, was the first police officer to arrive on the scene. He'd had to pry Jon Finch off his son. Despite his burly six-five stature, it hadn't been an easy task. Grief had a mad strength he didn't have to deal with often, something he was thankful for.

Small mercies. Thank God for small mercies.

The boy appeared to be deceased, and even if he wasn't, Shaw didn't want Jon adding insult to injury by handling his body as though Cody Finch was perfectly fine and just needed waking up.

A short time later, Sergeant Ross Harper pulled up in his cruiser and assisted his boss in separating the grieving father from his son. During the struggle, Shaw noticed the red blotches on the boy's right cheek. Tire marks. There was no doubt in his mind.

Shaw and Harper had walked Jon back to his house, not loosening their grip on his upper arms because they both recognized the wild hysteria in his eyes; there was no way to tell what he'd do. When the ambulance arrived, they sat Jon inside. Zoey Finch, on the other hand, appeared to be frozen in place where she stood, staring fixedly at her son's body in the road. There was another woman nearby, sitting on the sidewalk, funky hair, wailing at the top of her lungs. Shaw didn't know her, but he knew the old woman trying to console her.

His wife, Myrtle, used to attend a book club held by Mrs. Finch. She had stopped going recently, saying something about how Zoey was too busy. He didn't know Jon well, but he was on nodding terms with him. He had seen him around the Village on occasion. According to Myrtle, Jon was a gentleman, and yet someone had obviously murdered his son.

Now, both ends of Main Street were cordoned off, with traffic diversions in place. A tent had been erected over the victim. He had been glad when the Suffolk County PD showed up, three cruisers' worth of cops. Two unmarked sedans had pulled in behind them. Charlotte Lange emerged from one of the cars; she was a detective with the Homicide Bureau. Shaw approached her with his hand extended. She gave it a brief shake, and said, "What have you got so far, Chief?"

"It looks like vehicular homicide."

"What makes you think that?"

"The tire marks on the boy's face, on his right cheek. There are some ugly bruises there. Makes me think he might have been alive when he was hit first. Someone ran him over, then backed over him. Tire marks on the road suggest an instant increase in acceleration."

"We're going to take impressions of those marks ... did you get anything out of the parents?"

"Not much. They're in shock, as you can imagine." She eyed him steadily, all mountains of blonde hair and blue eyes, no makeup; she looked as if she had been sitting in front of the TV when she got the call. Detective Lange was dressed in jeans and an open-at-the-neck red leather jacket from which a blossom of royal blue ruffles of blouse emerged. She held his gaze, and Chief Shaw felt he was being assessed, as if his observations of the crime scene were being graded. She nodded at him, finally, as though she'd just gotten an answer to whatever question was in her mind.

"I need to speak to the parents, Chief Shaw," she said.

"I don't know …"

She looked past him at the ambulance and headed toward Zoey and Jon. Shaw didn't blame her. It wasn't going to be the right moment to talk to the Finches for a while. He understood that information provided by eyewitnesses in the immediate aftermath of a crime was probably the most accurate. Witnesses didn't have time to change their stories or consider the consequences of what they were saying. He walked alongside her, and two detectives from the Homicide Bureau followed them. Shaw glanced behind him. Most of the cops had gathered near the tent.

Shaw introduced Jon and Zoey to Detective Lange. They just stared at her, not offering their hands. But Lange didn't offer hers, either. She had probably done it one too many times as a rookie and been left hanging. Social graces didn't matter when your child was lying dead in the street.

"Mrs. Finch," Lange said, "do you know of anyone who'd want to hurt you or your family?"

Shaw glanced at her—she had accepted his assessment that this wasn't an accident, but a murder.

"Huh … uh, no. I don't—no, nobody."

"Mr. Finch?" Shaw was concerned about Jon Finch. He'd never seen a man as completely devastated, broken; he appeared dazed, face drained of color, confused.

Jon just shook his head, no.

Shaw glanced at Lange again, and knew she had decided to focus on Zoey instead. Jon wasn't going to be much use to her.

"Mrs. Finch, are you sure no one would want to harm your son?"

Shaw watched Mrs. Finch carefully. She was staring directly at Lange, and something flickered in her eyes. It was brief, but Shaw and Lange both saw it.

"What is it, Mrs. Finch?" Shaw said gently.

"Lizzy," Zoey said, "Lizzy Jenkins. She called me earlier, she's taking drugs for a mental illness. She wasn't making any sense."

"Did she threaten you?" Lange asked.

"Yes, but she's not well. Poor Lizzy ... she didn't know what she was saying."

"What did she say to you, Mrs. Finch? Take your time, but tell me exactly what she said."

"She said I was spreading rumors about her and I would pay for it."

"What rumors?"

"She didn't say. You have to understand. Lizzy is my friend, but she wasn't making any sense. She's on antidepressants or antipsychotics for her moods, but I don't think she's taking them. She said she was going to kill Cody because he's sweet on her daughter. I didn't believe her. They've been hanging out a lot. She didn't want Cody near Mia. I knew it from the start, but you know how kids are."

After a pause, Lange said, "She used those words? 'I'm going to kill Cody.' Did she say those words, Mrs. Finch?"

Zoey began crying and nodding, *yes*. Lange turned, and the detective at her side leaned toward her, one ear pointed at her mouth. Shaw caught the words she whispered to him—search warrant. He walked away at a brisk pace, phone out, and when he got to his car he left in a hurry.

Chief Vincent Shaw was troubled. Lizzy Jenkins was Myrtle's friend. He knew Lizzy, and she hadn't struck him as the violent type. Yes, she did have psychological issues, that much was clear. But violent? She was a librarian, for Christ's sake. She saw more of her own two feet whenever he had met her than of his face. A timid woman, wouldn't hurt a fly, as far as he could see. But Shaw knew there was no way to tell what a person would do, given the right, or wrong circumstances. He was willing to accept the possibility Lizzy Jenkins had run down a child in the road, although it seemed highly unlikely to him.

Charlotte Lange led him away from the ambulance, her hand on his arm.

"Thank you, Chief Shaw," she said, and shook his hand again, but held it longer this time.

By God, I can't wait to tell Myrtle the Big Cheese Cop has the hots for me.

He watched her walk toward the tent to look at the body. A sudden wave of sadness washed over him. He had been keeping it at bay ever since he'd arrived. Murder was extremely rare in these parts. The murder of a child was the worst, though. He had seen the expressions on the faces of the detectives who went in and out of the tent. He wasn't the only one who was going to see those horrendous crush injuries to Cody Finch's chest in his nightmares, and the tire marks …

He almost called Myrtle but didn't. He'd talk to her later.

Sergeant Ross Harper approached him as Shaw saw more cars and vans arrive.

"The media is here."

"Great," Shaw said, and as he walked toward the cordon, he was adding up in his mind the sum of how much he was going to give them.

Not much.

58

Lizzy had vacuumed and scrubbed the floors and the house smelled of the Citrus Fresh odor of Pledge multi-surface cleaner. There was a knock on the door. The knock had the weight of authority behind it, an official note that made her nervous. She'd barely had a minute to appreciate the order she had brought to chaos. If it was Marcus looking for his things, clothes and whatever godforsaken items he used to facilitate his acts of depravity on her *pretend friend*, he'd have to come back later. It had occurred to Lizzy that if Marcus owned a porn phone, he had probably concealed other sordid instruments in the house. Maybe Marcus was outside, hoping to reduce the trail of evidence against him, eager to remove the mementos of his infidelity.

She was startled as two policemen appeared in her backyard. *What in God's name …?*

The knocking resumed—impatient, demanding, urgent. Lizzy pulled her cardigan tight.

Who's afraid of the big bad wolf?

Lizzy came to an abrupt stop in the entrance hall, head tilted to the side as though the voice was outside her head. Why should she be afraid? *Not me*, she thought, *not anymore. I am the big bad wolf.*

A woman thrust a piece of paper at her when she opened the door. Lizzy didn't even glance at it. "Search warrant," she said, and Lizzy absorbed the red leather jacket. The tight jeans.

Oh my God, she thinks she's in CSI: Miami.

The nastiness in that thought, the scorn in its tone, prompted Lizzy to lick her lips and smile. She didn't care about this woman on her doorstep, this red leather whore, or the cops behind her. Lizzy Jenkins was done being scared.

A horde of policemen pushed past her and Lizzy stood aside. A tow truck pulled up on the street and backed into her driveway.

A man in plainclothes approached her. "Mrs. Jenkins, I'm detective Paul Wharton, Suffolk County PD. I'd like to ask you a few questions." Lizzy looked up at him and Miss Red Leather standing beside him.

She nodded and they followed her into the living room.

***

Mia heard the knocking and ignored it, at first. She had been trying to contact Cody all morning. His cell phone was off, and he wasn't answering on Twitter or Facebook. She'd sent a dozen or so messages and got no response. It was unusual. Cody was always quick to reply. Exasperated and a little worried, she rose from her bed and went to the window. Her mouth dropped open at the sight of police cars on Garden Street, their large number suggesting something serious had happened. She was rooted to the floor, watching as Mom's Spark was towed out of the driveway, covered in some kind of plastic, as though it was being protected from the elements.

The voices outside were now inside her home.

She went downstairs, confused, the little ball of worry in the pit of her stomach growing, moving higher, into her chest, settling in her throat, which was suddenly dry.

Mia walked past police officers on legs that seemed heavy, numb. She found Mom in the living room. A man and a woman were asking her questions, but Mia had noticed Mom had cleaned. A lot had happened recently, and she had kept to herself, stayed in her room most of the time, ignoring Dad's many phone calls. She would talk to him, just not yet. The fact that Mom had cleaned the house was an amazing development, a cause for hope. Mom often let things slide when she was ill, leaving Mia and Dad to straighten up. But when she was feeling good, when the clouds parted, Mom cleaned house. Now these police officers were turning it upside down, ransacking their home.

"What's going on?" Mia asked, and several pairs of eyes were instantly on her.

**

"These nice police officers just want to ask me a few questions," Lizzy said. Mia sat next to her on the sofa, and Lizzy put an arm around her shoulders and squeezed. "My daughter, Mia," she said, injecting a note of pride into her voice. Because she was proud of Mia.

"Mom," Mia said, "they took your car."

"Oh," Lizzy said, directing her questioning stare to Wharton, who was sitting on the edge of the sofa across from Lizzy.

"That's right," Wharton said, "we just have to run some tests and we'll have it back in no time."

"I need my car back."

Wharton looked at something of sudden interest in his notebook. Then Miss Red Leather Jacket, the woman who had introduced herself as detective Charlotte Lange, said, "How did the blood get on your bumper?"

"Excuse me?"

"Mrs. Jenkins—"

"Lizzy. My name is Lizzy. L-I-Z-Z-Y. Lizzy."

Lange stared at Lizzy for what seemed like an age, and Lizzy stared right back.

I'd scratch your eyes out and hand them to you, bitch, if I had half a chance. Coming into my house with your smug face and your bad attitude.

"There was blood on the left front wheel and on the bumper of your car," Lange said. "Lizzy."

Oh, you tramp. You're trying to provoke me.

It wasn't going to work, though. Lizzy wasn't going to fall for it. "Yes. And?"

Now it was the detectives' turn to show irritation; Lizzy saw it, and the satisfaction she derived from it was surprising in its power and intensity. Lizzy felt certain doors in her mind swinging open. She went through some of those doors, but some things also crossed the threshold in the opposite direction.

"Did you run over any animals on the road that you can remember?" Wharton asked.

"If I did, I don't remember."

Mia looked up at her. "Mom, what's this all about?"

"I wish I knew. I'm guessing it's some kind of trick."

"Do you know Cody Finch?" Wharton asked.

"Sure," Lizzy said, "he's ... he's Mia's friend."

Mia straightened. "Cody? Is he all right?" Lizzy heard the concern in Mia's voice; she was confused, completely baffled as to why her daughter was worried about the welfare of a boy who had tried to drown her, a boy who was the offspring of a lying, cheating *skank* and possible Satanist, the devil's mistress.

Wharton leveled his gaze at Mia. "Did you see Cody last night?" he said.

Mia paused. Lizzy said, "It's okay, Mia. Tell him what you know." Lizzy knew they had the information already; they were just waiting to catch them in a lie.

"You won't get upset?"

"No, Mimi, I won't."

"He came by last night," Mia said, "but he was only here for a few minutes. Is he all right?"

"He was here, in your house?" Lange asked.

Lizzy looked at Mia.

"We met outside. In the backyard. I'm sorry, Mom."

"It's all right," Lizzy said, squeezing her shoulders.

"Is Cody okay?" Mia asked again.

"Did you leave the house last night, Mrs. Jenkins?" Wharton said.

"No," Lizzy said, "I was here all night."

"You didn't drive somewhere? Went to a store or—?"

"I didn't leave the house last night," Lizzy said, and Wharton glanced at Mia. Lizzy felt Mia nodding against her shoulder.

"Did you call Zoey Finch last night?"

And this time Lizzy knew the *pretend friend* had put her in the frame. It wasn't good enough that Zoey had slept with her husband, engaged in perversions that would shame the devil, but now Zoey was plotting something even more nefarious, a plan so wicked she couldn't even guess the nature of it. Zoey must be conspiring with Marcus. Myrtle was probably in on it, too. Peyton was part of it because she was a follower; Zoey was a powerful friend to have, an influential ally in whatever half-baked scheme Peyton was daydreaming about. They were all going to trick her. It wasn't enough that she was humiliated, *violated*. They were determined to destroy her. She was overwhelmed by a sense of siege—a scared animal, cornered. But Lizzy hid it well. She wouldn't fall for any more tricks.

"*Is Cody okay?*" Mia's voice wavered with hysteria, something close to panic.

"Please," Wharton said, "your daughter shouldn't be here for this, Mrs. Jenkins."

"She has a right to hear whatever nonsense you're concocting," Lizzy said, keeping her tone casual. "You should answer her question."

"You called Zoey Finch last night?" Wharton said, as if Lizzy hadn't heard him the first time he'd asked.

"So?" Lizzy was looking at Wharton, refusing to dignify Lange with so much as a glance—the woman reminded Lizzy of Zoey. It was the high-fashion jeans and jacket, or maybe Lizzy just didn't like her face.

"What did you talk about?" Lange asked.

"Books," Lizzy said, looking at Wharton, directing her answer to him as though he had asked the question.

Lizzy could feel the detective's irritation. Good. She knew how women like Lange viewed her—from above, looking down. Because she wore cardigans and her hair was done up in a bun that more befitted an older woman and her shoes were plain and her dress was down to her ankles and she didn't wear makeup and she lacked the cool sophistication Lange seemed to believe she had monopolized. *Well, I don't have cops salivating as my ass pumps up and down like the pistons in an engine inside jeans that look like she's not even wearing them but like she was upholstered in them and I'm not putting out an air of superiority like this chinless cunt coming into my house with her fashionable clothes and her questions but I'm trying my best I'm a good person but this bitch is a manipulator—*

"Mrs. Jenkins? Are you feeling okay?" It was Wharton again, with more useless questions.

"I've had enough of this charade," Lizzy said. "Why are you here?"

"*Is Cody okay?*" Mia's voice had taken on a sharper edge.

"Please, Mrs. Jenkins, if you'd just answer a few more—"

"*IS CODY OKAY?*"

59

As he passed the chemistry department of Boston College on Beacon Street, Arthur recalled Roger telling him how lucky he felt to live here in beautiful Newton, one of the wealthiest suburbs in Massachusetts. And Arthur had smiled as if he'd agreed. But he didn't agree, and if he could have traveled back in time, Arthur would wipe that stupid smile off his own face by pinching the soft flesh on his inner arm to remind himself that just because someone else was fake it didn't mean you had to be fake, too. Luck had nothing to do with Arthur's rightful position on the top rung of the success ladder; there was nothing accidental about his mansion on Buckminster Road in Brookline, a mile and a half behind him—he deserved it. It was another addition to the long list in his mental ledger entitled *Reasons I Hate Roger Berris*: contrived humility. It was as though Roger believed it gave him the appearance of being just another down-to-earth humble success story, reducing his superior achievements in order to make himself look ... superior. Arthur snorted, clenched the marbles in his fist, one hand on the wheel, the muscles in his jaw twitching. He was grinding his teeth again, and even though he was aware of it, he couldn't stop. All he had to do was open his mouth, or risk yet another ferocious, evil headache.

What's one more goddamn headache?

He dropped the marbles into the cup holder as an idea occurred to him. He was on the road to his destiny, and a moment as momentous as this demanded he put both hands on the wheel; a man should drive toward his fate with both hands steering the way. He felt the ghost of Arthur Senior nodding agreement. His constant passenger was with him to witness the takedown of his tormentor, his bully, Judas Berris. He could feel Arthur Senior, an undeniable presence, a stubborn residue, somewhere in the murk, far back in the chaos of his thoughts, watchful. Ever watchful. He was at least sure of one thing—Mr. Pinch wouldn't terrorize him tonight. He was being a good son. It was Arthur Senior's Main Rule: *be a good son.* To obey his father's Rule meant not letting his inferiors trample him. *Son, if you ever let anyone take advantage of you, I'll kill you. If I die and you let someone win at your expense, I'll come back and fucking haunt you.* Arthur Senior was a man who didn't make idle threats and always kept his promises.

He couldn't sleep with the light on for the rest of his life. Arthur was going to kill Roger Berris and his wife. It didn't feel like an extraordinary thing to do, either. Arthur had already experienced the slow surprise at how natural it was to plan a double murder.

He had driven past his house on Buckminster, but there didn't appear to be any sign of media vans. Or police cars. But he wasn't taking any chances. He feared the police might be lying in wait, waiting for him to walk into their trap. And maybe the vultures had flown the nest when they realized the big bird wasn't there. Whatever the case, he had continued on, sunglasses on and baseball cap low. He was keen to avoid making the same mistake twice: if he'd remembered to conceal his identity, Jon Finch wouldn't have recognized him. The Finches' day of reckoning was fast approaching, too. Arthur hadn't given up on the notion of extracting further payment from them, however messy it became.

60

There was a small part of Roger Berris that believed Arthur wouldn't do anything crazy. But the larger, louder part of him suggested it would be unwise to take any chances. The gun stuffed between the hard leather cushion and the armrest of his office chair served as insurance; Regina was in bed, snoring like a sailor on shore leave, and she would have said he was the crazy one if she knew about the weapon tucked two inches from his hip. The TV was muted, and Roger clicked through the news channels. He was looking for reports on his old—former—friend. A snippet telling him Arthur had broken some law somewhere and was currently in police custody. He was keeping one eye open for reports on himself, too; even now, Roger was wondering if the deal he'd done with the Finches amounted to insider trading. But the more pressing question on his mind was what Arthur would do next.

Not so long ago, Arthur had dined with Roger and Regina. As a guest, Arthur was second to none. He was full of talk, humor, bantering back and forth with Regina. That Arthur was gone. The same Arthur whose eyes would widen when Regina brought out her homemade Black Forest cake, full of praise and delight, asking for the recipe, to which

Regina would only smile and point-blank refuse to give up her secret. That Arthur would take it in the good-natured way it was intended. What about now? The Arthur Now would probably rant and rave and complain and his eyes would shine with a peculiar black light he'd seen firsthand over the past few weeks. His dismay at the sudden change in Arthur had tapered off to a manageable level. He had spent too many days standing at his window overlooking the parking lot at Zinco, attempting to process why Arthur was steering their ship into the rocks. It would have been a relief to discover Arthur had an alcohol or drugs or gambling problem, something you could lay hands on; all three of those things held the possibility that they could be solved. But Roger sensed it was far worse—Arthur was dangerous, and Jon Finch's sighting of him in Sag Harbor was all the confirmation he needed. Arthur had no history with the place, no reason to be there. Unless it was to exact revenge on the Finches. However, Arthur appeared to have given up the notion of making the Finches pay, because he hadn't heard anything from Jon. He had advised Jon to keep his family close. He just hoped Finch had heeded his warning.

Arthur hadn't given him a choice, but he wouldn't see it that way. Arthur would see simple treachery, nothing less. And since Jon hadn't called, he figured Arthur was going to make him see the error of his ways first.

Come and get it, Arthur. I'll be waiting.

61

Benny Cooper was driving, using the hands-free kit; he'd been on the phone a long time. He didn't talk, just listened. Whatever one-way conversation he was engaged in, it only added an extra layer of tension to an already fraught atmosphere. When Benny became quiet, Ken Brooks became nervous. Not for the first time, it occurred to him that Benny was the most dangerous man he had ever met. He had encountered Mexican cartel members and not been afraid. But he had seen Benny's handiwork. Funny thing was, Benny had a sense of humor. He was easygoing, for the most part. Except when the laughter dropped from his eyes—then you saw the danger, the quiet menace simmering in those black eyes. In Benny's mind, killing a man quickly was a wasted opportunity. This, Ken had experienced up close. If it didn't take hours for the poor unfortunate focus of his displeasure to die … well, where was the satisfaction in that?

From his perch on the bench in the rear of the van, he glanced at his boss. His head was cocked—whoever he was listening to must have one hell of a story to tell. Ken was nervous about the job, true, but he would do anything for Benny Cooper. Even though it was the most insane job he had ever agreed to, he would see it through. Because without Benny, he'd be dead and buried a long time ago. And he paid well. He was just being honest with himself—no one paid like Benny, who had bought Ken's loyalty in more ways than one. At least it wasn't all for monetary gain.

He looked at the Bullet at his feet. It was similar to the ones used by SWAT teams for dynamic entry, as they called it. Except this one was different. There were four handgrips, two on each side of a thick cylinder filled with molten lead. Handmade by Benny, it required two men to use because it was heavy. Benny had explained his reasoning for producing such a weighty instrument: "You want to knock only once," he'd said. "If you have to knock twice, it might give the people inside a second to react. Knock once, and you're in."

He raised his eyes and stared at George Howard, who was eating quinoa from a plastic container that might have been Tupperware. The worst thing was, he was eating it with relish. He was enjoying it. His friend drank from a bottle filled with some green liquid, probably blitzed kale or avocado or a combination of same. There was a pack of dried apricots on the custom-built bench next to George. Ken's stomach cringed. George had told him that *eating clean*—whatever that meant, since Ken had been going through life accompanied by the working assumption that the food he ate *was* clean—was like wearing a Kevlar vest against pathogens, but for your insides. Eating clean was bulletproofing for the mind and body. Ken would have mocked him, except that George had become immune to mockery. Maybe George was on to something—perhaps the green drink and the apricots made him impervious to insults, because Ken launched as many as he could conjure at any given moment. Especially when his nerves were buzzing, like now. Another source of irritation was George's Instagram account—#greenandmean. He posted pictures there of his recipes. And, to Ken's amazement, he had followers. Thousands of them. Last time he'd looked, George had two-hundred-plus thousand fellow avocado fetishists.

"Seriously," he said, "how do you eat that shit?"

George frowned. "Same way you eat shit, with my mouth."

"Touché, motherfucker."

George lifted his T-shirt, which was truly disturbing: Tony Robbins's face covered the entire front of it, smiling out at Ken. Apparently, George needed a motivational speaker, maybe to get him through the torture of ingesting various vegetables and blended drinks throughout the day.

"See these abs," George said, "now show me yours." Ken looked at his best most hated friend, at his cargo shorts (what kind of man wore cargo shorts on his way to commit a crime?), at his sharply defined abdominals, and lifted his plain black shirt, unveiling the slope of a generous gut. "I do have abs," Ken said, "underneath prob'ly ten pounds of fat. Just because you can't see my abs doesn't mean they're not there."

George laughed, keeping the volume low. Benny was still listening.

Ken brought up a point of genuine curiosity. "Don't you get a lot of gas? Gas pains?"

"I use root ginger to tackle the worst of it."

Ken nodded. *Motherfucker has it all figured out.*

"You know," George continued, "let's get down to real talk here. Those ACE inhibitors you've been using for your high blood pressure could be a thing of the past if you tried some of this. Do you cough a lot?"

"No," Ken lied, "just in the morning, gets worse at night. What's it to you? You're a doctor now?"

"It's a bad side effect of blood pressure pills, Ken. Dry, hacking cough, won't go away. Even when you stop taking them, the cough can last for weeks, if you're lucky. If you're unlucky it could last for months."

"What makes you an expert?"

"Nothing. Nothing at all … okay. My grandma had to take those pills. I couldn't do much for her coughing except rub her back and make her a honey and lemon drink. Maybe I'm coming at this the wrong way. So here's something you'll understand—dollars and cents. Drugs cost money, and doctors, too. How much are you spending a month on doctors and pills?"

"None of your business, that's how much."

"All right. What if I said you could save thousands—literally thousands of honest-to-God dollars—every year by changing your lifestyle. Get rid of the belly fat, drop the salt—who knows? You might get a good night's sleep at last."

"Are you saying I look tired?"

"I am. Not sleeping well, huh? The coughing, Ken. My grandma, remember? She barely slept."

Ken was silent for a moment, staring at his most hated friend, hating him even more, because George had homed in on a terrible and ugly truth: the pills were taking the wind out of his sail. His stomach hurt from coughing and the headaches were more frequent and vicious.

"Okay," Ken said, "let's say I buy into your bullshit. How would I go about it?"

"You could start by following me on Instagram—"

"Go fuck yourself."

"Let me finish," George said, holding his palm toward Ken, "I meant to give you tips on diet. Exercise, too. Look at me. Take a good look."

"I'm looking. So what?"

"What do you see?"

"A talking asshole."

"I'm forty-two, Ken, and I'm *ripped.* You think I need Viagra? Goddamn straight I don't. I'm not spending perfectly good money on doctors that I could spend on myself. Why spend it on dick pills and blood pressure pills?"

"There's nothing wrong with my dick."

"I didn't say there was. But trust me, Ken, that's in the mail, on its way to you if you don't make a change to your lifestyle. Change your philosophy on life."

Ken wasn't aware he had a philosophy on life. He ignored the comment, and said, "It must be so easy for you, looking down on the rest of us mere mortals."

George raised his eyebrows, high. "Easy? You've got to be kidding me, right? I didn't say anything about easy. I can guarantee you this: it's horrible at first, the adjustment, but you do get used to it." That was another reason he hated George: you couldn't even argue with him. Sometimes, he was so reasonable Ken just wanted to punch him square in the face. On the other hand, he was in the company of the only two people he trusted.

As much as he hated to admit it, Ken thought George *had* figured out life, or maybe he'd just found the best way to live his. To look at him, in his cargo shorts, his tanned muscles, and his Tony Robbins T-shirt and an eight-pack with crevices deep enough to cast shadows, you'd never guess George Howard was a stone-cold killer. You'd never guess—

The van sped up, turned sharply. One of the earphones was dangling from Benny's ear. The Ford came to a hard stop; Benny climbed in back, crouched on the floor, and said, "There's been a slight change in our plan."

62

Arthur cruised along Bigelow Road, the sun flashing through the trees, the houses on both sides of the road becoming more expensive, larger, a pleasant slice of suburbia Roger had dreamed of owning as far back as his sophomore year in college. It was all Roger had wanted to talk about in those days, especially when he'd had a few beers. He had even described the house of his dreams: redbrick, black window shutters, white window frames, and the frosting on the cake—a white picket fence. How Arthur had laughed at him. *A white picket fence.* Who did Roger think he was, Tom Sawyer? But Roger hadn't seen the hilarity contained in sharing a dream. Arthur thought it was amusing simply because Roger's puny dream wasn't big enough. And Arthur had tried to smooth the ripple in their friendship by explaining to Roger the white picket fence should be a by-product of a bigger dream—running their own pharmaceutical company. It was easier to say he was sorry when he was younger; now, it was impossible.

He made the turn into Sylvan Avenue, a short road with generously spaced mansions, and Roger's dream house, just as he'd imagined it all those years ago. Roger's picket fence was the whitest one on the entire street. There was an empty lot next to Roger's home, a site being prepared for construction. The crime rate here was nonexistent, and there was no security keeping watch on the blue shipping container and its contents. Arthur parked behind it and killed the engine. He took the gun from the glove compartment and absorbed its weight, the deadly promise it held. He wondered how he was going to handle Missy, Regina's little dog, a Bichon Bolognese. The mutt was prone to fits of yipping and yapping.

Bolognese. What kind of animal names a dog after a pasta dish?

Arthur wasn't going to shoot a dog. He couldn't bring himself to do it. He had done some terrible things, was about to do something even worse, but killing a dog was the Line, and he wasn't going to cross it. Missy slept at the bottom of the bed, on Regina's side. Roger had mentioned it to him once, or three times, he couldn't recall, and in less than glowing terms. Something about how Missy snored, as did Regina, and Roger had had to suffer through yet another duet that caused him a sleepless night.

His thoughts and emotions were like a crown of thorns inside his head. Arthur was utterly helpless. Roger was responsible for it; he couldn't turn back now even if he'd wanted to. Arthur was eyeball to eyeball with the prospect of revenge, an overwhelming temptation. He was powerless to resist.

Through gaps in the hedges, he could see the house, but no movement. He waited for nightfall.

63

Benny laid it down flat: the consequences. Ken shifted on the bench to look at him.

"We're in the parking lot of the Hyatt Place Hotel in Garden City, which means we're not far. I'm asking both of you to think seriously about whether or not you want to do this. The job is going to attract federal attention. That's written in stone, you can bet on it. Our client has increased his offer due to the slight change in the plan."

"By how much?" Ken asked.

"Two million." Ken's eyes widened; he felt George shift again on the bench across from him.

"Your guy isn't fucking with us, is he?" George said.

"Three million each," Benny said. "He trusts me, so he's paid me already. He knows I'm going to do the job. If you're in, the money'll be paid to you when we get back down south. But there's always a catch, huh? A little fly in the ointment. If either one of you gets picked up by the feds, I need to know if you're going to accept the consequences." Ken was familiar with the consequences, and George had a keen understanding of them, too. Once the feds—or any other law enforcement agency—questioned either Ken or George or both, they were dead. Prison bars were meaningless if Benny wanted somebody whacked. In fact, prison bars made it easier. Benny, and some of his associates south of the border, didn't even have to visit the inmate who'd carry out the murder, just his family, pay them, and the family would pass the message on to their son, usually a life-without-parole prisoner keen to help those he'd left behind on the outside, because you could only sentence someone to life once. A guy with a ninety-nine-year sentence to look forward to wouldn't blink at the prospect of an additional ninety-nine years. Benny had had seven men murdered—that he knew of—in prisons around the country. He and George would be next if they were caught. Funny thing was, Ken reflected, Benny wouldn't enjoy it. Not like he enjoyed torturing the lawyer. Benny was offering him an out, and it was genuine, but Ken didn't want it.

"How much heat are we talking?" he asked.

"All of it, Ken. We're talking national news here, too."

Ken and George glanced at each other. George shrugged, and said, "Fuck it, I'm in."

Benny was looking at him. Ken said, "I don't want to hurt any kids."

"No one's hurting any kids, Ken. That's why I'm leaving that part to you, if you want it." Ken looked at the battering ram, the sports bag filled with guns. Funny thing about Benny was, he didn't force anyone to do anything they didn't want to. Benny was looking for volunteers; Ken understood it. The willing were reliable and tended to do a good job.

"Who are we doing this for?" Ken said.

"Does it matter?"

Ken kept his mouth shut and just stared at Benny, who let loose a long sigh.

"All right. Man runs a pharmaceutical company. I don't name names, Ken, as you know. I can't back out of a deal like this—word got around, no one would work with us again. You want to retire after the job's done, Ken, you're welcome to it. I won't like it, but there won't be any hard feelings over it. You too, George. You want to retire to some white sandy beach somewhere, I won't like it, either. But I'll live with it."

There was something different in Benny's face. Ken couldn't decide what it was, exactly. He'd known Benny ten years, and yet he hadn't fooled himself into thinking he actually *knew* him. Benny didn't let anyone peek behind the curtain. He could only judge him on his past actions: Benny had taken care of him in the decade they'd been friends, and as a result, Ken lived a good life.

"I'm in," Ken said, "I was always in, but you knew that already, didn't you?"

64

Roger poured three fingers of Johnnie Walker Black Label from his Waterford crystal decanter—three fat fingers. He returned to his chair, resting the tumbler on his knee. Regina had stopped snoring. She was moving around upstairs. He had hoped she would listen to his suggestion earlier that she not cook dinner and instead order some Chinese. But Regina was stubborn, flu or not. It was a particularly vicious strain, and so far, Roger had somehow dodged it. He continued clicking through channels on the TV. No news about Arthur. He checked his phone for news out of Long Island, scrolling until he had zoned out. Then something caught his eye. He sat up. His eyes fastened on the words *Suffolk County Police are investigating ... hit and run ... Cody Finch.* Arthur. He'd really murdered a child. He swallowed hard, about to call Jon, but paused. Regina was coming down the stairs, coughing, blowing her nose. She appeared in the doorway of his office looking exhausted, haggard, her bleary eyes watery with little streaks of red. "You're still up?"

"Can't sleep," Roger said, and Regina sat on the chaise longue across the room. Roger would have smiled at how considerate she was being (she didn't want him to catch her flu) if he wasn't in shock. Regina was staring at him and

Roger dropped his gaze to the floor.

"All right, Roger, what's wrong?" She sounded badly congested.

"I shouldn't have done it."

"What? Oh. You were right, baby. Arthur was wrong."

He held the phone out to her and she came over, took it from him.

"Oh my God, you don't think—"

"I *do* think," he said, and she handed the phone back to him and returned to the chaise.

"You didn't do anything wrong. You had to do it. It was your business, too."

"I keep telling myself that. I had to. Arthur turned me into a rat, and now it looks like he killed a kid."

"You don't know for certain it was him, Roger … and realistically, what were you going to do—let him ruin the business you helped build, let him destroy everything you worked for? Arthur doesn't strike me as a killer, babe. He's got a few nuts and bolts loose upstairs, but a killer?"

"I used to believe that, too. How can we know what goes on in someone's mind? I was worried about his mental state for a long time and I didn't do anything."

Roger heard the anger rising in Regina's voice. "Since when did you become a babysitter to a grown man?" she said. "He was going to bring you down and by the way you tell it, he wasn't going to lose any sleep over it."

"I know I did the right thing but … he hasn't mentioned his parents to me in the forty years I've known him."

"So?"

"I did some research to find out what happened to his mother. She was committed to Danvers State Hospital when

Arthur was two, so I assume he doesn't remember her."

"The state insane asylum? What did she do?"

"She murdered a woman in Bridgewater. And ate her."

He watched as Regina pulled her bathrobe tight around her shoulders.

"Arthur's mother was a cannibal? Oh my god, Roger, why didn't you say something?"

"The usual reason. I didn't want to scare you. When was the last time you saw Arthur?"

Regina paused while she tried to remember. Then she said, "A year or so, probably."

"It might be more than a year. If you met Arthur now, you'd recognize his face, but you wouldn't recognize *him*. I knew this man for forty years. The sudden change in his personality … I should call Suffolk County PD and let them know of my suspicions."

He didn't want to tell her any of this. Her face was drawn, anxious.

"Jon Finch called me some time ago and said he saw Arthur in Sag Harbor. Now Jon's son is dead. It can't be a coincidence."

Regina nodded. "I feel sick. I'm going to go back to bed." She held out her hand as she passed him and he squeezed it. Kisses were out of the question, too, at least until she was feeling better.

Roger drank the rest of the whisky in two gulps and dialed Suffolk County PD.

"I have some information about a hit and run in Sag Harbor," he said.

He spent ten minutes speaking to a detective, then poured himself four fingers of whisky, downed it, hesitated by the drinks cabinet and poured again, filling the tumbler halfway.

He unmuted the TV, kept the volume low. He was sure he had locked the windows and doors, but he got up to check.

65

Arthur couldn't believe his good fortune. He'd climbed the poor excuse for a wall that bordered the Berris's property, headed for the sliding door; two upright rectangles of yellow light spilled onto the grass in Roger's backyard. Roger was home. On the deck, Arthur passed the garden dining table and chairs (all cast iron. None of that plastic shit for Roger, the Success Story) and the redbrick barbeque, knelt beside the slider and pushed the handle. It gave enough to let him know it was open. He didn't believe it; it was too good to be true. Roger locked the doors in his house, despite living in a wealthy neighborhood. Arthur knew why—Roger didn't trust anyone, least of all the rich. He knew why Roger painted his picket fence out front, even if Regina didn't. It was because Roger believed the American dream required maintenance. You couldn't let the paint dry out, curl and flake off: Roger saw it as something physical to be protected from rot. Because, deep down, Roger believed it was an illusion, that his hard-earned, hard-won gifts would one day be taken from him when those in charge realized there had been a mistake.

He was about to reach for the handle again, and paused. What if it was a bear trap? What if Roger was the big juicy berry and all he had to do was walk inside? When he did, the door would lock behind him. He had expected to work to gain entry. He'd gone through several ideas on how to get Roger to open the door, each one more ridiculous than the last. The one that seemed feasible was knocking on the front door, hiding in the bushes as Roger came to see who was calling. But he knew Roger. He was too smart to fall for it. He wasn't going to come outside with a flashlight like a guy in a horror movie. Plan B was crude but direct: he had a hammer that would break the glass quickly, the kind with the sharp business end they had on some buses in case the bus burst into flames and you had to break a window fast.

He took one last look at the deck, the barbeque. How many times had he been invited here to eat? He and Roger flipping burgers and cooking the steak just right, drinking beer and exchanging stories they'd heard of what was happening in the pharmaceutical business, throwing the occasional rumor of a burgeoning scandal into the mix to spice things up. Good times, gone.

Get on with it.

He eased the door open, creating a gap wide enough for him to fit through. He closed the slider and crept forward, lightening his step, gun raised.

He came to a sudden stop as a tinkling sound reached him. It was unmistakable—it was Roger's wedding band striking glass. Roger was drinking. So that was why he'd forgotten to lock the doors.

Panic seized him. There was movement in the living room. His heart leaped, doing a frenzied drum roll in his chest.

Arthur headed out of the kitchen, away from Roger. In

the hallway, back against the wall, he peered around the corner. Roger was locking the slider. *Bear trap*.

He praised Regina for her love of carpet: the hallway and stairs were carpeted, and Arthur proceeded at a brisker pace, climbed the stairs, paused on the landing, listened.

He was drawn toward the soft guttural snoring noises coming from a room further down. Regina.

He continued along the hall. Her bedroom door was open. He craned his head around the doorframe, and there she was, a lump under the bedclothes. The mutt was at her feet, also asleep, and also snoring. But the dog couldn't compete with Regina. Arthur felt the vibrations of the noise she produced with each long breath. He stood in the doorway, his shadow stretching before him, cast by the light at his back.

He moved toward the bed.

66

Roger's moment had arrived, even though he could hardly believe it. Arthur was in his house. He'd not only seen Arthur's reflection in the mirror that hung on the far wall of the living room, but he had heard him. Arthur probably thought he was being quiet. But fabric and shoes made noise. He was so used to Regina's snoring that he could hear all other sounds beneath the endless aural assault of his wife's breathing. She refused to seek treatment for it, despite him recording the almighty, awe-inspiring respiratory rumblings and playing the evidence for her. Regina would not accept she snored like an overweight construction worker with sleep apnea. Even faced with proof, her infuriating, dismissive shrug was all Roger needed to drop the subject. Never mind that she choked in her sleep, waking and panting, her breath catching as if her airway had suddenly closed, and the whole unmusical nightmare would begin again a minute or less later and the discordant orchestra would continue until she choked yet again, woke and panted, and it was like God had singled Roger out for special punishment.

He locked the sliding door. The last thing he wanted was for Arthur to escape.

He went back to the living room, but he didn't sit. He

remained standing against the wall, gun raised. He guessed Arthur was in the entrance hall. He waited, wondering why Arthur hadn't crept up behind him and blown his brains out. He could have attempted it. But not Arthur. No. Because Roger knew Arthur better than anyone. Arthur was going after the person he cared about most, Regina, snorer extraordinaire.

Roger wished he'd set a trap for Arthur, but it wasn't the case.

Caught me slipping.

Indeed. And now Regina's life was in danger. He had considered the possibility that Arthur would stop by sometime, but he hadn't really believed it. Until now, when it was probably too late.

Roger wasn't about to give up without a fight, though.

He returned to the kitchen, gun now held in two hands, pointed at the dimly lit doorway that led into the entrance hall.

He moved forward slowly, his breath stopped. What if Arthur was waiting for him behind the wall?

His heart was the loudest sound, high in his chest, beating panicked rhythm into his neck.

Roger had experienced fear before, but the terror of a man with something to lose was unlike anything he'd had to struggle with in his life: the fear of losing Regina, the woman who massaged his head when he had a stress headache, the woman who loved him when he made a mistake, when he fell short of his own high expectations, the woman who told him everything was going to be all right when times were tough—the sheer terror at the prospect of losing her, the weight of it, was crushing him as he approached the doorway and what lay beyond.

He had to hurry.

Roger crossed the threshold in a jerky leap, the gun shaking in his hand, but he stilled the tremor with a supreme effort. Arthur wasn't behind the wall. He looked up at the upper hall and caught sight of Arthur walking along the wall, following his shadow.

Roger went up the stairs, and suddenly he was light-headed.

Breathe. Jesus Christ, breathe.

And Roger breathed, desperately trying to muffle the sound.

He was halfway up the stairs. If Arthur turned around now, he would see him.

Roger wasn't much for praying, but he prayed as each stair dropped behind him on his ascent to the top of the house. One good shot, well-aimed, would be enough.

He paused, a cold sweat breaking out all over his body like tiny pinpricks from small icicles. *Arthur was turning.* There was nowhere to hide.

Roger raised the gun, praying his aim was true.

His gut was knotted, and he could swear on a stack of Bibles that he'd just heard the pinging noises of hunger. If he had heard it, then surely Arthur had heard it, too.

But Arthur didn't turn. At least, not toward him. Instead, he entered the bedroom. Roger vaulted the remaining stairs in a single soundless bound, hurrying toward his bedroom.

67

Arthur leaned over the bed. Regina was in a deep sleep. He paused, in awe—the volume of the rattle produced by her snoring sent vibrations through the floor, filled the room. But it wasn't loud enough to rouse her. His shadow fell over her. Gun at chest level, he reached out with his free hand and clamped it over her mouth.

Her eyes flew open. Wide. He felt Arthur Senior's approval coursing through him, expanding blood vessels, dilating his pupils. He was taking action. He was standing up to the bullies.

Her eyes focused, fixed on him. "Don't make a sound," he whispered, "or I'll kill you." She stopped struggling when he showed her the gun.

He stiffened, froze. There was someone behind him.

Arthur launched himself across the bed. Even as he was airborne, he realized he'd be dead already if he hadn't been bending over Regina. He wouldn't have had time to dive out of the way. The bullet struck the wall inches from his head.

Regina screamed.

Roger fired again.

Arthur reached for Regina's ankle, grasped it. Pulled her toward him onto the floor.

He hadn't experienced this kind of physical strength before. Regina had all the weight of a ragdoll. He jammed the gun into her neck and prompted her to stand by grabbing a handful of nightdress around the neck and pulling it up.

Arthur Senior would be so proud. His son had climbed to the top of the food chain, demonstrated his fitness. And these bullies were going to learn the true meaning of natural selection.

"Roger, I have a gun pointed at your wife's throat. Come on out, now. Don't be foolish."

Missy, the Bichon Bolognese, was barking wildly, running in a shuffling circle.

"Roger," Regina said, "don't do it. He'll kill us both."

"Shut up! Come on, Roger, you don't want me to hurt her, do you? Drop the gun, make sure I can see it." He gave the handful of nightdress a vicious twist, cinching skin in its folds. Regina cried out in pain.

"All right," Roger said. He tossed the gun outside the bedroom door. He appeared in the doorway, a silhouette, the light behind him bright. Arthur couldn't see his face. But he was going to change that. He wanted to look into the eyes of the wrongdoer, another favorite word of Arthur Senior. *You must confront the wrongdoer, son. Failure to do so could make them see you like a lion sees a gazelle with a limp.*

"Downstairs," Arthur said, pushing Regina forward but not letting go of her nightdress.

"Take it easy, Arthur."

Arthur pointed the gun at Roger. "Move," he said, "walk backward. I swear if you twitch I'll kill her." Arthur pulled the bedroom door closed, locking the yapping dog inside.

Roger complied, and Arthur watched him try not to stumble as he backed down the stairs, glancing over his shoulder every few seconds as if he was checking for obstacles. It was funny, Arthur thought, how suddenly unfamiliar Roger seemed in his own house. Arthur knew it was raw panic. And he knew Roger was searching for a way out of his current, less than promising, situation. Arthur grinned, amused at Roger's optimism. *There's no way out.*

"Arthur, please," Regina said, "why are you doing this?"

Arthur ignored her question. The terror underneath the question didn't go unnoticed. The bullies were scared. Arthur Senior would be so, *so* proud.

At the bottom of the stairs, Arthur nodded toward the living room. "If you disappear from my sight once, Roger, she's dead. Understand?" Roger nodded. Of course Roger understood. Arthur could smell the booze, but the most important thing was that Roger understood: his life was hanging by a thread, as was his wife's. His appearance had seemed to have a sobering effect on Roger. He was wide-eyed, the eyes themselves watery, and Arthur recognized the film of moisture as terror. He'd felt his own eyes fill with a similar film whenever Mr. Pinch visited him.

In the living room, Arthur pointed the gun at a chair, and said to Roger, "Sit."

When Roger had lowered himself into the armchair, he said, "Arthur, it isn't as bad as it seems."

"How would you know?" Arthur asked, a sneer on his lips. "How would you know how anything *seems* to me?" He jammed the barrel of the gun into the side of Regina's head.

Roger's hands flew up. "Okay, *okay*! Tell me what you want. How can I fix this?"

Arthur laughed; it was derisive, but it wasn't without genuine mirth. "You always cracked me up, Roger. I'll give you that much. Fix? Can you time travel, Roger?"

"What?"

"Time travel. Can you go back in time and not conspire with Finch and his smug wife to cheat me out of the company I started?"

"*We* started, Arthur."

"There's no *we* anymore, Roger. Do you understand the position you've put me in?"

"Look, Arthur. I'm sorry. I had to do it. You were destroying Zinco."

"I was saving it, Roger. But you didn't answer my question. Or maybe you don't understand it. The position you put me in is one where I don't care about consequences. Do you know what that means?"

And, of course, Roger pretended to consider the question, but Arthur knew he was stalling for time, the way out, a painless exit. His gaze didn't waver from Roger.

"Dangerous," Arthur said, "a man with no fear of consequences … is dangerous."

Arthur cocked the gun. As he squeezed the trigger, he didn't blink, didn't tear his stare away from Roger. He wanted to see his reaction, all of it. He wanted to hear his pain, taste it.

Regina crumpled.

Roger screamed. "*NOOOOO!*"

Yes. Yes, Roger.

As he was turning to aim the revolver at Roger, his mouth dropped open. Roger had bent over, and now he was coming up, gun pointed at him. There was a brief moment of confusion: where did Roger get the gun? How had he reached for it so quickly?

His confusion was brief, but it was long enough for Roger to fire two rounds. One went wild, but the other hit Arthur in the chest. Then Arthur pulled the trigger, emptying the gun.

***

He was hit. At first, he didn't feel anything until he tried to stand. Then he felt the stinging in the side of his neck, and the dark blood shooting through his fingers. He staggered toward Regina's lifeless body. He didn't look at Arthur. Arthur was dead. He wanted to see Regina's face before—

Blood spurted between his fingers and the world swam in and out. Reality had taken on a peculiar dream-like quality. He felt as though he was trying to walk through quicksand. Roger knew it was over. He just wanted to touch Regina's face. Just one more time.

68

Only a few days had passed since Cody's death. Murder. Cody's murder, Jon reminded himself. He experienced those days through a haze of benzodiazepines; the doctor at Stony Brook hospital had pushed a bottle of pills into his hand and insisted they were for his own good. His memory of the hospital, his trip to the Suffolk County Coroner's Office for formal identification of the body, was like a projector show with some of the slides missing. Police officers and detectives had spoken to him in those few days, but Jon heard them as though they were speaking to him through a railroad tunnel. And they gave up on him, talked to Zoey instead.

He was in shock. It was the strangest feeling—it was easy to believe this had happened to someone else, that he'd left his body and was watching the horror unfold through the eyes of a bystander.

He held on to his tears, letting them fall when he was alone, caustic and bitter, but quiet. He was not inclined to share his feelings with anyone; he was determined to keep his pain, his grief concealed, not to inflict it on anyone else.

Underneath the artificial comfort blanket of the drugs, Jon knew he had to come back. At some point, he'd have to ditch the pills, because he had a family that needed him, a daughter who was mercifully too young to understand her older brother had been mowed down in the road like a rat or a possum or a squirrel—

His memory was patchy, but Jon remembered pulling the sheet back as his son lay on the slab. It was heartbreaking. He had looked so peaceful, nothing like the wreckage he'd held in his arms; no blood, no twisted limbs. As he'd looked upon his son's remains, Jon thought of all the things he'd never be able to teach Cody: beware of the wisdom of crowds, don't be a bully but don't allow himself to be bullied, but above all, he should form his own opinions and not receive them from others. He hadn't taught Cody those essential values yet because there was always time to find the right words and the right time … always time, until there wasn't.

Peggy had dropped by a few times, bearing casseroles, foil-wrapped lasagna—homemade—that just needed to be heated, pretending she was okay because someone had to be. And the strangest thing of all was that Jon had felt responsible for *her* grief, wanted to take it away if he could.

He spent most of his time upstairs, watching Jane in her crib. He held her tiny hand whenever she reached through the bars. He listened to her baby sounds, and wondered how he was ever going to let her out of his sight for a minute, a second.

Cody's body would be released to him soon. He had already made the funeral arrangements with Zoey, who had done most of the talking. He often heard her crying, sobbing quietly when she thought he was asleep. But Jon wasn't sleeping. The nightmare was too fresh.

He went downstairs to the living room. The TV was on,

and even though Zoey was watching some documentary, he knew she wasn't *seeing* it. Candice was scrolling through her phone, relaying nice tweets about Cody to Zoey, and how much he'd be missed. Zoey wasn't responding, although sometimes she issued a sound that couldn't be quite called a grunt—*huh*?

Jon sat next to Zoey and no one spoke. The documentary played on and no one was interested in it. Jon slipped another pill into his mouth and hoped tomorrow would be better. Or at least, less worse than today. Somehow, he doubted it was going to be any different from today.

69

Ken parked the van on Hollow Road near Stony Brook Cemetery, the left front wheel raised on a jack, and the wheel itself lying on the side of the road, the nail he'd driven into the tire visible to anyone curious enough to investigate. But the road was quiet, and access to the cemetery was easy. He vaulted a ramshackle obstacle that couldn't decide if it was a gate or a fence, or a hybrid of both.

The boneyard was surrounded by densely packed trees. As he wound his way toward Oak Hill cemetery, he heard someone speaking in righteous tones. A priest or pastor, Ken didn't care, he just needed to confirm they were burying the kid.

He kept his distance from the tree line, and through the binoculars he scanned the gathered mourners. He paused briefly on a woman; she was biting her lips and wringing her hands. Not the mother, he guessed; the parents were probably the man and woman with their backs to him and their arms around each other. He didn't know what Jon Finch had done, but whatever it was, it must have been serious enough that the mystery pharmaceutical CEO wanted major payback.

Some people you just don't cross.

He returned to the van and put the new wheel on.

Body snatching wasn't part of his criminal repertoire. And yet, here he was, adapting to changing times and attitudes. People wanted different things from the criminals they hired to do their dirty work these days. In the eighties and nineties, it was simpler: to make a debtor pay up, you broke their legs, robbed a jewelry store, provided papers for criminals on the lam, carried out a contract killing. Crimes he understood, could get his teeth into. There were easier ways for criminals to thrive that didn't involve grave robbing.

When Benny had first laid out the change in their plan, Ken had balked at the idea. At least he had an answer as to why two million had been added to the purse.

Purse? Like I'm a fucking golfer.

Benny had repeated his promise—no kids were getting hurt. The one in the coffin was already dead, so what was his problem?

If anyone other than Benny had been running this job, Ken didn't think he would have participated. But Benny was different, unlike any professional criminal he'd ever met. Benny was a planner, a sophisticated strategist. No detail was left to chance. Benny had adapted to the last-minute change quickly, not letting it throw him off his game. Most of the felons he had met in his lifetime were either dead or in jail. Benny had been in jail, but he had gotten out, with the assistance of some fancy legal footwork by his lawyer. He'd never returned to prison. And *he* hadn't been to the pen since he had been in Benny's employ; George was free as a bird, too. And yet Ken was uneasy about the job. He didn't want to desecrate the grave of a child. Another concern had risen to the forefront on his mental list of concerns: Ken wasn't as physically fit as Benny and George. He didn't think he ever would be, either. He accepted this fact grimly, and as much as he respected George, he would not adopt a vegan lifestyle. His diet was poor, dreadful, but it had a comfortable familiarity, even if it was clogging up his arteries. Ken would rather die satisfied than depressed.

I can't wait till this is over.

He put the wheel back on and as he was tightening the lug nuts he found himself out of breath. His bad diet was killing him, and digging up the kid tonight would more than likely finish him off. And he would do it anyway. He wasn't willing to turn up his nose at three million dollars.

Whoever the sick fuck was who contracted Benny for this job, I hope the sonofabitch dies from some necrotizing ass disease.

70

Ken's face itched as he watched Benny pour talcum powder in a rectangle, outlining the area for the dig. They had flashlights, but they were only to be used in an emergency. It was dark, and if there was a full moon, Ken couldn't see it; the canopy of trees overhead blocked whatever little light there was.

He glanced at George. The moron had turned up still wearing cargo shorts as if he was on some kind of excursion. Ken scratched his face, bracing himself for the maddening itchy prickle to come. He picked up the spade. George followed suit and, even in the gloom, Ken could make out the legs, and the thick, enormous quadriceps muscles. George was built for manual labor. Ken's eyes widened and his heart sank as George stepped on the spade's blade and it whispered softly into the ground with the ease of a knife through warm butter. Ken copied him, digging inside the white line of talc. *Oh shit*—the ground wasn't as yielding as George made it appear. It had rained the previous night. Ken decided it would be better to let his body weight do the work. He pushed himself forward, one foot on the spade, and the other foot lifted off the ground, enough so that Ken could direct all 285 pounds downward. He was in. Relief coursed through him. He had avoided embarrassing himself. He tossed his first wet clod of earth behind him.

Benny didn't waste any time. He started digging, and Ken's attention drifted back to George. The sonofabitch was a human backhoe, flinging mounds of soil past his knees. And Ken's confidence was losing its vitality; he was tired, sweaty and itchy. He was slowing down, and he felt panic rising in his chest. Benny and George were attacking the ground, their pile of black soil growing larger and *manlier.* Ken turned his head to gauge his progress: his pile of dirt was smaller, kid-sized. In full panic, he dug harder. The only sounds were the rasp of soil sliding off the blades of three spades and landing with a soft thump beside each man, and inside Ken's head, his own racing heart. Sweat flowed in rivulets down his legs, the jeans he wore trapping heat. He looked at George from the corner of his eye. *Oh, you smart motherfucker.*

Then, out of nowhere, George was standing near him, swinging the pickax at the spot Ken was digging. He couldn't see George's face in the dark, but he knew George wasn't looking at him, he wasn't making a *thing* out of this, he was helping a friend out and keeping his mouth shut about it.

He felt less like dying now that George was lending him a hand. They had made astonishing progress; Ken estimated they were halfway down.

A voice whispered in the dark. "Ken, it's time to go up." It was Benny.

"What? There's ten minutes left, by my watch. We're not done yet."

"Ken, I need eyes up top. Do it now."

He climbed out of the hole, holding on to the hope that Benny hadn't sent him to keep watch prematurely because he believed Ken was incapable of doing the job. That Ken was spent. That he had been unmanned by a simple dig.

As he stood on the edge of the graveside, looking at the top of George's head, he realized he didn't hate his old friend. He was just slightly envious of him, his lack of aversion to exercise, his dedication to keeping himself in prime condition. Ken was worried; Benny wasn't only concerned with the quality of a plan well laid and executed, but also the quality of the men he chose to be part of his crew. Ken was falling short of what was expected of him. No, Ken didn't hate George, he hated himself. He'd let his high standards slip, and maybe he wasn't the only one who'd noticed.

Ken lowered buckets tied to a rope into the grave. They were filled immediately and he hoisted them clear, dumped the soil behind him. This task was testing his physical capacity, too. As the buckets dangled briefly in the hole, either George or Benny tugged on the rope, signaling him to pull them up. His lower back and legs were screaming with the heat of pain. His entire body trembled at the insult of sudden exertion. This was the longest day of his life, and it was by no means close to being over … but they had to be close. In the dark, it was difficult to estimate depth; Ken couldn't see the floor of the grave because it had merged with the darkness.

There was a sudden pause below, followed by a soft hollow *thump, thump.*

Ken's heart rejoiced, but he couldn't enjoy it. A voice rose in a vicious whisper from the maw. "Wake up, Ken.

Lower the fucking ladder." It was Benny. Ken sensed there was no anger in Benny's tone, but he detected something else. He couldn't put his finger on it, couldn't find the word to describe it. He lowered the ladder and the ropes.

71

On his knees, Ken peered into the grave, watched as Benny and George looped the ropes through the four handles on the coffin. They came up the stepladder, George taking up the slack of two ropes and Benny and Ken pulling one rope each, tight.

"Hand over hand," Benny whispered, "begin on my count. One, two, three ..." As Benny counted, they began raising the coffin, watching each other's grip. If any of them was faster than the other, the coffin might tip over and the body could fall out.

The coffin was a strange sight. It was suspended over the open grave, and each man took the slack, taking a step forward, and another, until they had hands on the coffin's handles. They carried it to the graveside and laid it down. As Ken stood there, listening to these men breathing heavily and his own labored respiration, he realized he wasn't the only one who thought this was a bad job. None of them were enjoying taking a child from his resting place. He felt it. Benny and George didn't need to say anything. Ken tried to think of what he was going to do with his five million. A place on Key West. A quiet place to fish and watch the sun rise every morning. Somewhere to lay down a bad memory and hopefully forget about it. He hoped the scumbag who ordered this desecration would die in a car fire.

Ken's face was itching badly, but he didn't dare scratch it. He pushed the heel of his palm into the troublesome area below his cheekbone. He noticed George was pressing both palms into his face too.

"It'll pass," Benny said, "when we cool down, the itching will stop."

Ken looked forward to the aircon being turned up all the way. From here, he could see patches of white through the trees—the reefer truck. He couldn't wait to get inside.

Instead of carrying it by the handles, Benny seemed to think it was easier to carry the coffin on their shoulders. He refused George's offer to take the heavier end. To balance the coffin, Ken was on the left, with George and Benny on the right side.

It was slow going through the trees. No one wanted to trip and drop their end.

When they had passed the gray coffin over the fence, Ken hurried to the Ford Transit box truck to open the doors. He climbed inside; George and Benny lifted the coffin and Ken pulled it toward him, across the steel diamond plating on the floor. The blast of chill air from the refrigeration unit behind him cooled the itch a little, but not enough.

Ken handed the keys to George, who got in the reefer. Benny had asked Ken to hire it; they had no choice. It hadn't been part of the original plan; the client got what he wanted, though, especially when he was paying extra. Ken joined Benny in the van. The aircon was on, blasting cold air. Ken held his face close to the vent, and Benny leaned into it too.

"Not long to go," Benny said, "let's get this over with. It'll be worth it."

"Benny, I hope I'm not speaking out of turn, but are you all right?"

"A little under the weather. George recommended Goji berries for vitamin C."

They looked at each other and laughed. There was an instant release of tension.

Benny turned the key in the ignition. "Let's get closer to the target. We'll suit up then."

They left Hollow Road behind, Ken watching George in the side mirror following them in the reefer.

It's gonna be a long, long night.

72

Jon felt relieved as people began to leave. He didn't know how much more of *Sorry for your loss* he could take. The mourners in his home clearly sensed the wall he had built around himself, so they gravitated toward Zoey. *Sorry for your loss.* They meant well. Jon's level of consciousness wasn't at its best. But he knew he was being unpleasant. He wasn't tired of those gathered here to remember his son; Jon felt the need to snap out of it, even though he'd just buried his only son. He wasn't in the mood to examine this overpowering need to hold things together. He was losing patience with the unrelenting grief, the raw emptiness at his center. And it was normal, he knew. Yet, it wasn't. He had cried when they had played "Learning to Fly" by Pink Floyd at the church. It brought back Cody's love of flight, and the little dance he did whenever they were about to board a plane for a family vacation. It was a subtle shuffle of the feet, which had become less overt as the years had passed and Cody had developed new concerns: he didn't want to look like a nerd. Even though Jon had explained to him that nerds were a noble tribe. That was another thing Jon had seen take shape with stunning rapidity—Cody's increasing self-awareness. How he appeared to his peers, how he presented himself to the world. He was a kid in a big hurry to grow up. *Had*, he thought, he *had* been a kid.

But not your only child.

Candice was taking care of Jane. He still had a daughter. Jon would trade all his wealth for a guarantee that his one remaining child got through life safe. He smiled inwardly at his foolish wish, a humorless smile in the inner blackness. Maybe it was the booze combined with the pills. Even sober, reality had lost none of its surreal tint.

There are no guarantees. Life doesn't come with a warranty.

Indeed. He felt like laughing at himself, and if he did, there would be no humor in it. He remembered standing by the graveside, barely listening to the service, Zoey leaning against him. At one point, he'd had to put his arm around her waist and hold her up or she would have fallen. The last thing he had wanted was to create a scene at Cody's funeral. The faces around the grave were blurry but familiar. His mother had appeared, only for the funeral, and she had made a hasty exit when the ceremony was over. She had barely said a word. She was in shock, and it would take a while for her to come out of it. Lizzy had been there with her daughter, who had been sobbing uncontrollably. Myrtle and her husband, keeping a quiet, dignified vigil, eyes down; Peyton and her husband, who seemed to be *away on business* a lot. Marcus had been there, too, but he hadn't been standing next to Lizzy.

Now, in his living room, Peggy was walking around with a tray of food, asking people if they wanted some. He'd told her to put it down and sit down twice and twice she'd ignored him. Lizzy was sitting on an armchair on one side of the room, not looking at Marcus, and he was reclined in the writer's chair, not looking at her. He watched her get up and go in the kitchen to find Mia, who left with her, Lizzy giving Zoey a curt nod and not much else.

Ten minutes later, Marcus left, too, shaking Jon's hand and Zoey's, staring at the floor.

73

Ken parked the van in the lot that faced Mashashimuet Park. The reefer truck pulled in beside him and George got out, leaving the refrigeration unit running, and walked to the side of the van as Ken emerged from the passenger seat. George slid the van's door open for him, and eased it shut when they climbed inside.

"Here," George said, shoving a folded navy-colored boiler suit and ski mask into his chest.

"I just want to thank—" Ken began.

"Later, Ken. Let's focus here." He'd thank George later for helping him when he desperately needed it.

All three put the boiler suits on over their clothes, the ski masks sitting on their heads ready to be rolled down over their faces when it was time.

Even with the air conditioning cranked as high as it would go, it was stifling.

Benny crouched on the floor. Ken glanced at George. Benny remained silent until Ken and George looked at him. "Remember the details," Benny said, "*do not* deviate from the plan." Ken had no intention of deviating from the plan—it was reason enough to get whacked. Benny had drilled them on the plan so many times that Ken had lost count, making him and

George recite it back to him, throwing random questions at them when they least expected it, in an effort to weed out hesitation, uncertainty. "If you're nervous," Benny continued, "use it." Benny was smart enough to understand that fear wasn't an entirely negative emotion. He had explained it to Ken once, back when he was a lot younger, fitter, and prone to extreme nerves—*Lack of fear is like bobbing around on the ocean with no means of navigation. Let fear guide you, but don't let it master you.* Ken had thought it was all pop-psychology nonsense. Maybe it was. But he was sure of one thing: Benny was downright suspicious of any man who claimed he wasn't afraid of anything.

"Any questions, now is the time." Ken looked at George, then back at Benny. "All right," Benny said, "Ken, get in the driver's seat. When you're ready, start a two-minute countdown."

***

Jon made it halfway across the backyard before coming to a dead stop. He stared at the treehouse. At its dark windows. He couldn't go any further. This was his seventh attempt at crossing the yard and going inside his son's treehouse.

He returned to the house, paused in the kitchen, went upstairs. Jane was asleep in her crib. He listened to her small breaths. Looked at her little hands as they twitched, as though she was dreaming. Jon felt calmer, resolving to ditch the Valium tomorrow. If he tried to block the pain, mask its constricting power, how would he be able to appreciate the healing process? He couldn't cheat the natural order of things with drugs. Grief was indiscriminate, it didn't care how rich or poor you were or how good a human being you thought you were. Jon had tried to live a decent life, and figured that if he didn't harm anyone, he'd done all right. And yet he had harmed his family, the people closest to him, wagered their safety and happiness on a single bet. He had lost. Arthur Dunhill undoubtedly saw himself as the loser, but the Dealer had dealt him the worst hand possible. The only winner was Roger Berris; it was too late and useless to wish he had never met him.

The door opened and Candice walked into the room without asking if it was all right, if he wanted company. Since the day he'd fired her (and Zoey had rehired her) Candice had come to work late every day, sometimes not showing up at all. And she had given him a look full of challenge that seemed to say *So I'm late, what're you going to do about it?*

She sat beside him and said, "It's going to be okay, Jon." Not Mr. Finch, but *Jon*, as if they were friends. He didn't despise her for her electric blue hair, but because Candice took advantage of people and then shoved their nose in it, making sure he knew he had been taken advantage of. It was the insouciant grin, the impudent sneer as he handed over full pay for days she'd missed because Zoey had insisted she get paid, even for work she hadn't done.

"I'm really going to miss him, Jon," she said.

He didn't say anything. Instead, he watched Jane, sleeping soundly, hoping that whatever dreams she was having were good, hoping she would be spared nightmares.

Candice put her hand on his leg. "It's going to be okay," she whispered, and then her hand moved higher, towards—

He seized her hand, crushing her fingers. He swiveled towards her, and the sheer force of his fury must have scared her because she whimpered, and gasped as his grip tightened. He held up his hand, showing her the finger with his wedding band. "I'm married," he said, "and even if I wasn't, why the fuck would I dig in garbage?"

"I'm … sorry." He didn't believe her. He didn't believe Candice had been sorry once in her life.

"Touch me again," Jon said, "and I'll break your fucking fingers. Now get downstairs. Go."

***

Ken brought the van to a soft stop outside the house. He was worried the noise created by a violent entry would alert the neighbors. On the other hand, they had sixty seconds to complete the work once they were inside. He started the stopwatch. "Two minutes," he said, and Benny and George pulled the ski masks down over their faces. Ken kept watch in the rearview; they were poised at the van's door, ready to slide it back, the heavy doorknocker raised. Ken scanned the road ahead, checking all his mirrors. He saw headlights approaching, coming directly towards him.

***

In the living room, Jon walked past Candice, who gave him a sullen glance and continued scrolling through her phone. "Where's Peggy?" he asked.

"She went home," Zoey said, "she was tired." She didn't look at him. She sat on the sofa, feet tucked beneath her, pretending to watch TV. He knew what was on her mind, and he felt certain she'd get to it eventually—it was all his fault. Somehow, someway, she would find a way to blame him for their son's death. His murder. The police had towed Lizzy Jenkins's car, and when they had found no forensic evidence linking her to Cody's murder, they had returned it. It was ludicrous, anyway; Lizzy wouldn't have hurt Cody. The question was *why* Zoey thought her best friend was responsible for their loss. He'd ask that question, and many more, later. He had been calculating a few things in his mind and none of them added up. Zoey had barely spoken to him, before and after the funeral. Jon had to take a closer look at his wife, he realized as he sat next to her. She didn't close the gap between them by leaning into him, resting her head on his shoulder. From the corner of his eye, he stared at that gap.

***

Ken held his breath as the headlights washed over his face. The itch was back, but he didn't dare raise his hand to scratch it. Sweat broke out all over his body and was instantly chilled by the air conditioning. His armpits crackled with electricity and he squeezed them tight. His heart raced high and heavy in his chest. He listened to the surge of blood in his ears. Every muscle fiber was drawn taut; a vein in his neck throbbed in time to his elevated heart rate.

The car passed. He saw the brake lights fade and disappear in the side-view mirror.

He let his breath out in a shuddering gasp.

"Sixty seconds," he said, glancing in the rearview. Benny and George were coiled, ready to spring into action. They were relying on him, and again, his eyes flitted from the road ahead to the mirrors, making sure Benny and George were clear.

"Thirty seconds," he said, clenching and unclenching his free hand over and over, taking short, shallow breaths. As the seconds dropped away on the digital stopwatch, he felt his blood pressure increase, the sickening throb behind his eyes growing stronger ... but it was almost time.

"Nine, eight, seven ..." Ken leaned into the door, hand on the handle. "Three, two, one—*now!*"

74

An explosion startled Jon. He turned on the sofa toward the sudden influx of air and noise. His life didn't flash before his eyes, and time didn't slow down. The man wearing the ski mask was directly behind him, swinging the stock of what appeared to be a sawed-off shotgun at his face. It struck him on the forehead. He fell sideways, on top of a panicked body—Zoey. Somebody screamed—Zoey or Candice, he couldn't be sure. He was losing his grip on consciousness while simultaneously experiencing the horrible dream-like quality of one subjected to extreme violence.

Zoey was being dragged from beneath him, amputated from the warmth of a sofa they had bought together; suddenly, Jon was on the floor. A man stood over him; he was wearing a ski mask and a dark boiler suit, and drawing back to take a swing with a baseball bat. He glimpsed another man wielding a bat. A sickening, tuneless drumbeat began: the sound of wood striking flesh.

***

Ken had watched Benny and George run down the path, the Bullet between them. The door seemed to shimmer as the battering ram made impact, swinging inward with such force that it would have killed anyone standing on the other side of it. A chunk of wood flew over Benny's shoulder. Ken was out of the van, running. He headed for the stairs, taking them three at a time. As he reached the upper hall, he heard the distinctive snapping of bone from the living room. And the staccato thud of baseball bats ... he found the bedroom; the kid was already bawling. Ken picked her up, being careful to support her head. The baby was crying so hard that between each intake of breath there was no sound.

"It's going to be all right, kid," he whispered. "Shh, shh."

He put her in the Minnie Mouse rocker and carried her downstairs. Ken walked fast, not looking at the carnage taking place in the living room. He climbed in the van and put the rocker on the passenger seat. He turned. Benny and George were sprinting down the path toward him.

75

Ken drove back to the reefer truck where they had left it, outside Mashashimuet Park. Behind him, he heard the sounds of the Bullet being secured by Benny and George, fastening straps bolted to the floor to keep it from sliding back and forth with the motion of the van. He kept glancing at the baby in the passenger seat. Her crying had died down. He reached over and rocked her gently, searching his memory in an effort to find a song babies might like, but he couldn't think of any right now. He was waiting for the adrenaline to subside; Ken's heart was still racing. He wondered what the endgame was—what was going to happen to the kid? Why kidnap the baby in the first place? Ransom? It didn't sound like something Benny would do. He had no history of demanding a ransom. Kidnap and ransom had too much potential to go sideways.

He parked next to the truck, gave the keys to George. Ken followed him as he pulled onto Main Street.

He heard Benny moving around in back. "Benny?" he said. "Right here."

"The kid is gonna be all right. Isn't she?"

"I gave you my word, Ken. No harm will come to her. I promise."

"It's just—"

"I know, Ken. But you have to take my word. Those people in that house don't deserve to have a baby. I know more about them than you. This wasn't so much a kidnapping as it was a rescue." Ken didn't say anything after that. How did he know Benny wasn't lying to him?

His thoughts turned to Key West. Fishing on a lazy afternoon or in the evening, sitting on a folding chair with a beer within easy reach. Retirement seldom looked as appealing as it did now. And yet, questions tormented him: what was he going to do if he didn't believe Benny? He couldn't be part of hurting a child.

76

Jon didn't know how long he had been lying on the floor. It was difficult to breathe. He'd lost and regained consciousness so many times that he wasn't sure what day it was. He had to stay awake, even though the pain in his chest, right leg and arms was unbearable, made him want to drift back to darkness. The house was quiet … but he heard a sound—breathing: labored, hitching breaths. He turned his head to the side. Zoey's body was twitching; her arms shuddered and her feet jerked in a grotesque dance. He couldn't tell if she was awake or dying. Candice was lying face down, her legs twisted. She wasn't moving. She had the corkscrewed splayed posture of someone who'd been hit by a car … *Cody*. He knew his son was gone, he remembered that much. He hadn't figured out yet how he was going to get through the rest of his days when the world was full of reminders of Cody. First, he had to get through this day.

He attempted to push himself upright with his elbows, and the blinding white-hot heat of pain sliced through the center of his torso, wrenched a breathless gasp from him. He had to get help. He lifted his head; the effort caused him to groan, but he had to do it. He guessed the raspy, rattling breathing was coming from Zoey. He held his head upright long enough to see the rise and fall of her chest. If he could get to a phone … his left leg worked. He tested it by curling his toes. He raised his head again; his right leg was bent at an impossible angle—it was broken.

His arms were heavy, but he used them to pat his pockets. No phone.

He had to move. Zoey didn't sound good at all.

Jane.

The thought got him moving; as he used his left leg to push himself forward, bone scraped against bone in his other leg and he screamed … but he kept going, digging his heel into the floor, making sure he had enough purchase. Somewhere in the back of his mind he knew that if he passed out from the vicious pain, it was over. Panic, a low grass-fire in his gut, was rising. He held it down. Looked up and behind him. There, lying on the floor past the sofa, was a cell phone. It couldn't have been more than five feet from him, yet it might as well have been a million miles away. He bit down, clenching his jaw, bracing himself against the pain. Jon pushed his leg forward and he began to close the distance. He paused, breathing hard, the stabbing sensation in his chest making his eyes water. He paused, looked behind him again, and was stunned to see the first light of dawn spilling through the living room window.

Concentrate.

He was sweating profusely, face stretched in a grimace, and as pain sliced through him again, it left in its wake an unpleasant heat.

He reached for the phone. When his fingers touched it, he thought he had a chance. The screen was cracked. It belonged to Zoey. He tapped the screen; it was working.

After he'd made the call Jon passed out, screaming—he'd unintentionally moved his leg and the broken bone snagged something.

77

As she made the turn onto Joels Lane, Lizzy wondered how her alleged friends could harbor an adulterer ... but she was past the grieving process. There were more important things to do. All the windows in the Spark were down in an effort to get rid of the lingering odor of chemicals. Somebody had sent the police to her door, and she had run through the list of conspirators in her mind: Zoey, Myrtle, Marcus, Peyton, Sage and Lewis. It didn't matter now, anyway. She had already decided she was done being a victim. Done being *poor timid Lizzy.*

It was fun to think how her *pretend friends* probably believed she had retreated to a dark corner to tend to her wounds. Well, they were mistaken. As she closed the gates, retrieved the circular saw and pry bar from the trunk of the Spark, she felt good. Better than she had in weeks. The funeral of Cody Finch had been a low point. Lizzy was sorry the boy had died and wished he was still here. She had been too quick to judge him. Of all people, she *should know better.* Because people didn't waste any time when they judged her; they were out of the blocks in an instant. She'd had valid concerns, she reflected as she set down the tools on the porch and opened the door. She had tried to be a good mother, but the pills had skewed her view of reality. Now that the poison was out of her system, she saw everything in a new light. She had even apologized to Mia, who had simply stared past her, through her. Her daughter hardly came out of her bedroom. Lizzy was worried about her, and every attempt at speaking to Mia was rebuffed, either with silence or a gentle soft negative: *No*. Somehow, it was that single word, the way it was delivered with a thin, barely there smile on her lips that troubled Lizzy. She had found herself taking an involuntary step backward whenever Mia said the hateful word: *No*. It was unequivocal, total rejection. Lizzy really was sorry. If only it hadn't taken a tragedy for her to realize she had been wrong.

If only, she thought, considering the unrelenting cruelty of hindsight and its inability to solve anything.

Mia's behavior wasn't merely troubling, it was disturbing. She appeared to have spent her fear, all of it. And Lizzy wondered if that was the reason she was beginning to not only fear *for* her daughter, but fear her, too.

Ridiculous. I'm not afraid of her. I'm not.

She brought the tools in from the porch and stood in the living room, taking in the atmosphere—emptiness, absence: of people, of life. How many years had it been since she'd set foot inside her old home? If the musty odor was any guide, too many.

Marcus hadn't succeeded in convincing her to sell this house, the last standing monument to her mother. She was glad she had held on to it. Marcus didn't get it; she had her own way of paying tribute to loved ones long gone.

There was no basement. It would have helped a lot, made the job easier … Lizzy jumped, listening as she landed on the floorboards. She heard a dry creaking noise, but she would have to examine the boards close-up to confirm if they were rotten. She didn't want to buy new hardwood, especially given her intentions.

She rooted in the holdall, bringing out safety glasses, work gloves and a piece of broken white chalk. She laid the items on the floor, ready to be used just as soon as she moved the furniture.

She paused, felt her forehead crease with a deep frown. Was she really going to desecrate her home? The place she had grown up, the house her mother had loved?

What am I doing?

If she cut into the floor, that would be like cutting into her mother.

Her eyes widened, alarmed and dismayed at what she had been about to do.

Fists clenched, she went to the back of the house, through the kitchen.

As she looked out at the three-car garage that had stood at the end of the backyard for over a hundred years, Lizzy changed her plans. But she didn't have a change of heart.

78

Vincent Shaw had no leads on motive, but he was clear on the crime: three attempted murders, and the kidnapping of a minor child under the age of six years. That was the reason the FBI were gathered in a mini-conference down the hall, in a hushed huddle. Myrtle was sitting next to him on the hard chairs. She had insisted they follow the Finches to Stonybrook Trauma Center. After she'd been woken by her phone, she had called him. Vincent had left for work early at the time. Then Myrtle had phoned, telling him Zoey had called her, and there were choking sounds on the other end of the line. He had taken Sergeant Ross Harper with him, convinced someone in the Finch household had pocket-dialed his wife and that maybe Jon Finch was a snorer. But he hadn't suggested this to Myrtle—her voice had wavered close to the edge of losing control. Something was wrong.

When they'd pulled up outside the Finch residence, he and his sergeant had exchanged a knowing look, and both men had drawn their service weapons the moment they emerged from the cruiser, looking everywhere at once. Harper was on his radio, calling for backup. The front door was broken. As they had made their way up the path, Vincent felt the old restless fear in the pit of his stomach. He hadn't experienced it often as a cop, not in this relatively peaceful village. The last time it had raised gooseflesh on his body had been the murder of Cody Finch. And seven years before that when he had attended the scene of a road traffic collision on the junction of Hampton Street and Deerfield Drive, where two teenagers had slammed into a pole at what they had later estimated to be ninety-five miles per hour, and not the posted speed limit of thirty-five. He'd understood the crazy reasoning of the driver: it was past 2 a.m., the roads were more or less deserted, so why not open her up and see what she could do? He had done it himself when he was nineteen and not half as smart as he thought he was. As he had approached the smoking convertible, he'd felt his stomach coil and uncoil, knew he was about to see something utterly horrific. It was almost as though his body knew before his mind did because his legs had become heavy and uncooperative, so he had to force himself toward the wreckage. Inside the vehicle, he discovered a female passenger. She had suffered devastating crush injuries, her face twisted beneath a mask of drying blood. She had been wearing a seatbelt, but at those speeds … He had found the body of the driver fifteen feet away, on the verge. The slow walk toward the body of the young man hadn't taken as long as he'd thought it did—he had reached the body in seconds, already seeing the unnatural twisted legs and torso. The driver must have snagged his right hand in something because it had been completely amputated. He had found the hand under the driver's seat. He never discovered what the kid had been reaching for, or what had trapped his hand, although some of the firefighters had suggested the seatbelt, but no one had ever been able to explain why or how.

The fear Shaw experienced as he pushed the door, zigzag cracks extending outward from where the lock used to be, was similar to that dark morning on the corner of Hampton and Deerfield. But this time he might have a chance to help someone. The fear now was that whoever had broken into this house could still be inside. Harper was poised beside him, gun aimed, two-handed. The door swung inward; the hinges squealed, and both men stepped into the hall fast, looking around. Shaw found Jon Finch in his living room behind a large sofa, unconscious, a cell phone next to his head. There were splatters and pools of blood everywhere he looked. He glanced down at Zoey Finch. She was staring at the ceiling, her face covered in blood. Some of it was leaking from her mouth, which was moving, but barely. He had to secure the house. Harper went into the kitchen, came back, nodded at him, telling Shaw it was clear. Harper stepped over the body of a female near the entrance to the kitchen. The woman didn't appear to be breathing at all. Shaw thought she was dead. Even though Jon Finch was unconscious, he could hear his labored, heaving respiration. After they were satisfied the downstairs was clear, they headed upstairs. Shaw went first, Harper trailing, speaking quietly into the radio, demanding ambulances—one wasn't going to be enough.

They checked the upstairs rooms, entering with their guns raised, expecting trouble. The last room they came to was where Jane Finch should have been, but she was gone. Shaw had seen Jon carrying his daughter around the village in some kind of Disney rocker. This was her room, and the crib was empty. He looked around the room for the rocker, but it too was missing.

"Chief, what the hell happened here?" Harper had asked.

"I don't know." Which was true, but he was putting the basics together in his mind: someone had broken into the Finches' home and kidnapped their daughter, leaving the three people downstairs for dead.

He heard sirens and looked out the window.

Thank God, he thought. He glanced at Harper, feeling sorry for his colleague, and the shocked, bemused expression on his face. The violence that had occurred here was extremely rare, especially in Sag Harbor. Neither Harper nor Shaw had seen a crime scene like it before.

Shaw almost flinched as he was pulled from his thoughts by the touch of Myrtle's hand. She didn't look at him, just folded her hand in his. The Finches were being worked on in the operating theater, and if Jon and Zoey ever woke up, there would be a lot of people waiting to ask them a lot of questions. First, their son was mown down in the road. Now, their one remaining child had been abducted, Jon and Zoey beaten to the point where they could have easily died. He had gotten the name of the other woman from Peggy Dawson, the Finches' neighbor. But it had been a job getting anything coherent out of her. Mrs. Dawson had been so distraught he had needed Harper's help to get her inside her own house and sit her in a chair. He'd had to employ his best bedside manner, taking the patient approach. Peggy had told him, eventually, that the woman was Candice Fersh, the nanny, or babysitter, she would let them decide. Out of the three people who had been removed from the house, Candice Fersh was the most likely to die. He didn't need a doctor to tell me that.

79

Lizzy walked across the backyard. The overgrown grass caressed her ankles. Her gaze was fixed on the garage, although she had always thought of it as a barn: it was red with gray trim, gambrel roof, its gray weathered shingles like old cracked skin ... or scales. She'd had nightmares about this barn when she was a child, in no small part due to the movie *The Amityville Horror*. Her barn wasn't exactly the same as the house in the movie—it didn't have those windows that looked like eyes—but it was close enough. Abandoned to the night, it was easy for her to believe the wind catching a door left open and causing it to creak and slam was a baleful invitation to go down and close it. But in her young mind, she felt it was a trick. A trap.

A trap.

She paused, watching a rat sniff the air just a few feet from her in the tall grass. It scurried away. She had a vermin problem and had some humane rat traps that would solve it. She didn't want to harm the rats; she felt some empathy for them. Universally reviled, they were outcasts, unloved.

She struggled out of her thoughts, back to the surface. It was like climbing out of quicksand. She looked around for a ladder. It was at the rear of the barn, lying in the grass, its wooden rungs cracked and warped by sun and rain. She carried it toward the high fence, drawn there by a low drone. There was something almost hypnotic about the sound, even calming.

She positioned the ladder against the fence, grunting with the effort, and stood on the lowest rung, testing its stability. Lizzy climbed, each step careful and more apprehensive the higher she went. She peered over the top of the fence. Ernest Capaldi was pumping smoke into one of his beehives from something that resembled a copper jug. *He must be in his eighties*, she thought. And, in this heat, he was wearing the apiarist's white coverall and netted hood. He moved around his yard checking each of his four hives, although his movements weren't as limber as she remembered. But he could move under his own power. She cast her mind back, thinking that perhaps she had underestimated Mr. Capaldi's age. He'd been an old man when she was a kid. *Could be in his nineties.* She couldn't see his face behind the black protective netting. The sound of the bees filled her head as she backed down the ladder.

Lizzy headed toward the barn. She had waited long enough. It was time to turn the trick around on the tricksters.

Poor timid Lizzy, the victim ... Not anymore. She threw the double doors wide and went inside. The good news, as far as she could see, was that the dirt floor was mostly clutter-free. There was an old mildewed sofa against the far wall, a three-legged coffee table, a rusted lawn mower, hosepipes and their various attachments hanging on nails hammered into wooden planks on the walls, tools, shovels, spades. *You know what this place needs? A concrete floor.* Fragmented images melded into one coherent idea, like droplets of mercury attracted to the main puddle.

She was tackling the disgusting sofa, dragging it outside, when some disturbing questions stopped her dead: had Marcus kept her sick? Had it been in his interest to bring her to one doctor after another? Had it been the perfect ruse, orchestrated to keep her distracted, to take her mind off the Main Trick? She didn't have any more time to waste. Sweating and panting, she managed to wrestle the sofa outside the barn and stood with her hands on her hips, chest rising and falling as she stared into the dimness of a place that had promised nightmares when she was a child. A place where she'd sensed dark secrets, a place that housed bad dreams.

80

Chief Vincent Shaw had never known his wife to be so quiet. She sat next to him and barely said a word. Myrtle was pale, and if a doctor passed by him in the next few minutes he was going to ask for a Valium, something, anything, because he was worried that she was in shock. He held her hand, patted the back of it, and kept telling her it was going to be all right. Despite his fear that his wife was experiencing some kind of distress, he had questions for her. But they would have to wait. Why had she stopped going to Zoey Finch's book club? That one in particular was at the top of his list.

From the corner of his eye, he detected movement. He glanced in that direction; Charlotte Lange was walking down the hall, looked directly at him, gave a slight nod, and turned a corner. He told Myrtle he'd be back in a minute and strode casually down the hall; when he rounded the corner, Lange was waiting for him. He noted with some amusement that there was an old pair of sneakers on her feet. Quiet shoes. She didn't want to draw attention to herself by wearing anything with a heel.

He followed her further down the hall, around another corner. She turned to him and said, "I'll make this quick because I've got more than enough on my plate. Do you

331

know who Arthur Dunhill is? Roger Berris?"

Shaw shook his head. Already, he knew whatever information she was about to reveal to him was not because she thought he had a right to know, but because he might be able to help her investigation. After all, local knowledge was often the key to solving a lot of crimes. And Shaw was happy to help. Someone out there had a grudge against the Finches and they had perpetrated major crimes in his little burg in the span of days.

"Jon Finch shorted Zinco Sciences recently—"

"Let me stop you there," he said, "shorted?"

"You know Jon runs a hedge fund, right?"

"So?"

"One of the things they do is bet against companies they think are going to fail, or whose foundations they believe are less than sound. Anyway, Roger Berris dumped his entire shareholding in Zinco and a short time later the company's share price plunged. Jon and Zoey borrowed shares to short sell Zinco. In a nutshell, between the Finches and Berris, they destroyed Dunhill's business. Berris was the co-founder of the company. Arthur Dunhill was his business partner. Detectives in Boston discovered the bodies of Arthur Dunhill, Roger Berris and his wife Regina in a house in Newton. Dunhill got in and murdered them both, but it appears Berris got off a shot and took Dunhill with him." She was talking so fast Shaw could hardly keep up. But a picture of why the Finches had been targeted was forming in his mind.

"This is the part that concerns us—there was blood and ... um, *matter*, on the bumper of Dunhill's vehicle."

Shaw said, "So Dunhill murdered Cody Finch because

his father ruined his company?"

"The material on the bumper hasn't been confirmed as that of Cody Finch—"

"Oh, come on. You know it is."

"All right, yes, maybe, but it has to be confirmed."

"Just putting these not-so-puzzling puzzle pieces together, you think Dunhill had something to do with the kidnapping of Jane Finch."

She shrugged. "Maybe." Shaw couldn't pull back his dry smile—everything was *maybe* with Lange. She was being very careful not to give him firm answers. But he understood it, too. They needed all the facts.

"Right," he said, "so what do you want from me?"

She frowned and he watched her struggle to hold back a smile.

"You don't miss much, do you?" she asked.

"Wouldn't be much use if I did."

"Okay, look. When the Finches wake up—"

"If," he said, "*if* they wake up."

"They will. This was no random smash and grab. You were in that house. It was a professional kidnapping. If the perps didn't want the Finches to live they'd be dead by now."

"You think Dunhill really wanted them to suffer, to know what was taken from them?"

"Absolutely."

"Okay. Go on."

"When they wake up, talk to them. Find out as much as you can and let me know what you find."

"What makes you think they'll talk to me?"

"You're local. You were there when their son died. You just might have earned some trust points."

"All right, but let me know the results of whatever it is those Boston cops found on Dunhill's bumper."

"Fine. By the way, Chief Shaw—this story has exploded. The media are outside."

He squeezed his eyes shut. "How many?" he asked.

"All of them."

He stared at her. "I'm serious," he said.

"So am I."

"Jesus Christ," he muttered. "What are the chances the FBI are going to recover the child, alive?"

"Dunhill is dead, and I'm certain he's behind it. Let's hope when the perps discover their boss is history they'll leave the child somewhere safe. The heat could be too much for them. I can't stress this enough, Vincent—this is a *big* story."

"Jon and Zoey really messed with the wrong man."

She was quiet for a moment. He watched her turn his statement over in her mind.

"Yes," she said, "they did. Between you and me, I don't think Jon and Zoey Finch would've had anything to do with Dunhill if it hadn't been for Berris. Roger Berris knew Dunhill was dangerous, but he didn't warn the Finches. According to my sources, Dr. Berris was walking around his own house, armed. He had two guns, one in a shoulder holster, and he kept another on his ankle."

"He knew Dunhill was dangerous and just left the Finches swinging in the breeze ... *Christ.*"

"They couldn't have known how unstable Dunhill really was."

"That's why you don't mess with people. You never know what they'll do."

He told her the story of Terence Fisher. On the surface, Fisher looked nerdy, with his thick-rimmed glasses, pasty complexion, tall and skinny, always carrying an armful of comic books.

"Eight years ago, a kid up from Boston was on vacation. Philip Hayes, if memory serves. You know the type: jock, loud, plenty of muscle to spare, quarterback on his college football team. He literally walks into Fisher outside the Municipal Building and starts beating him. Fisher just had the look of a victim. Except he wasn't a victim at all. This kid was strong, so strong that he hammered Hayes's head into the sidewalk enough to leave him in a coma. Hayes is still in a coma, in this very hospital. His parents refuse to pull the plug. The whole thing was caught not just on storefront CCTV but on bystanders' cell phones. Hayes started it. In fact, he managed to break Fisher's nose and several bones in his face before Fisher took control. I can't forget the surprise on Hayes's face, the sheer disbelief. He really couldn't believe this nerd was kicking his ass. I saw something in Fisher, too. He was always going to win that fight, because he didn't care if he lived or died. Hayes tore those comic books out of Fisher's arm and stomped on them. I swear you should've seen the look that came into Fisher's eyes. I knew Hayes was in trouble the moment I saw it."

Lange nodded and said, "And that's why you don't mess with anybody, you never know what they'll do."

"Don't I know it." She shook his hand and he returned to the seat next to his wife. She was trying to smile for him, but it was weak and it broke his heart.

81

Lizzy had cleared out the barn in just over an hour. Her shorts and T-shirt were grimy and stuck to her skin. She was breathing hard and sat on the mangy sofa, looked around at the rotted artifacts like they were pieces of decayed memory, of a life that once was, but the world had moved on. And Lizzy would move on, too. But not before she made things right for herself and Mia.

Mia.

She patted her shorts, pulled her cell phone out of a pocket and called her daughter. To her surprise, Mia answered. Lizzy sat forward.

"Hey, Mia, uh … how are you?" Awkward. So awkward.

"Hi, Mom. I'm doing fine. I think."

She had a moment of panic as she realized she was grasping for something to say.

"Mom?"

"I'm here, Mia … I'm just glad you're talking to me." She took a deep breath.

"Are you still mad at Dad?"

Lizzy considered the question. She *should* be angry with him, and she was, but her approach to dealing with his betrayal was now a strictly practical one. "In some ways, I am," she said, "but with time, who knows?"

"You sound different, Mom. Calm."

"I'm not going to lie, sweetheart, I feel good. I'm just doing a little work on my old house, getting rid of the cobwebs and cleaning up. Doing some work instead of dwelling on what happened helps a lot … You sound different, too."

"I'm a lot happier, Mom. I talked to Dad on the phone. Hope you don't mind."

"He's your father, Mia. I don't mind at all … you really do sound, um … *breezier.*"

"Feeling much better, Mom. You know, I love you so much. Dad, too."

Lizzy gave up the struggle of containing her tears and let them fall.

She kept her voice as even as she could, and said, "I'll be home soon. I love you so much, too, Mimi. I'll make us a nice dinner."

"That's great, Mom. I have to go."

"Okay." When Lizzy hung up, she put her hand on her stomach as though to quell the shapeless dread that had settled there. She should be relieved; Mia had finally spoken to her and she'd seemed … reasonable. Better. But she didn't have time to examine her unease. A truck had pulled up outside. It was delivery day.

82

Although Chief Shaw was off duty, he was always on the job, he reflected. Always thinking about ways he could better serve and protect the residents of Sag Harbor. If he wasn't holding Crime Awareness seminars at the Municipal Building or handing out leaflets with advice on how to prevent theft, he was talking to people. For the most part, Sag Harbor had avoided crimes that plagued big cities, but now serious crime had encroached on his little patch of paradise. He'd driven by the Finch residence on his way home from the hospital. There was an impenetrable cordon around the house. The FBI's evidence collection unit was on scene. Vincent just hoped they found the child alive and well.

Myrtle was lying beside him in bed, propped up on pillows, reading a paperback novel, although he sensed she was looking at the pages rather than reading them. But he wasn't really watching Jimmy Kimmel on the TV, either. He had collared a doctor and convinced him to give his wife something to calm her down. Thankfully, the doctor had agreed, and Myrtle had swallowed the Valium without complaint.

Lange hadn't been exaggerating: the media were waiting

outside the hospital and for the first time in his career, he'd hurried from them, mostly to shield Myrtle from their shouted questions and jabbing microphones. He had gotten Myrtle into the car, looking back at Stony Brook's parking lot in the rearview, jammed with vehicles and reporters.

"Myrt, are you okay?" he said.

She turned to him and smiled, briefly. "I watch those true crime shows from the safety of my own home, not once thinking anything like it will happen on my doorstep. It always seems so far away. But it couldn't happen here. This is the Hamptons, where the rich and famous live. It wouldn't happen here."

"We're not rich, Myrt," he reminded her.

"No, but we made out all right."

"Can I ask you a question?"

"You're going to anyway, so just ask."

"Why did you leave Zoey's book club?" He felt her stiffen before she could stop it. It was a completely involuntary reaction. He stared at her, letting her know with his eyes that he'd caught it.

She put the book aside. "I love gossip," she said, "I'm not ashamed of it. But this is different." The cop in him restrained himself from prompting her—always on duty. She'd get to it in her own time.

"I couldn't go back there, Vincent. Because of Zoey." As he stared, he felt guilty. She found it difficult, as if she was about to reveal a secret shared in confidence. But he couldn't turn off being a policeman any more than one could turn off sadness or anger—there was no switch for it. "Poor Jon. That was the worst part of it. Seeing how clueless he was. He obviously didn't know."

"Myrt—"

"Zoey was having an affair. With Marcus Jenkins."

Vincent hid his surprise, keeping his reaction in check. "Okay," he said, gently, carefully.

"I knew it in my gut that woman was nothing but a whore. Her best friend's husband. Peyton knew Zoey was up to something, so she followed her. But Peyton couldn't keep her mouth shut, she goes and tells Lizzy, and now Lizzy won't talk to me or Peyton. It was none of my business. Just because Lizzy's my friend why should I get involved in her marital affairs? If only someone would teach Peyton the rules of keeping your nose out of people's business ... Jesus Christ, it was awful sitting in that house looking at Zoey. But even worse was seeing how loving Jon was, you just got the feeling he thought everything was fine. If Zoey wanted out of her marriage, there are other ways to do it ... Don't get me wrong, Vincent. I felt sorry for Lizzy, but it's not my place to tell her her husband is having an affair."

"No ... it's all right, Myrt. Try to get some sleep and we'll talk in the morning."

He turned his attention back to Kimmel, but it didn't take long for him to tune out the TV.

Interesting, he thought. *Very* interesting.

83

Lizzy was exhausted and covered in a film of grime by the time she got into her Spark and headed for home. It was full dark, and as she drove toward Garden Street, she realized something extraordinary—she wasn't afraid. For the past two years, the night had stoked in her an inexplicable fear, and her mouth opened at its sudden disappearance.

Is this what it feels like to heal?

As traumatic and difficult as life had become recently, Lizzy was astonished to find she was hopeful, nevertheless. It wasn't a bright, blinding light; rather, it was a weak beacon seldom glimpsed as she seesawed on heavy seas. But it was *there*.

She had to talk to Mia, tell her she was sorry. Lizzy wondered if she could find the words to express how mothers worried about their daughters ... she would stumble through it, somehow. She was sorry about Cody, too. Perhaps the boy hadn't only been interested in One Thing, after all. She hadn't changed her mind because the poor boy had died, she just viewed their relationship from a wider, sharper perspective: hindsight. They hadn't done anything wrong, and Mia had been happier. Lizzy had been selfish, wrecking the young romance in order to ease her concern, her fear, her anxiety.

Marcus and Zoey, on the other hand … she hadn't forgiven or forgotten the cruel trick they'd played on her. The deep burning embarrassment of having been fooled by people she had trusted, loved, remained as intense as when she'd learned of their affair. The sneering flavor in those photographs on Marcus's secret phone, the direct insult, the taunting look in Zoey's eyes—these were accounts worth settling. And when she was finished with him, he'd wish he had run out on her, run far, far away.

She turned into her driveway and got out, snippets of her earlier conversation with Mia surfacing and sinking in her thoughts. She was uncertain as to why she was suddenly walking faster, why her heart felt suddenly heavier, or why a strange, querulous sound had struggled out of her mouth as she hurried inside, slamming the door behind her.

"Mia?" she called, her voice shaking. There was electricity in the atmosphere, a disturbance, as though something unspeakably terrible had occurred.

There was nobody in the kitchen, living room or in the backyard. She went upstairs, taking them two at a time. The muscles in her legs convulsed as though her weight was too much to bear.

She went straight to Mia's bedroom, thinking about how positive she had sounded on the phone, thinking of the acceptance in her voice.

Lizzy opened the door.

Mia was lying on the bed, a plastic bag over her head. The opening of the bag had been taped around her neck, to prevent air from getting in. Or out. There were empty blister packs of antipsychotic medicine scattered on the floor, on the bed. Her wide, staring eyes paused on a pill bottle. It had contained at least a dozen oxycodone pills she had hidden at the bottom of a coffee tin in the pantry. Hidden from Mia. The bottle was empty. She had only taken six when she'd broken her leg skiing in Vermont four years ago. Back when Marcus had said she was normal, sociable, *pleasant.*

She knelt by the bed and ripped at the bag, tearing it open. Mia's lips were white, tinged bluish. She put her fingers on her neck, feeling for a pulse, hoping for even the faintest signs of life. But Mia was gone. She kept her trembling fingers on her neck for a few minutes and sank to the floor, against the wall, her vision blurred. She didn't know how long she sat slumped that way, but when she looked up again, she saw a piece of paper jutting over the edge of the nightstand. Lizzy reached for it.

> *Mom,*
> *Sorry I had to do this. Cody is gone and you and Dad are getting divorced.*
> *Don't be sad. I love you.*
> *Mia.*

She put the note back, stood, and carefully removed the bag from Mia's neck, filled a basin with water and soap, slung a clean towel over her shoulder, and returned to the bedroom.

After she had washed—gently, softly—Mia's face, hands, and feet, she closed the bedroom door. Walked downstairs, the spasm in her legs gone. Head bent forward, fists clenched, she got into the Spark. She had work to do. And she had nothing left to lose.

84

"He's awake!"

Jon's eyelids fluttered. He tried to locate the owner of the voice, but the light was too bright, as though he'd been trapped underground, in the dark, and was only now being brought to the surface, back to a world of color. Gradually, he noticed sounds: the bleep of something that could have been a machine of some kind, and a commotion that descended into an argument.

"We need to talk to him," he heard someone say, a voice of authority.

Jon raised one eyelid halfway, enough to see a scuffle in the doorway of a room with unadorned walls. He was in the hospital. Voices seemed to come from every direction; some were demanding and some were being calmed with the promise that they would get to speak to him soon. Although consciousness hadn't been completely restored, Jon thought there was a tone of urgency in those voices.

He focused on his body, on the numbness, the nothing he felt there. He had been drugged, which explained why the room appeared to float, the featureless walls seemed to shimmer.

His fingers moved, touched something. It felt like a wire,

or perhaps a tube. He tried to squeeze it but he had no strength.

He was in this room for a reason, and he searched his memory, desperate to learn why. Faces danced above him, blurred heads moving back and forth, hands touching him, adjusting whatever tubes or wires he was hooked up to. He faded out, but for a brief time, he thought. At some point, Jon regained consciousness and a new awareness of the waves of nausea in his gut. He opened his eyes wider, forcing his way out of the dark, determined to pull himself into the light.

Zoey ... Jane ...

Adrenaline flooded his body like a muted scream. His movements became purposeful, jerky. He tried to yank the tubes from his arms and a nurse shouted for a doctor.

"Hold his arms!" someone shouted, and the world swam away again.

85

Lizzy returned to Joels Lane with renewed purpose. She wasn't sobbing, no. The tears ran in quick rivulets down her face, and occasionally she rubbed a hand across her cheeks when they became itchy.

She looked up at the steel beam running along the length of the ceiling of the barn. The manual chain hoist was attached to a trolley that moved along the beam, which meant the mechanic's repair pit was somewhere directly below it. She stabbed a shovel at the dirt, listening for a hollow impact, like knocking on the lid of a coffin. It had to be here. She sank the shovel's blade into the dark soil and began to dig. This barn had, at some distant point in history, been used as a mechanic's repair shop. And a mechanic needed a pit to work on the chassis, although nowadays she thought they weren't strictly necessary, with all the fancy hydraulic lifts available.

She had removed perhaps a half-foot of black earth when she heard an empty *thump*. Lizzy paused for a moment and began digging again, this time in a frenzy, sweat flying off her in beaded strings, her hair damp, stuck to her face. She was so intent on uncovering the pit that she temporarily lost her uncomfortable awareness of the night outside, and the fear it instilled in her.

I'm not afraid of the dark anymore.

The lights overhead were dim, but she had found six old kerosene lamps that worked. Four of them lit the far wall, the gable end, the darkest spot in the barn, and two were placed near the door.

Lizzy scraped loose soil with the shovel and tossed it aside until the long rectangular shape of the pit's lid was a clear outline. In the center of the lid was a large, heavy-duty eye hook. She moved the hoist into place, the trolley above her squeaking, clipped its rusted hook into place and immediately began pulling the chain. The ratchets and cogs grated and chattered from years of disuse, but after a while, it became smoother, and the lid over the pit rose, releasing a breath of dank concrete and loam.

No more delays. There isn't much time left.

She had to hurry. With that in mind, she moved the hoist by dragging the chain toward the far wall of the barn, but not too fast. She was worried about the unbalanced lid swinging out of control and possibly damaging the hoist or jostling a ball bearing loose.

Slowly does it.

She eased up on the chain, went to the exhumed rectangular pit cover and turned it, bringing it closer to the wall.

She picked up a kerosene lamp and held it over the pit. It was unremarkable, just a long hole in the ground, concrete walls, some debris, but that was it. And that was all she needed.

She put the lamp next to the hole and climbed in, surprised at how deep it was. The top of the concrete walls was at eye level. A sudden wave of loneliness swept through her. Her eyes were blazing, and the loneliness was familiar, a consequence (or so one of her shrinks had told her) of being different. Lizzy didn't want to be different, but there was no denying that sense of *otherness*, the idea that she was a stranger among all the people she'd thought were her friends. The feeling of alienation, of terminal loneliness, passed eventually. She climbed out of the hole, left the barn for the kitchen, and carried one of the chairs that belonged at the dining table back to the barn, where she lowered it into the pit.

That'll work.

86

Chief Shaw was staring into the open grave when Ross Harper tapped him on the shoulder. Shaw glanced at him, and Harper pointed his chin over his shoulder. Shaw turned. Charlotte Lange was walking at a brisk pace toward him. The crime scene had already been photographed and agents from the FBI's evidence collection unit were on hands and knees poring over the ground. Shaw had spoken to one of the agents earlier as he'd introduced himself. He had made a casual, throwaway comment. "This is very strange," he had said, "grave robbing?" And the agent had replied, "It's not as strange as you might think. I've encountered a lot stranger. You wouldn't believe some of the stuff we see." Shaw didn't doubt him, but couldn't help being slightly taken aback: *body snatching wasn't the strangest thing this man had seen*. It brought home to Shaw how good he'd had it, how insulated, for the most part, Sag Harbor was. To him, everything that had happened over the past week was highly unusual. But his bubble had burst.

He went to meet Lange a discreet distance along the path. He felt the weight of many pairs of eyes on his back. "You don't answer your phone," he said. "Nice of you to grace me with your presence."

She held up her hands in a gesture of contrition. "Okay, hear me out," she said. "I had to be sure, that's why I haven't been in touch. The blood on Dunhill's bumper *is* that of Cody Finch ... We need all the help we can get, Chief Shaw—the FBI will contact you soon, so liaise with them. We can't do anything about Dunhill, but we might be able to find Jane Finch." He didn't believe her because she obviously wasn't convinced the child would be found. It was in the subtle downward flicker of her eyes.

"You don't think they're going to find her, do you?" he asked softly.

"Dunhill hired professionals, Vincent. We're not going to receive a ransom demand. The feds are on this case, around the clock, in fact. We can only hope somebody out there will see something. With all the news coverage, who knows? What's wrong, you look a little pale?"

"I can't believe what some people are capable of— digging up a child."

"Don't you read the newspapers? Watch the news?"

"I try not to."

"I don't mean to diminish this situation, but far worse and far more extraordinary crimes are committed every single day."

"But why go to these lengths? Even if it is revenge for Finch destroying Dunhill's company, don't you think it's a little extreme?"

"Not in the slightest. People have done a lot worse for a lot less ... also, if you knew anything about Arthur Dunhill, you'd know it's not that surprising. Dunhill had a long history of erratic behavior."

"So you're confident about motive?"

"Yes. Berris discovered Dunhill had fabricated the science behind one of their antibiotics, and Dr. Berris knew it was a matter of time before the chickens came home to roost."

"So he abandoned ship, and Dunhill didn't take it too well."

"Look," she said, after a pause, "I'll keep you informed as best I can, but don't expect too much."

"It's a federal case. I get it."

"That doesn't mean you can't help. Believe me, the FBI would love it if you could provide them with even the tiniest morsel of information that might lead somewhere."

He studied her face, catching the downward shift of her eyes. "You have no faith they're ever going to find Jane Finch," he said, "none at all."

"Do you know how many kids go missing every year? Jesus Christ. Some of those kids are never found, and if they are … Listen, I came here to let you know that Zoey Finch is out of surgery and awake. So is her husband. The doctors had to sedate her when she was told her daughter had been kidnapped—she was hysterical. Jon Finch isn't in much better condition. I can understand it, though. How would you feel?"

"What's your plan?"

"As soon as the Finches are mobile, or well enough to use a wheelchair, we're going to hold a press conference. If they agree to it, although I'm not sure they will. There's a lot of interest in this crime on the media's side, and when they hear about this …" She waved a hand in the general direction of what should have been Cody Finch's final resting place.

"So you're relying on the media—?"

"They can help, believe it or not."

"Okay … Myrtle's going to have to eat dinner without me tonight."

Her face softened. "How is she?"

"Shocked that her friend, people she knows, are at the center of something like this."

She nodded, and he noticed she was watching him as carefully as he was studying her.

"Something on your mind, Chief?"

He smiled. He couldn't help it, and quickly dropped it. Smiling felt inappropriate in such circumstances.

"Have you spoken to Zoey Finch yet?"

She shook her head, *No*. Her eyes brightened with curiosity. "Should I?"

"It might be nothing, then again, it could be something. Zoey was having an affair with Marcus Jenkins."

"Lizzy Jenkins's husband?"

"The very one. Like I said—"

"It could be nothing … but it could be *something*. I have to go. The FBI are waiting to interview the Finches, the first of many, and I'd like to sit in on it. You should, too. I'll let them know you're on your way. I'll see you around."

"You will," he said, and watched her go. Then he turned, stared at the FBI agents, some wearing the navy jackets with the yellow decaled letters on their backs, some in plainclothes. It was an odd sight, somewhat surreal because it was rare. So rare, in fact, that in his fifteen years on the job he hadn't seen a federal investigator in his village. He thought about the Finches, and how they'd react when they discovered their son's corpse had been stolen. What would it do to them? It was one shocking crime after another. How would *he* deal with it? He thought Dunhill had created the perfect conditions to cause the Finches a nervous breakdown. And it was possible that had been his intention all along. Rather than simply murder the people he held responsible for the downfall of Zinco, Dunhill had decided to make them suffer instead. If that had been his goal, Dunhill had succeeded.

87

Chief Shaw stood at the back of the hospital room, his back against the wall. Lange was standing next to him, writing something into a notepad. *Old school*, he thought, and returned his attention to the man in the bed. Finch's face was swollen, contused, two black eyes, a thick bandage high on his left cheekbone. He was pale, drawn. Shaw recalled news footage of a terrorist incident some years before, he couldn't remember which country had been attacked. However, he did recall the shocked, dazed faces of the survivors. Jon Finch had the same expression on his face, as though he'd just survived a bomb blast. There were three doctors by his bedside keeping a close eye on him, ready to intervene if the special agents present demanded too much of their patient.

Shaw felt sorry for Jon. He had no idea that the bad news showed no signs of slowing down. At some point during the investigation, either the FBI or the Suffolk County PD was going to question him about his wife's affair. His son had been murdered, his daughter had been kidnapped, and his wife was cheating on him. Jon Finch was rich, but Shaw didn't envy him in the slightest.

Two federal agents sat in chairs on either side of the bed,

approximately where Jon's kneecaps were. Shaw wondered how long it would take their main witness to recover. Finch was wearing a hospital johnny and his chest was bulky, as though he had body armor on, but it was a bandage or a cast of some kind. His legs looked huge underneath the sheets. According to Charlotte Lange, both his legs had been broken and had to be screwed back together. Someone really had made a respectable effort to kill him, and Shaw thought Jon had been lucky. But as the interview commenced, he became less sure of that.

The FBI agent on the left-hand side of the bed asked Jon to explain how he knew Dr. Roger Berris. Jon recounted his meeting with Berris, and Zoey's misgivings about having anything to do with him. Jon said he wished he'd listened. His voice was dry and cracked, and he kept taking sips of water from a bottle. Shaw watched the slow roll of Jon's eyes—these were not ideal conditions for an interview, especially since their witness was under the influence of whatever dope the doctors had pumped into him. Although, Shaw saw, the effects of the drugs appeared to be fading. Even that wasn't a good thing, because if he was in pain the doctors would give him more painkillers. They had to make the best of a bad situation. A baby girl had been kidnapped after a brutal home invasion, two people were seriously injured as a result, Candice Fersh was in the intensive care unit and the outlook was not optimistic. The doctors were doing everything to make her "comfortable," which in Shaw's view was a euphemism for *she won't recover*.

As Shaw observed the interview, it had become a slow tennis match. One agent asked a question and the other asked a follow-up question, Jon turning his head back and forth between the two men. Something dawned in Jon's eyes and Shaw stood straighter, his whole body tense.

"Why are you questioning me about Arthur Dunhill?"

Shaw sensed an immediate shift in the atmosphere, as though the federal agents knew the charade was up. When Jon spoke again, his eyes were wider, his voice higher, "What's going on? What did Dunhill do? *Answer me!*"

The agent on the left-hand side of the bed explained that Arthur Dunhill had murdered Roger Berris and his wife, Regina. DNA samples extracted from blood on Dunhill's vehicle matched those of his son, Cody Finch.

Shaw wanted to look away but he couldn't. The shock, the blinking surprise of a man who has heard the sound of laughter in a sad place was fascinating to watch. He had the distinct impression that he was witnessing a man experiencing total psychological ruin. Jon shuddered visibly and his hands trembled.

He looks like he bet against the devil and lost.

The moment Shaw's thought was complete, one of the doctors stepped forward, and said, "Okay, that's enough."

But the feds weren't going to leave easily. The one on the right of Finch said, "Jon, we're trying to find your daughter. We can leave, but the men who took Jane have a head start on us. We need your help." Jon nodded, and Shaw thought Finch was expending a lot of energy just keeping his head upright on a neck made rubbery by drugs.

Shaw was unable to take his eyes off the man in the bed, his dark shock of hair standing in tousled tufts, his complexion pallid. As he listened, he realized there had been no discussion of Cody Finch's missing body. Hadn't Lange or one of these agents told him yet?

The short interview was wrapped up and people began filing out of the room, including Lange. Shaw caught one of the FBI agents glancing at him and, as the door closed and he was the last investigator in the room, he was furious. He was the one chosen to deliver yet more miserable news. He cursed them all and quickly resigned himself to the task. Maybe telling Finch his son's body had been stolen was the push he needed, a helping hand off the ledge of sanity. He attempted to smile at Jon and dropped it instantly, feeling foolish. He crossed the room, sat uneasily on one of the chairs vacated by an FBI agent, the doctors eyeing him suspiciously. They wouldn't have to tell him twice if they wanted him to leave.

Shaw tried to avoid looking directly into Jon's eyes, where he could see the ruins of his spirit, beaten, ragged, in tatters. And yet, he was drawn, finding it impossible not to look at a man whose sanity he felt was threadbare and whatever remained of it would fray and break eventually.

He considered ways and means of easing into it, sidling up to a gentle delivery, revealing the horrific news by padding it, somehow, enough so that the blow, when it came, didn't hurt as much. He sighed deep in his chest, aware that there was no way to attenuate the theft of the body. Flowery words wouldn't mask the odor of a macabre truth. "Jon," he said, "Mr. Finch, I mean. I'm sorry to inform you that your son's body was stolen—" That was as far as he got before the scream tore loose from Jon's throat and the doctors swarmed around him and somehow Shaw found himself walking toward the door, the scream reverberating in his skull, haunting in its blackness, its abandonment of hope.

88

Lizzy crossed the Ferry Road bridge headed toward North Haven. The harbor lights twinkled in the dark, blurred and stretched through the lens of her watery eyes. The only sound in the Spark was that of her respiration, slow and even, in spite of the risky prospect ahead of her. She'd almost gotten accustomed to the spontaneous liquid burn of tears, and at least she wasn't sobbing. Even though she had carried her memories of Mia deep into a quiet compartment in her mind and closed the door, her only child knocked every once in a while, as if to remind Lizzy she still lived within her, somewhere in her dark interior.

A memory arose, unbidden, of her worst argument with Mia. It was over a year ago when Lizzy had taken her to see a therapist in East Hampton. Mia had been experiencing bouts of depression, and Lizzy was afraid she had passed the black baton to her daughter in a circular, unending race. Sometime after her first two therapy sessions, Mia had tweeted that she was being treated for depression. Lizzy had lost her temper, demanded she remove the tweet because any prospective employer in the future would see it, and why would a business hire somebody with a history of mental illness when they could just as easily find someone who was *normal?* Lizzy knew the media and celebrities acted as though the stigma of mental illness was a mere myth in the modern era, but they were lying. Lizzy had firsthand experience of the lie. She noticed how her colleagues at the library gave her the side-eye and *fake smiled* at her and were *fake nice* to her, but she was never in any doubt that she was just being tolerated, for now. Lizzy was marked by her own hand, and she regretted it. She should have kept her mental state to herself. She had tried to make Mia understand that the real world wasn't the same as that portrayed in glossy magazines and by celebrity culture. Celebrities could afford to be depressed, but not a kid from Sag Harbor whose career hadn't even started yet. And Mia had fought her every step of the way—Lizzy hadn't relented, she had insisted Mia remove the tweet. She had, eventually, after Lizzy had worn her down by her constant entreaties and promises of a fancy new cell phone. She was in awe of the fact that her daughter couldn't see that she was only trying to protect her, to safeguard her future.

Where are the good memories? She caught a glimpse of herself in the rearview mirror, eyes wide, stricken, as though she'd suddenly discovered a strange passenger in back, watching her. Where the good times should have been there was blankness, as though she were standing over a kind of psychic chasm, looking down into the infinite black, unbalanced by the gravity of its indifference.

No, not now. The good times are there, Mia, they are. *I'll find them later. I will.*

She turned onto Coves End Lane.

I'm coming, Marcus, ready or not.

It wasn't 3 a.m. yet, when Marcus, lifelong insomniac

and connoisseur of quality tobacco, went out on the porch to smoke those stinking cigars she'd stopped complaining about because she realized she was being selfish, that it was something he enjoyed and she really ought to drop it. Marcus was holding up his end of the bargain by being a good husband, and she hers by being a good wife and keeping her complaints to a minimum. But Marcus had quit being a good husband.

The road narrowed as she turned onto Coves End Lane, the trees thickened. She glanced at her wristwatch.

What if he doesn't appear?

It was possible, but unlikely. She knew Marcus. He was so predictable, which was one of the reasons she had loved him. Lizzy didn't like surprises. But, by Christ, hadn't he surprised her enough already, given her what her pharmacist would have described as an *adult dose* of surprise?

She turned the Spark in the driveway and pointed its nose toward the way out. She didn't want the hassle of Marcus doing it. He might trick her. *No, no, he* will *try to trick me.* After all, he had previous form in this area, and she had fallen for it.

Fool me once …

She parked on the grassy verge outside the house. For some reason, Lewis and Sage had decided to plant trees instead of installing a fence around their property. The trees stood in a neat row all the way down to the entrance of their driveway. All she had to do was walk through the gap between the trees toward the dark house.

The gun was slipping in the waistband of her shorts and she put it in her pocket. Its heaviness was reassuring. She avoided the front of the house, making her way across the soft grass to the rear, where hopefully Marcus was indulging his bad habit. She crouched behind a bush, pushed the button on the side of her wristwatch. It glowed, showing her it was 3 a.m. She rose from her crouch, and there he was.

Nothing left to lose.

But he was getting up, quenching the stub of his cigar in some kind of plant pot, turned on the porch, walking back into the house.

Fuck!

Her eyes flitted left and right, eyeing the pot Marcus had just set down.

She sprinted toward the porch, back against the side of the steps. She looked up. *The pot.*

She reached for it and pushed. It hit the porch floor and broke. She wasn't worried about rousing Lewis or Sage—their bedroom was at the front of the house. Lizzy waited.

Seconds passed and she heard the screen door open. Footsteps on the boards.

She listened as he muttered to himself, gathering the broken pieces of the pot into a pile. She sprang to her feet, ran up the porch steps, gun raised, pointed at Marcus's head.

"Hello," she whispered, her breath coming in hard gusts, her heart pounding. "We need to talk. Move and I'll kill you, shout out and your brother and his wife die, along with you. Get moving. Now." Marcus moved, mouth agape, hands raised. She recognized the look in his eye, the one that was confident he could talk her out of this foolishness. Good. She welcomed it. But Marcus was mistaken. Things had changed. If he only knew of the extent, the magnitude of the change, he would have made a break for it. As it stood, he was walking ahead of her, fingertips pointed at the sky.

"Lizzy—" he said.

"Shut up. Through the gap in the trees ahead of you. We've a lot to talk about."

She was giving him false hope, more or less the kind he had dispensed to her. Make him think she was willing to talk.

"Okay, get in the driver's seat. I'll be right behind you."

Marcus got into the car; Lizzy sat behind him, as promised. She pressed the barrel of the gun into the driver's seat, down low, so that if she did have to squeeze off a shot, lady luck might smile on her and she'd only cripple him. She wanted him alive—Marcus thought he was the king trickster, but she had a trick in mind to not only rival his, but surpass it.

"Put your seatbelt on," she said, listening for the click in the gloom. When she heard it, she pulled her belt across her chest. "Start the engine, Marcus. Slow, nice and slow ... by the way—if you veer off the road, towards a tree or a wall, there's more than enough time for me to kill you. Better get rid of those piggy thoughts right now, Marcus."

His head was cocked, listening to her. But he pulled away from the verge and they were headed back down the narrow road, the dark trees and thick vegetation close, looming over them. How ironic it must be for him, being kidnapped by his wife with the aid of the gun he kept for home protection. Must be galling.

"Where's Mia?" he asked.

"Sleeping," she said, and when his head swiveled toward her, she screamed, "*Eyes on the road!*" Marcus faced forward again, and this time Lizzy felt a change in his body language, his aura, as though he was only beginning to grasp the danger he was in. She pushed the gun harder into the back of the driver's seat.

"Couldn't sleep, Marcus?" she asked conversationally, "conscience weighing on you these days?"

"I'm sorry, Lizzy," he said, and it sounded so genuine—*heartfelt*—that for a moment she almost fell for it. She was done being tricked, by God.

"I'm curious, Marcus. I want you to think about your answer carefully. No rush—do you think *sorry* is ever going to be enough?"

It was almost funny the way he paused as if he was thinking seriously about her question, giving it due consideration. Almost.

Finally, he said, "No, I don't think sorry is enough."

Look at you, giving me all the right answers! Oh my, Marcus, you know just the right thing to say!

"Where are we going?" he said.

"To my old house. I need to show you something."

"What?"

"I'm losing patience with you, Marcus. I need to show you something important, even if I'm not sure it'll make a difference. But it could, and hopefully in the future we can at least be civil to each other." She watched him relax. Watched his shoulders loosen. *Good.*

"Lizzy," he said, and there was a quiet note in his voice, "you sound different."

"Really? I hadn't noticed. Different *good* or different *bad*?"

"Good, I think. You sound ... sure of yourself."

"Are you saying I sound confident, Marcus?"

She caught him glancing at her in the rearview. "Eyes forward, *now*!" she said.

"Okay, *okay.*"

363

The car turned onto Joels Lane.

You should have run, Marcus. You really should have run. A bullet in the back wouldn't have been half as bad as what you face now.

89

"Lie facedown on the ground," Lizzy said.

They were standing beside the Spark, Marcus staring at her. At the gun aimed at his chest.

"Lizzy, listen—"

"I can't talk to you if I keep thinking you're going to jump me, can I? For the last time—facedown or I swear to Christ I'll kill you now." His expression told her he believed the threat. Reluctantly, he complied.

"Hands behind your back and cross your legs, just like in the movies."

Lizzy took the cable tie from her cardigan pocket, already looped, ready to be closed.

"I'm going to sit on your lower back, Marcus, and when I do, keep in mind my finger is *inside* the trigger guard." As soon as she sat on him, she moved at lightning speed, pulling the cable tie tight around his hands. He grunted as she cinched it tight.

"Oh, don't be a baby," she said, "on your feet. Let's go." She watched him struggle into a sitting position, get his legs under him, and push himself upright. She opened the barn doors, releasing a warm yellow glow of light.

"Hurry," she said, "I don't have all night. Don't turn

around or you'll be sorry. Eyes front." She followed him into the barn, picking up a sock filled with sand and gravel, and struck him on the neck. His legs gave way and he dropped to his knees. He was conscious, but barely, making gargling, choked noises deep in his throat. She hit him again, putting all her weight behind it. Marcus dropped like a stone.

Lizzy set about getting Marcus sitting in one of the dining chairs. Chains rattled as she brought the hoist to the center of the barn, where she had replaced the cover over the repair pit. Marcus weighed somewhere around 220 pounds, and she wasn't putting her back out because of him. She looped a rope around his chest, under his arms and tied several knots in it, then clipped the hook onto the rope and positioned the chair underneath the hoist. She pulled the chains, hand over hand, and Marcus's unconscious body rose limply. Lizzy, fascinated, watched his boneless ascent, giddy with anticipation, looking forward to when Marcus regained consciousness and realized he was in more trouble than he had ever dreamed possible.

90

Now for the remaining conspirator, Lizzy thought, as she cruised down Division Street, slowing as she approached the brick building of Sag Harbor Police Department, across the road from the UPS Store, yellow light pouring out of the blue window frames. Was Chief Vincent Shaw's car in the lot?

She found what she was searching for and accelerated, headed towards Union Street. Something Marcus had said came back to her: *You sound … sure of yourself.* Did he mean she seemed confident? Lizzy felt *something*, an inexplicable but undeniable sense of *brazenness*. Or perhaps that feeling was audacity? Whatever it was, Lizzy liked it, welcomed the departure of fear and anxiety and a pervasive certainty of impending doom. Every day for the past two years had been that way. She shuddered at the thought of *them*, her persecutors, the cruel pranksters. The way *they* smiled at her and told her how brave she was and underneath the smiles she had mistaken for kindness and understanding was the sneaky glimmer of pity, *poor mad Lizzy*, inwardly shaking their heads at the tragedy of her illness. Yet, now she didn't feel sick. She felt alive, she had a renewed sense of purpose, she was, to use a word favored by the many faceless shrinks

367

she'd seen in the past, being *proactive.*

She took her cell phone from the glove compartment and scrolled to Myrtle's number and pressed Send. Three rings … four … five … six … Myrtle answered on the seventh, her voice thick with sleep. "Hullo?"

"Myrtle, I need to talk to you, I'm scared," Lizzy said, adding a sniffle, choking out a sob.

"*Lizzy!* My God, it's so good to hear from you, is everything all right?"

"I'm coming over to your house now, I need to talk to somebody."

"It's late—never mind, I'm just delighted you called."

"I'm turning into your street now." And she was, squeezing more tears from eyes that had become cold, stiff. She stopped outside Myrtle's house, looked up at the light in the bedroom window. The hall light came on, and Myrtle stood on her doorstep, bathrobe wrapped around her, slippers on her feet.

Lizzy got out, one hand on the gun in her cardigan pocket, the other wiping at her eyes. She marched up the walk, each step more confident than the last. Gone was her usual hesitant amble. She strode past Myrtle and closed the front door.

"Lizzy? What—"

Myrtle paused as the gun was thrust into her face. "Don't say a word. We need to talk. Get moving." And Lizzy surprised herself by grabbing Myrtle's arm, amazed at her own strength, almost lifting the older woman off her feet as she propelled her down the walk.

"Get in the driver's seat." When Myrtle just stared at her, eyes wide, mouth open, Lizzy opened the door and pushed

Myrtle into the car, as if she was packing away a sleeping bag.

"Try to get out and I swear to Christ I'll fucking kill you," she said in a tight whisper.

She got in the rear passenger seat, directly behind Myrtle, snaking her arm around the driver's seat and jamming the gun into the side of Myrtle's neck.

"Start the car," Lizzy said.

"Please, Lizzy, let's talk—"

"*START THE FUCKING ENGINE, YOU CUNT!*" Lizzy screamed, spittle flying, blood high and pounding hard in her face and neck. She caught sight of herself in the rearview, the bulging eyes that had taken on an eerie shine. *Who are you?*

There was no answer to her thought. The sound of the engine brought her back to herself. She told Myrtle the destination and assured her that she only wanted to talk, that she wanted an explanation. Lizzy could feel the intensity of her former friend's terror. *Now you know what it feels like, Myrtle.*

"Try to drive into a wall or a tree, I dare you. I've more than enough time to put a bullet in your back. I just want to talk, I promise."

A whimper escaped Myrtle's mouth, and Lizzy leaned forward, watching her throat work. Myrtle kept swallowing, as though her mouth had dried up.

91

As soon as Lizzy walked Myrtle into the barn, her hands bound, her former friend, a woman she had trusted with her life, tried to turn and flee. But Lizzy wrestled her to the ground, irritated that she had been *forced* to pistol-whip her until she lost consciousness. Once Myrtle had seen Marcus slumped in the chair, Lizzy thought Myrtle believed the same fate awaited her, and she was right.

She heaved Myrtle's dead weight toward the center of the floor. Out of breath, panting, she used the backs of her hands to wipe at the tiny spatters of blood on her cheeks from the blows she'd inflicted.

The chains rattled as she hoisted Myrtle's body off the ground. The rafters creaked, and suddenly she thought of Peyton Ellis. Was she in on the conspiracy? Lizzy doubted it. Peyton had somehow discovered Zoey was having an affair with Marcus. She started at the sound of a door slamming, but it came from inside her mind. It was Peyton storming out of Zoey's house. Peyton *had* been her friend, more than any of *them*. Peyton had a conscience, a moral compass. But these human vermin had no concept of loyalty. Myrtle was supposed to be her closest friend, and she had betrayed her, left her living in a house with a man who

had cheated on her, making her feel like the biggest fool—
poor dumb Lizzy. The embarrassment, the humiliation,
couldn't be scrubbed from inside her. There was no tonic for
it, no surcease. It clung to her like a rancid smell, haunting
her thoughts every second of every hour. Sometimes, she
fancied she could taste it, like black copper. They probably
laughed behind her back, too. Probably snickered in the cup
of their hands as they considered how stupid she was. How
did she not notice her husband was cheating on her?

"I was relying on other people to protect me," she said
out loud, and she paused in the process of taping Myrtle's
legs to those of the chair. The sound of her voice had a
peculiar, disembodied quality to it, as though it was coming
from someone else, something else, outside her. "I shouldn't
have relied on anyone to look out for my best interests," she
whispered.

She stood, hands balled into tight fists, and stalked across
the barn, past the two clear Perspex boxes she had made,
cutting the sheets to size and using Gorilla glue to fasten
them together. She picked up the shovel leaning against the
wall and began shoveling cement onto her mixing board, a
large square of plywood. She worked calmly, methodically,
listening to the low drone of the bees.

92

Marcus came to with a gasp as pain lanced down the back of his head into his neck. His senses returned slowly, but he couldn't understand what they were telling him. First, he heard a droning sound. Then he smelled something dry and gritty but somehow wet. His eyes fluttered, squeezed shut again as a bolt of pain shot through his skull. He raised his head on a neck that felt weak and stiff. Next to the yellow glow of a kerosene lamp, there was a glass jar filled with bees. He looked down, tried to move, and panic swelled in his chest, nearly developing into a scream. He couldn't have given voice to it, anyway. His mouth was taped shut and he was tied to a chair. He couldn't move his arms or legs. It all came to him in a sudden deluge of memory—Lizzy. She had brought him here at gunpoint, promising him she just wanted to talk. Marcus had no doubt now she had something far worse in mind for him. He looked at the jar of bees again.

Oh God, what is she planning?

There was another sound: digging, the unmistakable rasp of a shovel being plunged into soil. His eyes widened when he saw it wasn't soil at all, but cement. Lizzy was on the other side of the barn mixing … cement?

Jesus, help me.

Someone moaned beside him and he flinched.

What the—?

At first he didn't recognize the woman, who was staring at him with eyes as big and round as those of a frightened horse. There was tape on her mouth, too. Dirt on her face, and a darker substance that could have been mud or blood. He concentrated, searching his racing memory. Shaw, that was her name. Lizzy's friend, Myrtle Shaw. *What in God's name is going on?*

He tried to talk behind his gag, trying to produce some sound to get Lizzy's attention. He could talk her out of this, whatever she had in mind, he could talk her out of it.

But as he moaned, shaking his head in an effort to get Lizzy to just look at him, he watched her walk toward the chains. She attached the hook to the cover of the repair pit and began raising it. Marcus swallowed hard. Something in his throat clicked. All the spit in his mouth had suddenly vanished.

93

Myrtle screamed as the legs of Marcus's chair lifted off the ground. The sound of it was muffled, but the despair in it frightened her. The hopelessness in that imprisoned scream caused a wave of blackness to descend on her. Tears sprang to her eyes and a terrible sob wracked her body. There was no escape. Horrified, she watched Marcus hover over the pit; there was no doubt it was his grave. And hers, too.

The chains rattled and she glanced feverishly at Lizzy, the woman she had loved, a friend she'd only ever tried to protect. She had wanted the best for her … now Lizzy was going to kill her.

Marcus struggled in the chair, but Myrtle could see it was useless. He was going into the hole in the ground, and as the thought occurred to her she stared, terrified, heart slamming into the walls of her chest as he was lowered, disappearing from sight. Now Lizzy was walking to the edge of the pit, reaching into it with a shovel to make some kind of adjustment, went back to the chains, gave them one brief tug. Then Lizzy was walking towards her, eyes blank, black chips of anthracite. Myrtle pleaded with her, despite the tape over her mouth. Begged her. Turned her head to look up at her, get Lizzy to look at *her*, just maybe Lizzy would change her mind *if she would just look at me* …

But Lizzy didn't look at her. Incredibly, she was humming some kind of nursery rhyme. Myrtle would have sworn it was Humpty Dumpty. As Lizzy clipped the hook to the rope around her chest, she muttered, "All the king's horses and all the king's men …" She trailed off, and Myrtle prayed for a heart attack. For God to take her now.

Lizzy got on her knees and removed Myrtle's slippers.

Myrtle screamed, her worst fear about to be realized: she was going to die without footwear. Shoeless. Her cheeks puffed in and out as she screamed, ballooned out so hard she felt they would burst, a great tearing shriek of terror rising from the depths of her.

Lizzy went back to the chains and pulled. Myrtle jerked forward in the chair, the sounds of her own terrorized moans, the sweat stinging her eyes, and that disturbing, jarring line from an old nursery rhyme filling her head—*all the king's horses and all the king's men …*

The legs of the chair left the ground and she swung gently in the air. She stared at Lizzy, hoping to see any sign of life in those dead eyes. There was none. Lizzy lowered her into the pit, and Myrtle wondered if Lizzy was actually seeing her, because she got the impression that Lizzy was somewhere else, wandering through some confused landscape in her mind. Her head was tilted upward, ear cocked, as though she was listening to something, or someone. Every few seconds she nodded, as if acknowledging a voice only she heard. And yet her confusion couldn't have been too great, for Myrtle was descending. The legs of the chair scraped the concrete wall behind her, an awful grating noise. She looked down. Marcus was staring up at her, watching as she joined him, thick guttural whimpers working his throat. Myrtle recognized it—panic. Sheer, uncontrollable panic.

94

Mixing cement was not that hard, at least according to the man in the YouTube video she had watched. But shoveling it was an entirely different matter. Lizzy was exhausted, but she had never felt more awake, alive, *energized*. Her body thrummed with the low hum of electricity, and the drone of the bees in the jar was soothing—it summoned warm childhood nostalgia. With shadows closing in on her as she had tried to sleep, a terrified child clutching the blankets to her chin, the only barrier against the monsters that walked in the darkness outside, and possibly in her closet, the sound had calmed her fearful journey through the night, alone.

She blinked hard and the memory dissipated, focused on the wet rasp of cement leaving the blade of the shovel as she tossed it into the pit. The muffled screams drifted over the angular lip of the hole, but she paid them no mind. She hated Marcus, which was true. However, her hatred for Myrtle was on a higher plain, at an intensity level that made her eyes bulge just a little more whenever she thought about the older woman's betrayal: *she had expected more from Myrtle*. It was at the heart of the reason she was burying her now. Although Lizzy felt she was entombing the old Lizzy, too, even if it was only symbolically: the local victim, everybody's victim, *poor mad Lizzy, mad but harmless.* A friend didn't allow you to drown in your own ignorance, didn't stand by as the man you had loved had an affair with that Finch whore and then kept the information to herself. She had really expected more from Myrtle. It was shocking, in a way—she'd thought she had known Myrtle Shaw, but Lizzy was rapidly becoming acquainted with the idea that she didn't know *anyone.* Anyone at all.

She wasn't blameless, either. Lizzy had asked for far too much from life—a good husband. That and no more. Whatever else fell her way would have been a bonus.

Sweat dripped from her face and a vein pulsed steadily in the middle of her forehead as she slung shovelfuls of cement into the pit, which made impact with a wet slapping sound.

Lizzy blinked rapidly at the sudden memory of a picture she had found on Marcus's secret phone, filth of the purest form: Marcus with his hand raised as though he was about to slap Zoey Finch's bare ass. And smiling for the camera, in the bargain. She would deal with that dirty Finch slut, but she would make it her business at a more auspicious time to settle her account once and for all. *Don't worry, bitch, I haven't forgotten you.* Lewis and Sage had given succor to an adulterer, and they deserved a place in the hole right next to Marcus. Sadly, the clock was running down. Perhaps, someday, she'd have an opportunity to revisit them.

Who would have thought Peyton Ellis was the only one among these traitors who had a keen sense of right and wrong? Lizzy shook her head at the thought. Oh, how Myrtle and Zoey had gossiped about Peyton behind her back, remarking on her ability to fail at every turn. And what did it amount to in the end? The simplest explanation was usually the correct one—jealousy. They couldn't believe, couldn't entertain the notion that Peyton might actually be a good person. Worst of all, Peyton had accepted her failures, owned all of them, and made the mistake of telling Zoey and Myrtle; how they had fake smiled at her, and Peyton seemed unaware that she'd only stoked the coals of their jealousy and ordinary hatred. Peyton had come to her senses and seen Zoey Finch for who she really was—behind the money she was a soulless vessel, a wanton harlot all the holy water in a bottomless font couldn't wash clean. She had changed her mind about Peyton: she wasn't conspiring against Lizzy, after all; she had turned out to be her only real friend.

She paused, went to the edge of the pit and assessed her progress. If she kept going, didn't take a break, she could have the concrete up at chest level before long. Right now it was above their ankles.

Have to work faster.

They were looking up at her, the tape on their mouths puffing in and out. There was cement in their hair, on their faces.

They don't look human. With their gray faces, they look like monsters.

Lizzy picked up the shovel and resumed dumping clods of cement into the hole. Soon, she would have to mix a new batch.

95

Myrtle thought of the mind as a universe within the universe, equally vast and unknowable. She had believed she knew Lizzy Jenkins. If anyone had asked if she was dangerous, Myrtle would have been the first to say that Lizzy wouldn't hurt a fly. How could she when she jumped at her own shadow? Myrtle remembered the unnatural strength as Lizzy had dragged her down the walk in front of her house. A grip and raw power that had felt hydraulic, mechanical. If asked for an explanation of Lizzy's behavior now, all she could do would be to shrug and say she had snapped. Even *that* wasn't satisfactory. On the other hand, Myrtle read the newspapers and watched the news. Lizzy Jenkins wasn't an outlier, or the first person to crack under the creaky strain of a mind that had been poorly, shabbily fortified. The reasons didn't matter now, not to her. Her petty jealousies and over-the-garden-fence gossip seemed utterly ridiculous as she added up the total sum of her sins and prayed to God to forgive her. Not for anything specific, just … all of it.

Even as the concrete climbed above her knees, Myrtle hadn't lost hope. It was foolish, perhaps, but she clung to it desperately. The cruel irony of her present predicament wasn't lost on her, either. She had increased security in her home by adding more locks on the doors. She watched her crime shows (*48 Hours* being her favorite, of course) believing they would teach her what to look out for. Believing she would be able to recognize the murderer and the rapist before they could make her their victim. Forewarned was forearmed, after all. *And look how that had turned out!*

She imagined Vinnie was searching for her. Did he even realize she was missing? She pictured him bursting through the barn doors and rescuing her. And Marcus, who had become silent and just stared directly ahead at the wall in front of him. Even a cheating dirtbag like Marcus didn't deserve this.

The thing that disturbed her, made her stomach contract into tight bands of dread and sadness, was how Vinnie would cope without her. They'd had their marital issues like any couple who had been together for as many years as they had, but hadn't they always found a way through to the other side of the argument? She loved Vinnie, dearly loved him. If she could only talk to Lizzy, spark some compassion in her, persuade her gently to free them, but the tape over her mouth was fastened hard. It wouldn't budge. She would plead and beg for her life, and for Marcus's, worthless philanderer that he was. She would appeal to Lizzy's humanity, because she could not accept that it had taken a complete leave of absence. Would not accept it.

Myrtle had stopped screaming. She'd had no choice. Something in her throat had slipped, cracked. It was painful. But she was more worried about her legs, they were somehow both hot and cold. How could that be? She was shivering, but it was hot in here. The shivering bothered her because she couldn't control it. She recalled how Lizzy had removed her slippers. Lizzy knew her fear, irrational though it may be, but it was real to her. She was scared of dying with no shoes on her feet. It was stupid, but it mattered to Myrtle. It suggested to her that Lizzy was perfectly aware of what she was doing, that maybe she wasn't insane. How could a crazy person remember her dumb fear of dying without footwear? If the person above her dumping cold concrete on top of her was a thinking, rational individual who was fully conscious of the crime she was committing, that was chilling. Terrifying. She dismissed the idea. Some things just weren't acceptable. There were some things she simply refused to believe. If it were true, then Lizzy was cruel. Even after what Lizzy had done to her, the thought that she was *consciously* cruel was an outlandish one.

A clod of concrete hit her on the head with a wet *smack*. She felt it trickle down her face, fall in clumps into her lap, cold at first but oddly warming soon afterward. She turned her thoughts to Vinnie and prayed for him, and for herself.

When she was finished, she wondered if Lizzy had had any part in the break-in at the Finches' house. She had wondered a lot about that and had come up empty. Had Lizzy kidnapped baby Jane Finch out of revenge? Why not? She hated Zoey. The police had returned Lizzy's car, which had been big news around the Village, but what if Lizzy had concocted some kind of complex bait and switch? What if—?

There was a sudden pause on the barn floor. Myrtle listened. Something was being poured, then the sound of water, followed by a chopping noise. It didn't take a genius to work it out: Lizzy was mixing more cement, slicing the head of the shovel through it, which thumped the sheet of wood she was using as a mortarboard.

Oh God, please help …

96

Every few minutes, Lizzy stopped shoveling cement into the pit and spread it evenly around the rectangular hole with a rake, then tamped it with the back of the shovel's head, slapping it hard and sending sprays of wet cement into Marcus's face. He closed his eyes, wincing as the spatters stung his face. It was up to his neck now.

He listened. There was a scratching sound coming from somewhere inside the barn, but he couldn't tell what it was. He didn't have time to dwell on it because Lizzy was walking around the edge of the pit. She sat facing him, heavy-duty work gloves on her hands. She pulled them off. Her hands were red. Marcus held on to the flimsy hope that somebody would stop her in time. He didn't really believe it, though. Lizzy's eyes were blank, lusterless black orbs. Sweat rolled down her dirt-streaked face in rivulets. Her face twitched, the skin moving as though a nest of snakes had been disturbed. She became suddenly watchful, *seeing* him. Had she kidnapped the Finches' baby? She was currently engaged in a hellish act of cruelty, of pure evil. So why not? It didn't seem ridiculous now as he watched her watching him. He should have run. Being shot in the back couldn't be any worse than this. He had considered turning on Lewis's porch and bolting inside, diving through the door; he could have been lucky, gambled that her aim was off, she might only clip an arm or leg, something survivable, but it had happened so quickly. He had underestimated her, and he knew in his heart that if he had tried to escape, or made any sudden movements towards her, she would have killed him. That was one thing he hadn't doubted—Lizzy would have used the gun if she had been forced to. It didn't make him feel better.

It was spooky, the way she just sat there, legs crossed, hands folded primly together in her lap as if she was evaluating him. Despite his weakening state, and the effort needed not to drop his head and face plant into the cement and suffocate, he was awestruck by his wife. She showed no signs of her previous timidity. He searched his jumbled thoughts; it was a struggle, but he managed to pluck one out of the chaos: Lizzy had the calm watchfulness of a predator, of a wolf that has spotted prey. Marcus didn't know this woman. His mind reeled, shrank away from the stranger keeping her grotesque vigil, perhaps waiting for him to scream again, to show signs of pain. But Marcus was spent. Wrung out, wondering dimly why she hadn't just killed him already.

He blinked at another thought, this one more disquieting than the last—*where's the fun in shooting me dead, when she can make me suffer?* The least he could do was try to disguise his distress, mirror her often blank expression with his own. Why give her the satisfaction of showing her his suffering?

"Rapid Hardening Portland Cement," she said, and from the corner of his eye, he saw Myrtle was looking up at her, too. "I don't need it to cure, I only need it to be hard enough to stand on." Lizzy stood and left.

What does that mean?

Black waves of despair welled up inside him, and suddenly he was breathing too fast and too hard. No matter how much he gulped the air he didn't seem to get enough. He thought of Mia, of how much he'd miss her. Myrtle was moaning beside him. He looked at her; she was shaking her head at him, as if she wanted him to stop. Her eyes were huge, blazing balls streaked with red, hell's lightning.

Marcus made an effort to quell the surge of panic that had invaded every corner of his mind and body, and it was useless. Lizzy wasn't done with them. He heard the scratching noise again. He watched his wife carry a plastic box and set it down near the edge of the pit. Realization dawned on him, the coming horror. He screamed. Something gave way in his throat and he began choking. Blood squirted out of his nose. And still he screamed.

97

Myrtle didn't know how much longer she could hold her head upright. The cement looked hard, or harder, but she couldn't tell for sure. She only knew she couldn't move at all. Her entire body was numb, and the numbness was spreading to her neck. She tried tilting her head back, looking up at the rafters. It worked for a few seconds, then it became difficult to breathe.

It seemed an eternity had passed before Lizzy returned. A day? Two? It was impossible to know for sure. She had lost all sense of time.

She was up there now, somewhere, mixing more cement by the yellow glow of a kerosene lamp. Myrtle listened to the sloshing water and the chomp of the shovel slicing through the mixture, hitting the sheet of wood beneath it.

At some point, the sounds of work ceased, and Lizzy sat on the edge of the pit again, cradling a glass jar with bees inside it. She caressed the jar, staring directly at Myrtle, unblinking. "It calms me," Lizzy said, "the sound of them is a balm for a troubled heart." Myrtle hoped, *prayed*, Lizzy could read the desperate plea in her eyes. But Lizzy got to her feet with no warning, and when she came back she was carrying two clear plastic boxes. She set them down on the floor and retreated. Myrtle stared fixedly at the boxes, which were open at the bottom, a trapdoor at the top with a simple locking mechanism. Tiny holes were drilled low on the four walls of both.

Oh my God oh my God what—

Lizzy appeared above her. She was holding two large rocks, one in each hand. She put them on the floor, picked up the shovel, and pushed the back of the blade into the concrete. Myrtle could see she was testing its hardness, watched her shrug, neither satisfied or dissatisfied. She closed her eyes, prayed vehemently for a massive coronary to take her.

Something crunched and her eyes flew open. Lizzy had one foot on the concrete, pressing on it with a dirty sneaker. She seemed confident, pushed herself off the edge of the pit with her other leg and stood, both feet on the concrete, knees slightly bent. She was sinking a little, but not much. Terror flooded Myrtle's brain until she could no longer process any coherent thoughts, just images. Gingerly, Lizzy reached behind her and lifted one of the boxes, slowly taking a step forward and lowering the box over Myrtle's head. She repeated the same task, this time for Marcus. Lizzy hefted the heavy rocks, one at a time, onto the top of each box, setting them down carefully. The sounds of muffled screams filtered upward, filling the barn with a peculiar hum.

One clear thought did occur to Myrtle, underneath the cacophonous screams and clawing terror trapped inside her head. *I can swallow my tongue. Or I can bite off the end of it and inhale it ... choke.*

98

Chief Shaw was on his way to his car when Ross Harper came running towards him across the parking lot of Sag Harbor PD.

Christ, what now?

He had caught more overtime than he'd wanted or needed recently. He was tired and if he drank any more coffee it would come right back up the chute. Shaw opened the driver's side door, turned at the scuffling footsteps of Harper.

"What's going on?"

Harper said, "I got a call from Lewis Jenkins over in North Haven. His brother's missing."

"*Marcus* Jenkins?"

"Yeah. Lewis said Marcus went to bed last night and when he got up this morning he wasn't in his room."

"Doesn't mean he's missing." Even as the words left his mouth he realized he didn't believe them. The FBI hadn't said it outright, but Shaw knew Marcus was a suspect. They fully intended to interview him again, lean on him a little harder this time. Motive: jilted lover. Zoey Finch had sworn up and down that she had finished her affair with him, going so far as to say she didn't even like him anymore.

He slammed the driver's door closed and Harper took a step back. Shaw sighed wearily, and said, "Missing, or on the lam?"

"That's just it, Chief, I don't know, and Lewis Jenkins is adamant his brother wouldn't do anything like this, suddenly vanish and all." *Wouldn't do anything like this*, he thought, *that's what they all say.*

"Any of his belongings missing?"

"Nothing, Chief. All his stuff is where it should be, according to Lewis Jenkins."

It didn't mean Marcus wasn't on the run.

A car turned into the parking lot and he recognized it immediately. His heart sank.

Christ on a fucking trike.

It was Lange, and the second her foot touched the ground she was up and taking long strides towards him. He held up a hand. "No! Not now, I have to call my wife—"

"Chief, we need—"

"*I said not now!*" You sneaky bitch, he wanted to add but didn't. She stopped in her tracks, glanced at Harper. "What's wrong with him?" Shaw watched as Harper shrugged and stared after them as they went toward the police station.

He called Myrtle to tell her he wouldn't be home for a few hours. Either she had the cell phone turned off or she had forgotten to charge it again.

99

Lizzy stood over them as they stared at her from their concrete tomb. Stared at her through their Perspex cages. Blood trickled from the corner of Myrtle's mouth. Lizzy wondered idly if the new wooden box on the edge of the pit had piqued their curiosity.

Lizzy slipped her hands into a pair of thicker gloves. Her lower arms were wrapped in thick bandages. She opened the lid of the box, reached in, fumbled around and extracted a squirming rat, its pink tail slashing the air and its big yellow teeth snapping at the air.

"Rats, humanely trapped," she said to no one in particular, "*humanely.*"

She dropped the rat through the trapdoor above Myrtle's head. A spasm seemed to wrench Myrtle's head back and forth, thrashing it from side to side.

Lizzy dipped into the box again and this time dropped the rat through the opening in Marcus's box. "It was you, Marcus, and Zoey. Both of you pushed me into the pigpen. One hand each—one of yours and one of hers. How touching." Dampened screams rose all around her, and undamped *squeaks*. But the low drone of the bees kept her calm as she placed three more rats in each of the plastic boxes and finally closed the trapdoors.

Lizzy went up top to the mortarboard and its freight of freshly mixed concrete. She began shoveling.

100

Chief Vincent Shaw discovered his wife was missing when he returned from North Haven after questioning Lewis and Sage Jenkins, although it had been detective Lange and two FBI agents asking most of the questions. They had all left North Haven empty-handed. On the drive home, Shaw was convinced (even though he wasn't privy to all the details of their investigation) that the feds had nothing, and Lange was chasing shadows.

Arthur Dunhill had hired some of the best, most professional criminals in the business and they hadn't left any trace. Shaw knew one thing most of the public didn't know, something he wouldn't dream of telling Myrtle: some criminals escaped capture. For every serial killer caught, there were probably a dozen or more who weren't brought to justice. Not all victims of kidnappings were found, and most of said victims were murdered. Myrtle would have nightmares for months if he'd conveyed this bleak nugget of information to her. The TV shows in which the smart FBI agents located the kidnapper, took him away in handcuffs and walked the freed person to a waiting car, a blanket over their shoulders, were extremely rare events. Shaw kept his ear to the law enforcement grapevine. He attended conferences all over the country at every opportunity, and talked to other cops long into the night, usually at the end of a bar somewhere. The stories those cops had to tell were incredible, brutal, more extraordinary than anything one would see on a TV show. And all those stories were true, easily verified. Shaw was getting used to the fact that when he attended another of those conferences at some point in the future, he would have his own fantastic tale to tell. And yet this situation, the crimes that had been perpetrated here, paled in comparison when he recalled the stories told to him by cops from New York City, Chicago, Florida, and California.

As he sat in his car outside his house, bone tired, he remembered Lange detailing how the FBI had not only dismantled Arthur Dunhill's home in Massachusetts, but they had taken apart every item in his house, including electronic equipment, household appliances, floorboards, torn up carpets, and at one point had broken through some drywall in the mistaken belief that there was some kind of hidden compartment behind it. He asked her what they had found, and in a rare moment when her guard was down, she'd said quietly, "Fuck all. As in, nothing."

He got out of his car and went up the walk. He knew something was wrong the second he turned his keys in the door. The locks were open, and Myrtle never left them unlocked, whether she was in or out.

He had pushed the door, his hand dropping to his service weapon automatically. Gun drawn, he searched the house, but he knew. He *knew*. Myrtle was gone.

***

While a search party of police and local volunteers beat the bushes for Myrtle and divers searched the ponds around Sag Harbor, Chief Shaw drove down Main Street. Bleary-eyed and refusing to allow the low panic in his gut to grow, rendering him useless, he passed posters of his wife he'd tacked onto telephone poles and taped to streetlamps. He had done everything he could. He'd contacted everyone with whom Myrtle had even a tenuous acquaintance. The only person he hadn't been able to contact was Lizzy Jenkins. And now he was turning the corner onto Garden Street, the last light of the day fading. He had driven along this street more than any other, had even knocked on the front door twice. There was no one home. But as he got closer to the Jenkins residence, he spotted a vehicle in the front of the house. He got out of the car fast, not even bothering to close his door. The Spark was in the driveway, but the driver's door was open. There was no one in it. The engine was running. He drew his weapon, knocked, *pounded* on the door, his closed fist aching from the impact. He backed away from the door, looked up. The windows were dark.

He ran around back. He pushed the door handle. Locked.

He looked up at the window. And blinked.

What the hell?

One of the windows up there was covered in a black mass of flies.

They were crawling into the vent. And then he smelled it. His hand went to his nose and his stomach churned uneasily. He was no big-city cop, but he recognized the stench of death.

101

Three Months Later

Zoey was waiting for Jon on the sidewalk when he got out of the cab. She had been released from the hospital a month before him. Jon's injuries had warranted physical therapy and careful monitoring. Even though he was walking with the aid of a cane, the doctors had assured him that in time he wouldn't need it. He was happy to be home, even more so when he was sure the media frenzy had died down.

There were no news vans ... but there was a moving truck parked outside Peggy Dawson's house. The movers were closing the doors of their truck, and Peggy was locking the door of her house. There was a FOR SALE sign on her lawn. She gave them a brief wave and continued toward her car. Jon noticed she walked without grimacing, without a cane, and with brisk confidence.

"Where do you think *she's* going?" Zoey asked.

"To find her place in the sun," he said, and he caught the strange look she threw at him. He was standing about two feet from her and he could smell the booze fumes. She made no move to hug him. She hadn't visited him in the hospital, either.

"Well," Zoey said, "her loss, giving up a nice house like that."

"After everything that's happened, would you want to live beside us?" he asked, and limped into the house.

He sat at the kitchen table. Zoey sat across from him. Her eyes were shiny and restless. Was she taking something else on top of the booze? Pills of some kind, probably. As soon as Jon's pain was a dim and distant memory, he was going to flush his pain pills down the toilet. Zoey was half drunk and definitely stoned. She said, "It's time we talked, Jon. I'm sure the FBI questioned you about my affair?"

"They did," he said, watching her sway from side to side.

"Did it hurt, Jon? Be honest. Did it *really* hurt?"

"Yes," he said, honestly, "it did."

"Ha! I bet it did," Zoey said, her voice high, and Jon detected a scream in it somewhere. "I know how serious you are about the whole marriage business, like it's something sacred."

"It is," he said quietly, "it is to me."

"You don't look upset, Jon." She sounded disappointed. What did she want him to do? Throw things? Break some goddamn crockery? He *was* upset, he just didn't want to give her the satisfaction of seeing it.

She got up from the chair and took a bottle of whiskey from the liquor cabinet next to the refrigerator. Before she closed the door, Jon saw it was well stocked. She filled a Waterford crystal tumbler—*filled* it—and Jon almost asked her to take it easy. He didn't though, because Zoey obviously wanted to unburden herself. And he was sure she'd suggest (strongly) that he mind his business, anyway. She sat at the table again, taking long sips of the whiskey, her hand reaching for and touching the bottle, as if to remind her that it was there. The shine in her eyes was growing brighter.

"I fucked him in our bed, you know," she said casually, and her confession (he had no doubt this was what it was) didn't have the effect she was hoping for. He remained calm, even though he had to stifle the need to breathe harder. *Don't call her a cunt*, he urged himself, turning it into a repeating mantra. *Don't call her a cunt, even though she earned it.*

"I even blew him in this very kitchen," she continued, and Jon became very still. She was trying to provoke him, he could see that, and she would have liked nothing more than for him to get up and slam her head into the table. She'd call the cops and he would be hauled to jail in handcuffs. She would just love that. But Jon held on to his composure, even if it did require nothing less than the willpower of a saint.

Zoey's eyes darkened, and she focused on him. She said, "You got our son killed. I told you not to deal with Roger Berris. Didn't I tell you? Our baby is gone, all because you couldn't resist a lay-up. That's how you saw Roger's deal, wasn't it? It was there on a silver platter, how could you resist? Now that crazy Arthur Dunhill took our baby, he took Lizzy and Marcus—oh, you didn't hear? And I thought I was the only one the cops were keeping in the dark. Since I came home this place has been crawling with cops, the whole village. You know they found Lizzy's daughter decomposing in her bedroom? No? Suicide. I hope the SEC comes after you, Jon. I hope they officially let you know you made a *bad deal.*" Jon wasn't worried about the Securities and Exchange Commission. If they wanted to talk to him, they knew where he was.

"Want to give the money back, Zoey?" he asked.

Her eyes narrowed into beady slits. "Fuck you," she said. "After what I've been through, I earned that money."

"Why did you do it, Zoey?"

"What're you talking about?"

"The affair. Why?"

"You mean you don't know?" She laughed, a high, jagged sound that made him uneasy. "You really don't know? Who do you think you're fooling, Jon? All right. Okay. You remember the Christmas party two years ago at Aquarius?"

"Yeah. I remember. So?"

"I saw what you did."

Jon didn't know what she was talking about. He shrugged.

Exasperated, her face crimping into a scowl, Zoey said, "Wendy Chu. Wendy fucking Chu. I saw you two in the conference room."

Jon did a quick inventory of his memory. Wendy Chu, bright woman, paid intern, maybe twenty-two years old. "What did you see?" he asked.

"You two were kissing," Zoey said, although it sounded more like a hiss.

"Wait a minute," Jon said, "tell me *exactly* what you saw."

"I was looking for you, I wanted you to meet some investors, and as soon as I saw you kissing that whore I left immediately. I couldn't stand there and watch."

Jon was aghast. He shook his head, unable or unwilling to process this new information. He took a moment to get his thoughts in order, then he said, "*She* kissed *me*, Zoey. You didn't see that part, but she kissed me. Did you see the part where I pushed her away, held up the hand with my

397

wedding band and told her I loved my wife? You didn't wait around for that part. Instead, you just assumed the worst. Two minutes is all it would have taken for me to clear up the whole thing, but you made assumptions, Zoey. I *never* cheated on you."

Her face was twitching; it seemed to be undergoing a spasm. She lifted the half-empty tumbler and flung it at him. Jon leaned to the side, and the glass flew past him, shattering on the wall behind him. "You lying bastard," she said, between clenched teeth. "You dirty lying bastard."

"Am I lying? You were wrong, Zoey. I was faithful to you our entire marriage. I loved you. I *adored* you."

Her complexion was a waxen, pale mask. "You lying bastard," she said again, in a tone of utter disbelief.

"The day after the party," Jon said, "I let Wendy Chu go. Gave her a reference and even some extra money to get her started somewhere else. She was drunk, Zoey. But I wasn't drunk at all. What was I drinking that night?"

She hesitated, uncertain. Then her eyes widened slightly. "Orange juice, but that doesn't prove anything."

Jon ran his fingers through his hair. He was stunned, but he made an effort to keep it well below the surface. It was amazing, he thought, she believed I was cheating on her and decided to seek revenge rather than just talking to me. Incredible.

"I want a divorce," she said, her voice cracked, "and a fat settlement, too."

"Yes, I had no doubt this was all a preamble, the starter before you delivered the main course. I'll give you whatever you want."

He started to get up, and he watched her eyes flit back

and forth, searching for something. "He was a great fuck," she said quickly, "you wouldn't believe how filthy it got." Jon continued to stand, ignoring her now. He limped to the stairs, grimaced at the pain in his legs, and went to the spare bedroom. He locked the door.

102

Jon slept for twelve hours. He hadn't been able to sleep well in the hospital. And when he went downstairs he walked by Zoey, passed out facedown on the new sofa, one arm dangling over the side, a glass tumbler on the floor, its contents a puddle on the hardwood. He pushed her hair out of the way and held his first two fingers to her neck. Her pulse was fine, but her headache when she woke up would be a different story. He got a sponge from the kitchen and mopped up the spill.

Even though he'd slept for half a day, his mind and body were exhausted. He had been on his guard in the hospital. Now that he had been discharged, the innumerable hours he owed himself in shut-eye had caught up to him. Fielding an endless barrage of questions from the Suffolk County PD, the FBI and the assistant district attorney on an almost daily basis had left him drained. He had asked his own questions, and it hadn't taken him long to realize that law enforcement had come up empty. Arthur Dunhill was dead, and had taken the answers with him to the grave. A ransom hadn't been phoned in. The feds believed Dunhill's main goal in life before he was killed was to make Jon Finch suffer. Dunhill had achieved his aim.

He lived in the house on Main Street for five more days, mostly out of good old-fashioned curiosity. He wanted to see if Zoey's pill popping and boozing was a passing phase prompted by his homecoming, recalling the underwhelming welcome he'd received. He lodged in the spare bedroom for the most part. Zoey continued her one-woman party in the living room, drinking copious amounts of whiskey and coming to the foot of the stairs to shout up at him such random tidbits as "You're a liar" and "You killed our son" and "I'm making something to eat, do you want anything?" Jon hadn't responded. His only hope was that she didn't burn down the house.

When he did see her, after she had sobered up, they didn't speak at all. He knew the one thing she feared most was being alone. In fact, she'd had nightmares about it. She really didn't know just how close her worst fear was to becoming her new reality. He cooked his own meals and ate in the spare bedroom, bringing the plates down and washing them. Five days of this was enough for Jon, and he checked into The Herbert Hotel. Zoey had been right about one thing, though: he *had* killed their son. It *was* his fault. He would have to live with it, suffer through the nightmares of his mistake, his miscalculation. *Beware of strangers bearing gifts*, his mother had said in a dim and distant life.

He eventually moved out of the hotel and into a modest bungalow on Division Street, so close to the Sag Harbor PD building that he could throw a stone from his house and it would land on the step just outside the entrance door. He took walks in the evening as part of his rehab, determined once and for all to stop taking the OxyContin prescribed for pain. He was careful with the pills, taking them only when the pain was so bad he couldn't stand up. Those episodes were becoming less frequent, and he attended physical therapy regularly, never missing an appointment. It was on one of his nightly excursions that he heard his name being called as he was passing the Sag Harbor PD. He turned and saw Vincent Shaw waving at him. John waited, and Shaw joined him on the sidewalk.

"How're you doing?" Shaw asked.

Jon thought he was doing a lot better than the Chief of Police. Shaw's eyes were sunken, haunted; he had lost weight, and the eyes themselves were blood streaked. Jon hadn't been sleeping well, either, but he could see that Shaw's insomnia was far worse than his.

"All right, I suppose. Not great … managing."

Shaw nodded. "I can see you're back on your feet."

Jon grimaced as a bolt of pain shot down the entire length of his right leg and flashed hot waves into his toes.

Shaw held out a hand, almost as though to catch him if he toppled.

"Easy there," Shaw said, "maybe you should consider using the cane again."

"It comes and goes," Jon said. "It'd get a lot worse if I sat around. I know I'm healing, but the going's a little slow."

Shaw nodded again. "How's the wife?" he asked.

"Divorcing me."

"Oh, sorry to hear that."

"Yeah, well, it was coming … any news on … uh, I mean—"

"Myrtle? No. I often wonder if Marcus Jenkins murdered his wife and for whatever reason, did the same to Myrt." Jon was watching Shaw carefully, taking note of the way the policeman's eyes hadn't wavered from his face, and then it came to him: Shaw was *observing* him.

"Who knows," Jon said. "I'm sorry she's missing." And he was. The chief had no idea just how sorry Jon really was about Myrtle Shaw.

"Plans for the future?" Shaw asked.

"Once the divorce is finalized, I'm out of here. Too many ghosts. How about you?"

"I'm retiring soon. Best for everyone, I suspect. I'm not as focused as I should be."

"But it's understandable, given the loss you suffered."

"*Understandable* has a shelf life, too, like everything else. Well, I won't keep you any longer. Enjoy your walk."

Jon continued along Division Street, and when he came to the intersection with Main, he turned. Shaw was still standing by the streetlight outside the police station. Jon waved to him. Shaw returned the wave, a brief raising of his fingers.

Maybe you should consider using the cane again.

How did Chief Shaw know he had used a cane? The answer, Jon discovered, was disturbingly easy: Shaw had been watching him.

103

Key West, Florida

Ken Brooks had settled into retirement so comfortably that somewhere in a dusty corner of his mind he thought he should feel bad about it. He didn't, though. He had established a routine, bereft of excitement, and it suited him just fine. He ate breakfast first thing, walked around Bahama Village around noon, stopped for a coffee and people watched. Breakfast consisted of salad—no dressing—and two boiled eggs. Somehow, George had gotten under his skin. He would thank George if he was ever able to get in contact with him. It had been two months since he had last taken his blood pressure pills. He had lost thirty pounds, although he was too embarrassed to join a gym. Once he lost the wobble in his gut and the jiggle in his arms he'd do it, run on the treadmill next to the beautiful people. For now, his makeshift home gym would have to do.

He was sitting at his backyard dining table where he sat every morning, on a bluff overlooking the ocean. It was impossible to get tired of the ocean view. He turned his head toward the Gulf of Mexico and the haze hanging over the water. Ken was at peace here. The ocean had that effect, but sadly it wasn't lasting. Benny had kept his word and hadn't argued when Ken had decided he'd put in enough years as a professional criminal. But the itch on his face persisted, and he scratched at it absently, a maddening reminder of the adhesive used on the facial prosthetics Benny had labored for several hours to get right. It had been an equally painstaking process to get the masks off. But to his credit, Benny had started the process of removing the special effects makeup from him first, then George. It had felt as though a second skin was being removed. The multitalented Benny Cooper had made each of them look like entirely different people. The plastic prosthetics had looked so real. Benny had even used honest-to-God makeup. He could have worked in Hollywood, on any number of movies. But Benny wasn't built that way, the legit gene had skipped him.

It was at night when he thought about the final job. The strangeness of it all. He had no information on what Benny had done with the baby, or the kid's body. It was not knowing that had kept him awake; he wasn't worried Benny was going to harm the baby. He knew his old friend, better than anyone.

A cool early morning breeze slipped over the bluff and ruffled his T-shirt and shorts. He smiled, thinking about how much George had gotten inside his head—he wouldn't admit it to another living soul, but Ken missed his old friend, Mr. Self-Help. He had tried every cell number he'd had for George. Service had been cut off on some of those phones, and on others a robot answered, asking him to leave a message. He didn't. He kept returning to the night in the boneyard, where George had helped him and hadn't made a big deal out of it. And when Ken had thanked him later, quietly, George had pretended he didn't know what Ken was referring to. That was true class. Helping an old man like him and refusing to take the pat on the back. Good ole George. He would invite him over if he ever found him. He might even listen to George's diet tips, minus his customary grimace. Mr. Self-Help—

There was someone behind him.

He didn't turn, but he became very still.

"Hello, Ken," Benny said. Ken swallowed the morsel of chewed red pepper in his mouth, hard.

"Hello, Benny," Ken said, not turning around.

"Nice place. I knew you had taste, old buddy, but goddamn, this spread is something."

"Yeah … I was just thinking about my choices. Seems like I chose the right home."

"I'll say you did."

"Seen George around, Benny? I haven't been able to contact him."

"No … no, I haven't seen or heard from George at all."

George was dead. Ken knew. Christ, he *knew* it. He picked up his fork and continued eating. "Sure you don't want some breakfast?"

"No, Ken. I've had my fill … we've had some interesting times, old buddy."

"Sure have. Last job was the frosting on the cake, huh?" Ken had watched the news. He had gleaned two things from the coverage as days marched into weeks: Arthur Dunhill was crazy, and a fraud. He was also dead, responsible for the murder of Cody Finch, the boy whose body they had removed from his grave. The pundits and police believed Dunhill was the mastermind behind the kidnapping of Jane

Finch, the murder of Candice Fersh, and the attempted murders of Jon and Zoey Finch. Benny had been remarkably successful in sidestepping the heat. So adept, in fact, that Ken didn't know the whole story. The bottom line was irrefutable: Benny had gotten away with it. They all had. But it hadn't been enough for his former boss.

"Yeah," Benny said, "the frosting on the cake. I had help from two of the best people I ever worked with. Pros, the both of them."

Ken nodded. He couldn't turn to face Benny.

"I had no plans on talking, Benny."

"I know, Ken. That I do know. Thing is, I owe some debts that have to be paid."

Ken listened as metal was screwed into metal.

"Some things you don't want to do, *ever*, Ken, but sometimes you're not given a choice."

"I hear you," Ken said quietly, chewing rapidly. He was finishing his breakfast.

"If it makes any difference," Benny said, "the job was perfect. We got away with it, old buddy."

"But it's not enough?"

"I wish it was enough, Ken, but it isn't."

Ken put his knife and fork neatly on his empty plate. He turned to face the ocean. From the corner of his eye he made out the ill-defined shadow, but he could see the raised arm and the long barrel of the gun.

"Just do it," Ken said.

Benny did it.

104

Boynton Beach, Florida

Seven months to the day since he had spoken to Chief Vincent Shaw on the sidewalk outside the police station, Jon left Sag Harbor for good. His divorce from Zoey hadn't been spectacular, as he'd expected it to be, but a dull affair that had finally been settled, apart from an occasional spiteful text message from her in the small hours; those too had tapered to nothing. He hadn't replied to her. He had made certain that all his business, legal or otherwise, was over.

He turned off Old Boynton Road and parked in the lot of Ted's Homewares. Next to the homewares store was Boynton Retirement Village, a new independent living complex—it looked more like a resort to him. He watched the residents come and go, some still spry enough to play tennis in the two courts behind the main building. Some of the elderly clients were swimming in the large pool in back. Some ate a late breakfast in the dining area at the side, under a white awning.

He took a receipt for the burgundy Ford Expedition he had rented in Long Island out of his pocket, and the single button he'd found on his bedroom floor eons ago, the one that didn't belong to him, or his son. He crumpled the receipt around the bright black button, lowered his window and tossed them into the wastebasket beside him.

He kept his windows closed and the aircon cranked. After forty-minutes had elapsed, he was about to pull out when he saw an old woman take a seat in the alfresco dining area. The sun was too bright, throwing white reflections off every available surface. He shook his sunglasses open and put them on.

Ah, there she is.

Peggy Dawson was sitting at a table, alone. She was wearing shorts and an elegant blouse, both as white as the awning that sheltered her from the harsh sunlight.

His mouth fell open and a smile spread across his face, lightening the weight he'd begun to feel in his chest. She was joined by an older gentleman who was wearing a white baseball cap, tan slacks, and an open-necked sweater. He removed the cap, leaned down to kiss Peggy on the forehead, giving her a quick one-armed hug. Jon watched her face light up, and he felt the stupid smile on his face grow wider. Stupid or not, Jon felt real happiness and, for a moment, he was startled by how rare that feeling had been for such a long time. *God bless you, Peg*, he thought, *and you too, sir, whoever you are.*

They held hands across the table, and Jon didn't want to intrude any further. Peggy had made it. She had found her place in the sun, after all. It was all he needed to see.

105

St. Georges Island, Florida

The drive from Eastpoint over the Bryant Patton Bridge was scenic, beautiful as the sun sank low and dappled the waves bright gold and deep orange. Jon was in a good mood. Peggy was happy and whenever he thought about her, which was often, he couldn't help but smile. As well as Peggy living life and, from what he'd seen, finding love again (he hoped), Jon was pain free. It had taken months of physical therapy, but he had suffered through it and come out the other side sane and intact. The limp was gone, but the surgical scars remained on his legs and chest, and he didn't care. He was alive. More important, he had ditched the pills. As soon as the pain was gone, he had dumped the OxyContin. He didn't want to be a sad statistic—Jon had a lot of life left. Zoey was probably hooked on them by now, and he was surprised that if he knew for sure, he wouldn't take any pleasure in it. Anyway, he had played the game and won. Yes, it wasn't an unblemished victory, it had a bittersweet aftertaste. But he had played to win, had done so, and he didn't mind if the celebrations were muted.

He arrived on St. Georges Island and glanced over at the

lighthouse, then continued on up Gulf Beach Drive. He was only staying for one night. He had one more meeting scheduled for tomorrow in West Palm Beach, and from there ... he had no plans. Sometimes it was okay to wait. He wasn't in any hurry.

The houses and businesses thinned the further he went, and soon trees appeared on both sides of the road. He turned off, onto Watkins Cove. Here the trees were even thicker, and darkening as the sun went down. The isolation of this place was just what he needed. Even for one night.

He spotted the house and the man standing on the upper veranda, silhouetted by the lights behind him. Jon parked out front, looked up. The man was gone.

He switched off the engine and sat there. He'd waited a long time, had dreamed about this moment, had imagined what it would feel like. His stomach burbled, but not with hunger. He was excited. Jon got out of the car and walked slowly toward the house. The man emerged and ran toward him, grabbed him in a bear hug and slapped him hard on the back.

Jon laughed, and said, "All right, Michael. All right, that's good."

His brother stood back, looking at him, from his shoes to the top of his head, as if verifying that he was real. Once confirmed, Mike lurched into him again, hugging him hard.

"Jesus Christ, Mike, okay! You're squashing my ribs."

His brother stepped back suddenly, and said, "Oh. You all right? Are you in pain?"

"No, Mike, I'm fine."

"Okay. But do you think you could get used to calling me Benny?"

"As long as I don't have to call you Mr. Cooper."

"Come on around back."

"But—"

"Please, Jon. There's a reason."

Jon nodded and followed him into the backyard. Mike, aka Benny Cooper, had really found a private, quiet place. There were no houses overlooking the yard, which meant no *curtain twitchers*, his mother's term for nosy neighbors. Trees surrounded the roughly square yard. Mike (Jon thought he might have difficulty getting used to calling his brother by a different name, but there was time) headed for the tree line.

Mike looked down and Jon followed his gaze. He could make out a rectangular shape, indistinct now. An attempt had been made to conceal it with shredded tree bark. It was a good disguise; Mike had spread the bark all around the yard. You had to be standing directly over it to see it.

"He's under there?" Jon asked.

Mike nodded. "I buried him myself. I'm thinking about building a gazebo. Hand carve some airplanes into the design."

Jon sank to his knees and touched the ground. He said, "You know how to do that?"

"You know me, always trying to master a new skill … but yeah, I can do it. I just wanted your opinion before I got started."

"Sounds good, Mike," Jon said. "Thank you."

He felt Mike shift from one foot to the other. "He was your son, but he was my nephew, Jon. I didn't see him much in the past few years, and I regret it, I really do. I remember when he was small. Even then he had those toy airplanes— kid was obsessed."

Jon stood, looked at Mike in the gathering darkness. "Thanks, Mike."

"Don't thank me, Jon. You've done more than enough for me. You got me out of prison, for one. Here." Mike reached into his shirt pocket and handed an envelope to him. Jon had a brief look at the documents inside: passport, driver's license. "Better get used to calling me Benny," Mike continued, "because you're going to have to get used to your own new name." Jon wanted one last day to call his brother by his actual name. He was going to use it. He told him.

"All right," Mike said, "what's another day?"

Silence ensued. After a while, Mike said, "I can leave you alone if you want."

"No," Jon said, "it's fine. We shouldn't forget the dead, but we need to think about the living first."

They went into the house. Jon felt the excitement return. Mike led the way to the end of a hall, opened a door. Jon stepped past him into the bedroom.

"I'll leave you to it," Mike said, and Jon heard him walk back toward the living room.

Jon looked at the baby monitor, then back at his daughter, asleep in the crib.

He pulled a chair closer, and sat. She had grown, he could see that, and she had more hair on her head. He wasn't going to wake Jane, he would wait until she woke by herself. It took all his strength not to pick her up, hug her.

Jon sat there for hours.

106

The next day, Jon left St. George's Island after less than two hours of sleep. He was tired, but alert. He had left Jane with Mike (what was one more day?) and drove to West Palm Beach. He had racked up a lot of miles on the clock. It didn't matter; soon he'd settle somewhere new, he didn't know where yet, although it wasn't as though he was short of options.

He passed the Fourth District Court of Appeal on Tamarind Avenue, glancing at the high palms ahead, wondering if he was in the right area. *Ten palms, all in a row*, she had said, and Jon smiled. *You can't miss them.* Sure, he thought, can't miss the palm trees in Florida, shaking his head. But he was in the right place. He pulled into the parking lot of Lakeview Private Hospital. From his vantage point, he could see the entrance. He had described the car so she shouldn't have any trouble finding it.

When Jane had woken up last night, Jon had finally picked her up, cradled his daughter in his arms, hugged her. She had been in a good mood, patting his face with her small hands and speaking to him in baby language. Jon smiled again. He had smiled a lot more since he had left Long Island. Smiling felt strange, but he would get used to it the more he did it.

The sun was out, the sky was cloudless, and a moderate breeze shook the palms.

He closed his eyes for a moment. The relief at holding his only remaining child at last clung to him. Relief of the kind that had turned every muscle to jelly as the adrenaline subsided. Jon would sleep, yes, but he knew the price he had paid: the murder of his son, of course, but also the haunted, desolate look in Vincent Shaw's eyes. As long as he lived, Chief Shaw's face would haunt him, because a mistake had been made. He hadn't been able to stop it.

What would you have done if Cody hadn't been killed by Dunhill?

Mike had asked the question, and Jon had answered that he wouldn't have had much choice but to let his children continue to live with their mother. He could visit them whenever he wanted, but he wondered now if that would have been feasible … He watched as a woman exited the annex, the psychiatric unit attached to the main building. She wore blue shorts, sandals, a navy T-shirt and sunglasses. Even from this distance, he saw she had a healthy tan. Part of a conversation he'd had with Mike recurred to him: *She better be all right, Jon. Most people deserve a second chance. I believe in second chances. But I'll cancel her ticket if she becomes a liability. I'll be watching her.*

She was smiling as she approached and was still beaming as she got in the car and shut the door. "Hello, Lizzy," he said, and she leaned over and embraced him.

"Hello yourself," she said.

"Let's get going."

Jon started the car. At the stoplight on Tamarind, he turned to her and said, "How is your new doctor?"

"She's good. I'm getting better, Jon. I really am."

He paused briefly and had to ask, "Did you kill Myrtle Shaw?"

"Yes," she said, "I think I did." She removed her sunglasses.

"What does that mean?"

"I must have, Jon. Trouble is, I don't remember." He glanced at her. *Is she telling the truth?*

"But you remember Marcus? What you did to him?"

"Yes, I do. I'm sorry about Myrtle, Jon. I wish I could take it back. But I'll have to live with what I've done."

So will I, he thought.

Jon believed in second chances—for the lonely, the betrayed, the broken, the outcast, the frail. And if the conditions were right, some of them even found their own place in the sun.

The stoplight turned green.

Made in the USA
Middletown, DE
19 August 2023